I0656802

William John Lawrence, Gustavus Vaughan Brooke

The Life of Gustavus Vaughan Brooke, Tragedian

William John Lawrence, Gustavus Vaughan Brooke

The Life of Gustavus Vaughan Brooke, Tragedian

ISBN/EAN: 9783337142728

Printed in Europe, USA, Canada, Australia, Japan

Cover: Foto ©Raphael Reischuk / pixelio.de

More available books at **www.hansebooks.com**

THE LIFE

OF

GUSTAVUS VAUGHAN BROOKE.

Yours most sincerely,

Gustavus L. Brooke

THE LIFE

OF

GUSTAVUS VAUGHAN BROOKE,

TRAGEDIAN.

BY

W. J. LAWRENCE.

" Nothing in his life
Became him like the leaving it : he died
As one that had been studied in his death
To throw away the dearest thing he owed
As 'twere a careless trifle."

BELFAST: W. & G. BAIRD, ROYAL AVENUE.
1892.

[ALL RIGHTS RESERVED.]

PREFACE.

IN an age when it is fashionable for the well-graced player to indulge in autobiographical reminiscences, or to have his life written while in the meridian of his career, some apology may be deemed necessary for endeavouring to embalm the memory of a Triton of the past. There must be many, however, who still agree with Talleyrand, that to speak the whole truth, and nothing but the truth, concerning the life-work of any prominent personage, without wronging the memory of the dead or the peace of the living, it needs to remain silent for well-nigh three decades after the falling of the curtain. It was with this confidence, and under the assurance that the career of G. V. Brooke deserved treatment in full, that the present work was taken in hands some three years ago. In venturing to claim for it those merits which must be denied to the few fugitive biographical notices of the actor in existence—viz., accuracy and completeness—it is that I may testify to the generosity of a host of able correspondents who (in response to various letters of appeal considerately inserted by the editors of many home and foreign journals) have, from time to time, favoured me with their co-operation. Never, indeed, was actor so gratefully remembered, never biographer more magnanimously expedited. Material assistance was received at the outset from Brooke's old friend, Mr. W. H. Malcolm, of Holyrood, who placed his valuable collection of playbills, press cuttings, and autograph letters at my disposal. Thanks are also largely due to Mrs. Heatly (wife of the Rev. Canon Heatly, D.D., of Rosbercon, New Ross, and only surviving sister of the tragedian) for the unrestricted use of all the family papers relevant to the biography. Among these I may mention Forrest's characteristic epistle to Brooke, Brooke's lines on the death of Elton, and the

Australian correspondence so freely quoted from in Chapters IX. and X. Most of the particulars of Brooke's boyhood and family connections—except such as were vouchsafed by his old schoolfellow, Dr. Fox, of Greenock—were also furnished by Mrs. Heatly. Not a whit less important was the assistance of this lady in setting finally at rest certain moot points which have hitherto formed food for contention among green-room gossips and theatrical flaneurs.

For the use of upwards of forty letters, written at various periods by the tragedian and his second wife to the late Mr. Morris, of Ayr, I have to acknowledge my indebtedness to his nephew, Mr. James Morris, of 28 Canfield Gardens, South Hampstead, N.W. Among Australian correspondents, Mr. Joseph Blaschek, of Parkville, Melbourne, ranks easily first as an indefatigable helper. Mr. W. Dinsmore, of 16 Chestnut Street, Hightown, Manchester, was from first to last unceasing in his efforts to put me in possession of exhaustive details regarding the old Manchester stock days. Light on obscure points was also thrown by Mr. W. C. Day, of 24 Bedford Square, W.C.; Mr. William Douglas, of 1 Brixton Road, S.W.; Mr. J. A. Langford, LL.D., and Mr. Samuel Timmins, of Birmingham; Mr. James Sutton, of 31 Broomhall Place, Sheffield; Mr. J. O'Rorke, of 37 Belgrave Road, Rathmines; Mr. Gervais Bright, of Armagh; and Mr. W. Jackson Pigott, of Dundrum, Co. Down.

My attitude towards previous writers on Brooke having been for the most part aggressive, I find little occasion to make farther acknowledgment of indebtedness here. In the few instances where inspiration has been derived from public sources, ample avowal will be found either in the text or in accompanying footnotes.

The photogravure frontispiece represents the tragedian as he appeared after his return from Australia, early in the 'sixties. For permission to copy the photograph from which it is taken I have to thank my friend, Mrs. Swanton, who, in conjunction with her late husband, appeared with Brooke on his last night of acting. The autograph signature appended is from a letter of the same period, furnished by Mr. W. H. Malcolm.

W. J. LAWRENCE.

COMBEE,
JANUARY, 1892.

CONTENTS.

THE LIFE

OF

GUSTAVUS VAUGHAN BROOKE,

TRAGEDIAN.

CHAPTER I.

1818—1834.

Birth of the Tragedian—Not Christened Gustavus Vasa, according to
popular belief—His Father and Mother—Their Family Antecedents—
Brooke's Precocity as a Child—Is sent to School at Edgeworthstown
—Maria Edgeworth—The Rev. William Jones's Academy in Dublin—
Brooke's Youthful Prowess as an Athlete and Fencer—Acts and
Dances on a Private Stage—Influence of his Early Tutors—Russell,
the Professor of Elocution—The Stripling Interviews Macready and
J. W. Calcraft—His First Appearance at the Dublin Theatre, and
subsequent Tour through the Provinces—Anecdote illustrative of
his Large-heartedness—The " Hibernian Roscius " in London.

THERE are, in Ireland, two consanguineous Brooke families
of importance, the one of Fermanagh, the other of Donegal.
It was to the latter and elder branch that Gustavus Vaughan
Brooke belonged. Born at No. 40 Hardwicke Place, Dublin,
the residence of his father, on Saturday, April 25, 1818, as not
infrequently happened in those lax days, he was privately baptised,
and had for godfathers General Gustavus Vaughan Hart and
Thomas Brooke, Esq., of Lough Esk Castle, County Donegal.
In connection with the frequently repeated assertion that the
subject of this memoir was originally christened Gustavus Vasa,
after the famous tragedy of Henry Brooke (of whom he was a

B

collateral descendant), it is necessary to show how the names
Gustavus and Vaughan became associated with the Brooke
family. The facts are clear. Sir Frederick Hamilton, after
signalizing himself in the armies of Gustavus Adolphus, King of
Sweden, married Sidney, daughter and heiress of Sir John
Vaughan, and had as son Gustavus. Elevated to the peerage as
Viscount Boyne in the year 1717, the last-mentioned eventually
married Elizabeth, daughter of Sir Henry Brooke, of Brooke's
borough, County Fermanagh.

Described as " Esquire" in the Directories of the period, Gustavus
Brooke, father of the tragedian, was a graduate of Trinity College,
Dublin, and a Freeman of the city. His elder and only brother,
Henry Brooke, of Brookehall, had as son Colonel Henry Brooke,
C.B., who was on the verge of taking out the lapsed baronetcy of
Donegal when stricken with death at Holyhead.

It has been frequently stated in various accounts of the
tragedian's life that his father at the outset pursued the profession
of an architect. This was not the case. But the mistake is
pardonable, seeing that he had a hobby for trafficking in house
property and took great delight in altering and re-constructing his
acquirements. Inheriting the slender portion of a younger son,
he lost all, save what had been settled on his wife as jointure, by
injudicious investments in canal debentures and by "backing" bills
for impecunious friends. At this juncture—about the year 1824—he
left Dublin for Longford on his appointment as County Inspector
of Police for that district by the Marquis of Wellesley. It was a
time of great political excitement, and being clever with pen
and pencil he wrote and illustrated quite a number of racy
pamphlets and party squibs. His official career was, however,
short. He died at Longford in 1827, and was buried at Castle
Forbes, leaving a widow and four children, Gustavus Vaughan
(the eldest born), William Basil, Elizabeth, and Frances
Sarah (Fanny). Twin sons, Thomas and Henry, died in
infancy.

The lady whom Gustavus Brooke had taken to wife was
Frances Bathurst, youngest daughter of Matthew Bathurst, Esq.,

now of Ballinaskea House, and now of Summer Hill, County
Meath. The former residence was burnt to the ground in the
rebellion of '98. A woman of Gallic temperament and vivacity,
Mrs. Brooke is said, in the heyday of her youth, to have been
singularly handsome and attractive. Even in later life she
possessed remarkable grace and gentleness of manner, and from
first to last was perfectly idolised by her children. Lovable,
indeed, must have been the disposition which could have evoked
the brightest and best trait in the tragedian's character—a trait
which throughout all the blurring and hardening influences of
life shone luminously to the end: his intense child-like affection
for the woman who gave him birth.

From all accounts Master Gustavus appears to have been a
very precocious youngster. Surprising as it is to learn that at
the age of four he could read a newspaper, it is still more
surprising to find that at the same immature period his father
was wont to put him on the parlour table to recite before a circle
of admiring friends. So widely recognised, in fact, were the
child's mimetic powers that it was by no means unusual for the
military officers quartered at Longford to carry him off to the
barracks to enjoy a hearty laugh over his imitations of various
people in the town. On one occasion they treated him to the entertainment of a wandering ventriloquist, whose methods he so quickly
mastered that on his return home he nearly frightened his sister
Elizabeth out of her wits by making his voice come down the
chimney.

But these frolicsome pranks were soon to come to an end.
Having very good reason to fear that her child would be spoilt,
Mrs. Brooke made arrangements for his conveyance as a boarder
to a school in Edgeworthstown, originally established by Richard
Lovell Edgeworth, father of the famous novelist, and conducted
at that period by Lovell his son. Writes Dr. Fox, of Greenock, in
reply to our enquiries:—

"I went to that celebrated academy in the year 1826, and
remained there for two years; at that time there were upwards
of 500 boys, composed of boarders, out-boarders, and day scholars

The boarders occupied a large house adjoining the school, and paid a considerable sum for the privileges pertaining thereto. Master Brooke, however, owing to his youth and other circumstances, paid much less than any other boy in the house.

"The out-boarders were quartered through the town, and were looked after by the various ladies who accommodated them, and who were responsible to Mr. Edgeworth for their conduct and behaviour.

"The three classes of boys were dressed in nice well-made blouses, ornamented according to the taste of their respective mothers or guardians, and were inspected every morning on entering the school-room by Lovell Edgeworth himself. That gentleman lived outside the town in a beautiful large house, well wooded, with many ornamental walks and shrubberies.

"There was a room off the school-house called the *birch*, with which I was pretty familiar, having suffered there often for fighting with the day scholars and other minor offences. I must say, however, in justice to Master Brooke that I never saw or knew of his being in that hotbed of torture, and I venture to assert that he was an exception in general good conduct and behaviour.

"The course of study pursued was in strict accordance with the 'Lancasterian system' of teaching, and was very impressive, beside improving the retentive power of the brain. The classes, each composed of twelve boys, were arranged round the room in a semi-circular form, with a monitor to each; the board containing the lesson was suspended from an upright, and each boy read from right to left and from left to right, when the board was turned and questions asked by the teacher as to the nature of the subject. If the answers were not satisfactory, the same course was again gone through until the boys were masters of the subject.

"Master Brooke was a small boy for his years, but exceedingly nice, genteel, and interesting. I was his monitor at the writing desk, and had often been under the disagreeable necessity of correcting him for inattention and carelessness.

"In my second year I was enrolled as a reader, and in that capacity called at the big house every morning about eight o'clock to read in the bedroom and answer questions during the time Lowell Edgeworth was making his ablutions and dressing. Master Brooke was on the staff of readers, and was certainly a great favourite with the family."

So great a favourite, indeed, that he was selected as companion for young Essex Edgeworth. Maria Edgeworth, on the verge of sixty, still retained her great liking for children; and Brooke ever cherished deep remembrances of the penetrating grey eyes and sparse trim figure of the old lady who admitted him to her table and told him amusing stories.

At Edgeworthstown the boy remained until his mother deemed it expedient to remove to Dublin for the better education of her other children. Installing herself in a mansion in Marlborough Street, bequeathed her by her husband, Mrs. Brooke at once despatched Master Gus. to the Rev. William Jones's Academy in Gardiner's Place, where he received a classical education and was prepared for college with the view of entering the legal profession. Seeing that there had been three generations of judges in his mother's family, and as personal influence went for much in those days, it was far from idle to assume that his progress at the bar would be tolerably rapid. Events, however, soon occurred which diverted his ambition into another channel. As a matter of fact, he never entered at Trinity College. Statements to the contrary have frequently been made; but the registers, in their silence, show the fable is about on a par with the long exploded assertion that Edmund Kean was an Eton scholar. Such are some of the curiosities of histrionic tradition—green-room fungi, rotten to the touch, clustering round the root of a great name.

Among seats of learning in the Hibernian capital in those days Jones's Academy possessed one distinguishing characteristic. There the body underwent as systematic cultivation as the mind. Thanks to the able tuition of M. Satelle, the fencing master, Brooke made surprising progress, and as a runner, wrestler, and leaper soon became noted for his agility and endurance. His greatest delight, however, was in fencing, an art in which he had no compeer in the school. He came off victor once in a famous contest at singlestick between four hundred and ninety scholars, receiving so many ugly knocks in the fray as to suffer severely in the flesh for weeks after. Not aptly, indeed, has this trial of skill been compared with the famous struggle between the Horatii and Curiatii. There were three contestants on each side at the beginning, and bout followed bout until Master Gus. was left in undisputed possession of the field.

With the return of each succeeding Midsummer and Christmas came the half-yearly examinations, generally lasting four days in all. Of these, two were passed prosily enough, within closed doors ; meanwhile considerable pains were being taken to see what progress the pupils had made in the classical curriculum. On the remaining days things assumed a much livelier aspect, through the holding of public exams. in a large hall attached to the school, in which a platform and orchestra were erected for the occasion. Here the relatives and friends of the boys gathered in goodly array, to listen to the recitations in French, Latin, and English, and to undergo some modicum of excitement over the exhibitions of dancing, fencing, singlestick, and sword exercise. Occasionally, too, a House of Commons would be erected, when picked boys would spout some of the famous speeches of parliamentary orators, to the exceeding delight of papa and mamma. During his stay at the academy Brooke carried off no less than eleven prizes, the most coveted of which was the medal for elocution in the French language, won by an impassioned rendering of selected passages from the tragedy of *Zaïre*.

Mr. Montague, the dancing-master, who enjoyed great vogue in the Dublin society of those days (he was Master of the Ceremonies at the Almack), took it into his head to erect a stage in some building in North Frederick Street, where the boys of the academy were graciously permitted by their reverend master to perform in plays and execute fancy dances in costume. Mrs. Heatley has a vivid recollection of her brother dancing a sailor's hornpipe, dressed in character, and of his appearance in some female part in a dull tragedy. It is interesting to note that on this long-forgotten private stage Master Gus. first played Young Norval and William Tell, and in the latter personation astonished even his elocution master by his limpid and mellifluous delivery of the well-known apostrophe, " Ye crags and peaks, I'm with you once again."

To the praises lavished upon him in connection with these exhibitions and performances, the fostering of young Brooke's dramatic tastes has been very properly attributed. In thorough accord with the fitness of things, he was quite unconsciously receiving the best possible preparation for the career in which he was ordained to shine so conspicuously. Under the skilful tutelage of M. Satelle and Mr. Montague, he had acquired a grace of deportment which, combined with his classical features and beautifully moulded frame, subsequently rendered him a model of manly beauty. Mr. W. H. Russell, the elocution master at the academy, hailed with delight the dawnings of genius in the boy, of whom he predicted great things. A large measure of truth undoubtedly attaches itself to the charge brought against this worthy, that, without the knowledge of young Brooke's relatives, he took advantage of every opportunity to fan the dramatic flame into a blaze, giving the boy additional tuition after school hours, and encouraging him in every possible way to adopt the stage as a profession. With such tillage of rich soil small wonder that the boy's recitations soon became quite the feature of family parties. A favourite rendezvous of those who desired to get a taste of Master Gus.'s quality was the house of Mr. Collins, whose two sons were fellow-pupils and boon companions of the juvenile elocutionist.

Amid all this hubbub and pleasurable excitement, it chanced that Macready, on March 19, 1882, came to Dublin to fulfil a four-weeks' engagement. Hearing much talk of the great actor, Master Brooke must needs get permission from his mother to go and see him. It was his first visit to the theatre, and the result, as might have been anticipated, was a desperate case of stage fever. Next morning he had the audacity to wait upon the eminent tragedian, and found him busily engaged rehearsing *Rob Roy* for production on April 14. Macready received the aspirant for dramatic honours very courteously, and with paternal solicitude proceeded to impress upon him some idea of the trials and tribulations which beset the poor player. Gus. listened attentively to the homily (it was not the last he was to hear from the same lips!) and finding it was all the satisfaction he was likely to get for his pains, respectfully took his leave. Nothing daunted by the repulse, his resolution to become an actor remained unaltered.

But the stage as a vocation was not viewed in a favourable light by reputable families in those days, and Mrs. Brooke, after numerous consultations with friends and relatives, refused to countenance the project. Her son, however, was adamant, and only renewed his supplications and entreaties. At last, finding it perfectly useless to oppose the bent of his genius, the good lady gave way to his importunities, and "saying she would ne'er consent, consented."

A few days afterwards a tall, fair-complexioned youth of fourteen, with dark grey eyes and silken locks of a striking golden brown hue, was ushered into the august presence of Calcraft, the manager of the Dublin Theatre, and proceeded to astonish that gentleman by requesting that he might be allowed to appear as William Tell. Calcraft at the outset felt much inclined to show the rash intruder the door; but Master Gus. by dint of persuasiveness and resolute bearing induced the autocrat to give a patient hearing to his recitation of "Tell to his native mountains." Considerably to the manager's surprise the lad began the well-worn lines in a voice clear, firm, and musical, and without the slightest admixture of the brogue which had added to the glamour of his persuasive powers in the preliminary passage at arms. He noticed, too, that the youngster declaimed with good discretion and emphasis, suiting the action to the word with commendable neatness and precision. Puzzled to know what to say to the supplicant, the manager called in his

wife, who listened with interest to a repetition of the passage,
and rewarded the embryonic tragedian with some bread and jam
and a glass of wine. A vague promise of a distant engagement
followed, after which Calcraft dismissed his strange visitant.
But the interview was ultimately to accomplish its purpose.
Months rolled by. Edmund Kean, who had contracted to appear
in Dublin during the Easter week of 1835, found himself unable
to fulfil the engagement owing to rapidly failing health. Calcraft,
at his wits' end to know how to secure a novelty at such a
short notice, suddenly bethought him of his youthful visitor of
the previous year. Playgoers had not yet subjugated that
morbid hankering after young Roscii, which had its origin in
the precocious histrionic talents of the marvellous Betty boy.
Quite a host of infant phenomena had followed in his train ;
and so recently as 1824, one Master Joseph Burke, a child
of five, had played Tom Thumb in Dublin to crowded houses.
Others, too, of lesser note, such as Clara Fisher and little Miss
Mudie, were in the enjoyment of a fair measure of success
in the provinces. It is rational to infer that knowledge of
these facts urged upon Calcraft the advisability, in his dilemma,
of giving Master Brooke a trial. At any rate, to the boy's
inexpressible delight, negotiations were at once opened up, with
the result that his first appearance was fixed for Easter Tuesday,
in the part of *William Tell*. Those were anxious days in the
Brooke household. Endowed as he was, however, with a
remarkably quick study, Master Gus. had little difficulty, under
his mother's supervision, in swallowing the various parts in which
arrangements had been made for his appearance. Sometimes he
would slip away to Howth to give his lungs free play upon the hill.
At others he would become the prey of great fits of abstraction,
and would loll for hours upon the sofa utterly oblivious to his
surroundings. Although extremely methodical in his habits under
normal aspects, it was difficult at such periods to make him
remember his meal hours. Interrogations and remonstrances
were alike ignored until such time as whatever train of thought
his mind was pursuing had been followed out to the bitter end.

But at length the eventful day came, and with it the following announcement in *Saunders's News-Letter and Daily Advertiser:*—

THEATRE ROYAL.

EXTRAORDINARY NOVELTY.

This present Evening, April 9th, 1833, their Majesties' Servants will perform Sheridan Knowles' Historical Drama of

WILLIAM TELL, THE HERO OF SWITZERLAND.

William Tell by a Young Gentleman under 14 years of age. Emma, Miss Huddart.

A Pas de deux by Master and Miss Harvey.

The Entertainment will conclude with (second time these seven years) the Grand Melodramatic Spectacle of

THE FORTY THIEVES.

The Miss Huddart here referred to was afterwards better known to fame as Mrs. Warner the celebrated tragic actress. Calcraft would have acted more wisely had he chosen some lady of less robust frame to play the leading female characters during Master Brooke's engagement. Frequently when the exigencies of the piece required that Miss Huddart should faint or throw herself into the hero's arms, poor Gustavus had extreme difficulty in preserving his equilibrium, and the situation never occurred without a titter on the part of the audience. As for the remainder of the cast, Mr. King was the Gesler; Miss Harvey, Albert; David Rees, Strutt; and the other characters were principally supported by Messrs. Browne, Barry, Shuter, Coleman, Stodhart, Henry, Lambart, Shean, and Mrs. Pettingal.

"On last evening," says the *Freeman's Journal* of April 10, "the young *débutant,* who has been much spoken of, made his first appearance in the difficult character of William Tell. The powerful impression which Mr. Macready's recent personation of the hero of Switzerland must have left on the public mind was necessarily unfavourable for the youthful aspirant for dramatic eminence. His performance was very creditable for so young and so inexperienced an assumer of the buskin—occasionally, indeed we might say very frequently, it rose to a very high

degree of merit, and gave promise of future excellence which, if
the indication of dramatic talent which he evinced be not very
deceitful, will ripen at a future period into a fair harvest
of fame. To an agreeable face and a form which for the
young gentleman's years is well proportioned and rather gracefully
moulded, he adds respectable knowledge of the difficult secret
of acquiring what is, in truth, a considerable advance in
histrionic science, appropriateness of gesture and attitude, and
all the other almost imperceptible niceties which tend to produce
what is termed stage effect. For his voice we cannot say so
much; it is clear and sufficiently loud, but shrill, and occasionally
rather unmusical; its pitch was generally too high, and, at the
very striking passages, when he is carried off bound by the
satellites of Gesler, his repetition of the epithet 'slave,' three
separate times, in a shrill and grating key, produced an effect
which was very nearly dispelling our first illusions, and exciting
an ill-timed laugh. The address to the mountains of Switzerland
was given with good effect, and we would particularise the scene
in which Gesler's cap is raised for the obeisance of the Swiss
serfs as a piece of acting that does very considerable honour to
the young gentleman, to whose name we are sorry that we
cannot give publicity. One remark more we will make in the
hope that, if it be attended to, it will add considerably to the
effect of the young tragedian's efforts. The tone of his voice is
occasionally well suited to the expression of intense feeling in
the numerous passages calculated to call forth the very depth of
pain; but the muscles of his face are as immovable as if they
were formed of marble or adamant. The very first object of
his study should be to impart at least a reasonable portion of
expression to his countenance. On Friday he will appear in the
arduous character of Virginius (by the way, he is a close copyist
of Macready, as well in his style of acting as in the selection of
his pieces). Two such attempts within such a limited period of
time are sufficient proof that the talented young *débutant* is neither
destitute of considerable powers nor of the consciousness of their
possession."

Subsequently, in noticing Master Brooke's second appearance, the same paper railed at the blind partiality of the boy's friends in making him enact such unsuitable characters, and advised his withdrawal from the stage till his voice had reached its fulness and his figure its maturity, and, above all, till by study and observation he could discriminate for himself, and conceive a character instead of copying it. "Last night," says *Saunders's News-Letter*, of Saturday, April 13, in very much the same strain, "Last night we were spectators of the novel and interesting exhibition of the performance of Virginius by a boy not yet fourteen years of age. The enactment of such a character is in itself a task requiring the powers of a first rate actor, and we doubt if ever Sheridan Knowles or Macready felt fully satisfied with their personation of the Roman father. It was not, therefore, to be expected that a mere boy could do justice to the manlike sentiments, the matured actions and passions of Virginius, and William Tell—the two arduous and heroic rôles which this young aspirant for dramatic fame has selected as his stepping stone. His tones and gestures must necessarily be much weaker than what the parts require for proper scene illusion; and his personation of the impassioned father, or the vengeful patriot, must all consequently be (as the statuaries express it) 'far less than life,' and giving birth more to smiles than sympathy at the assumption. These tragic representations are, therefore, more properly matters of curiosity than of any deeper feeling; and in this view we are willing to concede that Master Brooke (for such we understand is his name) performed both characters better than we could possibly have expected; and evinces, altogether, a tact for scene oratory that gives fair promise of ultimate success if he perseveres in making the stage his profession. His memory is, in general, excellent; his confidence and self-possession never fail him; his conceptions of the authors' feelings, as clear as falls to the lot of childhood; and his action, which seems modelled on Mr. Macready's, partakes much of its graceful and temperate style. On Tuesday night, as William Tell, he was unfortunately chained too short in the scene where

Gesler confronts him with his son (Miss Harvey), and he could scarcely lay his hand upon her head."

Simultaneously with the appearance of the above, a local satirical journal (according to Ponsonby's "History of the Theatre Royal, Dublin," 1870) came out with the following lines :—

> "An 'under fourteen years' young gentleman,
> On Tuesday, made on stage his first congée
> As William Tell, and through his glib part ran,
> Such as one schoolboy out of every three,
> If taught and drilled so, might ; no one but can
> Admire the boy : but then, to you and me,
> Who've seen Macready, it is quite bewildering
> To have our best parts mimicked thus by children.
>
> . . . .
>
> "Last night young Master Brooke, our bold aspirant,
> Sought, as Virginius, more dramatic fame !
> His daughter slew—grew mad—then choked the tyrant,
> Swearing that kings were one and all the same :
> Sobbing aloud, with most pathetic high rant,
> And vowing vengeance in a voice as tame
> As a young bleating lamb, or dove a-cooing.
> Poor child ! his friends will be his sure undoing."

Under date Wednesday, April 17, we find the announcement in *Saunders's News-Letter*—" Most positively the last appearance, but one, of Master Gustavus V. Brooke, who has been received with most enthusiastic applause." He appeared on this occasion as Young Norval, "a character," according to the *Freeman's Journal*, "peculiarly suited to the young gentleman's powers, and one in which he acquitted himself in such a manner as to call down the general applause of a well-attended house." An extra attraction was afforded on this occasion by the appearance of W. H. Russell, Brooke's elocution master, who gave imitations of Kean as Othello, Young as Hotspur, Macready as Virginius, and Calcraft (the lessee) as Roderick Dhu.

On Tuesday, April 23, Master Brooke played Frederick in *Lovers' Vows*, to the Amelia Wildenhaim of Miss Huddart. After this he made no appearance until the 2nd of May, when he took his benefit to a well-filled house. This ended the Dublin engagement. In those days of half-price at nine o'clock, when the curtain usually rose at a quarter-past seven, playgoers liked value for their money, and generally got it. Hence there was a heavy bill on this occasion, Brooke's share in which consisted of two parts — Rolla in *Pizarro*, and Teddy the Tiler in the well-known farce. This, his first appearance in an Irish character, was probably made at the instigation of friends in generous rivalry with Master Burke, who, by dint of a good brogue and much natural intelligence, had effected his biggest hit in Irish comedy.

The result of his first appearance in his native city was such as to confirm young Brooke in his resolution to follow the stage as a profession. His decision fell like a bomb among his old schoolfellows, who had been taught to look upon the player's calling as an awful degradation for a gentleman's son— the only parallel for which could be found in the departure of a lady from the paths of virtue. So prejudicial, indeed, was the effect of Master Gus.'s action to the interests of the Academy that the Rev. William Jones thought it advisable to transfer his goods and chattels to Rathfarnham. To the sneers and entreaties of his friends young Brooke was alike obdurate, and moreover showed a lofty contempt for the proprieties by refusing (as was suggested for his family's sake) to adopt a *nom de théâtre.* His mother, however, remained loyal to him throughout, and, after packing off the other children to boarding schools, prepared to accompany him on a tour of the principal provincial theatres ; much the same plan of campaign being adopted as that followed by young Betty in 1803. Ever industrious in his studies, the boy mastered several new parts while travelling, and these proved very acceptable additions to his repertory. After a brief sojourn at Limerick, we find him in August appearing at Londonderry, where Seymour the comedian had gathered together a fairly tolerable stock company. The *Derry Journal* of Tuesday, August 27, in noticing his William Tell and Young Norval, considered that "The Dublin Roscius," as he was then styled, displayed talents of the first order as an actor. The critic condemned his tendency to over-emphasize, but confessed that

blemishes were overlooked amid the many good points made.
" He possesses an intellectual countenance ; his figure, though
slight, is good ; his action animated and convincing ; indeed his
tout ensemble is truly prepossessing ; and Master Brooke with
industry, care, and perseverance bids fair to arrive at the top of
his profession." Subsequently he appeared as Rolla, and on
Wednesday, September 1, took a benefit, when he played the
name-parts in *Richard III.* and *Teddy the Tiler.* This was
announced as his last appearance, but he took another benefit
on Friday, Sept. 20, playing Durimel in *The Point of Honour.*
" Tickets to be had of Master Brooke at 26 Ferryquay Street."

An anecdote related by James Morris (one of Brooke's life-
long friends), in his " Recollections of Ayr Theatricals " (1872),
shows that in after years the circumstance of Brooke having
played Irish characters in his tyro days had been completely
forgotten. " It was as a tragedian," writes Morris, " that he
became so widely known and his splendid talents so highly
appreciated, and yet the 'gentleman Irishman' was the character
in which he was most at home, and truly liked. A little incident
in his professional life, in proof of his partiality for that particular
walk, is worth notice, and became the means of 'bringing him
out' on a particular occasion, for one night in an Irish afterpiece.
Having arrived at Liverpool to commence a ten days' 'starring'
engagement in one of the theatres there, he was passing through
the lobby towards the green-room, for the double purpose of seeing
the manager and meeting as usual the outgoing star, when his
attention was attracted to a person sitting before the fire, apparently
in great distress. Brooke, being a humane man, inquired the
cause of the man's sorrow, which he thus explained :—' I had
given unwearied attendance upon Mr. ———— during his
engagement, and he, knowing that I have a large family, and from
other circumstances, promised to act for my benefit in the afterpiece to-morrow evening the character of Mr. O'Callaghan in the
Irish piece of his ' Last Legs'; but he has just informed me that
he requires to leave to-morrow.' 'Then,' says Brooke, 'put my
name in the bill for O'Callaghan, in the afterpiece.' With an

expression of gratitude the man replied—'That will *do me no good*. The public would not come out for *you!*' 'Never fear,' says Brooke, 'give it a trial, and a few may turn out for a laugh at my presumption, and it will, at all events, serve your present purpose.' The change was made accordingly, and a good house was the result, many theatrical critics being present, who had a desire to witness the 'breakdown' of an eminent tragedian in an attempt to assume a character in which his talented predecessor had carried all before him. It turned out otherwise, however, and the applause that greeted him was great. It may be noticed that the 'Irish star' did not depart next day, as he intended, but remained to witness from the gallery, *incog.*, the discomfiture, as he anticipated, of a young competing Paddy."

With so much enthusiasm was young Brooke received at Glasgow that, after fulfilling his original engagement of twelve nights, he was at once re-engaged on increased terms. On Friday, May 2nd, 1834, he made his first appearance at the Theatre Royal, Edinburgh, as Selim in *Barbarossa*, the announcements referring to him as "Master Brooke, whose performances in the Theatres Royal, Dublin and Glasgow, have distinguished him as the most talented youth that has appeared since the days of the young Roscius." After the following evening the theatre remained closed for a fortnight. On the 16th of the month, however, Brooke took his benefit, and made his farewell bow, appearing as Frederick in *Lovers' Vows;* Virginius in the third and fourth acts of Knowles' tragedy; and in the last act of *Richard III.* Shortly afterwards he made his first appearance in Dumfries, where he subsequently became a great favourite, and grew to be known as "the second Edmund Kean." Indeed, his popularity there was such that a street adjoining the theatre was eventually named after him. There are those still living in the town who have keen recollections of the great impression created during this first visit, when the theatre was crowded nightly, and of seeing the tall, slender, pale-faced youth walking quietly through the streets, accompanied by his lady mother.

Meanwhile, his fame had reached the metropolis, and negotiations with the proprietor of the Victoria Theatre resulted in an engagement. But the statement so frequently made in various accounts of Brooke's life that on his first appearance in London he played Virginius tri-weekly for a month, and gave complete satisfaction, is as far from the truth as the date (1837) usually assigned to the event.

Here is the announcement of Brooke's appearance :—

ROYAL VICTORIA THEATRE.

The Proprietor has the greatest pleasure in announcing that his efforts to improve the interior of the theatre have met with the most enthusiastic approbation from the Public and the Press, which unanimously pronounces the Victoria to be the most elegant theatre in Europe. In order to fulfil his pledge to the introduction of novelty, he has the honour to announce the appearance of the HIBERNIAN ROSCIUS, fourteen years of age, who will make his first appearance on the London Stage in the character of Virginius.

This evening (Thursday), October 2, will be performed

VIRGINIUS.

Appius Claudius, Mr. Selby; Caius Claudius, Mr. Griffith; Virginius, Master Brooke; and Virginia, Miss P. Horton.

At the end of the play will be exhibited the LOOKING GLASS CURTAIN, in front of which the celebrated Ramo Samee will go through a variety of extraordinary and novel Feats.

After which *The Man with the Carpet Bag*, Pluckwell, Mr. Doyne; Wrangle, Mr. Forrester; Grab, Mr. W. Keene; Grimes, Mr. Mitchell; and Harriett, Miss Foster. To conclude with

CAUGHT COURTING; OR, JUNO BY JOVE.

On the whole, the performance attracted little critical attention, and was passed over unnoticed by *The Times*, *The Sun*, and *The Observer*. "Last night at this house," says the *Morning Advertiser* of Friday, October 3, 1834, "the third, fourth, and fifth acts of Virginius were produced, and introduced for the first time to a metropolitan audience the Hibernian Roscius, Master Brooke, who, the bills inform us, is only fourteen years of age. The youth is evidently of tender years, but seemingly of some strength of mind; we would say he is rather tall of his years, but is an exceedingly clever boy, and evinces vast precocity of talent—that is, to see him perform, we would

c

never for a moment entertain suspicion that he had been merely
drilled to a task. His figure is neat, his demeanour graceful,
and he walks the stage with an air of experience and sufficiency
that bespeaks his performance is the emanation of his own mind.
The character of Virginius, which he personated, was a severe
ordeal for so young an actor to be tried by. It requires so
much passion and energy, and the continuance of so many
impassioned scenes in rapid succession draw heavily on the
physical force of the performer; and this was evidently felt by
Master Brooke: wherever his speech was of any material length
he had scarcely sufficient strength remaining at the finish to
make himself distinctly heard all over the house. It might
naturally be supposed, for youths who become actors, that they
ought to select juvenile parts; but unfortunately most of them
—such as Norval in *Douglas*, Frederick in *Lovers' Vows*, and
those of this class—require very superior skill in the profession
indeed, to make them tell upon an audience, and consequently the
very young actor, if gifted with superior talent, is likely to
produce a more striking effect in such parts as Virginius, and
become an object of wonder, and be much more attractive than
if he played with better judgment a quieter character. . . .
The performance of young Brooke was astonishingly neat, and
his business and bearing altogether was manly and characteristic,
far exceeding what could be expected from a boy of his years.
Those who are fond of witnessing essays of precocious genius
will experience a great treat in seeing the Hibernian Roscius.

"The play was cast with the whole strength of the
company, and was altogether produced in excellent style. At
the conclusion Master Brooke came forward and announced the
piece for repetition amidst immense applause. The young
gentleman met a most flattering reception from a very crowded
house."

Brooke's success, however, was purely one of esteem. Only
five or six performances of *Virginius* were given; and after the
ensuing week the name of the Hibernian Roscius disappears from
the bill. On the second night of the engagement the boy was

too ill to appear.   There was a large house, and the audience
grew so clamorous that Elton had to be sent for with the
view of his playing Virginius.   But the messenger returned with
the intelligence that the actor was not to be found, and
the piece was then changed. On Monday, October 6, a new
melodrama, called " The Purse of Alms, or, The Mendicant
Monk," saw the light. The *Morning Chronicle* of the following
day remarks :—" After the melodrama *Virginius* was produced,
the part of Virginius being undertaken by a Master Brook,
yclept the Hibernian Roscius.   .   .   We hardly know how
we can better characterise the performance of this young aspirant
to tragic fame than by saying, as Dr. Johnson said of the bear
that danced upon its hind legs—' He did not do it well, but
the wonder was that he did it at all.' "

It was certainly strange that Brooke's first appearance in
London should prove equally inauspicious with that of George
Frederick Cooke and Edmund Kean, the chequered course of
whose lives bore such a marked resemblance to his own. Nor
does the coincidence end there. As in the case of those fiery-
eyed geniuses, when next he appeared in the metropolis (after
much tedious but eminently useful strolling), it was to take the
town by storm and be hailed as the Coming Man !

CHAPTER II.

1834—1841.

Adventure at Dover—" Exit ' The Hibernian Roscius '; Enter Mr. Gustavus Brooke, Tragedian "—The Converted Manager—Re-appearance in Dublin—First Meeting with Mr. George Coppin—Brooke's Quick Study and Wonderful Memory—Remarks on his Delivery and Stage Deportment—His Physical Characteristics—Lord Lytton on his Claude Melnotte—Scene at the Birmingham Theatre—Two Tressels in the Field—Miss Marie Duret—Brooke's Drury Lane Engagement with Macready—Its Sudden Termination.

TRIFLING as had been the success of the metropolitan engagement, it at least enabled our youthful hero to become attached, for a time, to the Kent circuit, where he studied assiduously, and very soon added several new characters to his repertory. In some pleasing recollections of that period, contributed to the *Era Almanack* for 1881, Mr. Creswick, who was stage manager at the Dover Theatre, and had only just attained his majority, tells us that Brooke wore " a short jacket and peaked cap, and looked very boyish. He was announced as the young Roscius (?) and well deserved the name." Besides appearing in most of his old parts, he also played Looney M'Twolter in the well-known Irish farce, and Dennis Brulgruddery in *John Bull*. The theatre only being open four nights a-week, Creswick, Ternan, and J. Barrett took advantage of an off-day to accompany the youthful star on his first visit to Shakespeare's cliff. " He was brimful of excitement," writes Creswick, " and shouted, ran about, and climbed like a wild goat. He was then very wild—no one but his lady mother could tame him." There was a very exciting termination to the day's outing. Retracing their steps at a late hour, the little band came across a house on fire, down a narrow street in the suburbs of the old town, and were instrumental in saving the lives of a woman and child from imminent destruction.

In September, 1835, Master Brooke played a few nights at Leeds, where he made the acquaintance of a brilliant coterie of artists, in Chippendale, Compton, H. Mellon, Chute (afterwards the Bristol manager), and Miss E. Lee, better known now as Mrs. Leigh Murray. With Miss Allison, who played Amelia to his Frederick in *Lovers' Vows*, he was afterwards to find himself prominently associated at the Marylebone, when the lady and he were conjointly starred there in 1850. She was then to be recognised as Mrs. Seymour, the faithful friend of Charles Reade.

Although Brooke had now reached an age when he could no longer, with consistency, pose as "The Hibernian Roscius," no reliable record is extant to show that he ever went through the drudgery of stock work in any minor capacity. At this juncture, Fate merely wrote the stage direction—"Exit 'The Hibernian Roscius'; enter Mr. Gustavus V. Brooke, tragedian." In this latter capacity we find him starring at the Theatre Royal, Glasgow, early in February, 1836, in conjunction with Miss Clifton (of Drury Lane, Covent Garden, and the principal American theatres) and Mr. Mackay, the celebrated representative of Scottish characters. On Saturday, February 6, Brooke appeared as Henry Morton in *The Battle of Bothwell Brig*, and as George Douglas, of Lochleven, in another national drama, called *Mary Queen of Scots, or Lochleven Castle*. Mackay was in the cast of both pieces, and Miss Clifton played the name-part in the latter. During this engagement, which extended over a fortnight, Brooke appeared from time to time as Rob Roy, The Stranger, George Staunton (*The Heart of Midlothian*), and as Edgar Ravenswood in *The Bride of Lammermoor*. It is noteworthy that during the next thirty years the last-mentioned impersonation remained one of his most popular with provincial audiences, and was selected by him for his benefit on the penultimate night of his appearance on the stage. As early as this period, too, he had begun to study the character in which he was destined to make the hit of his life, at the Olympic. It was certainly something of an achievement for a youth of eighteen to give an acceptable rendering of the arduous and trying rôle of Othello. On Monday, April 11, he made his first appearance in Kilmarnock, playing there under the management of a Mr. Breyer, for six nights, in *Richard III., Douglas, Othello, Macbeth*, and other pieces. Seven months afterwards we find him at Perth, where he appeared, presumably for the first time, as Harry Dornton in *The Road to Ruin*. About this period, also, he played at Hawick for a few nights, under the management of Mr. W. Palmer, and was reminded of his sojourn there while performing in Manchester in the July of 1854, by the receipt of a letter from the quondam manager, who intimated that he had exchanged the boards for the pulpit, and, after the approved manner of such zealots, " most respectfully and earnestly begged his attention to the Gospel of Salvation." Brooke, who was accustomed to receive the most extraordinary communications, evidently took the appeal in good part; the letter in which it was made is preserved to this day.

Although upwards of four years had elapsed since Brooke made his first appearance in Dublin, the critics, on his return to his native city, in the October of 1837, still refused to listen to the voice of the charmer. " It is a very trite observation," says *Saunders's Daily News-Letter*, of Thursday, October 26, " that ' comparisons are odious '; but in some instances they cannot but be made, even if we were disposed to avoid resorting to such means of testing merit. The character of Virginius is so identified with the recollections of Mr. Macready, that when any other actor undertakes to represent it he must expect to combat with prejudices already formed, and opinions too deeply seated to be easily directed into another channel. But Mr. Brooke, who appeared last night as the hero of Knowles's tragedy, provoked comparison, for such a palpable imitation of a great master was never seen. It was an outline upon tracing paper of a beautiful picture, suggesting some idea of the original, but wanting the nature, the vividness, and reality which should impart life to the whole. Mr. Brooke has several qualifications for an actor; his voice is of a good quality, when too much is not exacted from it; his appearance is in his favour; and he has had sufficient experience to make him acquainted with what is generally designated the business of the stage, the knowledge of which, although it alone can never lead, may yet conduce to success. Why, then, lose his identity in wearing the mask of another? The ancients had their shades, who servilely followed them to their feasts, content to take share of what was given them, without much regard to reputation. But is that a reason why a performer upon the mimic stage should endeavour to obtain the sweets of popular applause upon grounds apart from his own intrinsic merit? We would not have spoken thus of Mr. Brooke did we not conceive that he has merit, and perhaps in some other character, less linked with powerful associations, he may prove deserving of higher praise. It is but justice to remark that he was greatly applauded by the audience."

Brooke's Ion, on the following Saturday, pleased the knights of the quill somewhat better; but although he remained until the 6th of November, and played Hamlet, Young Norval, and Julian St. Pierre to crowded houses, the critical thermometer never rose to summer-heat. On the 13th following we find him commencing a fortnight's engagement at Sheffield, where he quite exhausted his repertory, besides appearing in several new parts—Shylock, Sir Edward Mortimer, Jaffier, and Octavian in *The Mountaineers*, among the number. Here, too, he gave one of his earliest performances of Romeo—then and for some time afterwards a very fine impersonation; but one he was injudicious enough to repeat in later years, when his style and figure had grown utterly unsuited to the character.

During Brooke's sojourn at Sheffield he had as coadjutors Messrs. Brown, King, and Gibson, the celebrated Adelphi panto-mimists, who figured prominently in the pantomime of *Harlequin Marjery Daw*, which usually brought the evening's entertainment to a close. Judging by the frequency with which this worthy trio appeared as Second Actor, Bernardo and Francisco, and other parts in support of the tragedian, the resources of the local stock company were apparently of the slenderest. By the way, it is more than likely that in the Mr. Coppin who played Osric and Montano, Brooke for the first time found himself associated with the gentleman whose fortunes were subsequently to become so prominently identified with his own in the colonies.

An engagement in all respects noteworthy terminated on December 1, when Brooke took his benefit, playing the name-part in *Henry V.*, and Fitz-James in *The Lady of the Lake; or, the Knight of Snowdon.* Nine nights previously he had performed Iago, for the first time on any stage, to the Othello of Mude. In connection with this impersonation (by many of Brooke's admirers considered his best) Mr. Coleman, in relating an unhappy incident which occurred in the year 1864, tells us, strangely enough, that "he had never mastered the words of Iago textually, and was always afraid of being caught tripping with the text." Apart from the fact that from this time onwards Brooke was frequently seen in the part, and even played it at Drury Lane in 1853 — when his easy nonchalance and conversational flippancy aroused the bile of the critics—there is evidently considerable truth in Mr. Coleman's statement. Nature, in a prodigal mood, had nobly dowered him, and, as if jealous of the encroachments of art, had scattered gifts which eventually proved more of a curse than a blessing. Student in the sense that John Kemble was student he never could be. His genial, sunny, happy-go-lucky nature militated against this; and the barrier was rendered complete by a quickness of study and a retentiveness of memory well-nigh unparalleled. Mr. Morris, in the little book already referred to, relates that during Brooke's engagement in Glasgow in 1841, a gentleman, aware of his "peculiarly retentive memory, offered him one hundred guineas if he would undertake to read and repeat, on the same evening, the 'Glasgow Herald' published that morning. He wrote to ask my opinion, telling me that he was confident of success; but, as I advised him strongly against making the attempt, the matter went no farther."

The late Mr. Tom Chambers, treasurer of the Theatre Royal, Manchester, used to relate how Brooke studied *Richard III.* from a penny copy and learnt the part with all the errors and misprints. But there is great reason to doubt the story, because, in the first place, the tragedy had become part and parcel of Brooke's repertory long before he met the narrator. Moreover, the source was a jaundiced one, as Chambers had conceived a dislike to Brooke, and once spoke disrespectfully of him in public. On somewhat better authority, however, is it related that poor Gus. was at one time prone to make nonsense of Othello's speech—"Oh! the curse of marriage, that we can call these delicate creatures ours and not their appetites," by substituting the word *innocent* in place of "delicate."

On Tuesday, January 23, 1838, Brooke made his first appearance in Belfast—a city where he rapidly became the spoiled child of the play-going fraternity, and where his memory is still affectionately cherished. Commenting on his impersonation of Ion in Talfourd's tragedy, the *Belfast News-Letter* (which at that time seldom noticed the theatre) said:—"To personate the hero of the play with proper effect requires a highly cultivated taste, great professional experience, and a youthful and interesting appearance—all of which Mr. Brooke possesses; nor have we ever seen a character more felicitously embodied. The audience seemed fully aware of the treat provided for them, and evinced it by their earnest attention and warm applause." After his appearance in three characters, the *Northern Whig* of January 30 remarked—"The performances of Mr. Gustavus Brooke, we are glad to say, continue to attract large audiences; and judging from the high praise bestowed on his acting by some of our contemporaries, and particularly by the Scottish press, his claims upon the patronage of the lovers of the drama are by no means undeserved. Mr. Brooke, though he has scarcely reached that period of life when either the judgment or the taste of the actor can be expected to be perfectly matured, may yet be regarded somewhat as a veteran in the theatrical ranks, having entered upon his career at an age when boys of less brilliant

parts are usually sent to school. While, therefore, we are disposed
to be lenient towards the faults of this young and rising actor,
in candour we cannot ascribe them all to inexperience in his
profession. We point out what we regard as his faults the more
freely because we believe they are shared in common with actors
of far higher pretensions. We allude to that constant aiming at
effect by means of striking and picturesque attitudes, which is
certainly better suited to the melodrama than to Shakespeare's
heroes. This remark is particularly applicable to Mr. Brooke's
representation of Othello on Tuesday evening, which in some
respects possessed no ordinary merit. It was, however, marked
throughout by a manner which betrayed the effect of study in
every look and gesture, and a stage strut which would better befit
the dignity of a burgomaster than that of the noble-minded Moor
of Venice. With the exception of these defects, he manifests high
capabilities as a tragedian; and in some of the more passionate
scenes he displayed a power we have rarely seen surpassed.
We were particularly pleased with his admirable delivery of
Othello's apology." Two days later the same critic considers his
voice "unquestionably fine; but he partakes too much of the
spouter—or, if it pleases him better, the elocutionist; and at
times there is a want of nature in his tones, without which the
finest declamation falls feebly on the heart." Little idea of his
increasing popularity with each successive appearance can be
gleaned from these critical notices. It is best evidenced,
however, in an extension of the original engagement during
which he appeared in several new parts. Of these the
most noteworthy were, Selim in an Eastern romantic drama
called *The Bride of Abydos*; Rosenberg in the melodrama of *Ella
Rosenberg*; Julio in *The Foundling of Messina*; Sir Thomas Clifford
in *The Hunchback*; and Quasimodo in Fitzball's *Esmeralda*.

In connection with the *Northern Whig's* strictures on his
general style of acting, there can be little doubt that his
matchless voice—never afterwards so resonant and musical as
at this period—led him in his early and more exuberant days
to commit many elocutionary extravagances. Wrote "An Old

Fashioned Playgoer," in some pleasing reminiscences of the tragedian, which went the round of the press shortly after the loss of the *London:*—" A tolerable imitator of Brooke—and there are one or two of them on and off the stage—could recite several passages, notably the 'put out the light' speech in Othello, in which his vocal antics were of the most startling kind. First a few words were delivered in that tone of melting emotion which he made so effective; then his delivery rose to a fanciful falsetto, like scarcely anything in nature, and lastly it fell to a depth entirely *sui generis* and entirely unnatural. So, again, when as Sir Giles Over-reach he declared that he cared for nothing in heaven or hell, Mr. Brooke's gradual descent to unimagined depths of bass elocution was really not a whit more intelligent than the *tours de force* of a *basso profundo* in an opera. Contrast these examples with his later delivery of Othello's apology, and of the 'undone widow' speech in the *New Way to Pay Old Debts*, and you will understand that it is quite possible Brooke's voice, while establishing his fame, led him to play tricks with its foundations —the failure of his splendid organ synchronised, accidentally or otherwise, with a marked improvement of his latterly most perfect style."

By an irony of circumstance most of the other features in his acting considered as blemishes by the Belfast critic, were among those which ultimately assisted in the establishment of his reputation. In other eyes the "stage strut" (than which nothing could have been more leonine and rhythmic) became the very poetry of motion. Most indubitably not a little of his success was due to the graceful facility with which he assumed a series of picturesque and utterly unstilted attitudes. So natural, indeed, was this posing to the actor, that one might have photographed him at any moment with the certainty of obtaining an admirable picture. Turning the faculty to most advantage in classical characters like Virginius, Brutus, and Coriolanus, Brooke flashed upon the spectator a collocation of apparently unstudied attitudes, which, in the words of an admirer, "might have formed an extensive gallery of antique models."

A critical stage had now been reached in the tragedian's career. His mother, who never cared much for the strolling life, and pined for the society of her other children, deemed it expedient, as soon as he had attained his majority, to leave him to his own resources. Brooke did his best to repay all her loving kindness and attention by voluntarily resigning all claims upon her slender jointure: a generous action on his part, as it was doubtful whether the lady had the power of willing it.

Inevitable and just as was Mrs. Brooke's proceeding, it was none the less regretable. It was Hazlitt who, in defending the bohemian habits of actors, once said, "A man of genius is not a machine," and then went on to argue that "the intellectual excitement inseparable from those professions which call forth all our sensibility to pleasure and pain, requires some corresponding physical excitement to support our failure, and not a little to allay the ferment of the spirits attendant on success." Actors worthy of their salt are, as a rule, men of strong impulses and strong passions; possessing a keen sense of pleasure and full of the joy of living. Brooke was no exception to the number. The same frank, genial, good nature which earned for him the respect and friendship of all whom chance threw in his way rendered him an easy prey to the fascinations of conviviality. To the proverbial improvidence of a calling whose followers, seeing no way to make money breed money, for the most part live only in the Present, he added a large-hearted charity, which never turned a deaf ear to the distressed. Hence the man that made thousands seldom had a coin in his pocket. His future career suffered somewhat, likewise, from the excessive attention which his superb manliness won from the fair sex.

The tallest of tragedians, standing about five feet ten inches, his figure had now attained its ripeness and, though stoutly built, was extremely graceful in contour. With the limbs and

features of an Apollo, and the head and shoulders of a
Hercules, Brooke, as he strode the boards majestically in the
'forties, making the theatre resound with the music of his voice,
must have presented a picture of manly beauty, the like of
which has seldom been seen on the English stage.

During a ten-nights' engagement at Sheffield, commencing
October 29, 1838 (the manager being Mr. W. R. Copeland,
afterwards of the Royal Amphitheatre, Liverpool), Brooke
played a variety of parts, comprising Macbeth, Rolla, Shylock,
Henry V., William Tell, and Ion. After acting three characters
in *The Bride of Abydos*, he took his benefit on November 9,
when he aired his versatility by appearing as Rory O'More
in the Irish comedy so-called. But the engagement was chiefly
noteworthy for presenting him with an opportunity of making
his first appearance as Claude Melnotte. *The Lady of Lyons* was
then, of course, quite a novelty, as it had only seen the light
with Macready in the principal part at Covent Garden in the
February previous. Referring to the production of the play on
November 2, the Sheffield playbill of the following Monday said—
"*The Lady of Lyons* was received on Friday evening with the
most unqualified approbation. The interest excited by its
representation is unprecedented, and at the fall of the curtain
the applause was prolonged till Mr. G. V. Brooke, who was
loudly called for, made his appearance and acknowledged the
flattering testimony of public approval. *The Lady of Lyons* will
therefore be repeated to-morrow (Tuesday) evening." It was
performed also on Brooke's benefit and last night of acting.

Everything tends to show that, at this time and for some
years after, our hero was an ideal Claude Melnotte. London,
however, never saw him at his best in the part. When he
played it at the Olympic in 1850, his style had grown too
saturnine for the wild boyish enthusiasm of the ambitious
poet-lover. Mr. James Morris, presumably upon the authority
of the tragedian, relates that "upon one occasion, when Brooke
was performing in Portsmouth, I think, *The Lady of Lyons*
appeared on the bills of the day, and the gifted author (now

Lord Lytton) being in the town, was desirous of seeing Claude
Melnotte in new hands, saw the performance, and at its
conclusion waited upon Brooke and paid him the compliment
of declaring that he had not previously seen his 'Claude' so
well acted."

As illustrative of the interest taken in his impersonation
of this pinchbeck hero, we append some lines sent to Brooke
about this period by a fair wooer of the muses. The tribute
proved so flattering to the tragedian that he had a few copies
struck off for private circulation.

"TO G. V. BROOKE, AS CLAUDE MELNOTTE, IN 'THE LADY OF LYONS.'

" AYE, well has Nature in her mood assigned
        Tastes to beguile life's fleeting hours away
By feats of body or by charms of mind,
        With flowers of fancy thus to strew our way—
From earth-born fumes to bid our spirits rise
In passions pure as from our native skies.

" While some in arts abstruse would guide the age,
        Refine our manners, our enjoyments cloy,
Deeming life's horoscope a darkened page,
        On which no brighter beam marks 'to enjoy.'
Brooke! it is thine to choose a fairer part,
To guide the moral and to warm the heart.

" As some new star along the vault of heaven
        Bursts on the lonely gazer's pensive sight,
Streaming his soul with rays of splendour given
        From its own essence—such thou seem'st to-night;
But vain to trace each passion ray by ray
Like morn's young beauties stealing into day.

" Yes, I beheld thee, as the gard'ner's boy,
        Pour thy first offering at the shrine of love
To her, the idol of his youth—his spirit's joy—
        Nigh deemed by him a seraph from above;
Then, in each scene of feeling, falsehood, fame,
Still, Brooke! thy eloquence was still the same.

" The favoured suitor, the betrayer's wiles,
        The husband's agony, as he stands estranged
From all that he so loves, the very smiles
        Of Heaven, and earth's bright face are changed
To him, and then—but vainly words impart
The stern resolve, the rectitude of heart.

" Again—the hero from the battle plain,
　Who the long midnight of each hopeless year
Sighed to behold his loved one once again,
　With truth unaltered, and with heart sincere,
Now meets the past, the painful past, once more,
And all the anguish of that past is o'er.

" How comes it, Brooke, that thou can'st weave so well
　Thy witchery round us, and our senses thrill
As if some syren's charm, some wizard's spell,
　Were there to mould our feelings to thy will—
To bid our youth's impetuous pulses rise,
Or draw bright tears from beauty's gentle eyes?

" But fare thee well!　May fame round thy young brow
　Entwine her laurels, till thy course is past,
Still may'st thou shine admired and loved as now,
　May each new scene be happier than the last;
So may'st thou live, untouched by grief or pain,
Thy talents prized, thy love ne'er breathed in vain."

MARIE.*

Nor was this the only outcome of the lady's admiration of Brooke's talents.　Solely on his behalf she wrote the favourite school-boy piece, *The Outlaw*, which was first publicly recited by him during a brief engagement at Belfast, late in the summer of 1842.

In a " Memoir of Mr. Gustavus Vaughan Brooke," by " H. T.," prefixed to the first part of an edition of Shakespeare issued by the London Printing and Publishing Company in 1854, and evidently inspired by its subject, the following curious episode is narrated :—

" While still a mere youth he became a member of the company performing at the Birmingham Theatre, where he was concerned in an incident which is worth relating.　His engagement was prolonged for a considerable period, but after a short time the manager treated him in anything but a handsome manner.　He not only allowed the young actor but few opportunities of appearing before the public, but omitted paying him his salary during a period of eight weeks.　On the

---

* Said to have been a Miss Scott, a persistent wooer of the muses ; herself eventually wooed and won by a gentleman farmer named Henderson, at one time residing in the neighbourhood of Armagh.

last night of his engagement he was cast for the comparatively
trifling part of Tressel in *Richard the Third*, Mr. Charles Kean
being to play the blood-thirsty and crafty Glo'ster. During the
afternoon Master Brooke addressed a note of complaint and
remonstrance to the manager on the subject of his financial
claims, and intimated that he should expect the payment of
arrears. The manager either would not or could not pay; and
in the evening the young actor perceived another person dressed
for Tressel and every wing guarded by the stage carpenters and
friends of the manager. Determined not to be baffled in this
manner, Master Brooke, as soon as he heard the cue given for
the entrance of Tressel, vaulted over the head of one of the
carpenters at the upper entrance, and made his appearance on
the stage, greatly to the astonishment of the King and the
audience, who each beheld *two* Tressels in the field.

"Great confusion ensued; and Brooke, advancing to the
footlights, explained the circumstances, and threw himself on
the indulgence of his audience. The sympathy of the spectators
was enlisted on behalf of the lad and he was greeted with
thunders of applause, and with—what was equally acceptable—
a little shower of money. To the repeated demands made from
the wings that he should instantly leave the stage, young Brooke
replied by holding out his hand to the side for his arrears of
salary. At length the money was given to him, and he came
down to the footlights and leisurely counted it. Finding it was
not correct, he again stretched out his hand to the wing, and
would not withdraw it until he succeeded in obtaining the full
amount due to him. The play then proceeded; but the next
night the theatre remained unopened. Master Brooke had
ruined the treasury, and the season was closed."

Of this we can only say, *si non e vero e ben trovato.*
Unfortunately, the utmost endeavours on our part to verify the
details have ended in smoke. Although the incident, if true,
must have happened between 1834 and 1839 (in which latter year
Mr. Charles Kean left for America), the general consensus of
opinion among authorities on the Birmingham stage runs to the

effect that Brooke's first appearance in that city was made as a
star, many years after. Mr. Samuel Timmins, who very
considerately sifted the matter to the bottom, points out that
Charles Kean played Richard III. at Birmingham on October
24, 1834. But no evidence is forthcoming to show that Brooke
acted there at that period; which is not surprising, considering
that he had barely brought his engagement at the Victoria to
a close.

Commencing an extended tour through Ireland at the
Belfast Theatre on Monday, January 21, 1839, Brooke found
a somewhat altered condition of affairs in that city owing to the
crusade which the "unco guid" had unrighteously got up
against poor Burroughs the manager. After making several
indignant references in his advertisements to "the most unjust,
ungenerous, and persevering efforts" that had been made "to
injure his reputation, destroy his prospects, and cause him the
severest and most unmerited losses," the hapless lessee bethought
him of more salutary retaliation, and reviving *The Hypocrite*,
sarcastically invited his persecutors to call and see their friend
Maw-worm. Peace was then declared. Among the more
noteworthy parts played by Brooke during his fortnight's
sojourn here we find George Barnwell, Rory O'More, El Hyder
in a "Grand Eastern Drama," so-called; the three Lockwoods
in the drama of *The Farmer's Boy*; Reuben Glenroy in
Morton's comedy *Town and Country*; Petruchio in *Katharine
and Petruchio*; Alexander the Great in Nat Lee's famous
tragedy; and Duke Aranza in *The Honeymoon*. Mackay, the
great Bailie Nicol Jarvie, was performing there at the same
time, and Brooke for his benefit on January 31 appeared as
Mr. Bromley in *Simpson and Co.* Certainly the tragedian, if he
attained enduring popularity at this period in Belfast and
the minor towns of the north, worked hard for his laurels.
Frequently appearing in two heavy parts nightly, he would
also occasionally relieve the tedium of the entr'actes by reciting
"Lord Ullin's Daughter" and other favourite pieces. During
the summer he played a whole month in the primatial city

D

of Armagh, which, sad to say, like Newry, has long since ceased
to boast the possession of a theatre.

Always on the lookout for new blood wherewith to recruit
his company at Drury Lane, it was not in the order of things
that Macready could remain long ignorant of the growing
reputation of one who in his tyro days had paid him the
sincerest form of flattery. Fame had now blown such a loud
blast on her trumpet in Brooke's case that the eminent
tragedian was fain to send his agent to Scotland in the summer
of 1810 to report on the matter. So pleased was that gentleman
with Brooke's acting on coming across him at the Theatre Royal,
Aberdeen, that he engaged him forthwith to share "second
business" or juvenile tragedy with Mr. James Anderson during
the ensuing season at Drury Lane. According to agreement the
young tragedian was to proceed to London immediately after
the fulfilment of a short engagement at the Thistle Theatre,
Dundee. In the meantime, however, he received a severe injury
in the combat scene of *Richard III.*, which considerably delayed
him on his journey. Another and more dubious version of the
affair is related by Messrs. W. May Phelps and J. F. Robertson,
who start in their *Life of Phelps* by erroneously fixing the period
at 1812-13. In this work we are unblushingly told that Brooke
"had been smitten by a lady of Babylonian beauty belonging to
the Granite City, and she holding him fast in her toils arrested
his southward progress at Dundee. *One of the most promising
careers was thus blasted.*" This is entirely away from the facts.
Delays to the contrary notwithstanding, Brooke arrived in London
quite time enough for the Drury Lane rehearsals. It is
unfortunately true that while in Scotland he had contracted the
acquaintance of a fascinating actress of the Madame Celeste
school, known as Miss Marie Duret, who, as we shall see, for
some eight years travelled under his protection and occasionally
under the shelter of his name. But it would be as idle to impute
to the lady's influence the disastrous termination of the Drury
Lane engagement, as it is foolish on Messrs. Phelps and Forbes
Robertson's part to lay at her door the responsibility for the

"intermittent orgies" which the actor is said for several years to have indulged in.

When Brooke arrived in London early in the December of 1841, it was to find that Macready purposed opening his campaign at the National Theatre with a revival of *The Merchant of Venice.* On entering the green-room he saw posted up a cast of the play, with his own name opposite the ungrateful part of Salarino; together with a notice (according to Mr. Edward Stirling) that on Friday Mr. G. V. Brooke would play Othello. Unluckily for the newcomer, he had entered upon the engagement without giving careful consideration to all the provisions of the contract. Had he known himself properly when Macready's agent first crossed his path, he would at once have seen that nothing could well be more galling to him than the alternation of leading and secondary parts in a well-ordered London company. His was not the nature to play the triangles to any one else's first fiddle. Hence his gorge rose at the indignity which he believed had been thrust upon him. Pausing only to tear down the bill, he strode out of the theatre with lowering brow and menacing aspect, never to darken its portals again under Macready's management. In a brief account of Brooke's career which appeared in *Tallis's Magazine* for 1851, it is pointed out that the green-room gossips of the time absolutely stated that the actor, "on finding himself cast to play Laertes to Macready's Hamlet, immediately wrote to the manager, saying that he was only in the habit of performing one part, and that was Hamlet, and that Mr. Macready might play the Ghost if he choose." The writer, presumably on the authority of Brooke himself, denies this, and most emphatically lays down the Salarino version as the true one. The date of the occurrence and everything related to it has hitherto formed the subject of much dispute, principally owing to the fact that Macready makes no immediate reference to Brooke's conduct in his diary. But, taking the Salarino version as correct, there can be no two questions about the exact period, as *The Merchant of Venice* was only once revived by Macready, either at Covent Garden or Drury Lane.

Without any undue desire to exonerate Brooke in the matter, it remains to be said, in palliation of his offence, that Macready does not seem, at the outset, to have properly fulfilled his part of the contract. This is evidenced by the fact that an action for breach of engagement was at once withdrawn on Brooke's threatening to publish the whole of his correspondence with Macready, in self-defence.

Luckily for himself, Brooke lost little caste by his quarrel with the eminent tragedian. But after his return to the provinces, where he had no difficulty in getting eligible engagements, he looked askance at the tempting bait held out by metropolitan managers, and refused as many as thirteen promising offers before making his memorable appearance at the Olympic.

CHAPTER III.

1842—1846.

ABOUT the period of Brooke's rupture with Macready, Mr.
J. H. Anderson, better known as "The Wizard of the
North," and Mr. W. J. Hammond, the comedian, had entered
upon the joint management of the Theatres Royal, Manchester
and Liverpool. To these gentlemen the irate tragedian at once
declared allegiance, and during the greater part of the year
1842 was to be found acting at one or other theatre. The new
managers signalized their accession by a wholesome reformation
behind the scenes, evoking considerable praise from the critics
for scrupulous attention to the claims of *mise en scène*.
Commenting on Brooke's first appearance in Manchester, as
Richard III., on Wednesday, January 12, the *Guardian*, after
treating briefly (and erroneously) of the "new and young"
tragedian's antecedents, says :—"He has a good voice, which he
taxes heavily, and which consequently fails him towards the end
of a 'heavy part' like Richard III.; a tolerably good figure and
countenance, and has several good points about him without
attaining to the highest rank of our present tragedians. To
say that we think he will prove a better actor than Mr. Stuart *

---

* Probably the actor who played seconds to Brooke during his
Olympic engagement of 1848.

(who we see is now be-praised in some London papers), or than
Mr. Charles Kean, is not saying much. Yet it is all we are
disposed to say till we have seen more of him. He commenced
Richard with such *tours de force* that it was easy to predict that
his voice would fail him before the play closed. This is bad
husbandry of an actor in more senses than one; in fact, it is
the boy roaring 'wolf' before there is any need. Altogether
Mr. Brooke made a favourable impression, which it must be his
care to retain and strengthen. At the fall of the curtain he
was loudly called for and as loudly cheered."

Remaining in Manchester until January 26, Brooke grew
daily in popular, as well as critical, estimation, playing among
other parts Romeo, Rolla, Macbeth, Virginius, and Evelyn.
Accompanied by Miss Julia Bennett, the Manchester "leading lady,"
he opened at Liverpool on January 31, when Messrs. Anderson and
Hammond inaugurated their management at the Theatre Royal by
an elaborate revival of *Hamlet*. As the new lessees had two other
playhouses to contend with, they had very judiciously secured
the services of several old Liverpool favourities for their stock
company, Mr. Richard Younge and Mr. Bellingham among the
number. Says the *Liverpool Mercury* of February 4:—"We
now come to speak of the performers, and must first introduce
our readers to Mr. G. V. Brooke, who made his first appearance
here as Hamlet. He is a young man of great promise—nay, not
only of great promise, but even now of sterling abilities. His
performance was a masterpiece. With a clear and distinct
enunciation he adds gracefulness of manner and an admirable
conception of the philosophical Hamlet. He plays not to the
audience—he plays not for effect—he seems to be entirely
absorbed in the character, as every actor must be who wishes
to arrive at a high place in his profession. Some of his
readings are new and original, and we could not help but
admire the modesty and dignity—yet familiarity—with which
he delivered his address to the players. His encounter with
the Ghost was thrilling—every word seemed to have an impression
upon him, and the minor details of position and acting, the

result of much study and a just discrimination, are scrupulously attended to. We expect much from the young gentleman, who was called for by the audience, and are sure the managers will do well to announce a repetition of Hamlet."

The critical notices continued warm throughout. " Since our last," says the *Mercury* of February 11. " Mr. Brooke has played Evelyn in *Money*, Romeo, and has appeared again as Hamlet, in which he has given the most unbounded satisfaction; and the style in which the latter piece has been put upon the stage has received the warmest commendations of all who have seen it." Again, on Friday, February 25, the same paper says:—" The spirited manner in which the new managers have commenced their campaign has quite astonished the play-going public, and if any proof were wanted of this continued desire to please, it would be found in the style in which the tragedy of *Richard the Third* was brought out on Monday last, with appropriate scenery and new dresses, the elegance of which has not been equalled on the stage. . . . . We cannot speak too highly of Mr. Brooke's Richard; it was a splendid effort, crowned with the most complete success, and he was loudly called for at the close of the play. Never did any actor rise more rapidly in the estimation of the public than does this gentleman, and never did any aspirant for histrionic fame more justly deserve to do so."

After playing Macbeth and Othello, Brooke returned to Manchester for a few nights, and on May 16 reappeared in Liverpool as Ion. After the lapse of a week he retraced his steps to Manchester, and on June 14 figured as Iago to the Othello of Mr. James Anderson. Taking advantage of the off season to visit his friends in Ireland, he played a very successful engagement during the summer at the Cook Street Theatre, Cork; then under the management of Frank Seymour, the comedian, of whom so many funny stories have been told. Here he renewed his acquaintance with Mrs. Warner — the Miss Huddart of his early Dublin days— and, supported by Marie Duret (whose Juliet was very highly praised), ran the gamut of his histrionic scale, playing, among other parts, William in *Black-Eyed Susan*, and Don Felix in *The Wonder*.

Returning to Liverpool early in September for the opening of the winter season, we find him playing there (amid a variety of his old parts) Brutus in *Julius Cæsar*, Gambia in *The Slave*, and Rob Roy to the inimitable Bailie of Mackay. After a short visit to Manchester, where his Romeo was very warmly received, he reappeared at Liverpool on September 26 for Mr. and Mrs. Baker's farewell benefit. On this occasion he played Worthington in *The Poor Gentleman*, for the first time on any stage, to the Humphrey Dobbin of Mackay. Brooke little thought at this time how soon he was to find himself thrown out into the cold. Unfortunately, Messrs. Anderson and Hammond had commenced their reign in a spirit of liberality out of all proportion to the measure of support accorded them.

Returning to Manchester at the beginning of October, Brooke played Iago on the 3rd to the Othello of Woolgar, and remained there until the 22nd, when he made his last appearance under Messrs. Anderson and Hammond's management. The theatre was suddenly closed owing to the failure of the lessees; and when it re-opened its doors on December 24, with Robert Roxby as manager, Brooke was temporarily lost to Manchester playgoers, and Charles Pitt reigned in his stead.

Misfortunes such as these, however, are but "trifles light as air" when one is only five-and-twenty. Friends were not wanting to whisper in Brooke's ear that he had all the physical qualifications which go to make the great actor, and that with unceasing study and culture the ball was at his feet. Dissipation and elocutionary vagaries had not yet played havoc with a voice whose analogue had not been heard on the stage since the days of silver-tongued Barry. In no sense introspective, however, his devil-may-care nature spoiled all. If he burnt the midnight oil it was in excessive conviviality with the boon companions that fluttered around him. Thrown suddenly on his own resources, there was nothing for it, for the time being, but to return to his old strolling life. The victim of some strange caprice, we find him playing occasionally at this period as Mr. Gustavus *Vasa* Brooke—a circumstance which in after years evidently gave rise to the contention as to his real name. Emerging for a moment from obscurity at Brighton (where, supported by Marie Duret, we find him playing a few nights in February, 1843), he disappears again from sight, only to turn up later in the year at Berwick-on-Tweed.

Prominent among those places which lost their theatrical importance with the advent of the railway, the Border town during the first quarter of the present century was looked upon as an agreeable halting-place by the weary player in the course of his northward progress. Berwick owes her boast that the Kembles, the Keans, T. P. Cooke, Joe Grimaldi, and many other celebrities appeared on local boards, to the circumstance that the mail coach from Manchester once upon a time passed through the town on its way to the Scottish capital. The theatre, which had been originally opened by Stephen Kemble, of obese memory, was fitted up in a large building at the rear of the King's Arms yard. It was remarkable for its commodiousness, the stage being deep and well supplied with scenery of the old conventional order.

Thither the young tragedian, accompanied by Miss Duret, her maid Fanny, and some pet dogs, wended his way early in the summer, securing apartments at the house of the Misses Cameron in Church Street. A lady still living in Berwick happened as a child of twelve or thirteen to be residing under the same roof. Womanlike she has little remembrance of Marie Duret, save of her wearing "a beautiful pink dress covered with lace and garlands of flowers, and a large scuttle-shaped hat of light-coloured velvet." Things are different in the case of the tragedian, of whose liberality and extreme good nature the lady retains the most sympathetic recollections. This delight in the company of little children ever remained one of the most pleasing traits in Brooke's character. Few of those who knew him intimately but can testify to the huge enjoyment he derived from joining in their romps and helping them to set out their toys. Even when leaving the town with the slenderest of purses, he could not find it in his heart to say goodbye to his little playmate without giving her a bright half-crown as a keepsake.

At Berwick, we learn for the first time of his playing that arduous and searching character which few on the stage have rendered acceptable since George Frederick Cooke and Edmund Kean made it their own. Although many and various are the actors who have attempted to win renown as Sir Giles Over-reach since Henderson gave his elaborate conception and John Kemble failed in the part, only the names of Cooke, Kean, and Brooke will live in theatrical history as its interpreters.

In Berwick the popularity of Brooke and Marie Duret grew apace; so much so that when the lady took her benefit in her famous character of Jack Sheppard many were turned away from the doors. The casual wayfarer who happened to turn down Church Street in the day-time would sometimes get a glimpse of Brooke sitting at the open window attired in a gown of red cloth plentifully bespattered with black spots. Sometimes he might be seen rehearsing with his fair companion—sometimes playing with the dogs; and the spectator, if he cared to strain his eyes, might view with wonder the heap of rich dresses, swords, riding-boots, and rouge-besmeared towels piled higgledy-piggledy in the corner. Occasionally there would be a day's outing in a post-chaise, when Brooke might be seen shooting at sparrows along the Whiteadder burn what time the lady was beguiling the hours with a fishing-rod.

The circumstances under which their sojourn at Berwick came to an untimely end had somewhat of a tragic aspect. Brooke had grown so popular with the inhabitants that he was frequently invited out to dinner by the gentry in the neighbourhood, none of whom ever thought of including the name of his fair companion on the card. The slur seems to have left so deep an impression

upon the lady's mind, that on one occasion when Brooke was at
a dinner party at Dr. Cahill's she left her apartments and
poisoned herself in the public street. Repenting quickly of her
action she appealed to the timely assistance of a stranger, who
bore her into a neighbouring house and then set off, post-haste,
to fetch Brooke's host. Exerting all his skill the doctor
succeeded in saving her life. Although heavily in debt, Brooke
felt too much ashamed to perform in Berwick again, and at
once took his departure from the town accompanied by the
lady, but minus *his* boxes and *her* maid. Subsequently we
learn of him at Carlisle, where he made the acquaintance of
his life-long friend, Mr. James Rodgers (late the lessee of the
Prince of Wales's Theatre, Birmingham); and at Wigton, a small
market town eleven miles off, where he acted in a wooden
structure known as Thorne's Theatre. A Carlisle correspondent,
in informing us that he was among those who witnessed Brooke's
performances in the booth, emphatically gives it as his opinion
that, although he saw the tragedian many times afterwards at
Manchester and elsewhere, his acting never again appeared so
f rcible and vivid. The absolute truth of this statement is
corroborated by an anonymous writer in *The Australian Magazine*
for July, 1886, who, in some sympathetic reminiscences of
"An Old Australian Favourite," tells us of the excitement
occasioned some forty years previously in the little Scotch
town where he passed a portion of his school days, by the
arrival of the great actor. "Montgomery, Fechter, Irving, and
other exponents of the tragic art have I seen since then, but
there remains with me, embalmed in the clear amber of memory,
the eidolon of Brooke as far and away the best and noblest
representative of the romantic school of acting. Of the rival
school—the classic—with its traditions of the Kembles and the
Siddons, I can only judge by my recollection of old Vandenhoff,
once seen in Judge Talfourd's classic play of *Ion*. That I
remember as a noble and impressive performance, clear-cut,
statuesque, not without soul; but, compared with Brooke
at his best, it was as water unto wine, or as the cold

northern moonlight to the glowing sunshine of our Australian summer."

The comparisons and classifications here indulged in appear to us rather confusing, seeing that Brooke, after he had shaken off the thraldom of Macready, declared his allegiance to the school of Vandenhoff. We learn this from the revelations of the "Old Fashioned Playgoer," who says:—

"It has, however, been written since Mr. Brooke's death, that his style was entirely his own. I am enabled to say from personal knowledge that this was not G. V. Brooke's opinion. When not under the influence which was his bane, he was a remarkably modest man and seldom spoke of his own doings. But I was one day having a pleasant chat with him about great actors, and I tempted him into a piece of egotism by naming Mr. Vandenhoff. With certain limitations my mention of that actor was very eulogistic. Brooke seized upon my praises with avidity, treating them as if they meant more than I had expressed.

"I then added that I thought in a certain part he was very like Mr. Vandenhoff. 'I'm delighted,' said Brooke, in the husky tones and slightly Irish pronunciation which he so wonderfully got rid of on the stage, 'I'm delighted to hear you say that, for it was always my greatest ambition to resemble Vandenhoff.' But those who say his style was his own are, to a great extent, right nevertheless. He was too full-blooded a man to be very successful in imitating a model so comparatively cold and obviously methodical. Accordingly, they were most like each other in the Hunchback, for Master Walter suppresses his emotions or simulates others throughout the play. They were also somewhat alike in Brutus; but in Coriolanus the emotional power of Brooke and his vivid representation of the weaker and impulsive side of the Roman general's character left Vandenhoff's fine performances considerably on one side; while what I have called his full-bloodedness, rendered his Matthew Elmore, in *Love's Sacrifice*, a great deal more probable, more contagiously effective and more spontaneously affecting than that of Mr.

Vandenhoff, who was the original of the character. The two great speeches in this play—that on the horrors of a murderer's life and that describing the death of Count Du Barry—and the critical interviews with Lafont and with Margaret, constituted, in my opinion, Brooke's greatest triumph. I do not believe there ever was finer, more impressive, more overwhelming or better balanced acting since the stage became a profession."

But these were among Brooke's later characters. Resuming our narrative, we find that not long after Brooke's visit to Carlisle, Mr. James Rodgers (then the veriest tyro on the boards) was making his way from Glasgow to Inverness, and to his enjoyable surprise ran across his newly-acquired friend on the boat. On exchanging confidences they found that both were bound for the same destination; the one to open as Hamlet, the other as Laertes. "To tell you the honest truth," said Brooke to his companion, "I was due at Inverness three weeks ago; but faith I met three jolly fellows in Glasgow, and their company was too good to leave." Bubbling over with high spirits and good fellowship, he continued his conviviality on board the steamer, and quite demoralised the crew with his fascinating companionship and infectious drollery. A pleasant picture this—to those who can avoid looking at its pendant. With but poor husbandry of his financial resources it is not to be wondered at that the reckless youth, while playing in a notoriously untheatrical district, eventually found himself stranded. Whether the worthy inhabitants of Kilmarnock assumed an attitude of apathetic indifference towards the young tragedian, or were merely indisposed to flock to a theatre inconveniently situated in a loft over some stables at the bottom of a yard, is equally indeterminable. One thing is certain—that Brooke, from want of patronage while appearing there, after his Inverness engagement, had perforce to leave his apartments and take up his abode for a time in the green-room (!) of the playhouse.

Among the many managers who endeavoured to induce our hero to return to London, after his famous quarrel with Macready, we find Mr. Edward Stirling, who made him an offer for the Olympic, politely refused in the following terms:— *

TheaTre Royal, Greenock,
September 8th, 1843.

My Dear Sir,

Ever since the very disgraceful conduct of the Drury Lane Management towards me, I have almost buried myself in oblivion. With regard to visiting the metropolis, under existing circumstances it will be utterly impossible for some time; and even then I will candidly confess to you that nothing but a *most tempting* offer would induce me to leave the provinces. I am aware that a great number of persons think me little better than a madman for acting in the manner I have done and am doing, but I am determined to see my way clearly and 'bide my time.' I open the Ayr Theatre for the Caledonian Hunt on the 25th instant. However, I shall drop you a *weekly hint* of my locality, and shall feel happy to hear from you and profit by your counsel and advice, and in the meantime

I remain, dear sir,

Yours very truly,

Gustavus V. Brooke.

P.S.—I leave here on the 18th instant for Ayr.

It is a strange fact, that although more than four years elapsed before Brooke ventured to make an appearance in London, the theatre then chosen was the Olympic. Meanwhile his managerial venture at Ayr had proved disastrous; not very surprising considering that from first to last he never evinced the possession of any of the qualities requisite in a theatrical director. But his stay in Burns' town was not without its compensating advantages. It enabled him to acquire the friendship of genial James Morris, who throughout his chequered lifetime stuck to him manfully, and was ever ready to place his counsel and his purse at his disposal. Writes Morris in his little book of Recollections: "I have seen Brooke, when 'roughing it' as a manager, enact all kinds of parts or walks. As a sailor you naturally wondered whether he had ever been on shore, while from the gentleman to the robber he looked all the characters to perfection; indeed, with all that came in his way he was nature itself.' When things were at their direst extremity,

* See Stirling's "Old Drury Lane" (Chatto & Windus, 1881), vol. II., p. 224.

Morris, who was friendly with David Prince Miller (author of *The Life of a Showman*), then manager of a substantial wooden building in Glasgow known as the Royal Adelphi Theatre, induced that worthy to proffer Brooke, Miss Duret, and the Ayr company a satisfactory engagement. Rather unfortunate in his previous speculations, Miller was delighted to find that the Glaswegians had a thorough taste for the legitimate, as shown by the warm reception accorded to Gustavus. During a month or five weeks' sojourn there, commencing on Monday, May 6, 1844, the tragedian played to crowded houses nightly, appearing from time to time as Edgar Ravenswood, Othello, William Tell, Alexander the Great, Huon (in Sheridan Knowles's new play *Love*), Hotspur (*Henry IV.*), Tom Moore (*The Irish Lion*), Doricourt (*The Belle's Stratagem*), and Lothair in *Adelgitha*.

Lighter at heart and much heavier in pocket, the tragedian, accompanied by Miss Duret (who from her limpet-like qualities was now familiarly known among Brooke's cronies as "The Old Man of the Sea"), made his way southward to Manchester, appearing for the first time at the old Queen's Theatre in Spring Gardens on July 8. The Theatre Royal had been burnt down in the May previous. After starring at the Queen's in a round of stock characters, Brooke left there for Liverpool about the middle of August, having contracted to manage the Theatre Royal, Church Street (late Liver Theatre), in that city, for Mr. Malone Raymond, the lessee. At least, the bills of the period are headed, " Under the management of Mr. G. V. Brooke." His stay there, however, was short. On Friday, September 6, we find him playing Richard Shelly, the poacher, in Fitzball's domestic drama in two acts, *The Momentous Question*, for Mr. and Mrs. Malone Raymond's benefit; Miss Duret being the Rachel Ryland. By the 23rd following he had returned to the Manchester Queen's, where, during the month of November he played seconds to Vandenhoff for a considerable number of nights, appearing as Iago, Macduff, etc., etc. After fulfilling a similar office during Fanny Cooper's visit, he took a benefit, December 10, when *Ion* was in the bill. Beyond appearing as

King James in *Cramond Brig*, nothing of note occurred until
January 30, 1815, when he gave a fine impersonation of Sir Giles
Over-reach. So successful, indeed, was his first appearance as
Marc Antony in *Julius Cæsar* on February 3, that the play was
repeated four nights after, with George Preston as the Brutus
and T. H. Lacy as Cassius. Considered equal to the Brutus of
Vandenhoff, Brooke's superb Marc Antony is still well remembered
by old Manchester playgoers. Subsequently, he appeared thrice
as Martin Lessamore in *Pollar's Acre; or, The Wife of Seven
Husbands*, and took a second benefit on Wednesday, February 27,
when he played the name-part in the tragedy of *Bertram*.

Brooke's patience was now to undergo a severe trial. His
old enemy, Macready, had been engaged to appear at the Queen's
Theatre in March, when all the second parts, in the natural
order of things, would fall to Gustavus. A hoary tradition exists
in Manchester to the effect that Brooke at this period had ample
revenge for all the indignities thrust upon him by the eminent
tragedian. The story goes that Brooke, happening to be cast
as Othello to Macready's Iago, by a supreme effort put forth all
the power and pathos at his command, creating such an effect
upon the audience that his Moor-ship's ancient was well-nigh
overwhelmed. Without any undue desire to dispel such cherished
illusions, it is necessary to point out that, however feasible the
story, it is not borne out by any evidence at command. Beside
this engagement, Brooke supported Macready at the Theatre
Royal, Manchester, in April, 1847, and so far from endeavouring
to tower over his adversary, appears to have shown his contempt for
the star by, for the most part, " walking through " his characters.

In connection with this it is noteworthy that *The Star* of
February 21, 1890, contained an interview with Mr. Bruton
Robins, an old actor then at Drury Lane, from which we take
the following: — " During one of the season's excursions, Macready
went to Manchester to star. G. V. Brooke was leading man at
the time. A suit for breach of engagement had been entered
against him. The play was *Werner*, Brooke the Ulric. At the
end of the piece Macready sent a request to Brooke to favour him

with his presence in his dressing-room. Brooke was rather surprised, but complied. After the usual ceremonies, Macready thus addressed him:—'I deeply regret, Mr. Brooke, that any misunderstanding should have occurred between us, and shall take immediate steps to stay all further litigation. You have delighted me beyond expression by your masterly impersonation of Ulric to-night. A bright future is in store for you. Persevere in your studies, and you will be, or my judgment errs, a great actor.'"

Appealed to for his authority in this matter, Mr. Robins (who had played Iago to Brooke's Othello at Brighton in 1850) replied—"My informant was Mr. Cowper,* a leading member of the company at the time. Of course no third person would be present at such an interview, and only Mr. Brooke himself could have been Cowper's informant. When an eminent tragedian like Macready sends his messenger to an actor the members of the company are anxiously waiting to know the result of such an interview. Mr. Brooke was always an open-hearted good fellow amongst his brother actors, and, being so, made no secret of what transpired."

Mr. Robins' informant, we are afraid, got the story at second-hand, and garbled it in the telling. On the night he played Werner, during his first engagement in Manchester, Macready *did* send for Ulric, but with far different motives to those imputed to him. He had evidently felt greatly annoyed at the careless manner in which the actor had played his part, and under date March 27, 1845, enters in his diary:— "Acted Werner very fairly. Called for (trash!). Spoke in gentle rebuke and kind expostulation to Mr. G. V. Brooke."

Lest it should be argued that the real occasion referred to by Mr. Cowper was the *Werner* night of the second engagement (April 28, 1847), we may point out that the *Manchester Guardian*, so far from waxing enthusiastic over Brooke's Ulric, merely remarks that he was "effective, but not letter-perfect."

---

* Cowper does not appear to have been prominently associated (if at all) with any of the Manchester Theatres until 1856, when he was leading man at the Royal.

E

With the termination of Macready's first engagement, Brooke appears to have resumed his wonted vigour. On Thursday, April 17, he played Don Cæsar for the first time, and on the 23rd appeared as Orlando to the Jaques of Vandenhoff and the Rosalind of his daughter. On May 24 we find him impersonating Wallack's great part of Martin Heywood in *The Rent Day*—a character which he afterwards sustained with credit in America and the Colonies. Two nights later, an elaborate production of *Margaret Catchpole* took place; this, with Brooke as Will Laud, held its place in the bills intermittently for several weeks.

With the beginning of the autumn season, the Queen's Theatre had a formidable rival in the New Theatre Royal, which had just opened its doors with a great flourish of trumpets. It was a busy, eventful time for Brooke, but he bore his responsibility with an easy grace characteristic of the man. After repeating his admired impersonation of Marc Antony early in September (to the Brutus of Mr. James Anderson) he had the felicity of supporting Charlotte Cushman during her brief visit of six nights, when he appeared as Fazio (twice), Macbeth, Julian St. Pierre, The Stranger, and Duke Aranza.

Among all the actors who visited Manchester at this time, or played in the local stock companies there was none who could approach Brooke in melody, power and range of voice. Indeed it is doubtful whether he has ever been excelled in this respect save in the one noteworthy instance of Salvini. Notwithstanding all the good feeling evinced towards Brooke by his comrades-at-arms, a tinge of malice evidently entered into the raillery with which they plied him about the end of September. "Brooke, my boy," one would say, "look out; Forrest is coming." Then another would chime in with, "Yes, it's rather a shabby trick of his drowning the voice of everyone he comes across." "How can he help it?" says a third. "His lungs are simply frightful." To all of which Brooke would significantly make reply, "If he tries it with me I'll teach him a lesson." In due course the great American tragedian came to fulfil his engagement at the Queen's, and met with a good reception. For several nights he acted with moderation, Brooke playing Phasarius to his Spartacus in *The Gladiator*, and other parts of a similar calibre. On Wednesday, October 1, just as the minor fry were beginning to think all their trouble had gone for nothing, *Othello* was put up, with Forrest as the Moor and Brooke as Iago. If there was one part more than another in which the American actor let himself loose it was this. Consequently in the great scene in the third act where Othello seizes upon his ancient, Forrest put forth all the lung power at his command. With the gibes of his associates rankling in his mind, Brooke's combative instincts were at once aroused. No sooner had Forrest finished than Brooke came out with his speech, "Oh Grace! oh Heaven, defend me!" in a tone of thunder, which as it reverberated through the building at once dwarfed his colleague's delivery by the contrast. No one in the heat of the moment noticed the absurdity of the proceeding. Both behind and in front astonishment reigned supreme. Forrest himself stood perfectly stupefied. For the first time in his eventful career he had met with a man whose voice excelled his own in volume and strength.

Brooke, on reflection, seems to have repented his action, and by his friendly attitude towards the visitor apparently did his best to palliate the offence. Forrest, on the other hand, little mortified at the scene, met his advances half-way, with the result that they became firm friends. Each had a grudge against Macready, and the feeling united them in a common bond of sympathy.

On October 7 Brooke appeared to his friends as Huon in *Love*. Four nights after, Sloan, the lessee, took his benefit, and delivered a farewell address in rhyme, in which, after allusion had been made to the principal actors who had recently visited the Queen's, the doggerel went on to say—

> "Had I space, others, both 'stars' and 'stock,' might
>   justly claim a nook.
> But in my *stream* of rhyme I *must not* forget a Brooke."

The theatre then closed for extensive alterations, and reopened on Monday, March 2, 1846, with a seating capacity of about

2,800, the house when packed holding fully £127. Anything
but comfortable or commodious in the old days, the Queen's
even now, with all its vaunted improvements, was very badly
ventilated. It is noteworthy that this house dated from the
year 1775, and was in reality the first Manchester Theatre
Royal. But it fell at one time into bad odour, from which,
despite the efforts of subsequent managers, it never properly
recovered.

Meanwhile Mr. Sloan had for the most part done away
with the old stock company, comprising the names of Messrs.
Letchford, Melville, Hill, Fisher, Normanton, Redford, Denial,
Raymond, Watson, Mrs. Garthwaite, Mrs. Sloan, and Miss
E. M. Duret. With his re-opening, Brooke ranked as first
tragedian; Miss Angell as leading lady; Mr. Lester (Lester
Wallack) as genteel comedian; Henry Bedford as low comedian;
and William Artaud as first old man. The Theatre Royal stock
company, which in 1845-6 had for leading actors Charles Dibdin
Pitt and R. E. Graham (the latter of whom played Sir Giles
Over-reach at the Marylebone in 1848 in opposition to Brooke
at the Olympic), was, on the whole, considered immeasurably
superior to that of the Queen's. But the best stars of the time,
strange to say, preferred acting at the house in Spring Gardens.
Hence Sloan was enabled to announce engagements for the
forthcoming season with Macready, Charles Matthews, Forrest,
Buckstone, Madame Vestris, and many others of equal note.

Originally engaged merely for a few nights at the Queen's,
Mr. Lester (since better known to fame as Lester Wallack, the
celebrated American actor-manager) remained during the entire
season, becoming, as he himself styles it, a sort of semi-star or
asteroid. Afterwards he transferred his services to the Theatre
Royal. Referring to the circumstance that, during his stay at
the Queen's, Brooke and he shared the same dressing-room,
Mr. Wallack says in his "Memories of the Last Fifty Years":—
"Off the stage he had a particularly strong brogue. He was a
perfectly reckless man, who did not care how his money went
or what straits he might be in. He was an Irishman, one of the

generous, kind-hearted, whole-souled John-Brougham Irishmen.
During that engagement at Manchester we acted together. I
would often go into my dressing-room and find that certain very
necessary articles of my wardrobe were missing, and one night
in particular I remember I was playing Modus in *The Hunchback*,
while he was acting Master Walter, and Miss Faucit, Julia. I
went into the room and found Brooke ready to go on. I had a
costume I was particularly fond of, a chocolate-coloured, plain,
quiet sort of a dress, and I missed the tights belonging to it.
Brooke said, 'What is the matter, me dear boy?' I said, 'I
cannot dress—I can't find my tights.' 'Why,' said he, 'I took
the liberty to take your tights myself, they are on me. I couldn't
find my own.' Fortunately, I did not go on until the second
act, and by that time the whole theatre had been ransacked, and
I got somebody's nether garments, and he carried through the
performance with 'Lester's tights.' It was characteristic of
Brooke that he would have been quite as willing that I should
have taken his and have gone on himself without any. He was
one of those reckless, generous creatures, who would give anything
he had in the world to me, or to anybody else he liked."

Owing to the sense of discomfort produced by an overcrowded
audience in an ill-ventilated theatre, the critics on the opening
night were rendered grumpy enough to speak disrespectfully of
the equator. Next day they found fault with everything from
the scenery, which was condemned as "deficient in drawing, in
perspective, and in colouring," to the actors, whose lavish gagging
had certainly given cause for offence. "A lively but somewhat free
minor theatre of the Adelphi pattern" was the general verdict.

Beyond his great hit as Connor O'Kennedy in *The Green
Bushes*, and the reception accorded to his Romeo when placed in
juxtaposition with the Mercutio of Henry Farren, little of note,
so far as Brooke was concerned, took place during the season.
In it, however (as hinted by Lester Wallack), he appears to have
acted a round of characters in support of the divine Helen
Faucit, noteworthy among which may be mentioned his Mordaunt
in *The Patrician's Daughter* of Westland Marston. This was the

lady's first meeting with the actor with whom she was afterwards to be frequently associated on the stage. The impression left on Miss Faucit's mind by Brooke's acting was so favourable that she at once engaged him to support her in the lead during her forthcoming tour in Ireland. There was little difficulty in arranging this as things had been going badly with poor Sloan, who was eventually declared bankrupt in the February of 1847.

Before proceeding to Ireland, however, Brooke paid a visit to Sheffield to lend prominent support to Edwin Forrest, with whom he was on the best of terms. Some idea of the relations of the two leather-lunged tragedians may be gleaned from the following unpublished letter now in my possession :—

24 D'Olier [Dublin],
April 20 [1846].

My Dear Sir,

I have great pleasure in acknowledging the receipt of your favour of yesterday. If you can go to Cork for the five nights I should be well pleased ; if not, ask Mr. Bennett if he is at leisure and would like to go. My engagement is only for seven nights.

With much pleasure I will send the orders as you requested.*

If it be true that Mr. Leigh Murray *has* chastised that brute Macready for his insolence, he should be rewarded by the profession with a handsome and valuable piece of plate. The Actors here, men and women, say they will subscribe with pleasure.

I am glad you have received the sword.

Your letter containing the proposal from Mr. Copeland came duly to hand, but I must decline the offer. Should I act again in Liverpool, I should prefer Hammond's Theatre.

With kindest remembrances to Mr. Bennett,

Believe me,
Yours very truly,

G. V. Brooke, Esq.   Edwin Forrest.

I leave here on Sunday next for Cork by the mail coach. If you determine to come I would secure you a place in the same coach, which leaves here at half-past ten in the morning.

Helen Faucit had already made one appearance at the Theatre Royal, Dublin, when Brooke joined her there on

---

* Probably to Brooke's relatives in Dublin. The sword mentioned in the next paragraph but one was likely that of Edmund Kean, presented by someone at this period to Brooke (surely not Forrest?) and worn by him ever after in his impersonation of Sir Giles Over-reach.

Monday, October 26. *Saunders's News-Letter*, speaking of their acting on that evening in *Romeo and Juliet*, thought that the lady's impersonation of the confiding girl was finely imagined, albeit "it displayed something of study and not enough of the abstraction that speaks to itself, and asks not what effect it produces on others. With intuitive tact and knowledge she entered into the meaning of the text, and in the more energetic passages her spirit, animated by the occasion, lost not the opportunity of proving what it could do under the most agitating of influences. . . . . The part of Romeo, in which so many aspirants for dramatic fame make their *début*, Mr. Gustavus Brooke sustained. He has already acquired a considerable provincial reputation in the sister country, and, judging from last evening, possesses several requisites for the stage. His figure is good, and voice clear and sonorous, and his enunciation such as not to disguise the language of the author. To these requisites may be added a familiarity with the routine of the stage. But he wants the sincere and glowing fire of genius, and cannot so far forget his identity as to be the very person he would represent. This is the impression created by his performance last evening, but other characters will test the extent of his resources."

Supporting Miss Faucit regularly when she appeared, and acting even on her nights of rest, Brooke subsequently submitted his conceptions of Claude Melnotte, Orlando, Hamlet, The Stranger, Macbeth, Richard III., Beverly, and Sir Giles Over-reach to the notice of Dublin playgoers.

On November 9, Miss Faucit played Jane Shore to the Lord Hastings of Brooke, and on the following night (for the first time on any stage) appeared in the name-part in Southerne's tragedy of *Isabella : or, the Fatal Marriage*. Originally announced for performance on the 5th, with Brooke as Biron, the piece had to be deferred owing to Helen Faucit's sudden illness. It was favourably received, bearing six representations in all during the engagement. After the stars had conjointly appeared as Sir Thomas Clifford and Julia, Jaffier and Belvidera, Shylock and

Portia, and Brooke single-handed (so to speak) had played
Virginius and Petruchio, Helen Faucit's benefit and "last
appearance" took place on the 21st. Imogen and Leonatus
Posthumus in *Cymbeline* were the characters assumed on this
occasion by the stars. After four performances by Brooke solus
Helen Faucit (according to the accepted phrase of managerial
dodgery) was re-engaged, and on the 26th appeared as Lady
Macbeth. Two nights later an elaborate production of Euripides'
Iphigenia in Aulis, in English was effected. Announced as for
the first time adapted to the modern stage by Mr. J. W.
Calcraft (the lessee of the theatre), the classical tragedy was
given the adventitious aid of some original music by Mr. Levey,
together with new scenery, dresses, and decorations. Favourably
received in Dublin, especially by the *alumni* of Trinity College,
Iphigenia in Aulis held its place in the bills seven consecutive
nights, or eight in all. The cast was principally as follows:—
Achilles, son of Peleus and King of Thessaly, Mr. G. V, Brooke;
Agamemnon, Mr. Calcraft; Iphigenia, his daughter, Miss Helen
Faucit; and Clytemnestra, Mrs. Ternan.

　　Subsequently most of the old pieces in which Brooke and
Helen Faucit had already appeared were repeated. On December 9
The Winter's Tale (then a great novelty in the Irish capital) was
performed with the stars as Leontes and Hermione. Shakespeare's
comedy met with considerable favour; so much so indeed that
it was deemed advisable once or twice afterwards to perform the
latter portion by way of afterpiece. On the 14th another novelty
was afforded by the appearance of Helen Faucit as Lady
Constance in *King John*, to the Faulconbridge of Brooke. Nine
nights later, the engagement came to an end with Miss Faucit's
appearance, for her benefit, in *Isabella* and the second part of
The Winter's Tale. Seen most frequently in Achilles and Biron,
Brooke, during his noteworthy sojourn here of about forty-seven
nights, had played in all twenty-two parts, some fifty-one times.
What, it might well be asked, would a modern actor think of
such work?

CHAPTER IV.

1846—1847.

WITH the conclusion of the Dublin engagement Brooke accompanied Miss Helen Faucit to Cork, where they opened in Seymour's tumble-down playhouse in Cook Street three days after Christmas. Beyond mention of the fact that the actor here repeated his impersonation of Mordaunt to the Lady Mabel Lynterne of his fair colleague, there is little need to treat particularly of the visit in its professional aspect. Presenting an unbending front to the overtures of the surrounding gentry (nothing if not hospitable) the tragedienne had little patience with the vagaries of the convivial-minded Gustavus.

"Having a host of friends in Cork," says Mr. J. W. Flynn in an amusing little book recently published, entitled *The Random Recollections of an Old Playgoer*, "Brooke was very often late at the theatre, unable to tear himself away from pleasant company at the dinner parties he used to be asked to, or perhaps not having been able to get back from a long excursion into the country. He was very unpunctual, and Helen Faucit was quite the contrary. She could not bear to be kept waiting, and the love-making of Romeo and Juliet used sometimes to be preceded by decidedly acrimonious passages between the two great 'stars.'

"I remember well one evening I was in Brooke's dressing-room at the theatre. He was late and was dressing in a hurry.

The only others present were, one of the G——s, and Henry Roche, the hairdresser, who superintended the wigs. Brooke had been off in the country for a day's fishing with the G——s, and had dined with them in the evening. Sandy Seyton, son of the Mrs. Seyton I had told you about so often, came to the door twice: 'Mr. Brooke! Mr. Brooke! Miss Faucit's compliments; she's waiting.' And Brooke answered impatiently: 'Let Miss Faucit go to Jericho and wait!' We, I remember, did our best to get him out in time. *As You Like It* was the name of the play that night, and never before, nor since, did I see such acting.''

A few pages farther on Mr. Flynn (still posing as the interviewer of an elderly and deceased friend) says, " I have often told you how much Helen Faucit's patience was tried through Brooke's unpunctuality. One day when Brooke came to the theatre entirely late for rehearsal, the great actress gave him some wholesome advice about his want of punctuality. She had played, she said, with the greatest actor on the stage, Mr. Macready, and *he* had never behaved with such want of consideration. She was angry, and it is not to be wondered at, but Brooke answered somewhat sharply, 'Madam, G. V. Brooke has not yet had his day.' His words were prophetic. Even then people saw a great improvement in his acting."

Before closing Mr. Flynn's amusing little book, we cannot refrain from quoting a capital anecdote in connection with the impecunious manager of the Cork Theatre. "There is a story of something that occurred between Brooke and Frank Seymour on the occasion of one of Brooke's earlier visits, which is well worth relating. Frank Seymour owed Brooke a good deal of money on account of the various engagements of the actor. Owing to some 'chaff' from his friends, Brooke said one day—'Well I really must get some money from Frank; it is too bad my services should be going for nothing.' A few days afterwards he spoke to Frank, half in joke, and said it was quite time he paid something. 'My dear Gussy, you shall have a cheque for ten pounds.' Whereupon he gave the tragedian a cheque on one of the banks—the National— for £10. Brooke did not know where the bank was and he asked a friend to show him, and together they went to cash the cheque. The clerk to whom the cheque was presented looked at it meditatively and smiled.

"'What is the matter?' Brooke asked, 'Isn't that cheque all right?'

"'Oh, yes, the cheque is all right,' replied the clerk, 'but unfortunately there is no money to meet it—the gentleman has no funds in the bank at present!'

"Without a word Brooke left the bank. He was very indignant. That evening he met Frank and spoke his mind pretty plainly.

"'It is too bad,' he said, 'that you should serve me so about that cheque.'

"'But wasn't the cheque a good one, Gussy?' Frank said.

"'The cheque was good,' Brooke replied, 'but what was the use of that when they wouldn't cash it?'

"'What, not cash my cheque!' the other exclaimed indignantly. 'Who was he?—was he a low-sized stout man with a black moustache?'

"'I didn't notice,' said Brooke, 'but he wouldn't cash it anyway.'

"'Well, now,' said Frank impressively, 'you present that cheque on Monday, and if they refuse, you show me the man that refuses and I'll have him dismissed the bank.'

"That was on Saturday. On Monday following Brooke and his friend went again to the bank, and when the cheque was presented, the clerk proceeded to cash it. But he was laughing softly to himself all the while.

"'Why do you laugh?' Brooke said. 'What is it that amuses you?'

"'I can't help laughing,' said the clerk. '*This money hasn't been more than a few minutes in the bank.*'

"And at that Brooke and his friend laughed too."

Notwithstanding Brooke's conduct at Cork, Lady Martin does not appear to retain any save the most pleasing recollections of her many professional associations with the tragedian. Replying to our inquiries the Helen Faucit of old says—"He was a very fair actor; some thought a very good one: but never could be distinguished in his art because of his want of true dramatic instinct and imagination." He did not appear to her to give sufficient thought and study to the characters he undertook. "He would accept an idea from others gladly, but would not take the trouble to work it out for himself." Always good tempered and amiable, it was a pleasure to meet him. "He was invariably most attentive and obliging, accepting any hint at rehearsal which was offered for the better illustration of his character in the most kindly, grateful manner."

It is strange that one possessing so many qualifications for judging should have so profound a misconception of Brooke's great histrionic gifts. Not even the most enthusiastic of his admirers ever attributed to him transcendent intellect. Art could do little for an actor who was a master of natural and spontaneous feeling, and who, beyond most others of his time, had that gift of personal magnetism which at once grasps the attention of the audience and makes all hearts beat as one. In no sense psychological, his emotional powers were such that he arrived with ease at effects which others, like Charles Kean, were only able to accomplish by dint of much laborious analysis. On this head let us hearken once more to "The Old-fashioned Playgoer," who confessed he was a Brookite (although never knowing the tragedian at his best), because he was for dramatic convention, and because Brooke was the only man of his time "who could vivify dramatic convention with such a wealth of physical and elocutionary power and elegance as to convey an idea of the grand old days of the stage." Subtlety or originality in their deepest significance he did not claim for him. "A kindling glance at the bidding of the text; a softened tone as a line of his author shaded or digressed into pathos; an impatient agitation of his (when made up) splendid head at the crisis of a character's emotion; a grand stride or fall at the culmination of a scene—these were the only features of Brooke's acting in which he departed from, or rather went beyond, convention. But my

favourite had something better than subtlety." He then points
out, what has been frequently noticed since, that the ordinary and
purposely subtle actor is a man whose observation exceeds his
sympathies; one who holds his part at arm's length—regards it
objectively—and plays upon it as a musician plays upon a piano.
" When I think of Brooke's personal nobleness," he continues,
" and the ease with which he made it seem part and parcel of his
best characters, I am not at all sorry he was not a subtle actor; I
am very pleased to have had the opportunity of admiring in him
one who had a foremost place on the stage by right of a confluence
and affluence of natural endowments. Amongst these was *not*
reckoned an intellectually handsome countenance. Even before
dissipation had left its impress upon his face its handsomeness was
unintellectual. It was such handsomeness as might suit a Tom
Jones, a Faulconbridge, or an Othello, not such as would reveal
the poetic meditativeness of a Hamlet, the mystic ambition of a
Macbeth, or the fantastic passion of a Romeo. It was most ennobled
when aged by the dresser's art, and in Richelieu, Elmore, Master
Walter, or Over-reach, left nothing to be desired. As a rule,
however, it expressed, I consider, little more than dignity, tempered
as the case might be by anger, affection, impatience, or suspicion.
I have been told by an experienced actor who often played Iago to
Brooke's Othello, that his expression of face while listening to the
wily ancient's suggestions in the third act was a great incentive to
his play-fellow—so great that, in the language of my informant, a
man must have been a fool not to play Iago well to him. But this
actor was at the time a worshipper of Brooke, as almost every one
that ever played with him was; and certainly facial expression,
except of a very strong and simple kind, was not amongst Mr.
Brooke's claims to public admiration." *

What time Brooke was enjoying himself in the society of his
Cork friends, an announcement, to the exceeding gratification of

---

* Wrote a reviewer some years ago in the columns of the *New
York Dramatic News:*—"G. V. Brooke, as fine a tragedian as ever trod
the boards, albeit of the extreme old school, was spoiled as later, was the
graceful Walter Montgomery—by the fact that his eyes were small and
hardly ever beamed with the expression which the actor undoubtedly felt."

Manchester playgoers, appeared in the local papers to the effect that Mr. John Knowles, of the Theatre Royal, had secured the services of the old Queen's favourite as leading man. Accordingly Brooke made his first appearance at the new house on February 15, 1847, as Huon in *Love*, Mrs. Charles Gill, the leading lady, effecting her *début* there on the same occasion. The following evening Miss Fanny Kemble, who since her marriage to Pierce Butler, a Southern planter, in 1834, had been living privately in America, made her re-appearance on the stage as Julia (her original character) in *The Hunchback*. Evidently in the secret of the domestic troubles (culminating shortly afterwards in a divorce) which had induced Mrs. Butler to return to her old profession, the playgoers of Manchester crammed the house to suffocation and welcomed her, on her first appearance, with a volley of cheering, followed by rounds of applause. Such a reception could not fail to put heart into the actress. Although she had not trodden the stage in any capacity for over seven years, the critics gave it as their opinion there was little falling off in the exquisite music of her voice or in the fine poetic spirit which had been a prime characteristic of her earlier acting. All the other players too seem to have been affected by the healthy excitement of the evening. "The Master Walter of Mr. Brooke," noted the *Guardian*, "surprised us by its force, familiarised as we have so long been with the embodiment of Sheridan Knowles himself and Mr. Vandenhoff. With these two exceptions we have not seen so clever a personation as that of Mr. Brooke." Falling in line the *Examiner* remarked "of this very, very excellent tragedian," that "while impassioned and impressive he exhibited great good sense and good taste in his acting."

In the matter of rehearsals Brooke appears to have treated Mrs. Butler as cavalierly as he did Helen Faucit. On February 18, when Brooke supported the star as Duke Aranza in *The Honeymoon*, we find her writing to her friend "Hal.": "The company is a very fair one indeed, and might be an excellent one if they were not all too great geniuses either to learn or to rehearse their parts. The French do not put the flimsiest vaudeville upon the stage without rehearsing it for *three months*: here, however, and everywhere else in England, people play such parts as Macbeth with no more than three rehearsals; and I am going to act this evening in *The Honeymoon* with a gentleman who, filling the principal part in the piece, has not thought fit to attend at the rehearsal; so that though I was there, I may say in fact that I have had no rehearsal of it—which is business-like and pleasant." [*]

Notwithstanding Brooke's characteristic carelessness, the play was "all right at night," the *Manchester Advertiser and Chronicle* considering that his "personation of the Duke was very masterly though somewhat stern."

To a man of Brooke's convivial temperament a source of great temptation was at this time presented by the gatherings at the Kersal Moor Hotel, as presided over by the genial " Jem " Thompson, who also figured as mine host of the Concert Tavern, York Street, close to the Queen's Theatre. The former house especially was a great place of rendezvous for the members of both stock companies. Mostly every Sunday a regular theatrical dinner would be held, after which, provided the weather were fine, the assembly would adjourn to the bowling green to blow a cloud and enjoy the light afternoon breeze. Even on week days high revelry would be kept up before and after the actors' working hours, and Brooke often with difficulty tore himself away from his companions in time for the labours of the night. In after years old Harry Beverley delighted to relate how he had been out at all hours from midnight to break of day with the reckless tragedian, but never by any chance saw him with a book in his hand studying his part. This puzzled him very much, seeing that Brooke (in those days of frequent changes of bill) invariably turned up to rehearsal letter-perfect. Nor was his curiosity satisfied until he discovered the marvellous retentiveness of the tragedian's memory—so marvellous indeed that with a single reading he had mastered the text. Fatal proficiency! It is sad to think what heights Brooke could have attained had Nature thought fit to dower him less nobly.

---

[*] "Records of a Later Life," III., p. 163.

It is noteworthy that the youthful Miss Marie Wilton figured as a member of the Theatre Royal stock company at this period, and on February 20 appeared as Fleance to the Lady Macbeth of Mrs. Butler. Speaking of Brooke's Macbeth the *Guardian* says he "played the stirring scenes well; and his performance of the part had altogether fewer defects than any we have latterly seen here. It is the soliloquies in which he chiefly fails. They are more like set speeches than the spontaneous promptings of active thought, fitfully uttered aloud because so deeply interesting. And we take it that the same mental excitement which prompts a man to soliloquise would urge him to mitigate the peripatetic habit of walking while so engaged. Mr. Brooke commits the common error of speaking loud, for effect, in certain scenes when it is a violation of the consistencies of the scene—thus in the courtyard after the murder, as if his mental torture could not be sufficiently expressed in subdued tones; while his loud speech at dead of night must, according to all common-sense notions, have informed the sleeping retainers of the murder and its author. The same fault was practised in the Banquet scene." The *Express*, on the other hand, considered his Macbeth "a masterly performance—much the best that we have seen him give." If the metropolitan notices, however, of the succeeding year be any criterion, the Manchester critics at this period must, in all justice, have been exceptionally captious. Certainly an undue spirit of fault-finding reigned supreme throughout. When Brooke played Romeo to the Juliet of Mrs. Butler on February 22, the *Courier* considered the impersonation was, "as usual, manly and correct in the declamation, but wanted the romance of the beautiful poem."

Four nights after he played Cardinal Wolsey in *Henry VIII.* to the Queen Catharine of the tragedienne and the King of H. J. Wallack the stage manager. With a repetition of *The Hunchback* on Saturday the 27th, Mrs. Butler's sojourn was brought to an end. Besides appearing in a round of his old characters during March, we find Brooke, on the 2nd, figuring in the bills as Fabian in the new melodrama of *The Black Doctor*. Ten nights later he personated Evelyn in *Money* for Mr. A. Webster's

benefit, Groves on that occasion having his original representative
in Mr. Benjamin Webster—his first appearance in Manchester.
On the 13th following the Rev. James White's play *Feudal Times*
(which had only just seen the light at Sadler's Wells) was brought
out, with Brooke as Walter Cochrane, Earl of Mar. Owing to the
actor's exuberance of lung power the local press was unanimous
in condemning his impersonation of this character. After
accusing him point blank of ranting, the *Guardian* indulged in a
covert sneer at the old Queen's in asking, " Is it the effect of habit
in a theatre where the proprieties of the stage were far less
attended to than at the Theatre Royal, and where exaggeration
was an essential element of success?" This was "give a dog a
bad name and hang him" with a vengeance ! " Cochrane, Earl
of Mar," says the *Courier*, " is the leading hero, and was played
by Mr. G. V. Brooke with his usual dashing energy. We wish
he had more light and shade in his declamation, less of the
boisterous in passages where the purely poetical predominates
over the strictly passionate," etc., etc.

After March 19 (when Brooke gave one of his earliest
renderings of his great character, Matthew Elmore) nothing of
moment occurred until April 10, when Macready made his first
appearance at the Theatre Royal, playing Macbeth to the Macduff
of our hero. Judging from the notice in the *Express*, Brooke
evidently showed his contempt for his old adversary by walking
through his part. " It was not," says that journal, " equally
near to what he might have made it. He has great talent and
should respect it." Several off nights then succeeded, during
which Brooke appeared as Shylock and the Stranger to poor
houses, and on the 15th (for H. J. Wallack's benefit) played Don
Pedro in *Much Ado About Nothing*, to the Beatrice of Mrs. Butler
and the Benedick of Wallack. " According to the bills," says the
Courier, " Mr. G. V. Brooke kindly consented to play Don Pedro ;
it was a condescension the audience on this occasion could have
well dispensed with." Poor Gus.! Presumably he had not yet
recovered from his bad attack of Macreadyphobia. He was now
preparing for his own benefit on the 19th, when he purposed

playing Leontes in *The Winter's Tale* and Edgar Ravenswood in *The Bride of Lammermoor*. But two nights prior to that event he had once more to eat humble pie as De Mauprat to "the eminent's" Richelieu. His Laertes in *Hamlet* on the occasion of Macready's third appearance was spoken of by the *Guardian* as "somewhat too massive, but on the whole well played"—showing that the fit of sulkiness was slowly passing off. Playing Ulric to Macready's Werner on April 28, the same paper considered his acting "effective but not letter-perfect." On the following night he gave an unequal rendering of Edgar (Macready the Lear), good and bad points appearing in glaring juxtaposition.

On April 30 the Virginius of fourteen years' standing had to content himself with Icilius; and on May 1 played Iago to Macready's Othello. The *Guardian*, in saying good-bye to the great actor who had been drawing crowded houses nightly, incidentally pointed out that Brooke's Iago "wanted earnestness and intensity of malice; it rather assumed the levity of comedy."

This pithy criticism gives a just impression of Brooke's acting in the character from first to last. It is matter for regret that on the few occasions the tragedian ventured upon an original conception the critics failed to fall in line with his views. A little more encouragement in this respect might have urged him to continued study instead of throwing him back on theatrical conventionalism. But the time was not yet ripe for a Fechter or an Irving.

Albeit Brooke had presented an unbending front to Macready during this and a previous engagement in Manchester, it must not be imagined that an atom of professional jealousy influenced his attitude towards the tragedian. On the contrary, Brooke always spoke in the highest terms of Macready's acting, and openly confessed to his associates his doubts of ever approaching the excellence of the great tragedian in several standard characters. But it could not be without feelings of secret satisfaction that, after long years of waiting, Brooke eventually found himself hailed as

Edmund Kean's successor in Othello and Sir Giles Over-reach.
The former character was certainly Macready's poorest effort;
the latter he never dared attempt.

With Macready's departure Helen Faucit came to Manchester
on May 3 to fulfil a week's engagement in the characters
previously identified with her success in Ireland. According to
the local press, Brooke as Orlando, on the 5th, showed a tendency
to rant, and, moreover, was not completely grounded in his lines.
But his Master Walter, two nights later, proved a signal success;
and, wonderful to say, was unreservedly praised by the hypercritical
reviewers of the period.

On May 12 Brooke appeared for the first time as Sykes
in Boucicault's new comedy *The School for Scheming;* and on
Saturday, the 22nd, gave an effective performance of Waller in
The Love Chase, to the Wildrake of Robert Roxby, the Lydia of
Jane Mordaunt, and the Constance (her original character) of
Mrs. Nisbett. After Brooke had appeared twice in succession as
William in *Black-Eyed Susan,* the season terminated on May 31
with *The School for Scandal,* very strongly cast. Robert Roxby
was the Charles Surface; Mr. Ranger the Sir Peter; and Mrs.
Nisbett, Lady Teazle. Unlike the other actors, who were well
grounded in their parts, Brooke had never previously played
Joseph Surface, was unfamiliar with Sheridan's comedy, and
unfortunately had to swallow the part at a moment's notice.
While, therefore, to the *Guardian* the character afforded some
nice points, " it was certainly not so finished and effective as his
talents and a more careful study might have made it. In some
instances he seemed to be ignorant of the business, as when
he says to Sir Peter and Charles—' Gentlemen, I beg your
pardon, I must see you downstairs; here is a person come on
particular business'—intimating that he must show them to the
door, as he thinks it unsafe to leave them in the room together
with Lady Teazle behind the screen; whereas Mr. Brooke hurries
out of the room at the moment of uttering the sentence—a
palpable contradiction between word and act—and has to be
called back by the others."

During the off season at the Theatre Royal, Brooke, accompanied by Marie Duret, fulfilled a successful engagement of twenty-one nights, commencing July 13, at the Amphitheatre, Hull. Amid a variety of his old parts we find him appearing here as King John, Hotspur, Hastings (*Jane Shore*), Gambia (*The Slave*), Quasimodo (*Esmeralda*), Rob Roy, and Martin Heywood. Visits to Bolton and one or two other Lancashire towns followed, with but poor results. It is related, on fairly satisfactory authority, that one Saturday night at Wigan the house was so small that Brooke ordered the money to be returned, and, taken by a sudden whim, said to his business manager, "If these people won't come to see me act, perhaps they will come to hear me preach; go and get bills printed and posted at once, announcing that G. V. Brooke, the actor, will preach the Gospel of Christ to-morrow evening in the Primitive Methodist Chapel." No sooner said than done. The bills were printed and posted forthwith, and on Sunday the offended actor preached a sermon to a large audience of wondering deadheads.

From the apparent incredibility of this story, it is necessary to state that the responsibility for first putting it into print devolves upon Mr. Dinsmore, who gives us as his authority, one Healey, the tragedian's dresser about this period. After leaving the services of Brooke, Healey started in business for himself as a hairdresser in Manchester. He is now dead some years, but his widow still persists in maintaining 'the truth of the story, and adds that Brooke was a man of great courage and determination when his mind was once made up. The tragedian never paid a visit to Manchester in after years without looking up his old servant; and Mrs. Healey still cherishes a recipe for ginger beer which her husband's old master had copied out in her house and forgetfully left on the table when departing. In one of those intermittent spells of total abstinence to which he was prone in his hours of remorse, Mrs. Healey had thoughtfully supplied him with the un-intoxicating beverage, and he now desired to learn of the ingredients. Dropping in upon the Healeys on one occasion when he had not broken his fast for twenty-four hours, he discovered the whilom dresser's wife in the act of boiling potatoes, Irish fashion, in their "jackets." The good woman saw at a glance what was wrong, and holding out a large flowery potato on a fork said tantalisingly, "If you don't eat this I'll say you are no Irishman." Brooke laughed, took the potato, removed the skin after the primitive fashion of Adam, and finally devoured it with avidity. Then amid his mouthfuls he ejaculated that not for a long time had he relished anything so hugely. Keenly appreciative of the simple kindness of the Healeys, the tragedian, after Marie Duret's elopement, bestowed them a portrait of that fair deceiver which he had carried about in his breast pocket for years.

On appearing in Rochdale under the management of his old friend James Rodgers, Brooke was soon compensated for his chilling reception in Wigan. So great a favourite, indeed, did he become here that mine host of the Wellington, where he stayed, refused to take a penny for his board and lodging. Boniface evidently deemed himself sufficiently recompensed by the galaxy of choice spirits whom Brooke's genial presence attracted daily to his house. Mr. J. B. Howe, then a member of the local stock company, relates that on the night *A New Way to Pay Old Debts* was performed (with himself as Allworth and Brooke as Sir Giles), so terrifying in its reality was the tragedian's "death" scene that a well-known Rochdale physician, happening to be among the audience, hastened behind to give the actor his professional assistance, verily believing that simulation had merged into actuality, and culminated in a fit of apoplexy. One can realise the intensity of Brooke's acting in this scene when it is recorded that he has been known to lie prostrate for a quarter of an hour after the falling of the curtain — utterly dominated and overcome by the Frankenstein of his own creating. Well-nigh a quarter of a century afterwards Mr. Howe, when starring in Melbourne, had the pleasure of identifying the young medical man in Doctor Neild, then, and for many years previously, prominently associated with the Australian press as dramatic critic.

"The next night," relates Mr. Howe in his "Cosmopolitan Actor," "*Othello* and *His Last Legs* was the bill, in the cast of which I was included as Charles Rivers. Shall I ever cease to remember ('No, not while memory holds a seat in this distracted globe') the awe and wonder I felt as I saw the 'Dusky Moor' emerge from his little dressing-room, when a dark-faced, black-eyed woman, in black satin, Marie Duret, was easing his gorgeous robe to allow it to pass the little narrow passage on to the stage. As Grimaldi says, 'He was no more to me a *man*, he became a *god*,' and when he made his first entrance, with J. Rickards as Iago, from the right-hand side, I thought the applause would literally 'bring down the house, for it was not a commodious or substantial structure at that time, and had there been such an institution as the Board of Works, which nowadays (in London at least) so worries and perplexes theatrical managers, the place would have been condemned years before I was born, and I should not have had the honour of participating in the pleasure of acting with so great a genius.

"During the progress of the farce of *His Last Legs*, a funny incident occurred, which threatened at one moment to stop the piece. In one of the scenes, the Doctor O'Toole (? Felix O'Callaghan) is supposed to put Charles Rivers under the influence of mesmerism, and the irresistibly comic manner in which he made his 'passes,' and the extraordinary richness of an Irish brogue, had so powerful an effect on my risibilities, that I could not contain myself, and burst out into an immoderate fit of laughter on the sofa, so prolonged that poor G. V. joined in, and each was trying to outdo the other, until the very audience themselves caught it up, and it culminated in a general burst of almost inexhaustible mirth."

Returning to the Amphitheatre, Hull (then re-named the Queen's), on or about Saturday, September 25, for a few nights, Brooke proved very condescending, acting second parts to Stuart, who was subsequently to reverse positions with him at the Olympic. Thus on the 27th and 28th we find him

playing De Mauprat and Sir Thomas Clifford, to the Richelieu
and Master Walter of Stuart, and the Julie and Helen of Marie
Duret. On the 29th Brooke had a benefit, when *The Hunchback*
was followed by a novelty in the shape of *Tom and Jerry; or,
Life in London*, with the *beneficiaire* as Corinthian Tom.
"Tickets to be had of Mr. G. V. Brooke, 11 Osborne Street."
Henry Holl (who also supported Brooke during his famous Olympic
engagement) had his appeal on Thursday, October 7, when he
played Cassio to the Othello of Stuart, the Iago of Brooke,
the Desdemona of Miss Stuart, and the Emilia of Marie
Duret.

Although the winter season at Manchester was now about
to commence, Brooke still pursued the even tenour of his
starring course, absolved for a time from the necessity of
returning to the Theatre Royal by the managerial arrangements
concluded for the first and second weeks. Barry Sullivan had
now been engaged to share the lead with Gus., and it was he
who supported Mr. and Mrs. Charles Kean as Stukely in *The
Gamester* when the house re-opened on Monday, October 9. On
that day fortnight Brooke made his first appearance this season as
Claude Melnotte, Sullivan playing Richard Parker in the afterpiece of *The Mutiny of the Nore*. Subsequently Brooke played
the Ghost to Sullivan's Hamlet, Jaffier to his Pierre, and Hamlet
to his Ghost. "Mr. Brooke," says the *Guardian* of Wednesday,
November 3, "falls into what we conceive the common error in
his personation of 'the gentle Hamlet' by imparting to it too
much energy; and thus we have the anomaly of self-reproaches
for irresolution declaimed with the boisterous energy of a man
with whom manifestly 'all-ready *execution* on the *will* attends.'
Perhaps his best scenes were that in which he fools Polonius about
the cloud, and that wherein he receives the challenge through
Osric ; his quiet dignity in the latter scene was striking."

On the Monday previously Brooke had played Isaac of York
in *Ivanhoe* to the Front de Bœuf of Barry Sullivan and the Wilfred
of Henry Holl. The piece became popular, and was presented
several times ; but the *Guardian* considered that "Mr. Brooke and

Mr. Sullivan might have advantageously changed parts as the Jew and the Templar. We think Mr. Brooke would have imparted more of the chivalrous spirit to the latter; and Mr. Sullivan would probably have imparted more intensity with less physical vigour to the ancient Israelite."

On Monday, November 8, Miss Glyn, who had been ably schooled by Charles Kemble, made her first appearance on any stage as Constance in *King John*, giving, for a novice, an artistic and refined rendering of the character. Henry Holl was the Faulconbridge, and Marie Wilton Prince Arthur. "Mr. Brooke's King John," says the *Examiner*, "was, as is customary with that gentleman, a mixed performance—some passages of it, the famous one with Hubert for instance, being given with great delicacy and truth of conception." On the 15th following Brooke played Edgar to the Lear of Barry Sullivan, and on the 19th Leontes, in *The Winter's Tale*, to the Hermione of Miss Glyn and Mamillius of Marie Wilton. Subsequently he acted Brutus to Sullivan's Cassius, Romeo to his Friar Lawrence, and Ulric to his Werner. His last appearance at the Theatre Royal before entering upon his famous Olympic engagement appears to have been on November 25, when he played Durimel in *The Point of Honour*.

Either immediately before or after his engagement at this house (probably after—but the point is difficult to determine) Brooke performed for some little time at the City Theatre in Manchester—a wooden building, previously known as Cooke's Circus, occupying a site now covered by a warehouse adjoining the premises of the Young Men's Christian Association in Mount Street and Peter Street. Although nominally inferior to the two other houses, the City Theatre had the finest company in Manchester, retaining as it did the services of James Browne, Henry Bedford, William Davidge, and Sam. Emery. Opposite the theatre was a tavern known as the Alton House where the members of the three stock companies were wont to meet. Mr. John Coleman, who was acting at the Queen's Theatre at this period, tells us, in some sympathetic but not altogether trustworthy recollections of Brooke,* how he chanced to acquire the friendship of the tragedian. Returning homewards from the theatre one night he ran across Barry Sullivan in company with Browne the comedian, and the trio adjourned for refreshment to the Alton House. "Our principal topic of conversation," writes Mr. Coleman, "was the arrest of Brooke as he was going on the stage that night. It was his benefit, and the manager had been obliged to get him out of durance to enable him to keep faith with the public. While we were discussing the incident a row was heard outside, and a handsome young fellow entered the room, in animated altercation with a cab-man about his fare. The stranger, who spoke with a delicious Dublin brogue, was fair-complexioned, with an oval face, fair hair, and blue eyes.† He stood about five feet ten or higher, was broad chested, straight as a dart, and apparently was about five-and-twenty or thirty years of age. His dress was peculiar to eccentricity. He wore a drab cloth overcoat with a cape, a large blue silk muffler was twisted carelessly round his neck, and a white hat was perched on one side of his head. Although I had never seen him in my life I felt instinctively this must be Brooke. I was not left long in doubt upon the subject, for when he came to our end of the room Sullivan introduced us to each other, and a delightful time we had of it till we broke up about two in the morning."

While sharing the lead together at the Royal, Sullivan and Brooke were the best of friends. "It was in our joint dressing-room," said Barry Sullivan once to an interviewer, "that Brooke made his engagement with Captain Spicer to appear at the Olympic. He consulted me all through, showed me the letters, and asked my advice."

Captious and hypercritical as were the Manchester scribes at this period, there can be little doubt that the severe and not

---

* See "A Lost Tragedian," in *Longman's Magazine*, March, 1885.

† The lack of expression in Brooke's eyes (previously spoken of) appears to have arisen as much as anything from their indeterminate colour. His only surviving sister says they were "dark grey."

altogether undeserved strictures passed from time to time on Brooke's acting were not without their influence upon the tragedian when he elected to hazard his fortunes in London. Nothing, if not consistent in their attitude, and unconsciously jibing at their own power, the local critics were quite overcome with wonder at the result of the venture. "The leading journals," says the *Manchester Times* of January 8, 1848—"the leading journals are unanimous in their praise of his person, style, and manner, giving him, indeed, more credit for genius than we should feel disposed to allow."

CHAPTER V.

1848—1849.

AFTER biding his time with a patience that did him credit, Brooke had, all unconsciously, hit upon a very opportune moment for making his appearance in London. Everyone felt instinctively, in 1848, that Macready was fast approaching the period of his retirement; but popular acclamation had not as yet decided upon his successor in the tragic throne. Inclined for the most part to declare their allegiance to old faiths, playgoers had well-nigh despaired of once more beholding an unflinching exponent of the grand conventions of classic tragedy, when Gustavus Brooke burst upon the town. Possessing attributes of voice, gesture, and physique, entirely in consonance with the best-remembered traditions of the "palmy days," it is little to be wondered at that the new comer met with instantaneous success. But, alas! the event that looked like marking an epoch in the English drama proved a mere impermanent eddy on the current of theatrical affairs. All too soon poor Brooke tested to the full the truth of the Master's lines :—

> "There is a tide in the affairs of Men,
> Which, taken at the flood, leads on to fortune ;
> Omitted, all the voyage of their life
> Is bound in shallows and in miseries."

But we question if, with a happier issue, things would have turned out better in the end. Capable as he was by natural endowment of seating himself in the tragic throne, Brooke had none of the qualities which go to make the successful actor-manager. Unfortunate as was his after-career, it would have been still more unfortunate had advancing years found him at the head of a metropolitan theatre when the pre-Raphaelite spirit extended its influence to the drama, and, in smothering Shakespeare in archæological detail, demanded of the stage director something of the attributes of the pictorial artist and the antiquary.

Not the least prominent among the few persons living who made Brooke's acquaintance in London immediately prior to his memorable appearance at the Olympic is Mr. W. C. Day (the well-known amateur actor and theatrical collector), who tenders us the following appropriate reminiscences :—" My acquaintance with him was slight," writes Mr. Day. " A Mr. Calverley conducted the band generally engaged by an Amateur Dramatic Club to which I belonged, and hence our companionship. Calverley—an Irishman—was a bosom friend of Brooke, and led the orchestra on the Monday night of the latter's *début* as Othello. Brooke's name appeared in large posters on all the hoardings of the town, and of course I, as leading tragedian of my club, courted an introduction to the great man. This was given me on Sunday afternoon, January 2, 1848, at a tavern opposite Somerset House, in the Strand (either the 'Coach and Horses' or 'Edinboro' Castle'—I am not clear which), where the two friends had been dining after the final rehearsal of the tragedy on the Olympic stage in the morning. Both were 'pretty fresh' at the time I entered the house, and before leaving it all three were, to put it truthfully, perfectly 'fou.' We walked from the

Strand over Blackfriars' Bridge to Calverley's lodgings—a turning
out of Stamford Street—where we caroused till far into the small
hours of the actor's *début*. Of the conversation I remember little
more than that Brooke, in a strong Irish brogue, protested
Macready would find a doughty rival in him on the morrow;
and so impressed was I through the potations imbibed, and the
pride of a *tête-à-tête* with such a celebrity, that the pit of the
Olympic on the Monday night contained no more zealous partisan
of the Moor of Venice (when my judgment approved the scene)
than myself. His reception was enthusiastic and the applause
uproarious. The play over, I repaired with a party of young
companions to Jackson's, then a noted *à-la-mode* beef supper-
house in Blackmoor Street, Drury Lane, where the new
tragedian's merits and demerits were freely discussed."

Followed by Horace Mayhew's comic pantomime of
Harlequin and the British Lion (then running at the theatre by
way of afterpiece), *Othello* was produced at the Olympic on
Monday, January 3, when Brooke made his first appearance
in London, as an adult, in the name-part. The support was
fair, and comprised Mr. Stuart as Iago, Mr. Henry Holl as
Cassio, Mrs. Brougham as Emilia, and Miss Stuart (whose
recent performance of Julia in *The Hunchback* had been
eminently successful) as Desdemona. Fame had blown so loud
a blast on her trumpet concerning the merits of the new
tragedian, that a large and very distinguished audience,
numbering most of the celebrities of the hour, had assembled
within the walls of the old theatre. Latter-day accounts of this
memorable evening are for the most part conflicting; but it
would appear that not until the third act had been reached did
Brooke's success become assured. Mr. Coleman's version[*]
(related on the authority of Mr. Walter Lacy, an eye-witness,
but nevertheless on some points slightly inaccurate), proceeds to

---

[*] Allusions to Mr. Coleman throughout are to be taken as referring
to his article on Brooke in *Longman's Magazine*; the greater part of
which was afterwards republished in that gentleman's "Players and
Playwrights I have Met."

show how the house was bad, and the audience so unsympathetic
or antagonistic that the *débutant* made no headway until the
second act. At this juncture the ice was broken by a lucky
incident which we shall permit Mr. Coleman to treat in his own
words :—

" The newspapers of the day," he says, " teemed with
accounts of the gallantry of the Emir of Algeria, Abd'l Kader ;
more particularly of an exploit in which he had rescued a
number of women and children from being roasted alive, by
riding through his blazing camp, sabre in hand, cutting the
tent ropes, and carrying away the poor creatures clinging to his
saddle bow.

" In the quarrel scene, as Othello came rushing down between
the combatants, exclaiming, ' Hold ! for your lives !' as his
scimitar swept through the air it collided with their swords,
making a fiery circle in its flight. The picturesque grandeur of
the action and the magnificence of the pose so struck a fellow in
the gallery that he roared out, ' Abd'l Kader, by G— !' This
exclamation touched the keynote of sympathy : the house rose at
it, the pit sprang to its feet, the boxes swelled the general chorus
of applause, and from that moment the success of the actor was
assured."

From earlier accounts of that memorable evening it would
appear that after the bold, majestic figure of the Moor had been
hailed at the outset with a lusty shout of approbation, quietness,
the quietness of disappointed expectation, settled down like a pall
over the house. Possibly that obnoxious element known to later
times as " organised opposition" was present in considerable force;
at any rate there was a gradually increasing inattention, coupled
with conversation so loud as to interfere with the harmony of the
performance. Such conduct was certainly not in accordance with
the usual spirit of fair play. In the biographical notice in *Tallis's
Dramatic Magazine* (1851) it is pointed out that this distracting
hubbub continued until the beginning of the great scene in the
third act, when the uproar in the gallery grew so intolerable that
Mr. Perkins, the stage manager, came forward and complained

that they were not permitting Mr. Brooke to do justice to himself, and were acting without their customary generosity. Strange to say, the house took this well-merited rebuke in good part and set up a loud cheer to re-assure the insulted actor. Meanwhile poor Brooke had retired to a couch at the back of the stage and there sat him down, miserable and dejected, with a look of mute appeal in his eyes, which, despite his black visage, went straight to the hearts of the audience. After another encouraging round of applause, Brooke and Stuart proceeded with the scene amid the most respectful attention. Some corroboration is afforded us of this statement by the *Morning Post* of the following day, which points out that as Othello's suspicions of the fidelity of Desdemona gained strength "the acting was distinguished by a mental power that was extraordinary; and then the abounding trustfulness and the casting forth all doubts of her truth, seemed for the instant to quell the power of the tempter. The battling with the growing doubts, and the determination to believe no evil of the loved object were marvellously delineated."

At the termination of Othello's speech, commencing —

> "Think'st thou I'd make a life of jealousy,
> To follow still the changes of the moon
> With fresh suspicion?"

the audience, which at first had been so cold and froward, rose as one man, waving hats and handkerchiefs, and cheering so lustily as to startle the passers-by in the street. From that moment success was assured. Invigorated by this remarkable change of face, Brooke renewed his energies and played with a sublimity of passion that evoked round after round of applause, until the conclusion of the scene. "At the end of the third act," says Dr. Westland Marston in the chapter on Brooke in his scholarly work, "Our Recent Actors"—"at the end of the third act the house was in a fever of delight. The acclamations which recalled the actor subsided only into a restless murmur of applause. Knots of impromptu critics gathered together in boxes and lobby. In the pit looks and gestures and a hum of delight

expressed the general verdict; and outside the theatre a crowd,
attracted by the rumour of the effect produced, recalled the
account given of the scene outside Drury Lane on Edmund
Kean's first appearance." Acting with undiminished vigour to
the end, Brooke never loosened his hold upon the audience,
keeping them in a fervour of enthusiasm, the like of which had
not been paralleled within recent memory, save on the occasion
of Mrs. Nisbett's return to the Haymarket. Next day the
critics, with one noteworthy exception, joined in singing the
praises of the new actor. The dissentient was John Forster,
of *The Examiner*, whose violent partisanship of Macready was
patent in theatrical circles. To the abuse showered upon Edwin
Forrest's head by this eminent writer must be attributed those
regretable scenes of bloodshed and disorder which followed in
America, and left such a blot on international amity. Let us
hearken, however, to one or two of the most powerful voices in
the chorus. Said *The Times* :—

"It is long since a theatre has presented such an
appearance of excitement as that of the Olympic last night.
Mr. Gustavus Brooke had been announced to make his
London *début* in the character of Othello, and enough had
been said of his provincial celebrity to justify general
expectation. The house was crowded; but the mere statement
of this fact is not sufficient to convey a notion of the
peculiar aspect. There is a great difference in the people who
make up crowds; and the audience who were assembled to see
Mr. Brooke were just those persons who could be picked out by
an *habitué* as likely to interest themselves in theatrical affairs—
in a word, the connoisseurs of the metropolis.

"Mr. Brooke's first entrance created an impression in his
favour. He has a tall, commanding figure, and a face evidently
handsome, in spite of the disfigurement of the dark hue, which
gives somewhat of grace to every marked movement of Othello's
countenance. His voice is of excellent quality deep and
sonorous, and this quality is never lost, however strong the
utterance of passion.

" The first two acts rather gave the notion of an eloquent declaimer than of a man of fire and passion. The reading was excellent, the voice well modulated, the emphasis carefully adjusted. An air of commanding dignity was spread over all this early portion of the performance, and the only fear was that the whole would prove too quiet and measured, and at last seem monotonous. A well-conceived display of indignation at the brawl in which Cassio is involved led to a contrary supposition ; but still the third act was anxiously expected as a test.

" Through this great ordeal of the third act—of the dialogue with Iago—Mr. Brooke passed most triumphantly. Here he showed that he was a man, not only of form, but of substance. His bursts of jealous passion came down with terrific weight, and whether he soared on the wings of rage, or sank exhausted beneath its force, all was fresh, energetic, and genial. There was nothing in his points to suggest a reminiscence of other actors. Indeed, in the ordinary sense of the word, he can hardly be said to have made a ' point ' at all, of such a continuous, sustained character was his acting. And be it remarked, that the correctness and sound judgment which were visible in his earlier speeches did not forsake him when he abandoned himself to the more violent outbursts of passion. As he preserved his voice, so likewise did he preserve his head, however great the storm of emotion.

" But if we would mark the most striking features of Mr. Brooke's representation of Othello, we would indicate those passages in which the undercurrent of grief is forced up into the midst of jealous rage. Lines, and parts of lines, which he delivered were in this respect exquisitely touching, and evidently resulted from original conception. The exclamation, ' Damn her, lewd minx ; oh, damn her,' when he gave an expression of sorrow to the repetition of the curse, is a remarkable case in point. Indeed, all the mournful side of Othello's position he had conceived with great delicacy. The break of the voice into weeping at the words, ' Othello's occupation's gone,' and, above all, the deep anguish when he said, ' Fool, fool, fool,' after the discovery of the villainy that had been practised upon him, were touches of the deepest pathos.

"There is no mistake about the success of Mr. Brooke. It was not only a success marked by plaudits, but by the conversation of the old theatrical loungers. He was called with enthusiasm, and has excited an interest which will not speedily subside."

"With the single exception of Edmund Kean," remarked the *Morning Post*, "we have seen no such Othello. There is the same fierce energy—the same melting tenderness—the same lightning glance. There are no mannerisms, no traditional readings, no copying of the styles of this or that celebrated actor: the Moor of Venice is placed before us in his true dignity, his love, his doubts, and agony. As each passion is evolved, we are swayed hither and thither at the will of the actor, and are only awakened from the cunning of the scene by the loud bravos of the audience. The ruling excellency of Mr. Gustavus Brooke's acting consists in its manliness and truthfulness, combined with an amount of physical power equal to the sustaining the largest demands of the heroical drama. Every passage of the play has been studied with a full appreciation of its moral truth and poetical beauty. No one phasis of the character was rendered unduly prominent: the dignity of the noble Moor, the commander of the Venetian forces, was never for an instant forgotten. The famous speech to the Senate was enunciated with admirable effect, and the turning from the Duke to Brabantio at the words 'Her father loved me, oft invited me,' was admirably conceived."

Agreeing in the main with the opinion expressed by *The Times* critic, Dr. Westland Marston, in his admirable analysis of Brooke's first performance, points out that while his delivery of the line—

"O fool! fool! fool!"

was in accordance with the traditions of the elder Kean, the rendering was so far in harmony with the entire conception of the character that no suspicion of copying could be entertained. "The word fool," writes Dr. Marston, "was pronounced in the first instance with blended amazement and remorse, in the second with a musing, lingering sense of his own fatuity as Iago's dupe, and in the third with the quiet hopelessness of one who feels the past irrevocable." To which the writer might have added, as pointed out by an appreciative Melbourne reviewer, that Brooke uttered the first letter of the word, in its third repetition, with a quiver of the lip peculiar to himself, that seemed to accentuate the sob in his voice.

It is noteworthy, likewise, that although Dr. Marston saw Brooke's Othello on several subsequent occasions, he never knew it to approach the excellence of the first night, when the apathetic indifference of the audience acted as a stimulant and brought out the tragedian at his best. Afterwards we are told his Othello, "while retaining its mechanical outline and its elocutionary force, had lost much of that reality which the spectator feels when passion dictates expression."

While Mr. Coleman considers Brooke's Othello inferior only to the conception of Edwin Forrest, Salvini appears in critical opinion to bear away the palm. Not but the point has been hotly and very absurdly contested. Manchester playgoers were very much exercised in considering the matter when Salvini made his first appearance in their city. Even at that late day the Brookites—remnants of the "old guard"—were in strong force, and persisted in sending critical analyses to the papers, showing that remembrances of the stock favourite of '47 were still keen.

"It can hardly be said," writes Westland Marston, "that Brooke's Othello, even at its best, was equal to Salvini's. The former, for instance, could never have given us that grand piece of psychology which occurs in the third act, where Salvini, having trampled on Iago, stands awhile mute and vacant, then, with a distressed and courteous air, raises the fallen man and leads him to a chair. What finer illustration could be given of the mental chaos that follows the Moor's fury? For the moment Othello has forgotten his misery and his rage, and wonders at the sight of the prostrate tempter.

"There was, nevertheless, one feature in Brooke's passion which made me prefer it to Salvini's. It had more of the irregularity and the sudden contrasts which denote extreme tension of feeling. If excitement ran ever so high it would at times be driven back, as advancing waves are sometimes by meeting a gale. There would be frequently a momentary lull, a false calm of irony, ere the tide again gathered and leaped on. With all its grandeur and force, Salvini's passion lacked, I thought, at times the contrast and the variety I have indicated. It was somewhat too measured and uniform—a sea that rolled on majestically and irresistibly, but that had no convulsion; it did not turn and eddy with the wind."

Who shall decide? Mr. Edmund Yates in his "Reminiscences" gives the palm to Brooke, whose Othello, to his mind, had all the manliness, gallantry, and pathos of Salvini, without a suggestion of the repulsive violence that marred the Italian actor's rendering. Surely we have here the keynote to the radical difference between the two great conceptions of the character, which are not legitimately comparable in an artistic sense, and indeed would never have been pitted against each other had not the superb physical endowments of the two actors begged a comparison. Brooke's Othello was the climax of the conventional Moor as rendered by a long line of illustrious tragedians, who had sought by a slow process of idealisation— keeping pace from time to time with the progress of refinement —to imbue the character with a romantic spirit, and thus to mitigate the barbaric frankness and rugged animalism of the tragedy.

Untrammelled by tradition, Salvini arrived at the Othello of Shakespeare by resuscitating the mediæval Moor in all his elemental and brutal simplicity. With the single exception of Edwin Forrest, whose rendering of the character had something of Salvini's repugnant violence and sensuality, no other actor within living memory has dared to present the true and un-idealised Othello. The measure of the difference between Salvini and Brooke is as the measure of the difference between

the sixteenth and the nineteenth centuries. It is purely a
question of taste, and the modern stage seeks refinement in
poetic drama, not realistic brutality.

Beside the warm enthusiasm of press and public, Brooke
at once received material recognition of his success in the
raising of his salary. Mr. Coleman, on the authority of Captain
Spicer (the real head of affairs at the Olympic, although a Mr.
Davidson figured as nominal lessee on the bills), states that the
original agreement was £10 a week, and that the terms were
increased to £60 after the first performance. This would appear
conclusive. But it is singular that in the biographical notice in
Tallis's Magazine (evidently inspired by its subject) the writer
informs us that Brooke's original salary of £25 a week to play
alternate nights was at once doubled.

Brooke gave twenty-four successive representations of Othello
at the Olympic (not thirty as has so frequently been stated), or
twenty-seven in all, before the termination of his engagement
on March 25. On January 31, he appeared as Sir Giles
Over-reach, repeating the impersonation seven times successively,
or eleven in all. *The Times*, strange to say, neglected to notice
the performance, but the other papers were sufficiently enthusiastic
to make up for the deficiency. *The Sun* considered that his
acting " more than justified the most ardent hopes which had
been formed by all admirers of the drama from his impersonation
of Othello. No such actor has appeared on the boards since
Edmund Kean ; and Mr. Brooke's performance of Sir Giles did
not fall far short of that of Edmund Kean, in this his greatest
character. The third act was a masterpiece of wheedling and
villainy ; and in the scene with his daughter, the ' kiss close '
was given with immense effect. It is the closing scene of the
play, however, which is Mr. Brooke's great triumph. Here we
have a succession of violent contrasts, of bright light and dark
shadows, and it was in setting off these contrasts—in bringing
out these lights and shadows, that Mr. Brooke showed himself
so admirable. The madness of the triumph of the scoundrel at
the success of all his schemes for securing to his daughter

the hand of the popular Lord Lovell, and to himself the
fortune of the Lady Allworth, was admirably given, and
contrasted finely with the agony of despair at finding the deed
securing to him the Allworth property a mere blank, and the mad
fury of rage with which he rushes at his daughter, changing
suddenly into the paralysis of death, when he says, ' Some undone
widow sits upon my arm and takes away its strength.' In this
scene he was quite equal to Edmund Kean. Mr. G. V. Brooke is
far and away the greatest actor of the day." " He is stated in
the bills of the day," says the *Morning Advertiser*, " as ' being
universally acknowledged to be the greatest living tragedian,'
and certainly if his representation of other characters be equal to
his Sir Giles Over-reach of last night—if not the ' greatest living
tragedian,' he is equal to any that now tread the stage. Nothing
could be more exquisite than his conception of the wicked,
ambitious villain who spared no exertions to accomplish his
purpose, and laughed at all moral and religious obligations in the
pursuit of it, and the manner in which he portrayed his feelings
and passions proved him to be gifted with genius of the first
order."

It is necessary here to emphasize the good impression created
by Brooke in his second part, because Mr. Coleman, with a
guileless reliance in club-room gossip, has seen fit to put into
circulation a very different story. After pointing out that Brooke's
youth and high spirits were now leading him headlong into the
vortex of dissipation, Mr. Coleman continues :—" Sometimes he
sought relief from these ignoble occupations in rowing and
boating. One day he rowed up the river from Earl's Wharf Pier
to Putney and back; a jovial dinner and skittles and other
diversions followed; then it became necessary to ' put on a spurt '
to get back in time for the performance. *It was his first appearance
in town as Sir Giles Over-reach :* there had been no Sir Giles in
London since Kean's day, and it was characteristic of the man that
Brooke treated so fiery an ordeal so lightly. When he arrived
at the theatre, it was long past the time of commencement; the
audience (a densely crowded one) were already impatient ; it

was three quarters of an hour late when the curtain rose, but
the delay was condoned, and he was received with unusual
enthusiasm. He wore a new dress that night; the heat was
overpowering, and he was in a bath of perspiration, arising
principally from the hasty pull down the river. At the end of the
first act he desired his dresser to strip off his singlet; the new
canvas lining of the dress was damp; a chill struck to his
lungs; by the time he reached his great scene in the fifth act
he was totally inaudible, and his failure was as complete in Sir
Giles as his triumph had been assured in Othello. Instead of
resting and nursing himself, he tried to fight off his malady
with drink; but he got worse and worse, collapsed utterly, and
left the theatre."

It would be interesting to learn Mr. Coleman's authority for
this extraordinary effort of the imagination; likewise for the
statement that when Brooke became the talk of the town " his
admirers alleged that he was the greatest Othello since Kean,
that he was also the beau-ideal of Romeo, Claude Melnotte,
and Ion." It will be remarked that the three last-mentioned
characters were not among those presented by the tragedian
during his first Olympic engagement.

The announcement of Brooke's appearance as Richard III.
on Thursday, February 17, produced great excitement among
the frequenters of the little Wych Street Theatre, and caused
them to muster in such strong force as to crowd the very
lobbies of the boxes shortly after the opening of the doors.
" Mr. Brooke's performance," says *The Times,* evidently wakened
up at last—" Mr. Brooke's performance excited the greatest
enthusiasm, but still it is doubtful whether the parts that he
has acted after Othello have been wisely chosen. Whatever
may be said of the difficulties of Othello, it is a straightforward
character throughout. For Sir Giles Over-reach new qualities
were required, and though Mr. Brooke could throw much force
into the fifth act he made comparatively little of the subtle
usurer as displayed in the first four. Something similar may
be said of the Richard, which is played after Colley Cibber's

version. Mr. Brooke's best act was the last, in which the greatest physical energy is required, but there was a want of delicate discrimination in the earlier portions to give effect to all these little points of irony and sarcasm with which the character is studded. In physical qualities nature has been very liberal to Mr. Brooke. There is strength in his voice and form, and all that he does has certain weight. The combat could scarcely have been fought with a fiercer energy, and the convulsions of death were well rendered; but Mr. Brooke should husband his force to a greater degree. By employing it too early he produces a monotony of effect, and destroys the variations of the character. In the first scenes his best passages were those of quiet declamation. In all where mere subtlety is required he seems to aim at greater violence. His Richard is a strong, earnest, vigorous, but not a sufficiently intellectual performance."

After some half dozen representations of *Richard III.* the tragedy gave way on March 2 to *Hamlet*, which appears only to have been performed four times in all. Eminently princely and natural as was the characterisation, Brooke's over-studious attention to his personal appearance gave the spectator rather the impression of the Apollo Belvidere neatly arrayed in black velvet than of the distraught Dane. After pointing out that Hamlet was the highest test of the actor's powers, both intellectually and physically, the *Morning Post* proceeds to say—"Greatly as we thought of his Othello, and genially as we hailed his advent on London boards, we confess that we were little prepared for so lofty a conception, so scholarlike an appreciation, so consistent and artist-like development. Every point was carefully considered; there was an utter absence of stage mechanism, and there were no tricks of voice to astonish the lovers of startling effects."

The *Morning Advertiser* considered that "with all Mr. Brooke's gifts and talent, there appeared in his delineation a leaning more on physical display for effect than on the less corporeal, hence more spiritual, evolvings of the nicer, the deeper, and the darker shades of character. Mr. Brooke's personation of

the moody and philosophic Prince of Denmark was anticipated
with no ordinary interest. In all that could be acquired, even his
opponents accorded him the vantage-ground—'cunning of fence,'
a feather in the cap of youth, a good voice, fine person, nice
discrimination, and so forth; these are great adjuncts in the
personation of *Hamlet*, and Mr. Brooke possesses them all; and
in addition to them a tolerable idea of reading the author's text.
It must, however, be admitted that the conception was in some
degree imperfect; it was wanting in unity and completeness;
portions of it exhibited much careful study and intellect, while
others were less perfect and effective. With regard to originality,
the personation is strongly marked with it throughout, for in no
one scene does the actor for a moment forget himself by falling
into the vice of imitation. This was especially the case in the
reading of the play, as an instance of which we may mention the
speech which occurs immediately after the interview with the
Ghost, and when importuned by Horatio and Marcellus as to the
import of his converse with the spirit, he takes the former aside,
as if to inform him, and finding that the latter is about to follow,
he turns upon him sharply and exclaims—

> "' For your desire to know what is between us,
> O'ermaster it as you may.'

"This is usually addressed to both parties, but Mr. Brooke's
understanding of the lines appears to be more in consonance
with the after parts of the play, and accords better with the
spirit of friendship which is supposed to exist between the
Prince and Horatio. Again, the advice to the actor was given
seated, not in an overbearing manner, but gentle and persuasive,
each word having its full weight, and the whole apparently coming
from one who had been offended to the soul by the strutting
and bellowing of the players he had seen. The soliloquies were
uttered in an impressive and scholar-like manner, but in the
more impassioned scenes there was an absence of depth and
feeling, although they were energetic. The applause bestowed
upon Mr. Brooke was of a most flattering nature, sometimes

inconveniently so to the actor, for several passages were entirely lost by that means."

On March 13 Brooke played Shylock for the first and only time, and two nights after gave a sound characterisation of Master Walter. The engagement terminated on Thursday, March 23, with *Virginius,* in which Brooke approached perilously close to the excellence of Macready, though in a widely different manner. The former actor's was the more severely classic rendering; the latter's the more poetically-realistic.

During his off-nights at the Olympic (when Miss Glyn and others enjoyed a measure of popularity) Brooke occasionally performed elsewhere. Thus, supported by Marie Duret and the once celebrated Cobham, he played Othello at Brighton on February 16 to an audience representing some £110. After the conclusion of his Olympic engagement he made several one-night appearances here, always in association with Marie Duret. London-super-Mare saw his Master Walter on April 28; his Hamlet on May 3; and early in August he fulfilled an engagement there of six nights' duration.

Meanwhile his Olympic engagement had not created the sensation to be augured from his first-night reception. After defeating an audience whose callous indifference aroused all the combativeness in his Irish blood, he seems to have relapsed somewhat into the old happy-go-lucky methods so searchingly dealt with by the Manchester critics. There can be little doubt that the man whose portrait was in every shop window —whose name was on every playgoer's tongue—lost his head over the success to which he had looked forward so patiently during many weary years. It soon became apparent that the glamour which had thrown its terrible spells over George Frederick Cooke and Edmund Kean had claimed another victim in the new star, clouding his genius and rendering his future painfully uncertain. Beloved by all with whom he came in contact, as warm in his attachments as he was modest in forming them, Brooke never extended to himself the same fraternal solicitude he meted out to others. Alas! "No man's enemy but his own," has oftentimes the direst and most unrelenting of foes to contend against. What excessive porter drinking began, the ravages of bronchitis ended. The matchless chest voice, full and sonorous, with just a touch of nasality, was gone for ever. But there were crumbs of consolation for the admirers of Brooke, in the fact that with it went the rant born of excessive physical vigour and the elocutionary tricks which had previously given an artificial tone to his acting.

Years, however, were to elapse ere Brooke found himself utterly discredited in London. On the termination of his Olympic engagement, Benjamin Webster had made him the princely offer of £15 a night for one hundred nights certain, to place himself at the head of the fine company then playing at the Haymarket. This he was capricious enough to decline, preferring to make an immediate return to the provinces. After an absence of six or seven weeks, during which he appeared at the Queen's Theatre, Hull, and elsewhere, in association with the inevitable Duret, Brooke retraced his steps to the Olympic, where Anna Cora Mowatt and E. L. Davenport had meanwhile been appearing with satisfactory results. Uniting his forces temporarily with the American artists, he made his reappearance on Wednesday, May 17, as *Laurency* in Henry Spicer's new five-act tragedy, *The Lords of Ellingham*. Speaking of this piece in her "Autobiography," as published in 1854, Mrs. Mowatt informs us that while E. L. Davenport was considerably applauded in his portrayal of the confiding, noble-minded *Dudley Latigmer*, Brooke's rendering, on the other hand, of the audacious villainy of *Laurency* proved dangerously captivating. This, the first character "created" by Brooke during his fifteen years' stage experience, was indeed very favourably received, and would doubtless have left a more lasting impression had the play been strong enough to warrant an extended run. "On Wednesday," says the *Literary Gazette* of May 20, "the great test of Mr. G. V. Brooke's capabilities as an actor of the first rank was made at this theatre. A new play by the author of *Honesty*, *Judge Jeffreys*, etc., written long ago, but now first adapted for representation, and called *The Lords of Ellingham*, was the occasion, and we must say that the impression left upon us by Mr. Brooke's delineation of his first original part is very favourable. There were more study and carefulness in the delineation, nicer discrimination and appreciation of detail in his development of the character of Lawrency *(sic)* than have marked any of his preceding efforts; indeed, the whole was a fine, manly, forcible piece of acting, and the declamatory burst in the last scene was as effective as anything of the kind could be. *The Lords of Ellingham* is rather a heavy drama, and the plot does not develop itself with sufficient clearness during the progress of the play, though it is apparent enough when all is ended, and it has other faults which make it drag on rather heavily; still there are some well conceived situations, and the action is frequently well sustained, and there are many poetical beauties spread over the dialogue. The play has been well put upon the stage, is characteristically dressed, and the scenery is in every respect worthy of great praise. After Mr. Brooke, the principal parts were very carefully played by Mrs. Mowatt, Miss Marie Duret, Mr. Davenport, and Mr. H. Holl, not forgetting a minor one of a surly old gaoler, capitally done by Mr. Stirling."

After the brief run of the new tragedy Brooke returned once more to his old love, the provinces. Flitting hither and thither, we find him on Monday, November 20, making his first appearance as an adult actor at Edinburgh, where he was rapturously received during his fortnight's sojourn. The anonymous writer in the *Australian Magazine*, already referred to, was at this period one of the many students under Sir William Hamilton and the " old man eloquent," Christopher North, the humdrum course of whose winter session was pleasantly broken in upon by the arrival of the tragedian. " I was then," he remarks, " studying our English literature under the guidance of Professor Aytoun—Aytoun of *Blackwood* and ' Bon Gaultier's Ballads '—and was greatly struck with the clear light which my own experience of a great actor's power shed upon many a byway of literature; contemporary allusions to a Betterton, a Garrick, a Siddons. or a Kean no longer seemed written in an unknown tongue. Nor was I a solitary enthusiast. My fellow-students caught the infection; high discourse held we about the drama and the laws of dramatic expression and the unities; and still to one settled conclusion all our discussions led—that the great actor, and he alone, was the man most to be envied, his lot the most to be desired."

Sad to say, while Brooke was thus firing the imaginations of those still on the threshold of life, the ebbing of the tide found him experiencing those shallows and miseries of a stroller's course, which, although not new, came with added bitterness after the sweets of success.

Towards the middle of January, 1849, we find him acting at the Theatre Royal, Hull (under the management of Pritchard, then director of the York Circuit), where he gained considerable applause in his personation of Leontes in *The Winter's Tale.* After pursuing a somewhat precarious course in the provinces he returned to London with empty pockets and no immediate prospect of an engagement. This was some little time before the disastrous fire at the Olympic in March.

"His finances," writes Mr. W. C. Day to us, " had long been at a low ebb, and a few friends suggested that a benefit at the Olympic — the scene of his early triumphs — might possibly bring some grist to the mill. A scratch company was engaged, and *Richard III.* announced. By the way, I acted Tressel on that memorable night—memorable for the strange incident that follows.

"A lady with whom Brooke was then living attended him at the wing, a large black cloak over her arm, and a rummer of hot brandy and water in her hand; the former she threw over his shoulders with every exit, and the latter she handed him with every entrance. 'Hurrah!' exclaimed the Jezebel, as Glo'ster made his first entrance, 'Hurrah! Gustavus is on his own boards again!' As the play proceeded the glass was replenished more than once, and by the time the last act was reached the representative of the House of York was three sheets in the wind. He wore a jet black wig with ringlets, which, in the fight with Richmond, shifted its position; he endeavoured to set it right in vain; another trial and yet another; still the obstinate 'jazey' refused to be adjusted. At last, boiling with rage, and midst shouts of merriment, he forced it violently off his head, and finished the combat with his head-gear in his hand. When you remember that Brooke's own hair was *very fair*, the absurdity of the scene may be imagined. This I witnessed from the first wing, and though convulsed with laughter could not but feel grieved—remembering bygones—at the painful exhibition."

To add to these indiscretions the luckless tragedian was now about to permit Marie Duret, the lady in question, to act on the stage under the protection of his name. When they appeared together for one night at the Theatre Royal, Dublin, on Saturday, June 23, for J. W. Calcraft's benefit (before a distinguished assemblage, comprising, among others, the Lord Lieutenant and the Countess of Clarendon), it was as Mr. and Mrs. G. V. Brooke that their names were placed opposite the parts of Julian St. Pierre and Marianna in the programme. The *soi-disant* Mrs. also gave a capital performance of the Widow Cheerly in the afterpiece of *The Soldier's Daughter*. Brooke and the lady upon whom he had conferred brevet honours, received a call at the end of *The Wife* and were loudly cheered. The press notices of the following Monday sound the first note of warning regarding the breakdown in the tragedian's voice. While the *Freeman* was glad to perceive that he had "in a great measure acquired the clear resonance and fine intonation of voice that so pre-eminently marked his dramatic readings, but which has suffered for a time some detriment through his recent illness"; *Saunders's News-Letter*, on the other hand, says, "he seemed to be labouring under the effects of recent cold, for his voice was broken at intervals, but his delineation of the part was earnest and impressive; it abounded in fine and telling points—at times, perhaps, partaking of the melodramatic, but keeping the interest awake to the close. He was most favourably received and warmly applauded during the evening."

We have now occasion to refer to an extraordinary circumstance, which, as a link in a chain of startling coincidences, must appeal to all believers in the doctrine of fatalism. When Tyrone Power, the Irish comedian, was lost in the *President*, while returning from America towards the middle of March, 1841, Elton, the well-known tragedian, is reputed to have remarked, "I think I can imagine the exact manner in which Power must have felt when the waves first rushed over his head. I can fancy the lights of the Haymarket Theatre flashing before his eyes, and the roaring of the waves taking the sound of a burst of applause." A little more than two years afterwards (on July 18, 1843) Elton himself met with a similar dreadful fate when the *Pegasus* foundered on the passage from Leith to Hull. Brooke, who appears to have made Elton's acquaintance in Scotland (he spoke of him once as "a good actor and a good man"), was very much impressed by the circumstances of his "taking off," and evidently reverted to the subject again and again. Considering that he had no particular penchant for poetical composition, it is a strange fact that while sojourning in the bosom of his family about the period of his appearance for Calcraft's benefit, he went to the trouble of inditing an elegy on the death of the hapless tragedian. Seeing that he himself was fated to have his epitaph "writ in water," we think fit to append the hitherto unpublished lines from the original MS., merely premising that the strong religious tone throughout was eminently natural to the writer: —

LINES ON THE DEATH OF MR. ELTON, THE TRAGEDIAN.

WHEN tempted in the morn of life to roam
Far from the pleasures of our native home,
The path seems clear, the valley gemmed with flowers,
Refreshed and wakened by Hope's rainbow showers.
No cloud hangs weeping o'er the distant hill,
No wind disturbs the music of the rill;
Boldly we venture forth with laughing eye,
Joy in the heart and promise in the sky.
Too soon, alas! we reach the mountain's brow
Where serpents coil, and thorny branches grow,
Where hatred, malice, hollowness, and crime

In covert lurk, to sting us in our prime ;
And when we deem Fame's laurell'd wreath our own,
An earthquake comes and hurls us from the throne.
Thus, the "Poor Player," whom the Public mourn
(Pity shall hang [?] a tear upon his urn),
Commenced his early race with prosp'rous gales,
'Til sorrow whistled through his shivering sails
And laid him prostrate ; but the mighty power
Of Mind aroused him in that stormy hour,
And after years of toil on life's rude deck
He reach'd the gaol *(sic!)* and found his hopes—a wreck !
Oh ! who can tell the farewell agony
That shook his spirit as the thought of *thee*—
Wife of his bosom—fluttered o'er his mind,
When he to his Creator's will resigned :
What horrid terrors of the Ocean Queen,
What burning thoughts of what he might have been,
What rapid visions of his lonely home,
His orphans left in poverty to roam,
Press'd on him, as the stealthy [oozy] wave
Stifled his voice, and whirl'd him to his grave.
Yet to the skies did these mute words ascend —
"My children—bless them—God ! be Thou their friend."
The Pegasus went forth without a cloud
To cast a shade upon her swelling shroud,
She cut the wave as Queen of Neptune's realm,
"Youth on her prow and pleasure at the helm ;"
The farewell had been said, the last kiss given,
And blessings for her safety wafted up to Heaven !"
'Twas night, her mantle diamonded with stars,
Smiling like angels on the vessel's spars,
That swept along the bosom of the sea
As though in scorn of its immensity.
Of those within her some would seek releif *(sic!)*
In dreamy slumbers (destined to be brief !)
Some would engage to cheer the stilly hour
In holy converse (sweet entrancing power !)
Others would gaze upon the jewelled skies,
And ponder on their hidden mysteries ;
While some would seat them by the light's pale ray
With minds bent up to read 'til dawn of day.
All occupation had ; all sought for ease ;
No FEAR was on the wilderness of seas.
Suddenly shrieks are heard—"We split ! we split !"
Are cries that rend the air and startle it.
The deck is crowded ; forms half-naked stand
Straining the sight, to find one spot of land :
They see it not, and yield then to despair
And hurry to and fro, with horrid glare ;
When one loud voice exclaims, "To prayer ! To prayer !"

'Tis he; the man, from whom hope never flies,
The sinner's friend, the legate of the skies;
The minister of grace, ordained by ONE
Whose throne eternal knows no setting sun.
They kneel around him, and his words impart
Religion's cordial to the bursting heart;
Certain of death, he points to realms above,
Where they will meet again in peace and love.
'Twas thus they perished; in the act of prayer:
They turn'd to Heaven and found a refuge there.
No storm arose, no angry waters threw
Their fretted billows o'er the pallid crew;
No lightning flash the streaming canvas rent,
No howling wind the tapered mainmast bent;
No moaning thunder peal was heard to sweep
Its diapason o'er the restless deep:
But all was calm—around, above, below—
As twilight resting on untrodden snow.
Oh! boundless, wild, ungovernable sea,
Sublime in thine unbridled majesty!
Art thou enamoured of the sons of earth
To clutch them thus in thy capacious girth?
Or art thou jealous of the human skill
That dares to cope with thy gigantic will?
Roll on, deep sea; thou world of silence, roll!
An overwhelming wonder to the soul;
For thou art changeless; since the world began
Thou hast embraced it with thy mystic span
And laugh'd to scorn the petty power of man:
Time flies; thrones, kingdoms, kings—the good and just
Surrender to the mandate—" Dust to dust.'
But, Ocean, THOU' time works no change in *thee*,
Thou art ALONE—type of ETERNITY!
Peace to the dead! 'tis not for man to know
Why God afflicts His creatures here below;
Humility is taught us by the *Son*,
Then, mourners, orphans, let HIS WILL BE DONE.

GUSTAVUS V. BROOKE, *June*.

Were it not a foregone conclusion that Brooke has little literary reputation to lose, we should hardly feel disposed to give to the world this quaint gallimaufry of crude thoughts and infelicitous word painting, which, like many another act of its concoctor, speaks more for the qualities of heart than head. Viewed by the light of after-events these milk-and-water Byronisms will doubtless strike the purist with a force utterly lacking in many analogous productions of much finer fibre.

Following the Dublin performance, "Mr. and Mrs. G. V. Brooke," on June 29, gave some readings from *Othello* in the Corporation Hall, Londonderry, at popular prices. Next day the tragedian wrote from the City Hotel to his friend Morris, of Ayr, telling him the readings had been a failure, and asking the loan of a little money for immediate travelling expenses ; a request often repeated afterwards, and as often responded to by the kind-hearted Scotchman. He laments there is so little to be done in theatres during the summer months, and conveys the intimation that he has made an arrangement with Daly, of the Carlisle Theatre, to take him on tour through Penrith, Wigton, and Maryport, to lecture on Shakespeare. He thinks it will answer very well. On the same day Daly was writing to Brooke advising the postponement of his visit to Carlisle until the excitement of the impending races had subsided, and fixing the 9th of July for his appearance there. From the tone of Daly's note we can readily see that Brooke was very dilatory and careless in his business correspondence, and had left the bewildered Carlisle impressario to imagine for himself what he purposed reading during the tour. On July 3 we find the tragedian writing to Morris from the Maiden City, enclosing Daly's letter, and complaining that he cannot get a farthing from a certain manager, who, he says, is " deeply in my debt, not only for our services, but money lent." " Mrs. Brooke" has been taken suddenly ill with some affection of the heart ; he cannot leave as expected, and the money for travelling expenses will be exhausted before the end of the week. Will his good friend lend him another five pounds, " which shall be repaid with a thousand thanks." Needless to say, the money was forthcoming. Arriving at Carlisle on Tuesday, July 10, Brooke and Marie Duret gave two readings there ; " but," writes the tragedian to Morris, from the Angel Inn on the 18th, " from the extreme heat they have been comparative failures. We are going completely through the 'Lake District,' and I make no doubt some of the smaller towns will answer our purpose much better." When next he communicates with his trusty friend it is from the Saracen's

Head, Paisley, on September 22. "I fear you will think ill of me," he says, "for neglecting to write at the time you stated, but when you have heard how I have been situated, I trust sincerely your good nature will find some little excuse. I could not return the favour, and did not like writing. I have been a very severe loser since last we met; £53 by A ——,* and a much larger sum, a complete dead loss, in London, which I fully relied upon getting in a week or so after I wrote to you; added to which my mother, sister, and brother have been dangerously ill with the prevailing epidemic in Dublin, and I was compelled to assist them at a pecuniary sacrifice. The readings were a complete failure, and from the 1st of July to the end of August barely cleared expenses. But, thank Heaven, things are looking more favourable now, and my voice is much better. . . . . We have engaged here for twelve nights, and as trade is very good I have every reason to hope we shall have good houses." Eight days after, we find him writing to Morris from the same address, saying, "The receipt of your very kind letter on Tuesday morning afforded me the greatest gratification. I have only just time to save the post and say that Mrs. Brooke was seriously indisposed yesterday morning, and was in a very precarious state for some hours, but I am happy to say the doctor considers her out of danger. She still keeps her bed, and I have every reason to hope she will be able to resume her professional duties on Monday. I play at the Princess's Theatre, Glasgow, on Monday week."

Mention of Glasgow recalls an anecdote of one of Brooke's later engagements there, which vividly illustrates his carelessness in regard to money matters, and accounts in a measure for the dissipation of the three fortunes which he is said to have made and lost during his lifetime. A little time subsequent to the present period Brooke, it appears, had his headquarters at Cheetwood, Manchester, and while proceeding on his rounds took with him an actor for some time associated with theatrical affairs in that city, who played seconds to the tragedian and looked

* Manager of the Dundee, Perth, Montrose, and Inverness Theatrical Circuit; now deceased.

after business matters. Glasgow was visited in due course, and immediately after the termination of the last performance there Brooke informed his satellite that he intended returning forthwith to Manchester. "Then we must borrow money to take us back," said that worthy; "expenses have been heavy, the attendance but middling, and there's nothing in the exchequer." "That's strange," replied Brooke, in a tone of good-humoured perplexity; "the houses to me seemed very good. Why didn't you tell me sooner—I would have borrowed the needful? Go and see what you can do." No sooner had the financier departed than Brooke's dresser gave a significant wink to the tragedian, and without stopping to explain his conduct made his way into an adjoining lumber-room crammed with baggage. To Brooke's great astonishment he returned at once with a hat full of money, which he had found rolled up in some stage costumes in a trunk belonging to the actor-manager. Scarcely had he hidden this under a chair when "honest Iago" came back, pulling a long face, and protesting that he had tried his best and couldn't raise a farthing. "Oh, it's immaterial, Mr.——," blurted out the honest dresser, with a sudden familiarity that startled the actor. "A little bird has told me something"; and so saying he pulled the hat from under the chair and emptied its contents on the table. Taking in the whole situation at a glance, Brooke indulged in a hearty laugh over the discomfiture of his lieutenant, and then, much as his own Othello dismissed Cassio, quietly sent him about his business.

CHAPTER VI.

1849—1851.

WHEN Brooke reappeared in Manchester for the first time
since his departure for London (at the Theatre Royal,
on Saturday, November 24, 1849), it was with feelings akin
to pity that his old admirers remarked how great had been the
deterioration in the once magnificent voice, now, alas, broken
and husky. Owing to a squabble with H. J. Wallack, the
stage manager, Barry Sullivan had abruptly retired from the
theatre late in the previous March. He was succeeded as
leading man by R. E. Graham, who played seconds to Mr. and
"Mrs." Brooke throughout this engagement.

In a letter to Morris, written from the theatre on November 27,
Brooke says—"We opened on Saturday, and met with the most
tremendous reception from a crowded house I ever experienced ;
and I shall expect to clear from £120 to £140 by this engagement. I go to Oldham from here, where I am secured £60
for eight nights, and shall then remain quiet till five weeks after
Christmas, when I go to London. I have settled for the Olympic,
£100 a month, playing twelve nights in the month. . . My
engagement in London will last till the end of July."

A rather good story is told in connection with a sudden visit which Brooke's younger brother paid the tragedian precisely at this period. Invalided home by a bad attack of yellow fever from the island of Tobago, where he had held the position of private secretary to his Excellency the Lieutenant Governor, William Basil Brooke had conceived the idea of taking brother Gus. by surprise. Without stopping to change his travelling attire on arriving in Manchester he made all speed to the theatre, and walked into Gus's dressing-room just as the curtain was about to ring up. Somewhat startled by the apparition, the tragedian, who was putting the finishing touches to his make-up, petulantly inquired, "why on earth he came there to disgrace him in that rig-out." There was little time for much colloquy, however, as Gus. sallied forth shortly after to appear on the stage, leaving behind him a new suit in the latest and most luxurious style. Abashed by his reception, brother William, who was much the same build, and in appearance greatly resembled the tragedian, doffed the obnoxious garments, and arraying himself in Gus's choicer apparel strolled round to the front of the house and watched the entire performance from the boxes. Unfortunately, on his return to the dressing-room he found his brother there before him, and was greeted with a stentorian roar, "I might not well find my new clothes. What the devil do you mean by this sort of conduct?" "Ah, Gussy dear," insinuated William, "shure and you wouldn't have your own brother sitting in the boxes and disgracin' you with them ould things on!"

It must not be thought from this little skirmish that the brothers were anything but the very best of friends. Gus. had always William's interest at heart, and until the whilom private secretary received an official appointment in connection with the Dublin Courts, kept him by his side to look after business matters.

After appearing at Oldham, Brooke returned to Manchester for another week's engagement, commencing December 17. This had barely terminated when he received the first great shock of his life in the sudden departure of the woman upon whom he had lavished all his affection. After feathering her nest for years, Marie Duret, without a word of warning, ran off to America, where, as an actress of the Madame Céleste type, she passed through a number of vicissitudes, and finally died of paralysis in a San Francisco hospital in April, 1881. Much as this *liaison* was to be regretted, it appears to have originated and to have been maintained for a considerable period by sincere affection on both sides. But it ended as all such lawless unions generally end, no matter how plenteous the store of love at the beginning. And goodness knows it was abundant enough in the present instance. Our Manchester friend, Mr. Dinsmore, says—"to see her and Brooke in love-scenes, especially at the old Queen's, was a display that amazed the very gods. Her show of passion and the way she clung to him and wound her arms round his noble form was sometimes startling to witness." Happily for himself Brooke accepted the situation with true philosophy, as we can see by the following characteristic letter: —

> 10 YORK PLACE, FULHAM ROAD,
> BROMPTON, LONDON,
> *January 7, 1850.*

MY DEAR MR. MORRIS,

I have just arrived in town, and commence an engagement at the Olympic Theatre on Monday, February 4th, which will terminate the end of June, for which I am to receive £500. I am only to play three nights a week. The Town seems all agog, and very much in my favour. I have put myself under medical treatment till the appointed time, and my doctor, who is an exceedingly clever man, has not the slightest doubt that, with the rest, my voice will be restored to its wonted vigour.

I have not been acting since Saturday fortnight, and the alteration is wonderful. Pray write to me by return of post, and when I get a little more settled I will let you have a long letter.

I am sorry to say that *the lady* in whom I most confided, after having robbed me on all sides, eloped the other day (about eleven days ago), and is now on her way to America. But the world says, and I begin to think so too, that it is the best thing that could have happened for me—in one respect. She actually had money in the funds, and during my sojourn in Dublin, she came up here, and sold out. She has for years been making a purse, with which she has decamped, carrying with her a magnificent wardrobe; all the result of my laborious exertion and of placing implicit confidence in one who has been for years robbing me under the mask of affection. But though the shock was sudden and severe, I have put a stout heart upon it, and it shall serve as a stimulus to still further exertion, to gain a *name*, and become an ornament to the profession I have embarked in.

Believe me, dear sir,

Yours most truly,

GUSTAVUS V. BROOKE.

Poor Brooke! Like the Moor he so powerfully impersonated, he was—

. . . . . "of a free and open nature
That thinks men honest that but seem to be so ;
And will as tenderly be led by the nose
As asses are."

Writing again to Morris, under date "29 Arundel Street, Strand, January 31st, 1850," he briefly informs his friend of his removal into town, and concludes by thanking Heaven his voice "is now all right." Boasting a company as powerful and extensive as that of any other London theatre, the New Olympic had then been opened a little better than a month. All the available talent had been engaged at salaries well nigh ruinous to any management. Davenport, Conway, Belton, Compton, Mr. and Mrs. Alfred Wigan, and Mrs. Mowatt, formed the mainstay of the company; while among lesser lights enjoying a measure of popularity were Fanny Vining, Patty Oliver, Mrs. Seymour, Mrs. Marston, and the Misses Marshall. The new house had also a very accomplished stage director in Mr. George Ellis, who officiated in a similar capacity at Her Majesty's private theatre in Windsor Castle. At Mrs. Mowatt's suggestion the starring system was abolished, and a wholesome example set to the other metropolitan theatres in the printing of the entire cast on the bills without invidious distinctions in the matter of type.

When Brooke made his first appearance at the New Olympic on Monday, February 4, in a well-mounted production of *Othello*, he found himself adequately supported by E. L. Davenport as Iago, Fanny Vining as Emilia, and Mrs. Mowatt as Desdemona. The Press gave a hearty welcome to the truant, told him he had another chance to fulfil the promise of his *début*, and hoped he

would use it more wisely. Of a surety he made the most of his
opportunity on the opening night, when not even the striking
brilliancy of Davenport's Iago could serve to dwarf his noble
personation of the Moor.

On Monday the 18th, G. H. Lewes' drama, *The Noble Heart*,
which had previously been acted at Manchester, with the
author as the hero, was produced here for the first time in
London. Compressed into three acts since its trial trip in the
provinces, the new play was sumptuously mounted and well
acted throughout. Briefly put, the plot ran somewhat as
follows:—Don Gomez de la Vega, father of Leon, has
unknowingly fallen in love with Juanna, his son's betrothed,
and during the young soldier's absence in the wars, brings about
a compulsory marriage with the lady. With the immediate
return of Leon come many scenes of powerful passion, which
culminate in the father recognising as paramount the son's
claims to the affections of the unwilling bride. His is the noble
heart that dictates the terms of the treaty of peace. The
Pope obligingly gives a dispensation annulling the joyless union,
and poor Don Gomez takes himself off to the nearest monastery.
Despite its gruesome theme, the new play was well received by
a large audience, and the author called for and loudly cheered
at the end. Mrs. Mowatt evinced a delicate perception of the
strong and weak points in the character of Juanna, and acted
finely throughout. E. L. Davenport, as the ardent lover and
devoted son, showed much genuine feeling; while Brooke gave
an enthralling personation of the tempest-tossed father. His
Don Gomez, however, failed to evoke unanimous appreciation
from the critics, the *Literary Gazette* (for which G. H. Lewes
frequently wrote) going so far as to say that "he displayed
great vigour in those passages where there was opportunity for
loudness and action, but had none of the look or the manner
of the proud man he is constantly said to be."

The run of the new play was abruptly terminated on
March 7 by the sudden closing of the theatre. Up to that
period it had never struck anyone as particularly surprising that

a gentleman subsisting on the slender income afforded by a minor position in the Globe Insurance Office could live in regal style, drive a magnificent equipage, and simultaneously manage two such theatres as the Marylebone and the Olympic. Yet this was what the eminently agreeable Mr. Walter Watts was then doing. Thanks to his great adroitness in cooking accounts and the remarkable gullibility of his associates, Watts had succeeded in appropriating some seventy thousand pounds of the company's money before daylight was let in upon his actions. Owing to some technical quibble considerable difficulty was experienced in bringing the crime home to him ; but eventually the gentlemanly thief was sentenced to ten years' penal servitude, and commuted a few hours after the trial by hanging himself in his cell. At a time when all London was discussing the arrest, we find Brooke writing about it as follows :—

29 ARUNDEL STREET, STRAND,
Thursday, March 14, 1850.

MY DEAR MR. MORRIS,

You will no doubt be much surprised to hear of the sudden closure of the Olympic, which took place on this day week. If you will look at the *Times* of last Saturday you will find by the 'City intelligence' that there has been a considerable defalcation in the Globe Insurance Office, of which my late manager was a clerk and shareholder ; and by referring to the *Times* of Tuesday morning you will find the account of Walter Watts' examination at the Mansion House, he having been apprehended on a suspicion of embezzlement. He was remanded till Saturday next.

Here I am in *statu quo*, not knowing what to do till this affair is settled, and when it is some arrangement may be made for the opening of the theatre. My engagement was £25 per week up till the end of June. I was involved by a certain party before I came here, and have since been making that liability less weekly while in receipt of my salary, and now I am completely thrown on my beam ends. I will send you by next post my agreement with the Olympic management, which you will please to return to me. I now have to solicit that you will lend me some pounds to assist me till I see what is to be done, which I will repay with other favours when fortune places me in a more favourable position than at present.

In the present state of things I have thought it advisable to give up my apartments, and have ensconced myself in a single bedroom. Pray let me hear from you by return, and I will send you all the news that may transpire relative to the unfortunate affair.

Believe me,
My dear Mr. Morris,
Yours very faithfully,
GUSTAVUS V. BROOKE.

On his arrival in London to enter upon his Olympic engagement, Brooke (as we learn from another letter to Morris) had been arrested at the suit of the Messrs. Nathan, theatrical costumiers, for the hire of dresses from February, 1848, to February, 1849. Having suffered judgment to go by default, the sum with costs amounted to £123 odd; this the lavish Olympic manager advanced and procured the actor's release. Ten days afterwards the same firm served Brooke with a writ for £109 due, as they represented, for the hire of dresses up to January, 1850. Acting upon the advice of friends, Brooke had determined to defend this action; but it never came to a trial, as an arrangement was effected whereby the tragedian agreed to pay £100 in five monthly instalments. The closing of the Olympic shortly after threw poor Brooke completely on his beam-ends. Writing to Morris from Arundel Street, on April 4, he says:—

"I have had many little debts here and elsewhere which a certain party managed to contract for me; and in order to gain a little peace if possible, I can assure you that I have paid for the last two weeks I was at the Olympic £30 out of every £31 (having been allowed £6 for playing an extra night each week during the run of a play called *The Noble Heart*). So that I left myself with a sovereign pocket money to carry me through. I have now been five weeks without salary, and could not take any engagement with all these things hanging over me. So I at length resolved to take a desperate remedy and become an Insolvent. My petition was filed on Tuesday, and I got my protection yesterday. This morning two sheriffs' officers came into my bedroom at eight o'clock to arrest me at the suit of the Messrs. Nathan, but fortunately I had my protection.

"Nathan's first instalment of £20 was due on the first of April. He is the only creditor I have to oppose me, and his charge has been so out of all reason, and the measures he has adopted against me have been so harsh, that every one says, to use a technical term in the law, 'it won't hold water.' My hearing is fixed for Saturday the 27th inst., and as I have every reason to believe it will end satisfactorily I feel comparatively comfortable. This is the present position in which I am placed, and I assure you it will serve as a stimulus (when I am a free man) to make me strain every nerve to accumulate money and render myself an independent man, as I do not require a telescope to see through my past folly.

" Now for my future proceedings. I play at the Marylebone on Monday next for three weeks, and hope to realise something like £60 or £70 out of it; and I shall then be prepared with engagements for a tour through the provinces, which generally turns out more profitable, not being compelled to keep up the same appearance as in London.

" I have made arrangements for a wardrobe (not to hire, but my own); to be paid for at so much per month, which cannot hurt me, and I have every prospect of creating a sensation in the theatrical world and making a few hundreds in a short period."

Messrs. E. Stirling and J. Kinloch figured on the bills as directors of the Marylebone when Brooke opened there on Monday, April 8, as Othello to the Iago of James Johnstone. During this engagement the tragedian appeared in a round of old characters, and had for leading support Mrs. Seymour of the Haymarket, who played Portia to his Shylock on April 13, Edward Stirling being the Gratiano. Thanks to able management and an ever-varying bill, the pretty little theatre was crowded nightly. " On Brooke's return to London after a long absence," writes Westland Marston, " he made an approach in Othello to his first excellence. This might be due to the excitement of a reappearance. But his acting, like his person, was become coarse and his voice somewhat husky. I saw him at various times in Hamlet, in Sir Giles Over-reach, and several other characters. In all these were particular scenes in which he made an effect; but it was a great deal due to physical energy. He showed little subtlety of apprehension or emotion, nothing that recalled the first night of his Othello."

Happy in the issue of his suit in bankruptcy, we find him writing post-haste as follows:—

> 102 Lisson Grove, North,
> Paddington, *April 29, 1850.*

My Dear Mr. Morris,

I have only time to say that I think you will be pleased at the handsome termination of my insolvency case, the particulars of which you will find in the *Sunday Times,* which accompanies this letter. There is also a description in *The Times* of this morning, and, in fact, all the papers. The Commissioner complimented me highly upon the position which, as a young man, I held in my profession, and said he had not a doubt of my debtors being paid, provided I had good health. Excuse this short and hurried letter, and let me hear from you as soon as possible.

> Believe me,
> My dear Mr. Morris,
> Yours faithfully,
> Gustavus V. Brooke.

But the provincial tour looked forward to, after the Marylebone engagement, with so much joyful anticipation, failed to come off. Brooke's voice again held out signals of distress, and rendered him disinclined for a time to leave the metropolis. Hence from " 38 Prince's Street, Stamford Street," on July 6, we find him writing to Morris :—

My Dear Sir,

I was delighted to receive your kind letter this morning, and regret that I cannot have the pleasure of seeing you at Liverpool. I am happy to say that I have been under the first man in London for affections of the throat, &c.—Doctor Hastings, of Albemarle Street—and that he does not entertain the slightest doubt of the restoration of my voice. However, I am restricted to water only, and not allowed to play more than once or twice in the week.

Theatricals in London are at a very low ebb, and my position will not allow me to play on small terms. I have had £1,000 offered me to go out to New York and Philadelphia for twelve weeks. Charles Kean and Keeley are anxious for me to play a short time at the Princess's, and Webster is counting on my services for the Haymarket next season. So that until my voice is perfectly restored I cannot determine what I shall do. . . . .

> Believe me,
> Yours most sincerely,
> Gustavus V. Brooke.

To America, indeed, he was very soon to go; but Fate had willed it that he should never act at the Princess's or the

Haymarket. When the winter season opened he made his reappearance at the Olympic, under Farren, on Monday, November 4th, as Philip of France in Westland Marston's new tragedy of *Marie de Meranie*. "Not having been present at the reading," writes Dr. Marston, in "Our Recent Actors," "he asked me to go over his part with him. I was amazed to find a man who was, at all events, an accomplished executant so slow in forming his conception. Often, when the meaning of the text seemed to me too obvious for doubt, he would inquire anxiously and repeatedly as to the manner in which it should be delivered. He was at that time an established favourite, and it was curious to hear him asking questions that almost any tyro in his art could have solved. He had not a tinge of conceit; he threw himself frankly and unhesitatingly upon his author's guidance, which he implicitly followed, but showed at rehearsal a lassitude in going through his part which scarcely promised brilliant results. This possibly arose from the state of his throat. The powers of his voice were so much impaired that when he put a strain on them the effort seemed as distressing to the listener as to himself. However, on the night of production, by skilful management, an imposing bearing, and a dashing outline of the character, he accomplished far more than had been expected. His performance seemed to me to be wanting in subtle touches and an *innerness* (if the phrase may be used) of emotion. But this opinion may have been somewhat unfair. The acting of Miss Helen Faucit in Marie, who had fathomed every motive of a character which she expounded, not only with supreme truth and passion in the crises, but with a power to touch with the most delicate precision the right tones of feeling, tended to make an author unduly exacting as to the performer associated with her."

It is noteworthy that the impression conveyed to Westland Marston accords in the main with the opinion expressed by the various reviewers of his tragedy. Overshadowed for the most part by the divine radiance of Helen Faucit, and handicapped as he was by serious vocal deficiencies, Brooke still managed to give a very effective personation, and now and again rose to the extreme height of noble passion. Perhaps the severest stricture passed on his acting of this, his third original, character was that of *The Literary Gazette*, which, after conceding him the possession of a vast amount of energy, condemned his voice as "affected by so obstinate a hoarseness that all modulation is thereby destroyed. Of the harmony of the poet's numbers or of the various shades of passion nothing remains—all is wrecked and utterly lost ; the violence or the tenderness—the intenseness of rage or the pathos of sorrow are all destroyed by the physical effort necessitated to enunciate the mere words of the author. It is thoroughly painful and seriously damages the effect which the new tragedy would otherwise produce."

So much for the opinion of author and critics. The public, strange to say, were more widely tolerant ; one evidence of which was the number of engravings of Brooke as Philip Augustus, made to satisfy popular demand. Even so late as the middle of the following year a fine daguerreotype of the tragedian in this character was sent by Mayall to the Great Exhibition. With indications such as these to judge from, we cannot but consider the personation at least a success of esteem.

Passing an evening with Brooke at his own home about this period, Westland Marston found the tragedian a very agreeable companion: quiet, unaffected, and courteous ; and surprisingly devoid of egotism and stage airs. "He talked little of himself," we are told, "chiefly of things theatrical in Dublin, of those who had been special favourites there, and of the wild enthusiasm of Irish audiences, compared with which the approval of an English public, he said, seemed generally tame and dispiriting." Of Brooke's goodness of heart and simple convivial temper others have spoken in equally glowing terms. Says the "Old-Fashioned Playgoer"—"I had the pleasure of G. V. Brooke's personal acquaintance on those terms which rendered it most enjoyable. He kept out of the way when his society was not thoroughly acceptable to one who was not outrageously convivial in his tastes. At other times he was always glad to see me, and I have passed many happy hours in his company. My verdict upon him is that he had a heart of gold. I never knew a man who made one love him so, or whose simplicity and kindness better justified the instinct he created."

During November and December Brooke and Helen Faucit drew crowded houses nightly to the Theatre in Wych Street, in a round of legitimate characters, giving also occasional performances of the new tragedy. The support was brilliant throughout, as the Olympic company comprised such capable artists as Mr. Henry Farren, Mr. W. Farren, jun., Mr. G. Cooke, Mr. Henry Compton, Mrs. Stirling, Mrs. Griffiths, and Mr. and Mrs. Leigh Murray. On November 30 we find Brooke writing to Morris :— "I am, thank God, getting on as well as I can possibly expect, and mean now to maintain my position. My voice has at length been restored to me, and I do not see any one thing to prevent my having a very successful career. I am to play Claude Melnotte in town for the first time on Monday next, and we expect that *The Lady of Lyons* will have a run. Farren has made a re-engagement with us for three weeks, so that I shall remain in town till the end of January."

A glance around at the other London theatres will show that Brooke in those days had no pigmies to contend against in striving to maintain his position in the metropolis. In December Macready was acting at the Haymarket in *Richard II.* and *King John:* Charles Kean at the Princess's in *Henry IV.;* James Anderson at Drury Lane; Phelps and Miss Glyn at Sadler's Wells in *The Winter's Tale;* and Creswick and Tom Mead at the Surrey in *Coriolanus.* To shine amid such a constellation was indeed a triumph for one who had certainly seen his best day.

The Lady of Lyons, with Helen Faucit as Pauline, was brought out at the Olympic on Tuesday, December 3. Brooke as Claude was in capital voice, and played with great propriety. But his saturnine temperament ill-fitted him for the wild boyish enthusiasm of the ambitious gardener. He showed to much greater advantage as Master Walter, in which, according to current critical opinion, he approached nearest to his original excellence as Othello. Very striking, too, were his bursts of passion as Shylock on Boxing Night, when his voice had happily gained much of its old firmness and sonority. "The 'I thank God,'" says *Tallis's Dramatic Magazine*, "and the sudden falling upon his knees—the wild gratitude of the moment which makes his vindictive nature the more strongly developed—was actually wonderful. The wordless eloquence of his demeanour when buffeted and beaten, the frightful reverse of things to him, are strongly contrasted with the exulting malevolence with which he presses for his bond, and indicated a conception as vivid as it was elaborate and artistical.'

On January 2, 1851, he appeared as Sir Giles Over-reach, playing with such terrific force in the final scene as to conjure up visions to at least one imaginative spectator of "some incarnate demon, blasted and paralysed at the moment of triumph by the avenging lightning of Providence." Seven days later he gave a powerful, if somewhat uneven, rendering of Sir Edward Mortimer in *The Iron Chest*. This, his first performance of the part in London, attracted little attention, critical or otherwise, the truth of the matter being that playgoers were getting tired of these well-worn characters, and pined for a succession of strong new pieces.

Brooke's engagement at the Olympic was marked by the occurrence of a memorable and very pleasing incident. From what the tragedian subsequently told Morris and some of his Irish friends, it appears that Macready, on one occasion before its conclusion, visited the theatre, and after the performance waited upon Brooke in his dressing-room. The eminent actor was then giving a series of final performances at the Haymarket, and was in fact within a few weeks of his retirement from the stage. Although warped somewhat in judgment by a splenetic jealousy that made him, for instance, under-rate the powers of Charles Kean, no one was better able to appraise the qualities of the leading actors of the time. Hence we learn with satisfaction that Macready took advantage of his visit to inform Brooke he

I

was now the only English actor capable of upholding the grand
tragic line, and that, with proper care, he need fear no competitor.

Hungering greedily for the wild enthusiasm of Irish audiences,
Brooke commenced a week's engagement at Belfast on Monday,
January 13, when the critics adjudged his Othello "nearly
unrivalled," but gave it as their opinion that he was inferior in
Hamlet to Macready, Charles Kean, and Vandenhoff, and had
wholly misconceived the Shakespearian idea. Weighty accusations
of blustering were made, of giving one or two false readings, and
of misplacing the emphasis, or, worse still, of not using it at all.
To this formidable bill of charges the *News-Letter* added " a
laborious effort to supply the defects of a peculiarly rugged
voice by ventriloquial contrasts of sound." The tragedian,
however, was far too popular in Belfast, and unfortunately for
himself (in other respects) had too many friends there for the
receipts to be affected by critical condemnation.

As illustrative of his great popularity with the masses, the
late Mr. Brock, a well-known North of Ireland journalist, was
wont to relate a stirring incident which happened at the Old
Belfast Theatre about this period, and of which he was an eye-
witness.* It was Brooke's benefit night; the play Othello; and
the house crammed from pit to dome. Ensconced in the corner
seats of the lower boxes were a party of officers from the
garrison who had sufficient ill-breeding to maintain a sort of
after-dinner giggle throughout the opening scenes, to the great
annoyance of the audience. The tittering went on without
cessation until the dismissing of Cassio, when Brooke, no longer
able to restrain himself, rushed to the front of the stage hard by
where the offenders were seated, and, with a superb flourish of
his sword, exclaimed "Now, my fine fellows, if you don't stop
your blackguardism I'll put this through one of you." The
effect upon the audience, now justly incensed, was something
marvellous. The house rose as one man, and by its

---

*As similar stories have been related of Brooke in connection with
the Cork and Glasgow theatres, we think it better to give our authority
for placing the scene in Belfast.

threatening attitude compelled the shallow-pated ninnies to beat a hasty retreat. Cheer after cheer marked their departure, and then the play was proceeded with without further comment. It is only fair to Brooke to say that while his strength was commensurate with his courage he seldom gave way to the impulse of the moment. Once or twice his calm unruffled temper was mistaken for cowardice; but few indeed were the persons who found that he could be insulted with impunity. Mr. Dinsmore relates that once a mistake of this sort was made behind the scenes at Manchester, when a gross indignity, calling for immediate retaliation, was somehow thrust upon him. There was one blow and no more; like Mercutio's wound, it served.

Brooke was now at the height of his popularity in the provinces, where, whatever may have been the consensus of critical opinion, he was always hailed with enthusiasm by the public, who magnified his merits and had extreme toleration for his weaknesses. After playing an engagement at the Theatre Royal, Dublin, in conjunction with Mrs. Mowatt (where their attractions were supplemented by the feats of the sisters Ellsler, who ascended to the gallery amid a blaze of red fire on a tight-rope), Brooke paid successful visits to Glasgow and Edinburgh. During his sojourn at the Theatre Royal in the Scottish capital, he was efficiently supported by Powrie, Wyndham, and Miss Frankland, and received unstinted praise at the hands of the critics. His Richard III., they said, had no parallel in the performance of any living actor; and in the heavy part of Sir Giles Over-reach he was deemed equally unapproachable. For his benefit there he displayed considerable versatility in playing Rob Roy and Felix O'Callaghan—than which two more strongly contrasted characters could hardly be found. On Monday, March 31, he made what was announced as his first appearance in Birmingham, and had for leading support James Bennett, the well-known tragedian. Here, too, his masterly display of passion and power electrified the town and created such a sensation that he deemed it expedient to return there at the latter end of May, when he played another short engagement to crowded houses.

Possibly there are few actors who (living or dead) have had more tributes of verse addressed to them than the hero of these pages. Among a number of old family treasures placed at our disposal by Brooke's only surviving sister we find some anonymous and specially printed lines, bearing date "Aout 1851," and entitled "Vers Adressés à G. V. Brooke, Esq., le célèbre tragédien Anglais, apres l'avoir vu jouer plusieurs des grands caractères du célèbre Shakespeare." As this highly eulogistic offering was evidently the work of some enthusiastic Frenchman over on a visit to the Great Exhibition, the curious origin of the lines justifies their quotation :—

> "D'où te vient ce génie admirable poëte ?
> D'où viennent ces accents de ta sonore voix ?
> Toi qui de Shakespeare est le digne interprète.
> Toi qui nous montre encore ses Héros et ses Rois ?
> Le Parnasse joyeux acclame à tes succès
> Et en te couronnant sur l'Autel des neuf soeurs,
> Répond que c'est de lui qui viennent tis progrès
> Et qu'il te met au rang de ses nobles acteurs.
>
> "Oui, Brooke, est immortel, son nom et sa mémoire,
> Seront en lettres d'or gravés au Panthéon ;
> L'Angleterre en est fière et déjà son histoire
> Lui réserve une page à côte de Byron,
> Sa verve et son talent il prête à Melpomène,
> Et dans autre instant Thalie a ses ardeurs ;
> Alors vous le voyez égayer sur la scène
> Un théâtre rempli d'étonnes spectateurs.
>
> "Ah ! tu mérites bien les lauriers, les couronnes,
> Dont on jonche tes pas ; les applaudissements
> Mille fois répétés, des villes et des trônes,
> Seront un jour gravés sur nos grand monuments.
> Va, ne t'arrête pas, les Muses et leur lyre
> Sont toujours près de toi pour te dicter des vers ;
> Et Apollon leur frère est là, qui vous inspire
> A chanter les beaux traits dieux dieux de l'univers."

While touching the hearts of troops of playgoers during his recent visits to Birmingham, Brooke appears to have received a powerful impression upon his own. He was now to play a new and very important *role* in the drama of life. In short, on referring to the registers of Saint Philip's Church, Birmingham, we find that "Gustavus Vaughan Brooke, of Lambeth," was married there by special license, on October 17, 1851, to Marianne Elizabeth Woolcott Bray, spinster, aged 28, daughter of James Bray, of New Street, gentleman.

Five days after the wedding Brooke writes to Morris, from the Theatre Royal, Leicester, enclosing cards of the happy event, and informing him of his speedy departure for Glasgow, where he has arranged to star for a fortnight. He was then busily preparing for his transatlantic trip, and so tells his friend, "I sail for America on the 22nd November, having got what I call a small fortune for an engagement."

CHAPTER VII.

AFTER relating the Sir Giles Over-reach incident, which we
have already traversed in dealing with Brooke's first Olympic
engagement, Mr. Coleman goes on to say : —

" The manager of Drury Lane still believed in him, sought
him out, offered splendid terms ; he pulled himself together,
and, fortified by the accursed whisky bottle, attempted to retrieve
his fallen fortunes. There was an enormous house ; great things
were anticipated ; but, alas ! of the brilliant and accomplished
tragedian there remained only what George Lewes described to
be ' a hoarse and furious man, tearing a passion to tatters with
the melody of a raven.' . . . . This engagement culminated
in a miserable *fiasco*, in consequence of which he quitted the
theatre in disgrace, and sought refuge in an obscure tavern in
the immediate vicinity.

" Contemporaneous with these events, Mr. Phineas T.
Barnum had despatched one Mr. Wilton Hall to Europe, to
secure Jenny Lind for a tour in America. Having accomplished

this mission to the satisfaction of his chief, Mr. Hall was once more despatched to England to hunt up novelties to exploit in the States.

"Upon arriving in town this gentleman heard, of course (for the subject was rife on all men's tongues), of Brooke's sudden rise and equally sudden fall; and it occurred to the astute American that Gustavus was still a young man, that amendment was not impossible, and that what he had done before he might do again. Presenting himself at the H——, late in the day, he found the wretched object of his quest still in bed, and roaring out for a 'pot of four-half!' Upon explaining his business he met with but scant welcome, for the unfortunate tragedian's mind was unhinged by his reverses, and he had arrived at the conclusion that his career was over. Hall, however, would not take 'no' for an 'answer.' Instead of a 'pot of four-half,' he called for a bottle of Cliquot; under its benignant influence he soothed the fallen star, and in an hour's time it was arranged for him to leave the place on the morrow. Next day at twelve o'clock Hall came with a brougham, paid the tavern bill, and took Brooke to splendid lodgings in Belgravia. The day after, he was taken to a West-end tailor and 'figged out' in the height of the mode; and a few days later, to the astonishment of everybody, Gustavus was to be seen every afternoon lolling about in his chariot among the fashionable mob in the Ladies' Mile.

"After a month's recuperation, the tragedian and his mentor sailed for New York, where a series of engagements in all the principal theatres was speedily arranged. The tour commenced far away down South; the climate agreed with Brooke, who recovered his voice—that is, as much as he ever did recover it; he 'struck ile' immediately, and once more leaped into fame and fortune—the first tour alone yielding a profit of £20,000."

Once more we have to complain that Mr. Coleman has acted most ungenerously towards his old friend in giving to the world, without verification, the idle gossip of irresponsible chatterers. So absurd, indeed, are some of the statements just

quoted, that we should have been inclined to pass them by
unnoticed were it not that they have been widely and very
extensively reproduced in both hemispheres.   While allowing
that the circumstances of the American engagement were very
much as related by Mr. Coleman, it must first be pointed out
that the name of the agent referred to was Mr. J. Hall Wilton
(not Wilton Hall), who died at Sydney, N.S.W., on December
19, 1862.   In the next place, Brooke was never " expelled
from Drury Lane with ignominy," as Mr. Coleman states farther
on, and, so far as we can learn after prosecuting vigorous
inquiries, had never acted at that theatre previous to his
American tour.   So much for the subject that was rife on all
men's tongues.   Finally, his first appearance in America did
not take place " far away down South," but at the Broadway
Theatre, New York, on Monday, December 15, 1851, the play
being *Othello*.   Landing unheralded at a time when the orations
of Kossuth and the Forrest divorce suit were dividing public
attention, Brooke was received at once with genuine enthusiasm.
Taken very much throughout the length and breadth of the
States at his early British appraisement, the Americans, who
knew little of the misfortunes that had recently impaired his
powers, were sometimes puzzled to account for his great
European reputation.

   It has frequently been stated (we know not with what
degree of truth) that Edwin Forrest had several times of late
years urged upon Brooke the advisability of visiting America,
holding out dazzling hopes of his crushing the reputation of
their common enemy, Macready.   Be that as it may, it is
certainly significant that, in this, the year of Macready's
retirement from the stage— an event which must have brought
back painful reminiscences to New York playgoers—almost the
first person to welcome Brooke on his arrival in America was
his old friend Edwin Forrest.   Although much perturbed in
mind by his then impending divorce suit, Forrest found time to
promote the success of the English tragedian, took his seat
nightly in a prominent part of the Broadway Theatre, and was

graciously permitted by the audience to lead the applause.
Under such auspices it is not to be wondered at that everything
went off well. With Brooke taking three or four "curtains"
during every performance, success at once became assured.
After fulfilling a three weeks' engagement in New York (on one
night of which - December 23 - he played Claude Melnotte for
the benefit of "The Young Men's Hebrew Association"), he
left for Philadelphia, where he made his first appearance at
the Walnut Street Theatre, on January 5, 1852, as Sir Giles
Over-reach. Visits to Boston, Washington, and Baltimore
followed. Uniformly prosperous as were all five engagements
from a financial standpoint, none save the Boston critics went
into strophes of enthusiasm over his superb physical endowments,
or expatiated at length on the Rembrandt-like skill with which
he relieved the tones of his rich and sonorous voice by facile
transitions from high to low notes.

With the termination of his first tour Brooke found himself
once more in funds, and, like the child he was, sought some way
to rid himself of his superfluous cash. Possessing no appreciable
business capacity to speak of, he was injudicious enough to sever
his connection with Hall Wilton precisely at a time when the
services of that gentleman would have proved of most value. He
had now determined to embark upon the perilous waters of
theatrical management, and on May 2 installed himself as lessee
of the Astor Place Opera House, New York, with a company
made up principally of new faces and comprising the names of
Messrs. Lynne, G. C. Jordan, Harris, Arnold, and Mesdames
Wyette, Vickery, and Charlotte Hale. No novelty was afforded
at the outset, the actor-manager merely contenting himself by
appearing during the first fortnight in a round of his old
characters. Elaborate preparations were, however, being made
for the production of a new piece. Late in the February of this
year Charles Kean had brought out at the Princess's Theatre,
London, with considerable success, a cleverly adapted version,
by Dion Boucicault, of *Les Frères Corses*. Persuaded that
the Dei Franchi were eminently grateful characters, Brooke

(who had no desire to play second fiddle to his intellectual
but voiceless contemporary) had a literal translation made of
the original piece, as dramatised by MM. Grange and Montepin
from Dumas' famous story, and produced at the Théâtre
Historique on August 10, 1850. The only result achieved by
this lumbering version in five or six acts was to prove
the immense superiority of Boucicault's condensation. In
announcing *The Corsican Brothers* for production on Wednesday,
May 19, with himself as, the twins, Brooke had certainly
every right to make the most of the fact that his was (to all
intents and purposes) the original play. But the boast did not
end there. Mr. Gustavus V. Brooke, according to the playbills, was
also the original representative of the Dei Franchi. This was too
much for Hamblin, the Bowery manager, who some couple of
months previously had procured a copy of Boucicault's drama
and performed it, with elaborate scenery, to a succession of
good houses for fully five weeks. Out came Brooke's managerial
rival with a card in which, after stating that he had always
been under the impression that the Twin Brothers had
originally been played in England by Charles Kean and in
America by Edward Eddy, he showed his complete ignorance
of the fact that Boucicault's version was by no means literal
by a very incautious sally. "But for the originality," he says
in conclusion, "that's the grand question. He expects to find
some 'Grand Theban' writing a few introductory lines and a few
more additional clauses, omitting some of the principal features,
and add to and publish the whole as the Original Declaration
of Independence, never before published in France, England,
or the United States. The subscriber apologises for inflicting
this tirade upon his readers, which he certainly would not have
done, but that his silence might have been deemed an
acknowledgment that he had been imposing on that public that
have believed in him and so nobly supported him for five-and-
twenty years." Mr. Hamblin should have known that *The
Corsican Brothers* of Dion Boucicault was at once something
more and something less than the original play. While

eliminating many excrescences from the plot, the astute English playwright had also added the Ghost Melody and the mysterious sliding trapwork. These extraneous features contributed materially to the success of the melo-drama at the Princess's, but they were utterly repugnant to the artistic sense of Fechter, the French original of the Twin Brothers; so much so that he eliminated them from the piece when revived under his management at the same theatre in 1862.

Things had been going badly enough with poor Brooke without Hamblin's interference. Considering the bloody memories attached to it, the unlucky Opera House might well have been rechristened "The Dis-Astorous" Place, as a wag suggested. Financial mismanagement had brought Brooke's resources to a very low ebb. Deeply involved in debt, and with his spirits at zero, he vacated the theatre on June 5, just as a vein of hot weather was beginning to make playgoing intolerable. Still struggling on manfully, however, he, on Tuesday the 8th, transferred *The Corsican Brothers* and his entire company to the boards of Niblo's Garden, but was only able to maintain his position there about half-a-dozen nights. Another shift was made to Brougham's Lyceum Theatre, where Brooke appeared on the 14th as Othello, remaining there with his company for a week, and giving representations of several stock legitimate pieces. But these further exertions merely served to sink him more deeply in the mire. His, however, was not the nature to sit down under misfortune. With a much-needed rest of a couple of months he soon recovered heart, and by the end of August had wisely secured the services of Hall Wilton to make all arrangements, and assume the entire control of financial matters during his ensuing tour through the West. Nothing could have answered better. Few men were more conscientious or indefatigable than Barnum's whilom agent. Wilton entered with enthusiasm upon the management of Brooke's affairs, and during a period of four or five years proved himself indispensable to that volatile spirit.

Another turn of fortune's wheel placed the tragedian once more on the pinnacle of prosperity. Philadelphia, Albany, Buffalo, and Cincinnati were visited to a monotonous succession of crowded houses. Indeed his triumphal progress through the States was only marred by a serious illness contracted shortly after his arrival in St. Louis. Attending the funeral of Mr. James Bates, son of the manager of the Cincinnati, Louisville, and St. Louis Theatres, he stood bareheaded at the grave during the last solemn rites, and received a severe chill, owing to a sudden thaw that had set in after a heavy fall of snow. Within a few hours the disorder resolved itself into a malignant attack of inflammatory rheumatism, and increased in virulence day after day despite the skill of the best physicians attainable. After numerous consultations the Faculty confessed their inability to cope with the ravages of the disease, and told the little circle of anxious friends the worst might be expected. By an irony of circumstance a sudden change for the better took place with this announcement. A good constitution and the admirable nursing of his wife rendered Brooke's recovery as rapid as his illness had been sudden. Little time elapsed ere he was enabled to resume his professional duties. The sympathies of St. Louis had gone out to him while he lay hovering between life and death. They were now palpably expounded in the People's Theatre, where his performances were so well attended that his original engagement of a week blossomed into a stay of fifty-two consecutive nights. Desirous of presenting some slight souvenir of his visit to his many friends in St. Louis, Brooke, just before leaving, had a number of daguerreotypes taken of himself in stage and ordinary costume, by Fitzgibbon, of that city. From these, several fine engravings on steel were subsequently made, copies of which are still to be found, among other memorials of the tragedian, in the theatrical taverns and oyster-rooms of our provincial towns.

Seen off the stage at this period, there was little about Brooke's appearance or bearing (save perhaps the abundant curly locks which flowed in careless profusion over his ears) to denote the "deep tragedian." Beyond the merest apology for side whiskers the face had no suspicion of hair, and the soft semi-humorous expression of the features was somewhat accentuated by the quivering eagerness which lurked in the corners of the mouth; a marked indication of volubility and fun thoroughly characteristic of the Irish race. To the superficial observer, however, the G. V. Brooke of a decade later was a very different personage. The cultivation of a thick moustache cut short at the ends did much to alter the expression of the features, which in themselves had become more serious and self-possessed. Hence his whole bearing while in Australia was that of a soldier, rather than the poor player fretting and strutting his hour upon the boards.

On returning to Boston, Brooke was made the recipient of a welcome from the patrons of the National Theatre, equally affectionate with that tendered him in St. Louis, and on the occasion of his farewell benefit there on May 27, 1853, was presented with a magnificent service of silver plate—in seven pieces, all suitably inscribed—as a mark of esteem from his American admirers. After the performance of Hamlet, Mr. Fleming, in making the presentation on behalf of the donors, read the following quaintly-phrased address :—*

TO GUSTAVUS VAUGHAN BROOKE, ESQ.

DEAR SIR,

With feelings imbued by respect and honour, warranted by the histrionic genius and superior power of delineation portrayed by you in your profession as a representation of Shakespeare and the Drama, the Undersigned, feeling that we express the sentiment of many thousands of your warm admirers, cannot allow you to depart from our shores without conveying to you the high appreciation entertained for you, not only as a great actor, but to testify to your invariable urbanity and gentlemanly demeanour, by which you have "won golden opinions from all sorts of people." It seldom falls to our lot to witness such truthful illustrations of the Bard of Avon as are so universally and brilliantly given in your truly great rendering of his grand ideas; and we feel it our duty to enable you to carry with you to your country some tangible mark of the high favour your superior talent is held in this. We therefore solicit your acceptance of the accompanying Silver Service as a slight token thereof, and to add our heart-felt wishes for your

* An excellent engraving of this presentation (from a daguerreotype by Mayall) is to be found in Halliwell's edition of Shakespeare, as published by John Tallis & Co., of London and New York, in 1854.

continued health, happiness, prosperity, and safety, hoping soon to welcome you back again to this our native land; but, should we never see you again, we say, "*extinctus amabitur idem*."

We have the honour to subscribe ourselves very respectfully and truly yours,

R. I. BURBANK, Boston,
E. P. STEVENS,
W. THOMPSON, Providence,

} *Committee of Presentation.*

As soon as the cheering and uproarious applause of the audience had subsided, Brooke made reply as follows, in a voice quivering with emotion:—

"MR. FLEMING,—I feel inadequate to express at this moment what my heart dictates. This is indeed a mark of esteem which, although bearing the immaculate glitter of precious metal, cannot render me more deeply sensible of the honours and kindness I have had conferred upon me by my friends in Boston and Providence. I receive your testimonial in the spirit of a heart overflowing with gratitude, so much so as to be unable to convey to you the sincerity of its acknowledgment. I hope that this token of your appreciation shall be handed down an heirloom to posterity, and be valued with pride by those I leave behind me. Now, with your permission, I will take this opportunity of requesting the ladies and gentlemen before us to accept my unalloyed thanks for the patronage I have hitherto been honoured with, as well as their presence on this occasion. I shall leave this country in a few days, and I shall do so with regret—with deep regret. Who, having travelled it, could do otherwise? I have visited several important cities of the Union, and I feel much gratification and pride in saying that I have been treated with the greatest degree of hospitality, liberality, and attention—not only professionally but in private life. I have, traveller-like, made my observations as I went along; and what is the result? 'Tis briefly told. I found a vast and glorious country—a large and powerful nation proud from industry, independence and education; imbued with honour, hospitality, and affluence, and—I may use the term universal equality, forming a grand chain of union, which is strength; each son

a link, feeling an individual responsibility for the protection of
his country, made invulnerable by a constitution founded on
principles of honour, as set forth by its immortal father,
Washington. This is the result of my visit; and so deeply am
I impressed with admiration of your country, that I hope to
return to it, and I have to regret all do not feel as I do. And
I have but one maxim to lay down for those who contemplate
visiting you—to first divest themselves of all prejudice, and
indelible satisfaction must follow. I am unwilling to trespass
any further on your patience, and, reiterating my deep sense of
gratitude to my donors and to all, I am compelled to utter that
impressive word 'farewell'; but I trust only for a short time.
The ties of kindred and home command me, for a time, to leave
you. For as Eliza Cook beautifully expresses it :—

> "'There's a magical tie in the land of my home,
> Which the heart cannot break, though the footsteps may roam ;
> Be that land where it may, at the line or the pole,
> It still holds the magnet that draws back the soul.'

" May heaven bless you ! And that prosperity and happiness
may reign uninterrupted among you shall often be my prayer
when far away. Allow me, then, with every feeling of sincerity,
reluctantly but most respectfully to say farewell— farewell!"

Farewell it was indeed, for Brooke was fated never to
renew his acquaintance with his whole-souled friends across the
Atlantic. Making his last appearance in America on Tuesday,
June 14, at the Walnut Street Theatre, Philadelphia, as Othello,
he set sail immediately for England, leaving nought but
pleasant memories behind him. That his final tour had proved
uniformly prosperous is shown by the fact that from the 6th of
September previously he had acted something like 180 times at
an average nightly profit of about £15. All told, his repertory
during this period consisted of twenty-four parts (of which
Richelieu and the Guerilla Chief had been newly added), the
largest demand being upon Fabian and Louis Dei Franchi (14),
Othello (15), Sir Giles Over-reach (11), and Shylock (11); the
figures in brackets representing the number of repetitions of

each character. Considering that the tour had brought him in upwards of £8,000, it is not surprising that, after settling all the liabilities incurred in connection with his unfortunate managerial experiences in New York, he was enabled to return home with a substantial sum in pocket. Evidently sincere in the sentiments expressed in his farewell address at Boston, he ever retained the most grateful recollections of his reception throughout the Union. A slight exchange of amenities in after years vividly illustrated this. Among the many setting high esteem upon the friendship of Brooke was Mr. R. C. Burke, proprietor of the Cork Theatre, who once sent the tragedian an agreeable keepsake in the shape of a dagger which had belonged to Edmund Kean. Superstitious to a nicety, like most actors, Brooke remembered him of the old idea that gifts of this kind sever friendship unless nominally purchased by the exchange of a coin. To effect his purpose without giving offence he unfastened a dollar piece of the year 1849, which he had worn on his watch-chain since his return from America, and forwarded it to Mr. Burke, together with a note explaining his whim, and referring to the indemnifying trifle as "the coin of the country where every man, whether English or Irish, receives the best reward for his labour."

CHAPTER VIII.

1853—1854.

Brooke Reappears at Birmingham, and Enters upon a Short Provincial Tour—A Successful and Protracted Drury Lane Engagement—*The Betrothal*—Presentation at the Coal-Hole Tavern—Brooke's Christmas Boxes to the Poor—Reappears at Drury Lane—Production of *The Vendetta*—An All-night Sitting in Manchester—*Ocnano* Brought Out for the First Time at Birmingham—Brooke Meets Coppin and Arranges to go to Australia—His Third Drury Lane Engagement—First Appearance in London in Irish Comedy—Accedes to a Public Requisition to Act at the City of London Theatre, and says Good-bye to his Friends in England.

MAKING his reappearance in England at the Theatre Royal, Birmingham, on Monday, July 25, Brooke fulfilled a ten-nights' engagement there, and departed for Dublin with the assurance from *Aris's Birmingham Gazette* of "having proved by the assumption of the most difficult characters within the range of the drama that he is without doubt the greatest tragic actor on the stage." After passing a few days tranquilly in the Irish capital, whither he had gone mainly for the purpose of introducing his wife to his circle of relatives, Brooke repaired to Cork, where he was joyously received, and drew crowded houses for a week despite the intense heat. Recalled after the performance of Sir Giles Over-reach for his benefit on Friday, August 26, he said:—

"LADIES AND GENTLEMEN, Fatigued as you see I now am, I cannot forego the opportunity of endeavouring to express to you the great gratitude I feel in responding to your most warm and enthusiastic call, and more so as it emanated from an audience which twelve or thirteen years ago encouraged and fostered the talent they thought I possessed. (Cheers.) Since

K

I last had the pleasure of visiting this city, I am happy to say that my star has been in the ascendant. (Cheers.) I have just returned from America, where I met not only with success but with the greatest degree of courtesy, kindness, and hospitality from our brethren across the Atlantic; and it is my intention in the course of a few months to leave Europe again for some years, for the purpose of exercising my professional abilities in a far distant country. (Cries of—' Success attend you.') I am sure that I carry with me your good wishes for my success—(cheers, and cries of ' You have always had them ')—and wherever I may be the recollection of your kindness shall never be forgotten. (Cries of ' We never will forget you,' and applause.) And now, ladies and gentlemen, in endeavouring to express my gratitude for past favours, and for the compliment you have conferred on me by your presence here this evening, allow me in return sincerely to wish that increasing prosperity may attend the commercial interests of the city of Cork, and at the same time allow me to wish that happiness may reign uninterrupted among you. (Applause.) Ladies and gentlemen, I am due at Belfast on Monday evening, but owing to the solicitation of a great number of admirers and friends I have been induced to appear here again on to-morrow evening—(cheers, and ' You are welcome ')—which night shall he set apart for the benefit of the worthy manager, Mr. Poole." (Cheers.)

Brooke then retired amid great applause, only to return immediately to pick up a laurel wreath that had been thrown to him, and to apologise for the absence of mind which made him overlook it. After the performance on the following evening he came before the curtain and spoke a few words by way of farewell in a voice full of emotion. "I didn't wonder at Brooke's emotion on this occasion," says "The Old Playgoer," as interviewed by Mr. J. W. Flynn, " because he had a host of friends in Cork, and it must have been a source of real pain for him to part from them. He was very often at the G——'s, I met him at dinner there often. In private life Brooke was a

man of delightful manner, frank and hearty. He always gave
me the idea of a man who thoroughly enjoyed his professional
success. I remember one night at G——'s, someone asked him
to recite and he very gracefully complied. Someone asked him to
give 'Othello's Defence,' and he did so in his own grand style.
Later he gave us 'Lord Ullin's Daughter.' In those days we
had not the extensive selection that reciters have now, when
almost every week sees a score of new pieces brought forward
to c'aim public favour. It is needless to say we were all
delighted with Brooke's recitation of the lachrymose lay of the
lover and the lady who went under the 'waters wild.' I can
never forget the infinite pathos he infused into the line, 'My
daughter, oh, my daughter!'"

Meantime the tragedian, little recking with what red-hot
enthusiasm his reappearance in London was to be greeted, had
settled with Mr. E. T. Smith, of Drury Lane, for a twenty-four
nights' sojourn at that theatre. Acting somewhat nervously in
the opening scenes on making his first appearance there, as
Othello, on Monday, September 5, he soon warmed to his work,
and, thanks to the sympathetic attitude of a crowded house,
gave on the whole such a stirring personation that the cheering
at the end was agreeably mingled with cries of "Bravo, Brooke."
From the theatre the next morning he wrote a brief note to a
Cork friend, saying, "Just a line to tell you of my splendid
success. Audience most enthusiastic. All the morning papers
speak well of me."

Although Brooke's old provincial admirers maintained that
his voice was never the same after the year 1848, the critics at
this period considered that it had now to all intents and purposes
recovered its normal power, and was enabling him to repeat
those somewhat uncommon feats of elocutionary force and finesse
to which his early success was largely attributable.

"Mr. Brooke's Othello," says the *Illustrated London News* of
September 10—"Mr. Brooke's Othello is a piece of acting possessed of many beauties; the pathetic delivery of the great speeches
being remarkable for the quality of tone and tenderness of the

expression. It was well chosen for the opening night, it being
generally appreciated as his best character. It certainly possesses
all the characteristics of his style; and in none is he so equally
excellent.   His other characters, such as Shylock, Richard
III., and Sir Giles Over-reach, are charged with physical
exuberance, which not seldom degenerates into violence and
extravagant excess. Nothing of this sort attached on Monday
to his Othello, which deservedly extorted from the house the
most enthusiastic applause." Supported by a powerful company,
prominent among whom were Mr. E. L. Davenport, Mr. George
Bennett, Miss Leslie, and Miss Anderton, Brooke continued to
act to uniformily crowded houses. On Saturday, September 10,
he gave his first rendering in London of the character of Iago;
an original conception which by many of his provincial admirers
was then and is still placed on a plane of excellence with his
Othello. Brooke's idea was to show that Iago was not naturally
of a fiendish disposition, had no sordid hope of advancement,
and was malicious only because a deep-seated feeling of
revenge for wounded honour prompted him to be even
with the despoiler, wife for wife. With his interpretation of
the character, however, the critics entirely disagreed. " In
Iago," says the *Illustrated London News*, " Mr. Brooke had a
character rather of intellect than passion, and one that required
subtle elocution, as distinguished from vehement demonstration.
The performer here, accordingly, is to be seen in quite another
light than Othello, and Mr. Brooke affected an air of easy
nonchalance and familiarity of speech that brought him to the
ordinary level of stage power. The assumption of character
proved flippant; there was no exaggeration, but there was no
profundity. Deep-seated malice was not indicated, though great
emphasis was judiciously given to the passages in the soliloquies
expressive of his jealous suspicions regarding both Othello and
Cassio. Mr. Brooke is far from the best Iago we have on the
boards; that of Mr. Marston is much superior, and Mr.
Vandenhoff's leaves it at an immeasurable distance." The
selection was unfortunate in other respects, as the change of

parts gave E. L. Davenport an opportunity of showing, by an
impersonation full of majestic grace, pathos, and cumulative
power, how perilously close he could go, in Othello, to the
bright particular star of the moment.

After this nothing of paramount importance took place until
Monday, September 19, when a new poetic play called *The Betrothal*,
by Mr. G. H. Boker—an American dramatist, whose *Calaynos* had
seen the light at Sadler's Wells a little time previously—was
produced at Drury Lane. Albeit the later piece had considerable
literary merit, its structure was too artificial, and its situations
(more especially the catastrophe) too puerile to admit of any great
success upon the stage. Seemingly unable to develop a theme
naturally by a succession of climaxes, the author had contented
himself in saturating his mind with the essence of the Elizabethan
drama, many striking passages in which were reproduced with all
the marks of modern super-refinement, but with little of the breadth
and masculinity of the golden age. Moreover, the elements of the
theme were not homogeneous; though the ring was Shakespearian,
the metal on examination proved base. The large audience,
however, attracted to the theatre by the announcement of
a novelty was in nowise captious, and while far from unduly
demonstrative received the piece with considerable favour. The
character of Marsio the usurer, which evoked reminiscences now
and again of Shylock, Sir Giles Over-reach, and the Luke of
Massinger, was played by Brooke with much rugged force. His
acting reached the extreme height of power in the scene where
the guests whom Marsio has attempted to poison turn the tables
by administering a soporific drug in his goblet, the action of
which causes all the physical agonies, and all the fears, of the
horrible death he had contrived for his visitors. But the loudest
applause of the evening was bestowed upon Mr. A. Young for his
exquisitely humorous rendering of a Lancelot Gobbo-like character
—Pulti, the usurer's unfaithful servant. The play, however, was
so devoid of dramatic grip and sequential interest, that not all
the fine acting of Brooke, Young, E. L. Davenport, Mr. and Mrs.
Belton, and Miss Fetherstone could give it enduring popularity.

On Saturday the 24th we find Brooke appearing as Virginius, in which he had no rival, now that the great original had departed from the scene. Holding his audience in the hollow of his hand from the outset, he had not proceeded farther than the end of the third act when his appearance before the curtain was strenuously demanded. Says the *Illustrated London News* (October 1). "The paternal character was especially illustrated; and indicated with so much conscious ease, as well as apparent impulse, that critics have formed from it a higher estimation of the actor as an artist than they had received on previous occasions."

On Thursday, September 29, Brooke's great success was celebrated by his numerous friends and admirers at a *déjeuner* held at the Coal-Hole Tavern, when Mr. E. T. Smith, supported by Messrs. E. Stirling and G. Wild, presided over the distinguished company, including John Oxenford of *The Times*, that had assembled to do honour to the tragedian. After the chairman had presented the hero of the hour with a splendidly mounted dagger and a diamond ring, and had been thanked in a short but eloquent speech, Mr. Renton Nicholson, the host, delivered a powerful eulogy on the talents of Edmund Kean, and was feelingly responded to by Mr. John Lee. Mr. E. T. Smith, replying to the toast of "The Chairman," explained at length the difficulties he had to encounter in forming a company for Drury Lane, and confessed that he was doubtful about the policy of his venture until assured by the great success of Mr. Brooke's engagement. He then announced, amid vociferous applause, that he had secured the services of the tragedian for another three weeks.

Apart from the evidence afforded by this immediate re-engagement, signs are not wanting to show that Brooke had now renewed the triumphs of his early Olympic appearances. Vast as was the theatre, the management had found itself unable to cope in an ordinary way with the persistent demand for seats. Finally, several morning performances of *Othello* and *Virginius* were given to large and fashionable audiences; a rare thing in the days when the *matinée* was quite unknown as a regular theatrical function.

Satisfactory as it must have been to Brooke to mark the thorough re-establishment of his reputation in the metropolis, he could hardly have been aware at the outset of the magnitude of his achievement. For some considerable time previously the fortunes of Drury Lane had been at a very low ebb. The so-called National Theatre had passed rapidly through the hands of a succession of managerial adventurers, who evinced but scant respect for its glorious traditions, and turned the temple of art into a vast raree-show. Without any extraneous aid, Brooke by the glamour of his acting had enabled Mr. E. T. Smith to stem the tide, and despite the growing importance of Spectacle, had shown (what Helen Faucit at the same theatre in January, 1852, had failed to do) that the legitimate drama could still be made attractive without a gorgeously exuberant *mise en scène.* How great, indeed, was this purely histrionic triumph can only be conceived by remembering that Charles Kean at this period was in the heat of his elaborate archæological revivals at the Princess's Theatre, and had quite recently drawn all London to see his magnificent production of *Sardanapalus.*

Taking his benefit on Monday, October 3, Brooke, after the performance of *Virginius,* delivered the following eloquent address, amid the ever-recurring plaudits of a crowded house:—

" LADIES AND GENTLEMEN,—I can recall no instance in my whole career when I found it so difficult to give adequate expression to my feelings as on the present occasion. The immense crowds that have thronged this vast theatre through a long engagement, at the worst season of the year, and the enthusiastic acclamations that have hailed my appearance in every variety of character, have so completely outstripped my expectations and desert that I find myself at this moment, when I most need it, without the power to convey in commensurate terms my fitting acknowledgment or my fervent sense of gratitude.

" The applause and honours I was so fortunate to receive at the hands of warm-hearted strangers, whom I so lately left, were most grateful to me; but this glorious welcome back to the stage of my country is doubly dear, not only as a mark of your personal esteem, but as a proof to my American friends that I am not without some small merit in the eyes of my countrymen.

"There are considerations, however, connected with this event far beyond my individual success, that touch my heart more nearly. My reception in this metropolis at this particular juncture, when the theatrical world is worn out by a variety and excess of amusements that accumulate during the feverish months of a London season, is a sure and consoling sign that the noble art to which I belong is not dead; that, in spite of all seductions, the Bard of Avon still lives in the eternal admiration of my countrymen, and that the wonderful creations of his genius, however feebly portrayed, are still followed by congregated thousands.

"This is creditable, in the highest degree, to the pure taste of my countrymen. It is, besides, a national tribute to that marvellous intellect which has given such elevation to the dramatic literature of England, as to leave it, for upwards of two centuries, unapproached amid the rivalry of nations.

"The dramatists of France, of Spain, of Germany, have sent forth productions that will endure—that shed honour upon themselves, and fame upon their countries; but the glory of our country is still undimmed. Nay, it only grows the brighter as we contemplate the immeasurable distance between the height his genius scaled, and that of all his competitors. The homage of his countrymen is justified by the universal admiration of all men; for, in every tongue and every land, Shakespeare is declared to be the sole heir to immortality. I feel it an honour and a privilege to interpret, however unskilfully, the inspirations of this mighty mind; and my vocation is not without its value if it serve to perpetuate them in all their imperishable beauty. This is, indeed, an arduous task.

"But if the toils and exertions of my difficult profession required a new stimulant—if my energies demanded a new incentive to greater effort, I could not fail to find them in the crowds that have followed me, in the applause that has been so kindly, so prodigally showered upon me to-night, and week after week, since I first appeared before you.

"It will be a reward beyond my hopes if, in the estimation of this vast and brilliant assemblage, it shall be decreed that I have contributed something to the revival of a noble entertainment — that I have earnestly sought to 'hold the mirror up' to the majestic proportions of our national bard; and that, for a time at least, I have aided in restoring to its pristine and loftiest use the lovely temple of art now irradiated by your presence."

Mr. E. T. Smith, the manager, made a personal appeal to the public on Wednesday, October 19, and in a speech delivered after the play referred to the rumour then current in the papers that the tragedian was under agreement to return to America for a period of four years, and hinted that nevertheless there was just a possibility of his appearing again on the boards of old Drury after the run of the pantomime in the ensuing year. The occasion was marked by Brooke's appearance as Macbeth—a character on which he had not been inclined hitherto to risk his metropolitan reputation. "Certainly," says the *Illustrated London News* of October 22 —"Certainly it requires a subtlety of delineation, alien from his general style, and not quite in accordance with the peculiar physical power to which his effects are generally due. Wisely, however, he has adopted an interpretation of the character which gives him, at the beginning, an opportunity of assuming the noble and heroic bearing predicated by the poet of the warlike Thane previous to his fall. The remorse that accompanied the progress of the assassination was something, therefore, very different from and much better than that craven fear with which the act is absurdly accompanied by performers in general."

Beyond the occasional appearance of the tragedian in one or two unsuitable characters, nothing whatever occurred throughout to mar the brilliance of this long extended triumph. Nevertheless, the impression of inequality thus given served as a handle to the few dissentients from the general verdict, who contended that, stripped of his great physical advantages, Brooke was an unintellectual actor. The personal equation cannot, of course, be ignored in summing up the merits and demerits of a great player. Allowing, for argument's sake, that Brooke's Iago was quite as indifferent as Macready's Othello, surely the deficiency in both does not warrant us in placing either on a lower grade in the histrionic scale than some less noted actor who could play both characters with equal facility.

During the succeeding provincial tour, Brooke appeared in no part of any particular newness save Richelieu, which, after the retirement of Macready, he had wisely added to his repertory. Differing essentially on many points from the presentment of the great original, Brooke's rendering of the Cardinal was "lit up by flashes of genius," as an Australian critic once put it, "as though he were controlled by some unseen intelligence, greater and stronger than himself, who played upon his vital functions as a fine musician plays upon a grand instrument." Commencing his tour at the Royal Amphitheatre, Liverpool, on Monday, October 24, and visiting Birmingham and Sheffield in rapid succession, Brooke's progress through the provinces was, as Mr. Coleman points out, the march of a conqueror. Every town was entered in a superb equipage drawn by four horses, and embellished by two outriders in scarlet. Whether going to or proceeding from the theatre his carriage was always surrounded by a ragged retinue of admirers, who delighted in unharnessing the horses and drawing the tragedian through the town unaided. The newspapers for the most part, however, professed to see great inequality in his performances; but with this reservation confessed that, taken for all in all, he was the best actor then on the boards in his range of characters. "None of the faults usually imputed to his acting were apparent," says the *Belfast News-Letter* in treating of his Claude Melnotte; "there was not a trace of rant; there were no abrupt or ventriloquial tricks of voice; no rude or ill-ordered gestures; all was graceful, suitable, intellectual, and truly manlike and natural."

According to his usual custom at Christmas time—no matter where he might find himself situated—Brooke while in Belfast distributed some 125 blankets to the deserving poor. His method was to forward tickets to three or four clergymen of different denominations, with instructions to bestow them where they thought proper. Each ticket when presented at a certain local shop entitled the bearer to receive a blanket in exchange. It was a strange whim, but Brooke's charity was certainly genuine, and in most instances utterly unostentatious. Sometimes the gift was varied, and coals, soup, or tickets for the play substituted for the blankets. Indeed, his kindness to the poor in Ireland was such that a sub-stratum of truth underlies the humour of the well-worn statement that the lower classes in his native country used to teach their children to pray for "father and mother and Gustavus Brooke." To the humbler members of his own profession whose distress became apparent, he was equally humane and generous: a quality which, combined with his comparative freedom from professional jealousy, contrived to render him in purely theatrical circles the best-beloved actor of his time. As illustrative of his large-heartedness Mr. W. Dinsmore relates an anecdote which strikes the keynote of Brooke's character, and accounts in great measure for the financial straits in which he ever found himself. Always helping others and always needing help himself, the tragedian was never without a friend ready and willing to respond to his appeal. Riding one day in an open carriage in the neighbourhood of Manchester, with Walter Montgomery and another friend, Brooke rather surprised his companions by abruptly breaking off the conversation and commanding the driver to stop. Without deigning a word of explanation, Gustavus, as soon as the vehicle drew up, ran swiftly down the road and paused before a miserable looking woman, who in company with two puny, half-starved children was resting herself dejectedly by the wayside. Having eased his mind by emptying the contents of his pockets into the astonished vagrant's lap, the tragedian ran back as quickly as possible, and telling the driver to go

ahead, at once took up the conversation where he had
ruptured it.

Notwithstanding he had already said "good-bye" to his
friends in Cork, Brooke was easily induced to return there
immediately after his Belfast engagement, and was received
with great warmth on making his reappearance on Boxing
Night. Some idea of the interest taken in the tragedian's
career in the southern city at this period may be gleaned from
a powerful article, entitled "Mr. G. V. Brooke as an Actor,"
which appeared in the *Cork Southern Reporter* of December 31,
1853. In the course of a long and searching analysis of the
tragedian's characteristics, his style is thoughtfully and by no
means invidiously contrasted with that of Macready, for whom
the writer has equal admiration. "In Macready," he says,
"we always perceived the highly-polished, educated, and careful
artist, whose greatest achievements are due to the study of the
closet and the effects of scenery and costume. In Brooke we
have a man who, while assiduously cultivating these aids, at
the same time evinces his opinion that they are, after all,
only secondary, and relies mainly for a triumph on that
brilliant genius wherewith he is endowed. This is proved by
the intrepidity with which he has undertaken his finest parts,
not alone unsupported, but absolutely seriously embarrassed and
foiled by the other performers, and yet succeeded in calling
forth an amount of applause as enthusiastic and cordial as it
was deserved. . . . . He, in common with others who have
preceded him, can boast of delicate perception of character,
readiness in appreciating 'points' (a trick which he only
resorts to where it is absolutely necessary to redeem the
dialogue from tameness), and boldness and breadth of
conception. In this latter quality, indeed, he excels those of
his predecessors we have seen, and the only one of his
contemporaries who could fairly be named in connection with
him, Mr. Phelps." After playing four or five nights at
Limerick, Brooke returned to Cork, and in accordance with
a requisition of the citizens, as made through the Mayor and

Corporation, reappeared there on Saturday, January 7, 1854. Recalled after the performance of *Richelieu*, for the manager's benefit, he was received with a shower of bouquets from all parts of the theatre, and finally presented with an artistically-constructed laurel crown. "Brooke made a short speech," records Mr. J. W. Flynn, "in which he referred to the flattering compliment paid him by the citizens, and said he should be proud to inform his wife, the partner of his cares and his hopes, who was prevented by illness from witnessing it, of a triumph which should be remembered while memory held her seat."

On the penultimate day of the month Brooke reappeared at Drury Lane as Brutus, in the tragedy, so called, by Howard Payne. Miss Fanny Cathcart—whose services for the projected American tour had been previously secured at Liverpool—was in leading support. Unfortunately a breach of good taste at the outset seriously imperilled the success of the engagement. Mr. E. T. Smith had injudiciously exceeded the bounds of play-house panegyric in announcing the return of the star, and the press at once took umbrage at the ready-made encomiums. Rendered somewhat petulant by this ill-advised puffery, the critics spoke of Brooke's rendering of Edmund Kean's great part as striking, if palpably unequal in the earlier scenes. He was found to be lacking in skill in the assumption of idiocy, and too impatient in his desire for the production of vehement effects to await fitting opportunity. They allowed, however, that when this excess of physical vigour was displayed in its proper place (the malediction in the third act being a case in point) the effect on the house was electrical. Equally impressive was the deep pathos of the final situation, where the actor is called upon to depict the strife between paternal solicitude and judicial duty. Brooke's old friends had assembled in overwhelming force, and were remarkably demonstrative throughout. But despite the bouquets and the applause the critics disallowed a triumph and spoke only of a success of esteem. They were much better pleased with his Master Walter on the succeeding evening. And well they might: he was then quite unapproachable in the character.

On Wednesday, February 22, Cibber's version of *Richard III.* was brought out in opposition to Charles Kean, who had just revived the spurious piece at the Princess's Theatre. Phelps had previously produced the orthodox Shakespearian play at Sadler's Wells; but the clap-traps of Pope's old antagonist were too precious to the plaudit-loving tragedian to allow of any immediate emulation of this praiseworthy action. Blundering again, the Drury Lane management evoked odious comparisons by neglecting to furnish the play with a new and appropriate *mise en scène*. This policy had its redeeming merit, as a wag remarked at the time, because the old stock scenery had its enjoyable associations in reminding the spectator of many a previous night spent at the play. Possibly if the ensemble had been powerful and complete, no invidious allusions would have been made to the spectacular splendour of Charles Kean's revival. The play is, after all, the thing; and Brooke had already shown to good purpose that large audiences could be attracted nightly by the unaided brilliance of fine acting. But on this occasion he appears to have given a very ineffective performance; allied to which the support accorded—excepting the Richmond of Mr. T. Mead and the King Henry of Mr. George Bennett—failed to rise above the level of a third-rate provincial theatre.

The true secret of E. T. Smith's carelessness in mounting the play probably lay in the fact that elaborate preparations were being made for the production of the version of *The Corsican Brothers* performed by Brooke in America upwards of 100 nights. Under the title of *The Vendetta*, this piece was first introduced to the notice of an English audience on Monday, February 27, and well-nigh damned at the outset owing to the incompleteness of the mechanical arrangements and other defects arising from a want of thorough rehearsal. The audience had evidently become grounded in the mystery of the story from Boucicault's well-knit adaptation, and took advantage of the numerous scenic hitches to express their disapproval of the long, cumbrous version in five acts and nine tableaux. A vigorous use of the pruning knife soon brought things more ship-shape. But the fiat had gone forth that the piece was a failure; and not all the fine acting of Brooke as Fabian and Louis Dei Franchi, and Mead as Chateau Renaud, could suffice to hold it on the boards longer than twelve nights.

The management was now all at sea. Two new plays, announced as in rehearsal for immediate production, and as expressly written for the bright particular star of the moment, never saw the light. During the last two weeks of his engagement, Brooke appeared on alternate nights in a round of well-worn characters, bringing an ill-ordered campaign to an end on Saturday, March 25, with a performance of *Hamlet*.

Among the Morris correspondence we find the following:—

THEATRE ROYAL, DRURY LANE,
16th March, 1857.

SIR,

Mr. G. V. Brooke desires me to present his kind regards and to ask you to inform him what he is indebted to you. Although you are down in his schedule of insolvency as a creditor for £10, he wonders whether it is so or not—as your many acts of kindness to him left no other record but gratitude; and I am one of his true friends (I hope) and am desirous to take the schedule off the file at once, but cannot do so unless I hand in the necessary releases of the creditors. The favour of your sending such a release or receipt on receipt of this, and letting him know what he is indebted—which he will remit—will expedite this very necessary affair and be esteemed a further obligation.

Mr. G. V. B. desires me to add that being so overwhelmed by business and study is why he does not write himself now, but will do so in a few days.

I am,
Yours very obedient,
J. H. WILTON, for G. V. BROOKE.

Returning almost immediately to the provinces, Brooke on May 19 wrote to his friend Morris from the Theatre Royal, Glasgow, acquainting him of his whereabouts, and promising to run down to Ayr as soon as opportunity offered. "Our houses here are very good indeed," he continues, "and my engagement will turn out very well. Everything has been going on (thank

God) most prosperously with me, and the only inconvenience I feel is the constant and successive exertions of my mental and physical faculties, which perhaps require a little relaxation. However, I am determined to reserve to myself the month of August for a pleasant tour, which will no doubt renovate me and prepare me for a fresh campaign." So attractive were his performances in Glasgow that before the termination of his engagement the management had secured his services for another twelve nights, commencing Saturday, June 3. Following on the heels of this came a month's sojourn at the Queen's Theatre, Manchester, the result of which is given in the undernoted letter :—

> 7 QUEEN'S TERRACE, VICTORIA PARK,
> LONGSIGHT, NR. MANCHESTER,
> *July 4 [1854].*

MY DEAR MR. MORRIS,

    I have been as busy as a bee since I left you, and am happy to inform you that, notwithstanding every opposition from the Theatre Royal here, our efforts have been attended with the most triumphant success—our house having been nightly filled, while the Royal presented a beggarly account of empty boxes. Helen Faucit opened there last evening as Pauline to about £35, while our house was jammed. We shall finish here on Saturday week, and commence on the same principle at Birmingham for a month on the 24th at the new theatre there, in opposition to the Theatre Royal, which will not give me my terms. I am sorry to say that Sultan has turned out no use as a carriage horse, but is a most beautiful saddle one; and I have got a nice grey to run with Prince. Both of them are in splendid condition. We are living about two miles from Manchester, in the Park, a delightful place, and as retired as if we were fifty miles from any large town; and sleeping in the country air has wrought a most material change in me. My wife is still delicate, but the weather has been so very uncertain here that it has had a singular effect upon all our constitutions, and when we are blessed with sunshine for an hour or so it is hailed with rapture. I will feel very much obliged if you will ask Mr. —— (I forget the gentleman's name whom I had the pleasure of meeting at your table, but I know he was an architect, and lived, as also did his father, in the road to Burns's monument) for the plan of his father's house, as I have taken a most extraordinary fancy to it, and should like to build one for myself by the banks of the Hudson River. Believe me, my dear Mr. Morris,

> Your very sincerely attached friend,
> G. V. BROOKE.

   Let me, if possible, have the plan and specification of the house.

It is to be feared that on more than one occasion during his stay in Manchester Brooke did not reach his suburban residence, after the performance, until a very early hour in the morning. Mr. William Stafford, a veteran journalist and poet, in relating how he renewed the tragedian's acquaintance, after having first met him years previously in Glasgow, has kindly furnished us with the following reminiscences of this engagement:—
" It was the midnight hour," he says, " when I found him, with many other gentlemen, comfortably seated in the cosy smoke-room of a hotel near the theatre. He had that evening been playing Julian St. Pierre, in Knowles' fine play of *The Wife.* Jollity and good humour reigned supreme. Brooke was in grand form. He had been playing night after night to crowded houses. A large amount of money had been, for want of room, refused at the doors; and throughout the night or early morning all went merry as a marriage bell. After two o'clock a.m., the company began to disperse, and one by one they went away, till at length there were but three people left in the room. Of course poor Brooke was one of the trio; the second individual was an employé—a scene-shifter, I understood—at the theatre, and the writer of this completed the party. Brooke and the jolly scene-shifter had for some time been indulging in whiskies hot, and it was evident that their deep libations to the 'jolly god' had begun to tell upon the delicate network of their craniums. Brooke was certainly 'o'er all the ills of life victorious,' and his companion was not a whit behind. Brooke and I had a pleasant chat about bygone times, when he was with David Prince Miller in Glasgow. 'The woe short hours ayont the twal' flew by on rapid wing, but Brooke, who appeared to be in the seventh heaven of delight, remained brimming over with conversation and good fellowship. 'So you consider Julian St. Pierre one of my best performances,' he said, smilingly, to his companion. 'Most certainly,' replied the scene-shifter; 'I have seen other big stars in the part, but you bear away the palm.' Do you like my Othello?' enquired the actor. 'Well *raythur*,' with great stress on the *raythur*, was the answer. 'I saw you play Othello some

years ago, and even now I fancy I can hear the deep wail of anguish which you put into the words, 'Desdemona dead! O! O! O!' I cordially endorsed the opinion of the scene-shifter, and said that none could readily forget the impression created by the intense feeling which Brooke threw into the brief passage. And still the 'whiskies hot' kept coming in and going down, till at length the scene-shifter, in his lethargy, put the burning end of his cigar into his mouth, which made him very wroth and angry. However, when he had sufficiently cursed the weed he closed his dull eyes and fell fast asleep. Shortly after this poor Brooke also gently sunk into the arms of the drowsy god; and as the clock struck five I went leisurely home to my lodgings."

The new theatre in Birmingham, referred to in Brooke's letter to Morris, was in reality the Bingley Hall which Mr. John Tonks, a busy, bustling, spirited little man in the printing trade, had fitted up for dramatic performances in the December previous, with a seating capacity (it is said) of some 4,500. Considering the season of the year, Brooke's engagement at Tonks' Theatre proved immensely successful. After playing a round of his old characters, the tragedian on Wednesday, August 9, appeared for the first time in the name-part of a new tragedy called *Ornano*, the work of Mr. S. Hillis, a Dublin barrister. Although favourably received during the two nights it was played here (as evidenced by the fact that on both occasions the author was loudly called for and as loudly cheered), the piece was not strong enough to retain a permanent place in Brooke's repertory. Replete with powerful situations, and playing well despite its slowness of action, *Ornano* had little literary merit to commend it to critical notice. The author had indulged in a redundancy of language, and was far too exuberant in his use of tropes, figures, and rhetorical phrases. That he had steeped his mind in the essence of the Elizabethan drama there could be no doubt. Passage after passage cropped up in the play that were little better than mild paraphrases of some of the best remembered lines in *Macbeth*, *Othello*, *Romeo and Juliet*, etc.

Here is an example, the source of which is too apparent to need mention :—

> " Oh ! Venice, still beloved,
>   Farewell ! I bid thee one last, long farewell !
>   No more for me the cannon's distant roar
>   Shall wake the memory of the thunder's bolt !
>   For me no more the glowing steel shall burn
>   To rush amid the foe. No more in me
>   The trumpet's blast shall wake the fiery breast ;
>   Nor the shrill fife, the drum's loud echo,
>   Nor the bugle's sound, arouse my soul to arms."

The following account of the plot and acting of the tragedy is taken from the notice in *The Birmingham Journal and Commercial Advertiser*, August 12, 1854 :—" In the war between the states of Venice and Genoa, Ornano, a young soldier, married to Vanina, a Genoese, is appointed second in command of the army. On his departure he leaves with his wife his signet ring to ensure her protection and free passage through the ranks on her visits. While the war is being waged, Lovigo, the brother of Vanina, unconscious of hostilities, arrives in Venice, is pursued and seeks refuge with his sister. To save his life she entrusts him with her husband's ring, by the aid of which he escapes. But it appears that subsequently he avails himself of the signet to play the spy in the Venetian ranks. He is arrested, and whispers the secret of his possession of the ring into Ornano's ear. As communication with a Genoese was death, he refuses to inculpate his wife, is supplanted in his command, and sent home to Venice. He is arraigned as a traitor, and the last sentence of the law is about to be passed upon him, when Vanina rushes in and avows that she alone is the unconscious culprit. Ornano stands acquitted, and his wife takes his place. She is led to execution, but to save her from an ignominious death she falls pierced by her husband's hand. The blow is scarcely struck when intelligence arrives that the Venetian army are mutinous, refusing to meet the enemy unless led by Ornano, and a respite for Vanina is announced. Ornano rushes to the gates, and in the victory he there achieves receives his death-wound and dies as the spirit of Vanina is borne upwards.

This is, very briefly, the outline of the plot. There is, to be sure, the commencement of a bit of underplot, and a conspiracy in addition; but they have, in reality, no purpose in the play. The piece was put upon the stage in very creditable fashion, and was well acted, as may be imagined when we state, in reality, although the canvas is crowded, there are only two figures in the piece; and these were Mr. Brooke as Ornano and Miss Cathcart as Vanina. In some of the scenes, however, Mr. Brooke seemed to be improvising rather than working out a conception. The first two acts went somewhat heavily, if we except the parting interview, and the struggle of affection with duty in Vanina's heart when her brother pleads with her for his life. A really good, though by no means original, effect is produced by Ornano's dream, which Mr. Brooke gave very finely; a remark which applies to his meeting with Vanina, and to her anguish and self-accusation. This, perhaps, is the most powerful passage in the piece."

The Birmingham engagement was otherwise noteworthy for Brooke's meeting with Mr. George Coppin, the famous Australian manager, who after a chequered experience of some eleven years in the Colonies had just returned to the old country in search of novelties. As a first-class tragedian naturally came within the category, Coppin made it his business to induce Brooke to sign articles, whereby he agreed to give two hundred perform- ances in the principal cities of Australia and New Zealand at a nightly salary of £50 clear of all charges, the other taking all responsibility and risk.* One result of this was that the Australian manager expended £1,000 shortly afterwards in the construction of the shell and framework of a portable iron theatre, capable of holding an audience representing £300, the contract for which was undertaken by Messrs. Edward T. Bellhouse & Co., of the Eagle Foundry. Another was the issuing by John Tonks, of Birmingham, on Monday, August 21, of a circular soliciting subscriptions to the Brooke Testimonial

---

* These terms are given in accordance with the newspaper announce- ments of the period; but Mr. Coleman tells us the engagement was for two years certain at a nightly salary of £100.

Fund, it being "contemplated by some of the friends and admirers of the above eminent actor to present him with an appropriate memento of the high sense entertained for him as a man and an actor." In the printed appeal it is further stated that an appropriately designed candelabrum was in view, the presentation to take place "on the occasion of his farewell in London on the 11th of October." But as the newspapers of that period (theatrical or otherwise) are completely silent regarding the proposed mark of esteem, we must take leave to doubt whether Mr. Tonks' efforts ever had practical issue.

After giving six performances on alternate nights in the Coventry and Leamington Theatres (where he was efficiently supported by Miss Fanny Cathcart, Mr. Belton, Mr. A. Young, and Mrs. Selby), Brooke repaired to Ireland for a brief holiday. Writing from 3 Marine Terrace, Kingstown, in reply to an application from Messrs. Johnson & Nelson Lee, asking his terms for a few nights at the City of London Theatre, he says :—" Having for the last thirteen months been constantly engaged (although, thank God, I never was so well in health as I am at present), I feel I should like a few days on the Continent, and propose going thither after the 11th of October, for about three weeks, at the conclusion of my Cambridge engagement, or I should be tempted to visit you, as I have had so many solicitations to do so, and really feel awkward in my incessant refusals ; but my every hour that could be rendered available for professional services has been seized upon, and I am at this moment thronged with applications for even a single night in the towns surrounding, but being under contract to sail for Australia I am reluctantly compelled to decline."

In consonance with a prior arrangement Brooke reappeared at Drury Lane on Monday, October 2, and notwithstanding the fact that the trouble in the Crimea was absorbing public attention, gave a brief series of farewell performances to substantial houses. Enthusiastically recalled by an overflowing assemblage after the performance of *Macbeth* on October 9 (nominally the last night of the engagement), Brooke took advantage of the favour to deliver the following speech :—

" LADIES AND GENTLEMEN,—It is little more than fourteen months since I had the honour of appearing before you on my return from the United States. The welcome which then greeted me within these walls I shall never forget. It repaid me in the emotions of a moment for the many trying vicissitudes of my previous career, and aroused me to new and unimagined efforts. During the interval I have given in Great Britain and Ireland 371 personifications, and notwithstanding the mental and bodily fatigue attending on such a task, I feel grateful to say I have managed to preserve my health. I say this in no boastful spirit, but rather in the hope of showing that I have struggled hard to merit the patronage and applause so heartily bestowed on my humble efforts ; and I can only account for the buoyancy which has borne me through it by the constant and heart-stirring encouragement that met me in every town where I appeared, and sustained me with unceasing warmth to this last hour of my engagement. Under ordinary circumstances such strong and general tokens of public estimation could not fail to impress me deeply, but on the eve of my departure for a far-distant land, with the certainty of a long absence from my native country, it is impossible to recall the intensely gratifying recollections of the past year without giving way to feelings I shall not attempt to describe. Ladies and gentlemen, in uttering that short but lingering word, ' Farewell,' I do so in the hope that I may be spared to return and become again a candidate for your favour ; and allow me to assure you, and my generous patrons throughout the length and breadth of the land, that neither distance nor time shall subdue or weaken my profound and grateful sense of your past kindness."

On the following evening Brooke appeared as Claude Melnotte, giving his services voluntarily on behalf of the Licensed Victuallers' School and Asylum, which had been tendered a benefit at the theatre.

But a surprise was yet in store for his Drury Lane admirers. Saying " good-bye " in real earnest on Wednesday, October 11, he appeared in *The Stranger*, and signalised the occasion by giving his first performance in London of an Irish character. Challenging comparison with Tyrone Power by electing to figure as O'Callaghan in *His Last Legs*, he came satisfactorily through the ordeal, receiving high praise for a forcible and original rendering, but being deemed, on the whole, inferior in *vis comica* to his lamented compatriot. Only in the provinces and Australia were his merits as a natural Irish comedian, devoid of all stageyness, appreciated to the full. Speaking of his Captain Murphy Maguire, his O'Callaghan, and one or two other Irish parts, the "Old-Fashioned Playgoer" says:—"In these performances there seemed to be no acting; all was apparently the outcome of animal spirits and the inspiration of the moment. This was a very distinguishing feature indeed of his acting in all his parts; the only difference was that in the grand parts his copious animation and manly amplitude corporealised and breathed soul into the dry bones of the poet's valley of vision; while in colloquial rollicking parts, especially Irish ones, he had simply to be himself without even those golden shackles of convention and tradition which he wore so gracefully. It were a curious speculation to imagine what might have been done by a man so magnificently gifted with ductile powers if he had the originality to anticipate or the aptitude to meet that demand for quieter and more natural tragedy which is so general, but which no living actor in the least degree satisfies, simply because those who try to be natural cease to be tragic."

Meanwhile a requisition,* signed by upwards of 400 influential merchants, bankers, and traders of the metropolis, had been forwarded to Brooke, soliciting a few performances at the City of London Theatre on behalf of many living in the East-end who, "owing to the distance, business hours, and other circumstances," had been debarred from the pleasure of witnessing his performances. "Were I to refuse so marked a token of respect," writes Brooke in reply, under date Drury Lane, October 6, "I should feel myself

---

* A copy of this, signatures and all, together with Brooke's reply, appeared in *The Times* of Thursday, October 12, and was afterwards reprinted for distribution by the City of London Management.

unworthy of the unparalleled encouragement bestowed on my humble efforts in this country. I therefore cheerfully relinquish my premeditated trip, and have instructed my agent to close with your liberal offer, and will perform at your establishment for a limited number of nights." After fulfilling a short engagement at Cambridge, which evoked much interest, he at once repaired to the East-end theatre, where his old repertory proved so attractive that hundreds were turned nightly from the doors.

In taking leave of his "many kind and liberal friends," in an advertisement in *The Era*, before embarking for Melbourne, Brooke lays bare his mind in a manner entirely *un*characteristic of the genus actor. He most respectfully returns his sincere thanks "to the press in general for the very great kindnesses which they have shown him in their frequent notices of his professional efforts, notwithstanding the many expressed differences of opinion regarding his endeavours." Continuing in this strain, " he begs to assure them that in no wise does chagrin arise, for in very many instances where criticism has thought proper to censure he has found suggestions of worth, and wherever possible, has taken advantage of them with great benefit; for experience alone can teach, and he desires most emphatically to thank all for their great liberality towards him, and trusts that, if the old adage ' Practice makes perfect ' may come to him, nothing shall be wanting on his part to use his every endeavour to become more worthy of the noble profession he has the honour to belong to." We find him furthermore " imbued with the fervent hope that in 1857, after having fulfilled his engagement already made (D.V.) in the colonies of Australia, California, and the United States, he may again have the honour of appearing in this country and merit a continuance of their recognition." But Fate had decided otherwise. He was not to revisit the United States or to win additional laurels in California, any more than he was to return homewards within a space of two or three years. So the pleasant residence on the banks of the Hudson, like many another project conceived by the same mind, proved a mere castle in the air.

CHAPTER IX.

AFTER spending a few happy days in the family circle in
Dublin, Brooke left for Plymouth, *via* Holyhead and
Bristol, on November 22, but owing to a vexatious delay on
the road, only arrived at the southern seaport on the evening
prior to his departure. Feeling rather gloomy he betook himself
to an American circus which was enjoying great favour there,
and found the place crammed, it happening to be a benefit
night. "During the scenes in the circle," wrote Brooke to his
mother from the Royal Hotel, " the clown began to give some
quotations from Shakespeare, and alluding to a gentleman in
the circle, whom he had never before seen in a private capacity,
mentioned my name, paid me most marked compliments, and
concluded by wishing me every success in the land of gold, at
which the audience cheered most vehemently." Promising in
the same letter to drink his good mother's health every day at
five o'clock, and to keep a log-book for her amusement, he
affectionately subjoins, "I pray to God that we may meet again
round a nice family fire, and 'I have a saving faith within me
tells me that we shall.' '

Accompanied by Miss Fanny Cathcart, Mr. Richard Younge, Mr. J. Hall Wilton, and two servants, Mr. and Mrs. Brooke sailed from Plymouth in the new steamship *Pacific* at four o'clock on the afternoon of Saturday, November 25. During the first week, and on several occasions afterwards, the usual routine of the voyage was diversified in anything but pleasant fashion by the repeated breaking of the connecting rods of the paddlewheels, which delayed the steamer very considerably. Happily the weather proved fine, and grew so sultry as they approached the tropics that Brooke found it necessary to take his rest at night on deck. The condition of his wife's health, now for some time delicate, was causing him much anxiety; but, apart from this, he enjoyed himself serenely, pronounced the captain and officers "trump cards," and was soon on agreeable terms with most of the passengers. In the evening they would have singing and dancing on deck—the latter very hard work, calling for copious libations of soda-water and lemonade. "At half past five," records Brooke in his log-book under date December 3, "we saw a strange thing. The moon in her brilliancy on the larboard side of the vessel, and the sun just within half-an-hour of setting on the other side; the sky the most beautiful thing I ever beheld; not a breath of wind stirring, and the sea like a mirror."

Arriving at St. Vincent two days afterwards, Brooke went on shore to escape the dirty, but necessary, process of coaling, was cordially received by the Commandant and suite, and wiled the time away generally in watching the antics of the natives, whose naked picaninnies tried their best to steal his pet dog. By the 29th of the month the vessel had reached the Cape of Good Hope, where, as soon as the passenger list was made known, a number of residents, who in bygone days had enjoyed Brooke's acting in the old country, gladdened his heart by coming on board to give him welcome. Like Charles Dickens, he discovered that the world was a very small world after all, and that one fell across acquaintances in the most unlikely places. In a long letter to his mother, dated "Melbourne, March 10, 1855," he says—" A deputation waited on me at Capetown, requesting me either to read a play or enact one. There was a small garrison theatre in the barrack, and a number of gentlemen amateurs volunteered their services to assist. I complied with their request, and we played *Othello*, *The Lady of Lyons*, and *The Stranger*. The theatre each night was crammed to suffocation. The tickets were sold by auction, and brought as high as thirty shillings each. One day we started from Capetown, but had not got above ten miles from the harbour when the paddle-wheel rods broke and we were obliged to return; in consequence of which we were compelled to give another night at the theatre, which consisted of selections from different authors." Previous to the departure of the steamer on the following day, Miss Fanny Cathcart was waited upon at the hotel by a deputation representing the leading members of the Colonial Legislature, and presented with a gold watch and chain as a mark of their gratification and esteem.

Before the close of the voyage a similar but more dubious presentation was made by the passengers to Hall Wilton, Brooke's agent, who had contrived to keep himself in evidence through acting as auctioneer of the tickets sold daily in connection with the pool held over the vessel's progress. As the tragedian had an idea that the testimonial was more or less of Wilton's own getting up, the incident only served to add to the annoyance he had already felt over an attempt on the part of that gentleman to pose as the impresario who was about to exploit the actor's genius in the Colonies. A growing dislike of Wilton's professional methods (which were of the school of his old employer, Barnum) begot in Brooke mistrust of the man; and this eventually led to serious and unfortunate rupture.

After many vexatious and expensive delays, caused by defective paddle-wheels and a shortness of coal, the *Pacific* at length reached Melbourne, having taken eighty-five days to complete the passage. "On Thursday, the 22nd of February," writes Brooke to his mother, "we made Melbourne Heads, and about ten o'clock came into Hobson's Bay, where an express steamer with Coppin and the leading members of the theatrical profession in the colony came alongside. After an introduction to the latter and an affectionate farewell to the passengers we went on board. When we landed [at Sandwich] there was a coach-and-four waiting for us, beside divers and sundry other vehicles, and off we started for Melbourne, about three miles distant, and arrived at the Prince of Wales's Hotel. . . . . On the evening of Friday Mr. Coppin announced his benefit at the Theatre under my patronage; and at the conclusion of the first piece, the house being full, some people got a glimpse of me in a private box, whereupon they shouted 'Three cheers for Mr. G. V. Brooke.' I was obliged to bow from the box, but as all the house could not see me I was at length compelled to appear on the stage, led on by Mr. George Coppin."

About nine o'clock on the following evening, Mr. and Mrs. Brooke and Fanny Cathcart, who were occupying the apartments lately held by Catherine Hayes the Irish songstress, were serenaded by the theatre orchestra with some music from Locke and Bishop, arranged specially in the tragedian's honour. There were close on two thousand people present, and in answer to their clamours Brooke and Fanny Cathcart appeared on the verandah and bowed their acknowledgments. A torchlight procession then followed.

It is necessary at this juncture to indulge in a little retrospection. To such an extent had the adventurous and profligate youth of Great Britain rushed to the goldfields of Bendigo in 1852, that by the time of Brooke's arrival in the Colonies the population of New South Wales was fully five times what it had been a quarter of a century previously. Most of those rash spirits who saw fortune in the venture never cared to return homewards, preferring to settle down in opulence in the country of their adoption, and to become the progenitors of a sturdy and independent race. What time the gold fever was at its height playgoing proved a delightfully free and easy occupation. No one ever thought of wearing fine clothes. Even in the most expensive parts of the theatre, cabbage tree hats, top-boots, red shirts, and cutty pipes were more the rule than the exception. Utterly unconventional in their habits, the diggers would occasionally demonstrate their approval of some favourite performer's exertions by pelting him or her with half-crowns and nuggets of gold wrapped up in one-pound notes, and thrown with all the dexterity of a bouquet-lavishing exquisite.

Melbourne in those days could only boast of one theatre, the old Queen's, situate at the corner of Little Bourke Street and Queen Street. Originally the property of Mr. John Thomas Smith, for many years Mayor of the city, the Queen's had an excellent stock company, prominent among whom were Mr. and Mrs. Charles Young, the latter better and more prominently known now as Mrs. Herman Vezin. Mr. George Coppin, until recently the *doyen* of the Australian stage, had landed at Sydney in 1843. After a career as actor and manager replete with vicissitude he built a theatre in Adelaide towards the end of 1846, and soon acquired a large fortune. Subsequently he lost every penny through speculations in copper mining in connection with the discovery of gold in Victoria, and after going through the bankruptcy court made his way as best he could to Melbourne. He then tried his luck for a fortnight at the diggings, the only material result being a couple of blistered hands and a terrible backache. Reverting to his old profession, he, in 1852, assumed management of the Great Malop Street Theatre, Geelong, on but slender capital, and prospered exceedingly; so much so that in less than two years he had returned to Adelaide and surprised his creditors by inviting them to a dinner, at which all his debts were discharged in full. Sailing for England in January, 1854, he fulfilled several successful engagements as a starring comedian in London and the provinces; and after securing the services of Brooke and others, returned to the Colonies in the December following.

Brooke on his arrival in Melbourne was charmed with the climate and more than delighted with the rough and ready tone of the people. He noticed that everyone he met had a self-reliant and well-to-do air, and was inclined to think, considering the exorbitant prices charged for all liquors (*e.g.*, porter half-a-crown a bottle), and the amount of drunkenness prevailing, that the publicans had struck upon the richest vein of the precious ore. A digger at this period thought nothing of spending five pounds a day, and many of the luckier ones frittered away as much as one hundred pounds a week. There were known, and by no means rare, cases where men holding bullion to the value of a thousand pounds made their way on arrival to the nearest public-house and never sallied forth until all was exhausted. A dangerous atmosphere this for a man of Brooke's temperament! But he had gained wisdom for the time being by bitter experience, and had landed in the Colonies with the firm resolve of banking his money regularly until his final departure homewards. To his mother, who knew of this determination, he wrote regularly by every mail (seldom without enclosing a handsome remittance), now and again complaining, half jocularly, that although trade was somewhat duller than usual everything remained comparatively dear. Pineapples, he says, are 8s. 6d. each, oysters, 5s. 6d. a dozen, and "one cannot get into a cab without making a considerable hole in a pound." Hence his living expenses from the beginning averaged fifty pounds per week.

The following bill of the Queen's Theatre, Melbourne, heralded Brooke's first appearance on the Colonial stage:—

QUEEN'S THEATRE.

MONDAY, 26TH FEBRUARY, 1855.

First night of the Great Actor, MR. G. V. BROOKE, whose extraordinary powers are universally acknowledged to have no compeer since the days of the elder Kean. In order to render the pieces, in which Mr. Brooke will perform, complete, the celebrated artistes, MISS FANNY CATHCART and MR. RICHARD YOUNGE, from the THEATRE ROYAL, DRURY LANE, LONDON, have been engaged, in addition to a new and costly Wardrobe and Properties purchased, with entirely new Scenery.

Mr. Brooke's engagement in the Colonies being limited, the more so in consequence of the long protracted passage of the steamer "Pacific," he will appear in a round of his great characters, which will seldom, if at all, be repeated.

On Monday will be presented Shakespear's Tragedy,
"OTHELLO,"
with the following powerful cast :—

Othello,	Mr. G. V. Brooke.
Iago,	Mr. R. Younge.
Brabantio,	Mr. G. H. Rogers.
Cassio,	Mr. Burford.
Roderigo,	Mr. J. P. Hydes.
Duke,	Mr. Hooper.
Desdemona,	Miss Fanny Cathcart.
Emilia,	Mrs. C. Young.

To conclude with the very laughable farce,
"A. S. S."

Diogenes Hunter,   Mr. G. H. Rogers.
Prices—Boxes, 12s. 6d. ; Pit, 7s. 6d. ; Gallery, 5s.

"In remarking upon Mr. Brooke's Othello," says *The Argus* of the Wednesday following, "faint praise would not be just. It was a performance such as on leaving our English home we never expected again to witness. It was the creation of Shakespere, but an essentially original rendering. It was the noble presence, the unaffected orator—skilful through very simplicity ; the stalwart soldier, prepared even to surrender love! —and what love!—in obedience to the call of the country of his adoption. It was the confiding, unsuspicious friend, the devoted husband, the watchful and just governor. And when goaded on to suspect the fealty of Desdemona—not more by the hints of Iago than by doubt of his own worthiness to possess such a being—Othello demands palpable proofs of her incontinence, nothing could have been finer conceived than the expression thrown into—

'Be sure you prove my love a wanton.'

The fierce Arab blood, excited by the seeming confirmation of his wife's want of chastity—the deadliest crime in Oriental morals—gleamed from the eyes of the actor, and scarcely needed further language to tell the final catastrophe of the story. The sacrifice of Desdemona—for sacrifice it is—was almost too painfully portrayed ; and we suggest upon the repetition of the tragedy on Wednesday, that its fearful consummation should take place behind the curtain and out of sight. Mr. Brooke was gorgeously attired, and although apparently a severe sufferer from those pests to new arrivals, —mosquitos—looked in excellent health.

"The tragedy has been well put upon the stage, much of the scenery being entirely new. At its conclusion, Mr. Brooke was loudly called for, and that gentleman at length came before the curtain with Miss Cathcart. When the applause had somewhat subsided, Mr. Brooke, addressing the audience, thanked them for their enthusiastic reception, which, he said, had almost caused him and his companions to forget that they were so many thousand miles from home. He expressed himself delighted with the town and all he had seen since his arrival, and paid a handsome compliment to the actors with whom he found himself associated. Mr. Brooke then retired amidst loud cheering, waving of handkerchiefs, etc."

Subsequently the same paper considered his reading of *Hamlet* that of a gentleman and a scholar. "The sublime soliloquies were given by Mr. Brooke with proper emphasis and spirit, and the famous advice to the players was, in his hands, the facile analysis of a highly educated critic. The scene with his mother was perhaps the finest piece of acting throughout the tragedy, and it would indeed be difficult to imagine anything more perfect than the exhibition of terror and awe which proceed from this splendid actor upon the abrupt entrance of the Ghost."

In looking over Brooke's colonial correspondence with his relatives in Dublin, it is amusing to note the ever-recurring allusions to the doings of a pet dog which had evidently enjoyed high favour in the family circle; so much so that on one occasion the pampered animal is made to append its signature to a letter, the tragedian thoughtfully guiding the pen as held between its claws. "Little Pepy is very well and was quite a lion on board," writes Brooke to his mother, under date March 9. "Last night in the first scene of *Virginius* the little rascal got away from Polly [Mrs. Brooke] and ran on the stage to me. He jumped up at my legs and then lay down at my feet, and when in the dialogue with Icilius I had to cross the stage he came with me. Strange enough I had to say— 'Well, 'tis true, dog fights with dog, but honesty's not a cur doth bait his fellow; and e'en dogs, by habit of companionship, abide in terms of faith and cordiality.'* The audience did not laugh, but at the conclusion applauded vehemently. So that you see Pepy has made a successful *début*."

Playing at the Queen's Theatre with increasing favour until March 23, Brooke ran skilfully over the gamut of his histrionic scale, appearing from time to time in *Othello* (3), *The Hunchback* (2), *Richard III.* (2), *The Wife* (2), *Hamlet* (2), *The Stranger* (2), *Virginius* (2), *Macbeth* (2), *Rob Roy* (1), *New Way to Pay Old Debts* (1), and *The Bride of Lammermoor* (1). Irrespective of Fanny Cathcart and Richard Younge (the latter of whom, as stage manager, instituted many wholesome reforms), the support accorded throughout was very strong, and indeed was considerably above the level of what would have been given to a starring tragedian at Drury Lane about the same period. Particular mention must be made of Mr. G. H. Rogers, a genial, well-informed artist, then in the enjoyment of great popularity in Melbourne. It is not too much to say, that as an actor of character parts and old men this gentleman had few, if any, superiors on the stage of Greater Britain during his epoch.

After a sojourn of nine nights at the Theatre Royal, Geelong (in the course of which Brooke appeared as Claude Melnotte and Felix O'Callaghan, for the first time in the Colonies), a return was made by the Melbourne stock company on Easter Monday, April 9, to the Queen's Theatre, when *William Tell* was presented for the first time on local boards. Robert Heir, the affianced husband of Fanny Cathcart,

---

* . . . . . " Well, 'tis true,
    Dog fights with dog, but *honesty is not*
    A cur, *that* baits his fellow; and e'en dogs,
    By habit of companionship, abide
    In terms of faith and cordiality."

who had been delayed somewhat in leaving England, made his Australian *début* on the following evening as Icilius, to the Virginius of Brooke. The company was further recruited by the enrolment of Mr. George Coppin, who appeared to much advantage as Launcelot Gobbo, General Dumas, and in a variety of other important characters. Besides repeating many of his previous impersonations, Brooke, during this second season, gave performances of Shylock, Richelieu, Iago, Romeo, Martin Heywood, Pizarro, and Duke Aranza. The fourth on the list was certainly injudiciously chosen, his rendering of the love-sick Montague proving too mature to hit the fancy of *The Argus;* but with this solitary exception the tragedian carried both press and public with him throughout. Taking his benefit on May 4 (the last night of the engagement), he appeared in *The Stranger* and *His Last Legs,* and was honoured with the largest audience ever seen within the walls of the old theatre. Considering the size of the house more than the prices of admission, he was astonished to find the receipts amounting to some £406. In obedience to a summons before the curtain, after the performance, Brooke made a short speech, in which he thanked the Melbourne public for the patronage that had been bestowed upon him, adding that after the fulfilment of his Sydney engagement he hoped for a renewal of their favours at Coppin's new theatre, of which he had laid the foundation on April 18.

As an average specimen of the many poetical tributes lavished upon him during his prolonged stay in the Colonies, we append the following lines, sent to him on his birthday, while playing in Melbourne :—

TO GUSTAVUS V. BROOKE,

On his Thirty-seventh Anniversary,
25th April, 1855.

WHEN thy brave namesake* free'd his native land,
Tearing its Sceptre from the Danish hand ;
And He† still greater, who on Lutzen's field
The cause of Freedom with his life-blood sealed,

---

* Gustavus Vasa—the Liberator of Sweden.
† Gustavus Adolphus—the "Lion of the North."

They left thee loftier triumphs yet to find,
Not over vanquished *matter* but o'er *mind :*
To show us Nature, despite pedants' rules,
And the dull jargon of Theatric schools ;
Which all acknowledge thou hast nobly done,
While gazing, eagle-like, on Shakespeare's sun,
A bold undazzled, yet adoring one ;
Fit to expound those superhuman pages,
The oracles of past, and future, ages.
'Tis said " The Gods" upon Olympus late
In conclave sat, to fix the Drama's fate,
When " He of Avon's" ghost, with aspect grave,
A passing glance at modern actors gave,
Then said—" Where's *my* Othello—where Macbeth ?
Such clowns as these inflict a second death."
Apollo smiled, then, with benignant look,
A spark ethereal breathed, which called up *Brooke.*

Geelong, Victoria.   W. E. H.

Crossing over to New South Wales, Brooke opened at the
Theatre Royal, Sydney, on May 10, as Othello. personating
much the same round of characters during his lengthened
engagement as had been previously performed in Melbourne.
But on Tuesday the 29th a genuine novelty was afforded in
the shape of *Henry IV.,* cast as follows :—Henry IV., Mr. R.
Younge; Henry Prince of Wales, Mr. Robert Heir ; Prince John
of Lancaster, Miss Julia Matthews ; Earl of Westmoreland, Mr.
Maynard ; Sir Walter Blunt, Mr. Richardson ; Thomas Percy,
Mr. C. Evans ; Henry Percy, Mr. G. V. Brooke ; Sir John
Falstaff, Mr. Lambert ; Lady Percy, Miss Fanny Cathcart ;
Mrs. Quickly, Mrs. Lambert. Several other novelties followed
in quick succession. On June 4 Brooke played Faulconbridge to
the King John of Richard Younge, and seven nights after
produced Howard Payne's *Brutus,* apparently for the first time
in the Colonies. As if to supplement the many favourable
comments which had been made in the local press on Brooke's
acting, we find a correspondent writing to the *Sydney Morning
Herald* (June 12) affirming of the tragedian that " to a figure
of fine and manly symmetry he unites a countenance of agreeable and varying expression and great intelligence. Besides,
his voice is full and flexible—the tones soft and silvery as those

of Belial—sometimes reminding one of the voice of O'Connell in his palmy days of eloquence ; and all who knew that remarkable man were sensible that his voice was one of the principal means by which he achieved oratorical renown. Mr. Brooke's enunciation is so clear, distinct, and audible, that, whether ' in the whirlwind of a passion ' or in the soft depths of a pathetic passage, every word reaches the ear and the heart." After remarking that he had seen the actor in some half-dozen characters, the writer adds—" Virginius struck me as the part most genial to his taste and genius, and from beginning to end it was a noble and almost perfect performance."

Black-Eyed Susan, with Brooke as William and Fanny Cathcart in the name-part, came as a welcome relief, on July 7, to the long succession of blank-verse dramas ; and on the 9th the tragedian appeared as King Lear for the first time on any stage. Shakespeare's tragedy was repeated on the 12th, and on the following night the season terminated with Coppin's benefit, when Brooke played in the first piece, assuming the character of Pierce O'Hara in *The Irish Attorney ; or, Galway Practice in 1770*. " His performance," says *The Illustrated Sydney Journal*, " was a rich piece of acting, and quite equal in merit to his O'Callaghan in *His Last Legs*."

In response to an unanimous call from an inconveniently crowded house, the tragedian appeared before the curtain at the conclusion of the performance and delivered the following speech in his usual impressive manner :—

"LADIES AND GENTLEMEN,—With this evening my labours in this city will cease for some time, if labour it can be termed, for ' the labour we delight in physics pain.' This is my one hundred and fifth performance since I arrived in the Colonies, and I shall need a little quiet and repose till the 30th instant, when I shall resume my avocations at Melbourne. It now devolves upon me, in the name of Miss Cathcart, myself, and the gentlemen who accompany me, to thank you briefly but sincerely, not only for the patronage but also for the marked approbation which has attended our efforts during our prolonged stay; and to assure you that the tangible flattering testimonials of approval we have received in Sydney shall ever be dearly remembered and proudly acknowledged. And now, ladies and gentlemen, indulging in the hope that I may soon have the pleasure of visiting you again, in the name of Miss Cathcart, myself, and my confederates, I most respectfully say 'Farewell.'"

Paramount among the "tangible flattering testimonials of approval" referred to was a highly ornamental silver candelabrum, standing nearly three feet high, which had been presented to the tragedian towards the close of the engagement. The *Illustrated Sydney Journal* of July 21, 1858, in giving a woodcut of this testimonial, says:—"The stem springs from the pedestal, and is surmounted by seven branches; at its root are the full-length figures, most beautifully wrought, of a Nymph struggling with a Satyr at the side of a fountain. The whole stands on a superb plateau, and weighs 270 ozs. It was imported by Flavelle Brothers, and is the largest ever sent to this colony." There is just a possibility that this was the piece of plate originally selected by Mr. John Tonks for presentation to the tragedian on his departure for Australia, subscriptions for which had hung fire at the outset. But what proportion of the sum had been contributed by English and what by Australian admirers, or whether Brooke (as hinted of him by Mr. Coleman in other instances) had eked out the cost from his own pocket, will probably never be determined.

It was with feelings of genuine regret that Brooke said good-bye for the time being to his many friends in Sydney. As an actor his self-esteem had been flattered by their nightly attendance at the theatre in large numbers at a period when trade was much depressed through the market being over-stocked with English goods. In his private capacity, likewise, Society had lionised him to his heart's content. He had not been more than a fortnight in the city—whose magnificent harbour, by the way, greatly lessened his admiration for the Cove of Cork—before he was on easy visiting terms with Sir Charles Nicholson,

Speaker of the Legislative Council, the Chief Justice, the Judges, and the Attorney-General. But he was most at home in the company of the little band of artists who had temporarily united their fortunes with his own. There was, of course, much merrymaking over the marriage of Fanny Cathcart to Robert Heir, and on Sundays the labours of the week would be agreeably diversified by excursions of a placidly enjoyable nature to Botany Bay and elsewhere. Under the spells of a genial climate, the tragedian and his wife found themselves growing somewhat obese; a state of affairs jokingly alluded to in the "joint-stock letters" regularly sent home to his brother and sisters in Dublin. In one of these we have the first serious note of warning in connection with Brooke's impending rupture with his agent. Writing on June 1, he says, "Mr. Wilton is in Van Dieman's Land, managing the Wizard Jacobs, which is a speculation of Coppin's and mine. It has answered hitherto remarkably well. I do not like Wilton near me. He is not the man I thought he was; and, much to his chagrin, I have sent him to attend to my interest in another quarter. I had at one time a personal respect for him, but now have none, and hold no communication with him but on matters of business." After this expression of opinion it is not surprising to find Wilton in the course of a few weeks seceding from the service of Brooke to manage the affairs of the Wallers. Subsequently, however, the tragedian evidently repented his action, and in writing home on November 24, announces his quondam agent's departure for England in the following terms: "Wilton, *I find, is not a bad fellow after all*, but very expensive. He returns by this mail and will no doubt call to see you. *Treat him as of old, and make the most of him.* He will amuse you with a description of our adventures in the land of gold."

One of the principal members of the Sydney stock company at this period was Mr. H. T. Craven, who was afterwards to develop into a powerful actor of the Robsonian type, and to become widely known as the author of *The Chimney Corner* and *Milky White*. Trying his hand at this early date at play-writing,

Mr. Craven made a fine and very effective adaptation of Schiller's *Robbers*, which, under the title of *The Brothers*, was purchased by Brooke, a little previous to his departure from Sydney, for the sum of fifty guineas.

Meanwhile Coppin's new Olympic Theatre, erected at the corner of Stephen Street and Lonsdale Street, Melbourne, had been informally opened early in June to permit of the Wizard Jacobs giving a series of entertainments there. Referring to this structure, which was afterwards to become familiarly known to local playgoers as "The Iron Pot," Brooke, in his letter home of July 20, says—"It is a most beautiful place; fitted up with great taste, and will hold three hundred and fifty pounds." Then actively preparing for the ensuing theatrical campaign, he was apparently all at sea as to his future arrangements, and adds—"You will perhaps be surprised when I tell you that our stay may be shorter than I anticipated." Ten days afterwards the Olympic was formally opened for theatrical performances, on which occasion Brooke spoke the following address :—

> "Kind friends, upon your hospitable shore,
> 'Neath Coppin's standard I appear once more.
> Here for a brief time is my little world,
> Where he his flag Theatric has unfurled.
> Cheered by the memory of your past applause
> He marches onward in the Drama's cause,
> And hopes for that—if not himself—to gain
> Still greater triumphs in his new campaign.
> His forces are a small but chosen troop,
> Yet all their powers without your aid must droop.
> Amid the thousands who life's battle fight
> The actor's struggles are not few or light,
> And although you find him in your golden land,
> E'en there, believe me, he needs a helping hand.
> Shall it be said he seeks it here in vain—
> That his best efforts meet with cold disdain?
> That none look on where art and genius strive
> Such scenes as Shakespeare drew to keep alive:
> Scenes which alike refine, exalt, engage,
> And all but make a pulpit of the stage?
> Oh, no! where'er beneath your skies I roam
> I find to all comes nature's language home,

That ever better feeling of my kind
Dwell in each heart—however rough the rind,
And like your gold, though hidden deep from sight,
Wants but a touch to bring it forth to light.
Fostered by you then may our present field
Fruit, both to actor and to author yield ;
And, spite our iron sky and wooden soil,
Prove not in vain our tillage and our toil ; —
Light, moisture, warmth, that soil must draw from you,
Your smiles its sunshine, and your tears its dew—
Till on these boards the Drama wins its way,
With root too firm to perish or decay.
Our space is small, but if, my friends, you prize
Things by their merits, rather than their size,
And are content to meet us where at least
Two of the muses spread their choicest feast,
We'll dare to hope no rival, far or near,
Will ever tempt you to desert us here."

The original programme, here appended, serves to show the
constitution of the company : —

COPPIN'S OLYMPIC.

Monday Evening, July 30, 1855.

God Save the Queen,	By the Band.
New Act Drop, -	By Mr. W. Pitt.

The Opening Address (written by an Admirer of the
Legitimate Drama) will be spoken by
Mr. G. V. Brooke.

The performance will commence with Bulwer's play,
The Lady of Lyons,

Beauseant, -	Mr. R. Younge.
Colonel Damas, -	Mr. G. Coppin.
Glavis, - -	Mr. Robert Heir.
Mons. Deschappelles, -	Mr. Leslie.
Gaspar, -	Mr. Robins.
Claude Melnotte, -	Mr. G. V. Brooke.
First Officer,	Mr. Webster.
Second Officer, -	Mr. Seyton.
Third Officer,	Mr. Percy.
Notary, -	Mr. Lester.
Madame Deschappelles,	Mrs. Brougham.
Pauline, - -	Miss Fanny Cathcart.
Widow Melnotte,	Miss Herbert.
Marian, -	Mrs. Avins.

To conclude with a new Farce, called
To Oblige Benson,

Mr. Benson (a barrister), - -	Mr. R. Younge.
Mr. Trotter Southdown (his friend),	Mr. G. Coppin.
Mr. John Meredith (a pupil of Mr. B.'s),	Mr. R. McGowen.
Mrs. Benson, - - - - -	Miss Herbert.
Mrs. Trotter Southdown, -	Miss Glyndon.

Doors Open at a Quarter to Seven ; Commence at Half-past Seven.
Boxes, 7s. 6d. ; Stalls, 5s. ; Pit, 3s.

Subsequently, nothing of more than passing note occurred until August 9, when *The Serious Family* was produced with Brooke as Captain Murphy Maguire, and proved so attractive as to hold its place in the bills for nine successive nights. Owing probably to this unexpected hit, the star's appearances in Irish comedy were very frequent during the season. On the 20th, *The Vendetta, or The Corsican Brothers* was brought out and enjoyed a run of six continuous nights, or eight in all. This was followed on the 27th by the production of the Princess's drama, *The Courier of Lyons*, in which Brooke appeared for the first time in the dual parts of Lesurques and Dubosc. After seven performances the novelty gave way to *Money*, presented on September 5 with a very powerful cast. Mr. R. Younge's Stout, Mr. C. Young's Graves, and Mrs. Young's Clara Douglas, were all equally admirable in their way. Indeed, so thorough was the *ensemble* that the character of Evelyn, as delineated by Brooke, shone like a diamond of the first water—much the better for its setting. Commenting upon the production of *Love's Sacrifice*, a week afterwards, the *Argus* says : —" Mr. Brooke, as Matthew, portrays with exquisite skill the varying emotions of the conscious homicide, bearing constantly about with him the remembrance of his crime, seeking to atone for it by heaping benefits on those whom he has bereft of a father, and anticipating in the union of his idolised daughter and the injured son of his foe, the completion of that daughter's happiness and of his life of atonement. The discovery that he is known and that his secret will be made public, comes upon him like a thunderbolt, and the generous sacrifice which Margaret (Mrs. Young) is willing to make in order to secure her father led to a succession of emotions on the part of father and child which displayed the power of both performers."

Subsequently there were productions of *Macbeth*, *Richelieu*, *King John*, and *King Lear*, of which the first ran seven nights, the second and third three, and the last four.

"We have been playing," writes Brooke in a joint-stock letter to his relatives in Dublin, under date September 28—"We have been playing in our Iron Theatre since the 30th of July, and it is getting on famously. There has been a very fine, large theatre opened here, which had been built during Mr. Coppin's absence from the Colonies, and which opened about the same time; but we have the lion's share of patronage and support. Miss Catherine Hayes has returned here from India, and called to see us yesterday with her mother. She is a remarkably nice person. . . . . We are as comfortable as it is possible to be under the circumstances. We have a detached cottage about a hundred yards from the theatre, containing six rooms, kitchen, out-houses, stabling, coach-house, fowl and pigeon-house, with a very large yard, for which we pay two hundred and fifty pounds for nine months. Polly amuses herself by breeding ducks, chickens, and geese, but I am sorry to say she has not been very well for some time past.

"Fanny Cathcart, a short time after her marriage with Mr. Heir, was compelled by him to withdraw her services from me, and has broken her contract, notwithstanding that on her marriage I increased her income from one hundred a year to twelve pounds per week. They went immediately to the other theatre, and as soon as I saw the announcement that she was to act I procured an injunction to restrain her from so doing. She acted in defiance of that injunction, and the next day I obtained an attachment against the persons of Mr. and Mrs. Heir, but did not allowed it to be served, as they would have been lodged in gaol for contempt of court. They then, by the advice of persons connected with the other theatre, endeavoured to get the injunction dissolved, but failed in the attempt. The consequence is that he is engaged at the other theatre, and they are obliged to live on his salary; and she cannot act in the Colonies without my permission till after the fourteenth of next September. Mr. Heir was not satisfied with the parts we gave him. He wanted to play some of the first parts, and got dissatisfied. He thought that if he could break her engagement with me, they might go starring about the country. They have involved themselves in one hundred and fifty pounds costs, and I believe they will have to return to me at last. Ingratitude has been exemplified to a very great degree, and I can never feel the same interest I did as to her welfare. I wish we had some *good* utility actors out here, but they must be *good*. They could get five times the amount that they do at home. . . . . George and I watch over and protect the advancement and interest of our theatre as a parent would watch his child, and everything has as yet exceeded our anticipations."

Brooke was probably the first to introduce the Irish jaunting-car into the Colonies. On leaving home he had given Mr. Grady, the coachbuilder, of Dawson Street, Dublin, *carte blanche*, to construct one of these peculiar vehicles and send it out after him. Many anxious inquiries are made in his letters from time to time regarding it, and in one we find him enclosing a bill of exchange for £47 odd to defray the cost. In sooth, a strange whim!

The new playhouse referred to in the above extracts was the magnificent Theatre Royal, which Mr. John Black had erected in Bourke Street. So many attractions were afforded to local playgoers by the contest between Black and Coppin that the old Queen's gradually became deserted, and was eventually turned into a carriage factory.

At the Olympic during November *Macbeth* was again revived, with Brooke and Mrs. Waller in the principal parts, our hero likewise giving several performances of Pierce O'Hara in *The Irish Attorney*. On December 1st the season terminated with a

performance of *Love's Sacrifice* for Brooke's benefit.   Delivering
an address, as usual, the tragedian was frequently interrupted by
the deafening applause of the audience, and was saluted on
retiring with a shower of bouquets from the boxes.

Following this came a fortnight's sojourn at Ballarat, which
he describes as " the oldest of the goldfields; a city of wood
and canvas, with sixty thousand inhabitants." Here the diggers
testified their approval of his performances by presenting him
with four large nuggets, worth about seventy pounds.

On returning to Melbourne he was made the recipient of
a similar mark of esteem from the members of the Olympic
stock company, who, on Saturday, January 26, 1856, asked his
acceptance of a splendid testimonial, consisting of a figure of
Shakespeare in gold, resting on a volume of his works, supported
by nuggets, the whole standing on a tablet of gold. " In token
of their admiration of his talents as an Artiste, his conduct as
a Gentleman, and his worth as a man"; so ran the somewhat
infelicitous inscription.   In connection with the avalanche of
testimonials that now descended upon him it is necessary to
explain that, according to previous arrangements, he was soon to
depart for California.   Although never carried into execution,
some time elapsed ere he finally abandoned the project.

When Coppin's Olympic reopened for the second season on
Monday, January 28, several improvements in the arrangements
had been effected, not the least noteworthy of which was the
introduction of gas.   Speaking of the performance of *Julius
Cæsar* on that occasion, *The Argus* says, " Mr. Brooke, who, as
the bills set forth, impersonated the character of Brutus for the
first time on any stage (?) was on his entrance flatteringly
received, and by a very clever reading of the part succeeded in
eliciting the approbation of the audience.   The interpretation of
this finely-drawn character by Mr. Brooke impressed us with
great satisfaction.   With considerable temptation to rant, the
actor carefully eschewed it, and by a judicious management of
voice, gesture, and attitude imparted to the splendid declamatory
passages a proper and natural effect."

During the season, lasting until April 26, a few novelties were agreeably interspersed between the performances of well-worn plays. Owing to the growing popularity of his Irish comedy personations, Brooke was constrained to appear in his old character of Rory O'More, and at this period gave his first performance of Sir Lucius O'Trigger in *The Rivals.* Much appreciated likewise were his finely discriminated assumptions of Hotspur, Jacques, Henry V.; of Alexander the Great in Nat. Lee's old tragedy and John Mildmay in *Still Waters Run Deep.* The month of March was marked by the occurrence of two noteworthy events. Brooke, on the 4th, appeared for the first time on any stage as Benedick in *Much Ado about Nothing,* and on Wednesday the 19th was presented at the Olympic with a gold cup and salver (value 250 guineas) from the playgoers of Melbourne. Mr. James Smith, a prominent member of the colonial press, who was deputed to act as spokesman for the testimonial committee, addressed the tragedian in the following terms, the speech being delivered with a quiet earnestness that gave the air of sincerity to his words : —

"I have been requested by a number of your friends and admirers, Mr. Brooke, to present you, in their name, with this testimonial, not as the measure, but as a mark, of the high opinion they entertain of your talent, as an actor, and your worth, as a man. We owe, sir, to your visit to these colonies not only a renewal of the refined and elevating enjoyments we have been accustomed to derive from the acted drama, in the other hemisphere, but the foundation—if I may so say—of a national theatre in Australia. If some of the Shakespearian dramas which have been produced in this theatre with so much care, mounted with such historical accuracy, and performed with so much intelligence, have been less successful than they deserved, you may depend upon it that an explanation of the circumstance is to be sought in the fact of their being so entirely new to the colonial stage, and is certainly not owing to any defect in their interpretation by yourself and the talented ladies and gentlemen by whom you are so ably supported. We

are anxious, sir, on this occasion to mark our high appreciation
of the wide range and the remarkable versatility of those powers
which you have brought to bear upon the illustration of the
British drama.   Few of the actors who have ennobled your
profession have exhibited so much versatility, or so great a
fertility of mental resource as yourself.   Permit me, in the name
of the subscribers, to offer you this testimonial, and to hope that
you will long continue to delight and instruct us by the display
of those eminent and varied faculties with which nature has
endowed you, and that, whenever circumstances shall recall you
to Europe, this memento may remind you, not inappropriately,
of the golden land at the Antipodes, and of the many warm
friends and earnest admirers whom you will leave behind you
here, and who will always cherish the most agreeable recollections
of your visit to Australia."

Although strongly affected by the tone of the address, and
the ever-recurring applause of the audience, Brooke's practised
self-command stood him in good stead, and enabled him to give
an admirable delivery of the following reply :—

GENTLEMEN,—If I could put my heart into my tongue, and
could crowd into one word all the emotions which I now feel, it
would relieve *me* of much embarrassment and *you* of the task of
listening to an inadequate expression of my heartfelt thanks.
Gentlemen, an occasion like the present touches me nearly, and
all the more so because it follows an already lengthened
experience of your kindness and applause.   To me, as to my
professional brethren, that kindness and applause are beyond all
value : for you must bear in mind that the actor's reward is
the PRESENT ONLY.   Whatever distinction the actor may obtain
becomes a tradition merely—when he dies.   The glowing canvas
and the breathing marble perpetuate the reputation of the
painter and the sculptor.   The poet, the musical composer, and
the orator become immortal in their published works.   The
fame of the great dramatist endures to all time; but the
reputation of the actor who interprets his works is as brief and
fugitive as his own life.   When the tongue lies motionless, and

the plastic features become rigid beneath the touch of death, his name ceases to be anything more than a tradition; and therefore, Gentlemen, we prize still more highly these cheering—these splendid recognitions of our poor endeavours and our humble worth. Upon the arduous and chequered path of our professional life occasions like the present shed a glow of sunshine which reaches forward even to the evening of our days. Whenever the time arrives for me to bid adieu to that stage which it was the ambition of my youth to tread with honour—which it has been the pride of my manhood to occupy with credit to myself and satisfaction to the public, and which will always be identified with my fondest recollections of the past—I shall be able to recall to mind no brighter scene or more gratifying remembrance than that of the present hour. I shall be able, " in the silent sessions of sweet thoughts," to summon up the images of no friends whose opinion I prize more warmly—whose generous appreciation of my humble efforts I value more highly, or in whose worth I more entirely believe, than those of my warm-hearted and munificent friends in Australia. I accept, with pride, this flattering testimonial, and, in conclusion, can only say, in the language of the poet, we all love and venerate—

> " Kind gentlemen, your pains
> Are registered where every day I turn
> The leaf to read them."

Although kept very busy for some weeks afterwards, owing to the severe indisposition of Coppin, Brooke still found time to furnish his Dublin friends with all the news, and wrote a "joint-stock" letter from Melbourne, on April 20, stating, *inter alia*, " I shall finish here next Saturday, the 26th instant, and then proceed on a tour to Geelong, Bendigo, Hobart Town, Adelaide, and Sydney; and then I think it is more than probable we shall return home *via* California and the States. This Melbourne is really an astonishing place, and though it is only fourteen months since I landed, its enlargement and improvement seem to me almost magical." After remarking that the approach of winter had been heralded by extremely wet weather, one surprising feature of which was that, while it might rain an entire day, on the next the dust would be blowing in your eyes, he adds, "I have had the good fortune to meet some exceedingly nice families here. We do not go much into society, and our associates are *few* but *select*. We are very much in want of actresses out here. Even with mediocre talent they would make five times as much as actresses can get at home. I am afraid I have spoiled the colony, for they have seen plays so well done that they will not be satisfied with anything that is not *bona-fide*, respectable, and good."

While at Hobart Town Brooke was much distressed by the intelligence that his brother's life was despaired of. The poor fellow had incurred a severe chill through driving home from Kingstown regatta in damp clothes, after having been instrumental in saving the occupant of a capsized boat from a watery grave. The tragedian had opened a very successful fortnight's engagement at the Victoria Theatre, on Monday, June 9, with *Othello*. Two days afterwards we find *The Tasmanian Daily News* saying:— "If it be true that 'ars est celare artem,' Mr. Brooke is an artist indeed. Quiet, easy, self-possessed, natural, the Master Walter of the poet spoke and moved before the audience. The most remarkable feature in Mr. Brooke's acting is what is technically denominated 'bye-play.' In this respect Mr. Brooke has few equals, probably no superiors. It is not so much what he says, and the elocution with which he delivers it, as it is the look, the attitude, the gesture, which convey all that is intended, and so much that language alone can never impart without such aid. And yet there is a remarkable absence of stage effect. All seems spontaneous, unstudied: the result of who shall say how deep reflection, and what elaborate training? This is the highest and real triumph of art."

Having now, by unremitting attention to his professional duties, amassed a handsome fortune (some say £50,000), Brooke, in spite of his woeful experience in America, must needs enter once more upon the perils and anxieties of theatrical management. Joining himself in partnership with Mr. George Coppin, he purchased, in association with that gentlemen, the lease of the Theatre Royal, Melbourne, and the freehold of Cremorne Gardens, Richmond, expending upon these acquirements something like £100,000. A serious mistake was made at the outset in having too many irons in the fire. And the best that can be said in mitigation of the disasters that ensued is, that greater masters of managerial strategy and finance than Messrs. Brooke and Coppin have since burnt their fingers in attempting to control a multiplicity of speculations.

Simultaneously with Brooke's first appearance in Hobart, the Melbourne Theatre Royal opened its doors under the new management with *She Stoops to Conquer*, and a musical entertainment, to an audience representing £478 15s. 6d. Two nights afterwards the first grand opera season ever given in the Colonies was inaugurated, and following this came performances of English opera. Although an excellent company of vocalists, musicians, and dancers had been engaged (among whom may be mentioned Madame Anna Bishop, Madame Caradini, Mrs. Fiddes, Julia Harland, Sarah Flower, Mr. Laglaize, Mr. Howson, and Mr. Walter Sherwin), and despite the fact that ten operas in all, ranging from *Norma* and *Der Freischutz* to *The Bohemian Girl* and *Maritana*, were presented, the result was a loss to the treasury of about £3,000.

Passing through Melbourne on his way to Sydney, Brooke appeared for one night at the Theatre Royal on July 2, playing Captain Murphy Maguire to a full house, the receipts amounting to £531 odd. Of his subsequent doings the following extracts from a letter home, dated "Melbourne, September 27," give a satisfactory account:—

" Your letters, containing an account of the death of my dear brother William, shocked us indeed, though from the tenour of the last letter previous to the melancholy event I was in some measure prepared for it. Still we cherished a hope that the Almighty would have spared him to us; but *the Lord's will be done*. I have ever entertained a strong affection for poor William, and although circumstances attendant on my wandering and wayward fate in early life prevented me from showing my love and affection as my inclination prompted me—I did look forward in the hope that I should have had it in my power one day (not distant) to have made him, with those that are dear to me, happy and comfortable, as far as this world is regarded.

"I have now abandoned all idea of visiting California, and shall return direct to Europe next year. Mr. Coppin and myself have become the lessees of the Theatre Royal here, which we have had open for four months successfully. We have jointly purchased the Cremorne Gardens, about two miles from Melbourne. It contains ten acres of land, laid out as a Botanical Garden, and part of it devoted to a collection of Australian birds and animals. There is a nice house—which will be used as a hotel—and a large dancing platform, quite equal to the London Cremorne. We have laid down a gasometer, and the gardens will be brilliantly illuminated. We have also built there a theatre for Concerts, Vaudevilles, and Ballet, and there is a large sheet of water, on one side of which will be an immense picture representing the City of Naples and the eruption of Mount Vesuvius, which will be accompanied by enormous discharges of fireworks.

"We have now the Theatre Royal, the Olympic, Astley's Amphitheatre, Cremorne Gardens, and four very large hotels all *in full swing*—and Cremorne will be shortly. It is a great speculation, but with every certainty of success.

"With the exception of home thoughts I only think of my profession and making money, and look forward with anxiety to returning to Europe. We have lately been to Sydney, where I opened a new theatre called the Lyceum, and brought full and fashionable audiences for six weeks. On the 21st of next month I recommence my tour, visiting Geelong, Hobarton, Ballarat, Bendigo, Launceston, Adelaide, and Sydney, returning here to play a farewell engagement. I am not certain whether I mentioned in any of my former letters that Mr. Coppin and myself are more closely connected than we were. We are masonically *brothers;* and we have been since July twelvemonth *brothers-in-law*, he having married Polly's sister. The result is that on the 26th of May he was presented with a fine daughter: indeed, the finest child I ever saw. It is only four months old and it looks more like thirteen. She is a great pet, and often serves to afford much amusement to her *nunky*.

"I have been acting every night that I possibly could, and do not feel myself at all worse for it. It is wonderful how much can be done—if *systematically*.

"My dear Elizabeth has my blessing and so has her husband elect. We shall remember the 31st of November* and at half-past eleven at night shall wish them health, happiness, and prosperity. This epistle is indeed a hurried one, for, as I said before, I have had very little time to myself, and last night on the occasion of my benefit I played Werner for the first time. The house was *full in every part*."

In connection with the occasional lapse into the first person plural in these "joint-stock" letters (as he delighted in calling them), it may be advisable to point out that in most cases Mrs. Brooke's signature followed that of her husband, the whole usually concluding with "Believe us, your affectionate son and daughter, brother and sister, Gustavus V. Brooke, Marianne Brooke."

Harking back a little we find that the tragedian had returned to Melbourne in time for the opening of the regular dramatic season at the Theatre Royal, reappearing there on August 25, as Matthew Elmore. With the receipts for some considerable time averaging three hundred pounds nightly and the expenses never exceeding four hundred pounds weekly, Brooke was certainly justified in holding out great hopes of the success of the venture. Taking only a secondary position in the management of affairs, it was by no means apparent to him that money came in at the window and poured out at the door.

Although the tragedian's old repertory continued to prove an unfailing source of attraction, several praiseworthy attempts

---

*An extraordinary slip. The date intended to be alluded to was that on which the marriage actually took place, viz., October 30, 1856.

were made during the season to whet the public appetite with
novelty. Owing to the fact that colonial playgoers had not
been educated up to a proper appreciation of the more
unhackneyed plays of Shakespeare, these efforts seldom met
with the measure of success deserved. Hence the management
became prone to fall back on Irish comedy, which, with Brooke
to the fore, invariably drew crowded houses.

On Monday, September 1, the tragedian appeared as Leontes
in *The Winter's Tale*, and on that night week played Leonatus
Posthumus to the Imogen of Fanny Cathcart in the first
production of *Cymbeline* in the Australian colonies. Despite the
novelty afforded the house on the latter occasion was by no
means well filled, the occupants of the dress circle, for instance,
only numbering five-and-twenty. In the judgment of local
critics, however, Brooke made the most of his opportunities,
investing the character with an importance which none but an
accomplished artist could have given it. His delineation of
Posthumus' tardy change from boundless confidence in his wife
to full belief in her infamy ; the bursts of frenzied passion which
followed ; the bitterness of his remorse and self-reproach on
hearing Iachimo's confession, and the ecstacy of joy which
thrilled through his being on discovering his unsunned wife in
the "scornful page"—all commanded the attention of the audience
and won for the actor unstinted applause. It was a rare
performance in more ways than one, for the tragedy was not
seen again on the Melbourne stage until November, 1880.

Commenting upon Brooke's first appearance as Werner, *The
Argus* of September 27, says, his "delineation of the 'soul-sick
and miserable' nobleman, morbidly sensitive and with a mind
full of sickly fancies, struggling with the toils of fate, a prey to
remorse and an abject believer in destiny, was worthy of the
actor's well-earned reputation. His passionate pleadings with
Ulric in the second scene in the second act, where the beggared
father endeavours to extenuate the crime of which he has been
guilty ; the agonising struggles of his mind in the colloquy with
Ulric in the garden ; the overwhelming anguish which he

experiences on discovering who was the murderer of Stralenheim, were all portrayed with a consummate skill; and the breathless silence of a full house during the most interesting scenes, was the best tribute that could be offered to the power and ability of this eminent tragedian." On the 30th, *Much Ado About Nothing* was revived, the performance being under the immediate patronage of the five election candidates for the city. Brooke and Mrs. Heir (as Fanny Cathcart was now called) divided the honours between them as Benedick and Beatrice, and according to *The Argus*, "infused as much animation into their auditors, as into the dialogue, action, and by-play of the piece. Both performers were so easy, natural, and yet earnest withal that they carried the audience with them throughout, and it was interesting to listen to the exclamations which ever and anon broke forth from the spectators, demonstrative of the pride felt in their own superior sagacity which enabled them to see through and chuckle over the plots which Benedick and Beatrice were incapable of detecting." Efficiently supported by Mr. and Mrs. Robert Heir, Mr. R. Younge, Mr. Rogers, Mrs. Charles Young, and Miss Herbert Josephine, Brooke appeared subsequently in many of his favourite characters, and on October 14 increased his Hibernian repertory in playing Sir Patrick O'Plenipo in *The Irish Ambassador*. With the termination of the engagement on October 18 the tragedian, in conjunction with the principal members of the stock company, at once left for Geelong, to commence the tour spoken of in his letter. This was interrupted, however, by his return to Melbourne on Thursday, November 20 (a general holiday and race day), when he played Captain Murphy Maguire at the Royal to the Aminadab Sleek of Mr. George Coppin. On the following night *Richelieu* was performed in commemoration of the opening of the New Houses of Parliament; and with Brooke's appearance in *The Stranger* at Castlemaine on Saturday the tour was at once resumed.

CHAPTER X.

OPENING at the Lyceum Theatre, Sydney, on New Year's
Day, 1857, as Felix O'Callaghan, Brooke continued to act
there until January 24, when he transferred his services to the
Royal Victoria Theatre, in the same city. In treating of his
impersonation of Leontes, at the latter house, the *Sydney
Morning Herald* says it "was graphic, earnest, and picturesque
—more vigorous, if less refined, than that of Mr. Phelps—a
performance, the period of the age which the play is supposed
to depict, strong, bold, and manly." Subsequently, Brooke
appeared as Hotspur, Posthumus, Sir Lucius O'Trigger, and (on
February 28) as Jaques in *As You Like It*. Of the last-mentioned
personation *The Empire* says:—"He made him an abstracted
person, contemplative and passive, with a taste for music and a
contempt for pleasures. His delivery of the speech 'all the
world's a stage' was very fine, and we may pronounce it the
most finished specimen we have heard from Mr. Brooke. At

its conclusion the actor was greeted with a round of applause
from the crowded audience."

The most noteworthy feature of this engagement, however,
was the production, on March 30, of *The Tempest*, in which
Brooke played Prospero for the first time. Owing to the fact
that the principal Sydney journals had taken umbrage at the
showmanlike strategy of the manager of the theatre in devising
a thousand-pound prize lottery scheme on behalf of local
playgoers, no criticism appeared on this or any other of Brooke's
later performances. Nevertheless, the engagement ran its course
prosperously to the end, terminating on April 6.

Seeing that Mr. and Mrs. Robert Heir were in leading
support to the tragedian throughout, and bearing in mind that
the original contract with the actress had expired in the
September previous, it may be assumed that all concerned had
readily patched up their old differences. Writing home from
"St. Kilda House, Wooloomooloo Street, Sydney," on February
9, Brooke again speaks in hopeful strain of the various
enterprises which Coppin and he are controlling, and
continuing says—"I am sure you will be glad to hear that it
is more than probable we shall, by the end of July, wind up
our affairs in so satisfactory a manner as to enable us to sail
for England about August or September. I have worked very
hard but systematically, and it is indeed a source of great
gratification that every speculation which Coppin and [I] have
entered into has been successful. I am induced to think
that my reappearance at home will cause a great deal of
curiosity."

Deposing Mr. and Mrs. H. P. Craven (who had been
attracting fair audiences, principally in dramas from the actor's
own pen), Brooke, on returning to Melbourne, reappeared at the
Theatre Royal on Easter Monday, April 13, in his old characters
in *La Vendetta; or, The Corsican Brothers*. It is noteworthy that
the engagement was announced as "prior to his farewell—for
one month." This statement was evidently made in good faith,
but the nauseous iteration of these leavetakings in process of

time disgusted the public and went towards depriving the tragedian of much of his hard-earned popularity. On the 21st and 22nd of the month, Brooke played Othello to the Iago of Mr. Buchanan Read, who had been tendered these two nights as complimentary benefits prior to his return to England. So far, however, from following suit, our hero remained at the Theatre Royal until December 24, and during his lengthened sojourn was seen in many important productions. After adding still another grateful character to his Hibernian repertory—Gerald Pepper, in *The White Horse of the Peppers*—he aroused a good deal of attention by appearing on Monday, July 6, as Prospero in a tasteful production of *The Tempest*. In treating of the first performance of Shakespeare's comedy in Victoria, *The Argus* says: "Well does the grave and finished style of Mr. Brooke's acting illustrate the conception of the poet. His opening narrative to Miranda at once gave the tone to the audience, which listened in hushed attention as if loth to break the spell of the poetry. Indeed, we observed several times throughout the evening, that the applause was subdued by the same powerful spell—it was the genius of Shakespeare exciting its mighty fascination."

Not the least memorable of the many important productions of the season was that of *Henry VIII.*, on August 31, in which Brooke appeared as Cardinal Wolsey to Miss Goddard's Queen Catharine, Heir's Cromwell, and Richard Younge's Buckingham. In the course of a long notice testifying incidentally to the splendour of the mounting and the general all-round excellence of the players, *The Argus* says:—"Mr. Brooke's Cardinal Wolsey we must rank, in point of excellence, with—though perfectly distinct from—his Cardinal Richelieu. His elocution and acting in the second scene of the third act were literally magnificent, and called forth repeated and rapturous applause, followed by his recall before the curtain at its fall. All the complex emotions by which the Cardinal's mind is actuated in the hour of his fall—his amazement at the discovery he has made with reference to the misdirected documents—his grand scorn of the malice of

his enemies, his withering contempt, which finds expression in
the words:—

> 'How much, methinks, I could despise this man
> But that I'm bound in charity against it!'

And in the ironical observation—

> . . . . . 'If I blush
> It is to see a nobleman want manners.'

The exquisite pathos of his lamentation of his fallen greatness
– the anguish with which he exclaims, when told of the King's
marriage to Anne Boleyn—

> 'There was the weight that pulled me down! O Cromwell,
> Had I but served my God,' etc.,

were exhibited with consummate skill, and combined to produce
one of the most finished displays of histrionic ability which even
Mr. Brooke has favoured us with since his residence in the
colony. To listen to his delivery of the beautiful but hackneyed
passage—

> 'Farewell! a long farewell to all my greatness!'

Would alone repay anyone for a visit to the theatre, and it was
gratifying to observe how great and general was the enjoyment
of the actor's masterly elocution."

Meanwhile Coppin had left for England with the hope of
inducing other stars to visit the Colonies, and the entire control
of the Royal had devolved upon Brooke, who exerted himself
strenuously to maintain the prosperity of the establishment.
Hence novelty after novelty followed in quick succession. In
reviewing the production of Lalor Sheil's tragic play, *Evadne:
or, the Hall of Statues*, on September 7, the *Argus* says:—
" Mr. Brooke's Colonna was in all respects a satisfactory
impersonation. The loyalty which has come by inheritance,
almost a passion, the daring courage which leads him to
impeach the powerful favourite before the whole Court, the
deep and proud affection for his sister, the agonising revulsion of

wounded honour on discovering that the monarch for whom he would have shed his blood is the would-be betrayer of that sister's innocence, the feeling of lofty revenge which will not endure that any hand but his own shall slay the tyrant, the refusal to become his assassin, and again the resolve to be so, lest his sister should survive him only to encounter disgrace— all these were depicted with unfailing truth and vigour. Mr. Brooke's delineations are always portraits boldly drawn and highly finished, and his Colonna is by no means one of the least successful of them." Equally fine in its way was the Evadne of Mrs. Heir. Although the production was received with acclamation by a crowded house, Sheil's old play proved too stagey and artificial to take a permanent place in Brooke's repertory. On the 21st following, the Adelphi drama of *The Marble Heart* was brought out with Mrs. Heir as a satisfactory exponent of Mademoiselle Marco, the callous woman of the world, to whom the acquirement of wealth is the sole purpose of existence and in pursuit of which she stubbornly resists all the promptings of her better nature. In the eyes of the Melbourne critics, however, Brooke's Raphael Duchalet, retained all the ineradicable defects which marked his Romeo and Claude Melnotte. While it was properly agreed on all hands that the actor's physique was too mature to enable him to do full justice to the youthful vehemence of the sculptor's passion, it was just as freely conceded that the personation was, on the whole, a vigorous and spirited display of histrionic skill. As a matter of fact, *The Argus* records that "the earnestness of feeling which he infused into his acting, and the vividness with which he depicted the conflicting emotions by which the unfortunate sculptor is supposed to be actuated, so strongly enlisted the sympathies of the spectators that an emphatic 'hear, hear,' and 'that's true!' broke forth occasionally from the pit and gallery after the delivery of a moral sentiment or the utterance of some strong argument in favour of natural affection as opposed to avarice and worldliness." Seven nights afterwards

Brooke gave a racy delineation of Connor O'Gorman in a new Irish play, called *The Groves of Blarney*, bringing down the house in the first act by his vivid relation of the incidents and accidents of a steeplechase. Meanwhile elaborate preparations were being made for the production of Lord Byron's tragedy *Sardanapalus* on a scale of magnificence unprecedented in the Colonies. In view of the extra attention bestowed upon the accessories, most of the company apparently approached their work with unwonted carelessness, the result being that when the piece was presented on Monday, October 19, the *ensemble* proved weak and the performance tediously long. However, as the critics did not spare the rod, considerable improvement was soon effected; but the fact that the tragedy had a run of fifteen successive nights must be attributed purely to its merits as a spectacle. Beyond the Myrrha of Mrs. Heir hardly a single character was adequately sustained. Reviewing the production for the second time, on the 26th, the *Argus* says:—" Mr. Brooke's we regard as an entirely erroneous conception of the character of that Imperial Voluptuary and careless trifler who perished with his dynasty. There is more of the melancholy and solemn north than of the brilliant and glowing south in Mr. Brooke's Sardanapalus. Such a sad, slow, sombre reveller was not the man to crown himself with flowers, to bask in the smiles of the beautiful Ionian, and to utter such fervent praises of the juice of the grape. Mr. R. Younge's Salamenes is still more ponderous, and from such a preaching, prosy brother-in-law it was very natural that the King should take refuge in suicide. The best portions of the play are those in which Mr. Brooke relates the dream and in which his dormant courage awakens into fiery life." The production was probably based to some extent on Charles Kean's celebrated revival of Byron's tragedy at the Princess's Theatre in June, 1853. This Brooke may have seen immediately on his return from America, but even in that case, and admitting his propensity for reproducing Kean's successes in the Colonies, his repugnance to the excessive display of scenic archæology, in which the other delighted, must have forbade any servile copying of the English production.

Beyond Brooke's first appearance as M'Shane, in *The Nervous Man*, on November 7, for Mdlle. Miska Hauser's benefit, nothing occurred of more than passing importance after the run of *Sardanapalus* until his last appearance on Christmas Eve. Resting on his oars, our hero elected to appear during the latter part of his sojourn in a round of old characters which, to the motley Melbourne public of the time, proved quite as attractive as the more pretentious productions of the season. Writing home from "Cremorne Gardens, Richmond," on November 16, we find him saying of Coppin—"I expect him out by the next (December) mail. He has been making very extensive arrangements for our next campaign, and in a short time after his return we shall start for England. Since he left I have had my hands full in conducting our joint properties—the Theatre Royal, the Olympic Theatre, and Cremorne Gardens, . . . and the latter I am very busily engaged with, as we open for the summer on Monday next, November 23rd. I like this place amazingly, but, come what will, we must have a fireside muster (God willing)."

Repairing to Ballarat with the opening of the new year, Brooke laid the foundation stone of a new theatre on January 20, 1858, and apparently remained there in the exercise of his profession for some little time. Towards the end of February he was rather surprised to learn that, much to the consternation of his friends, an extraordinary telegram had appeared in the *Melbourne Evening Mail* giving a detailed account of his supposed illness, and concluding with the intimation of his death. To this he made the best of all denials by returning to to the Theatre Royal on March 1, to give six farewell performances in his old Shakespearian characters, and was naturally accorded a tremendous reception on effecting his reappearance. In announcing *Richard III.* for Saturday night the newspaper advertisement ran—"Positively *the last* of the greatest tragedian in the world, fully confident that it will be many years, if ever, the colonists have a similar opportunity of witnessing the works of Shakespeare illustrated by so celebrated an artist." In spite of this statement, Brooke appeared throughout the following week in a round of exclusively Irish characters, and remained at the theatre until the 23rd of the month, when he took his " Farewell Benefit," and made his " last appearance in Melbourne " as Matthew Elmore. Placing implicit reliance in the good faith of the managerial announcement the local public crammed the theatre to suffocation, recalling the tragedian, with immense enthusiasm, several times during the evening, and listening with every token of sympathetic affection to the touching speech in which he said " Good-bye." Poor Brooke ! He little knew it was only *au revoir* after all, and that many darker days and drearier were to pass ere that sad little word should be said in reality.

In the course of a " joint-stock" letter sent by the tragedian to his mother and sisters on June 9 from " Hobarton, Tasmania," we find him writing :—

" I have no doubt that you have wondered at not having heard from me long before this, but Mr. Coppin's visit to England and his protracted return, caused by the irregularity of the mails (he having been delayed in Egypt six weeks) placed me in the position of an Atlas, having had the Theatre Royal, Argyle Rooms, and Cremorne Gardens to look after in Melbourne, and the Theatre Royal, Geelong. So that, independent of my professional duties, I have had, thank God, a good share of wholesome mental and physical labour. But now since his return I have yielded up the managerial reins, and am, as you may perceive, pursuing my professional avocations and taking my farewell tour. . . . . The Governor patronised me a few weeks ago at Launceston, laughing at Felix O'Callaghan till his sides were sore, and I have this morning received a note from him requesting me to play Sir Giles Over-reach on Wednesday next From this place I shall go to Sydney for a short time, from thence to Adelaide in South Australia, and then sail from Melbourne for England, ho !

"I am sorry to say that poor Coppin has since his return lost a dear little girl, the most delightful and interesting child I ever saw or knew, and the admiration and wonder of all that looked on her. It was a sad blow to us all, but more particularly to him, poor fellow. I felt it sorely, too, for during his absence I supplied the place of a father to her, and she was attached to me as much as a child could possibly be. So much so that on George's return she would not leave me to go to her father for a week or so. She was only twenty-two months old.

"It is probable you may not recognise me when you see me, as I have grown a tremendously *big fellow*. Polly is also getting stout and preparing herself for *Fat* and *Forty* which, with the addition of *Fair*, I was on the 25 of April last."

Supported by Mr. Henry Edwards and Mrs. Poole, Brooke opened his Sydney engagement at the Prince of Wales's Theatre "under the management of Mr. Charles Poole, of the Theatre Royal, Melbourne," on July 19, as Othello. With the exception of a couple of nights towards the end of the season (when a physician's certificate was published testifying that the tragedian was incapacitated by a severe attack of influenza) he performed there continuously until October 21, on which occasion he took his benefit, playing Edgar Mordaunt in *The Patrician's Daughter,* and Paddy O'Rafferty in the farce *Born to Good Luck.* It was a night of unbounded enthusiasm and good fellowship. A great treat had been anticipated; eager crowds of playgoers jostled round the doors for hours before the advertised hour of performance; and for once in a way the mountain brought forth something more formidable than a mouse. In a brief speech, made during the evening, Brooke regretted that the state of his health demanded immediate rest, but assured them, amid hearty cheers, that a few weeks would see him back again in their midst. Although his appearances during the season had been for the most part in his old repertory, a few new characters were occasionally presented. Of these the most noteworthy were Zanga in *The Revenge,* Paddy O'Donovan in the one-act comic drama *Paddy the Piper*, and Major O'Dogherty in Tyrone Power's drama *St. Patrick's Eve: or, The Order of the Day*.

On November 12, Brooke reappeared as Captain Murphy Maguire, for one night only, at the Melbourne Theatre Royal in graceful acquiescence (if playhouse advertisements are to be relied upon) to a requisition signed by a number of local gentlemen immediately on learning that the tragedian purposed paying a flying visit to the metropolis. This announcement was soon capped by another, setting forth that owing to the *Wonga-Wonga* having been despatched with mails to New Zealand, thus upsetting the arrangements made for Brooke's departure, he would continue to appear until the end of the week. Giving his last performance on Saturday the 20th, as Tim Moor in *The Irish Lion*—a piece new to Melbourne—he was to have sailed for England on the following Monday. But despite his seeming anxiety for "a fireside muster" in Dublin he still procrastinated, and by December 1 had made his reappearance at the Prince of Wales's Theatre, Sydney. Wisely abstaining from performing there more than four nights a week, he brought his engagement to a close on the 22nd, and returned shortly afterwards to Melbourne.

Paramount among the things which contributed to detain Brooke in the Colonies at this period was the difficulty experienced in arriving at a definite settlement with his partner in regard to the disposal of their joint properties, a moiety of which had absorbed all the profits derived from the remainder. Confronted suddenly with the appalling fact that the bulk of his hard-earned money had been swallowed up in these hare-brained enterprises, is it to be wondered at that the hapless tragedian returned like a dog to his vomit, and became from this time forward practically a lost man.

On January 26, 1859—or two days after Coppin had set Melbourne all agog by advertising for tenders for the purchase or lease of the Theatre Royal, Olympic Theatre, and Cremorne Gardens—Brooke reappeared at the first-mentioned house as Othello, supported by Mr. and Mrs. Robert Heir, Mrs. Mortyn,

and the regular stock company. He played there uninterruptedly
in *King Lear*, *The Tempest*, and other old pieces until Monday,
February 21, when *The Argus* announced that in consequence of
his indisposition the part of Richard III. would be taken by
Mr. R. Younge. On the Saturday following the rumoured
dissolution of partnership, which had formed the chief topic
of public conversation for some weeks previous, became an
accomplished fact. To mark the occasion Coppin gave a
farewell address, and Brooke appeared as Duke Aranza in *The
Honeymoon.*

Assuming entire and undisputed control of the Theatre Royal,
our hero at once installed Mr. R. Younge in the position of
managing director, and inaugurated his reign on Monday, February
28, by introducing Hudson, the celebrated Irish comedian, to
the notice of the Melbourne public. As usual with Brooke,
however, one difficulty was no sooner surmounted than another
cropped up. Taking advantage of his absence on a starring tour
in the provinces, certain persons holding responsible positions
under his command had contrived a nice little plot to rob him
of the profits of the theatre. But a flood of light was let in
upon their movements shortly before the termination of the
season, on May 30, by the timely arrival of an anonymous letter,
which is still preserved, strange to say, among the family papers.
Opening the new season on Thursday, June 2, with Mr. R. Heir
as acting-manager, Brooke, previous to the singing of the
National Anthem by the entire company, made a long and manly
speech, in which he alluded to "the gloomy subject" of his
quarrels, and dwelt with eloquence on "the wearisome history
of injuries received by me at the hands of persons who, during
my unavoidable absence from Melbourne, abused a trust unhesitatingly reposed in them, and bartered the interests of their
employer for prospective and shadowy gain." In concluding,
he spoke with emphasis of the drastic changes he hoped to
effect in the management of the theatre, and trusted before
long to "entomb the melancholy past." Four nights afterwards he played Valentine to the Proteus of Robert Heir in

The Two Gentlemen of Verona: his first appearance in the part, and the first performance of Shakespeare's comedy in the Colonies.

Writing home to Dublin in a "joint-stock" letter on June 16, Brooke says, " I am afraid that you have been very uneasy about us of late, but I have had a great deal to do and a very difficult game to play. Coppin did not behave well to us ; but, thank Heaven, I have got the best of it, and have taken possession of my property. the Theatre Royal and Royal Hotel, valued at £30,000. I have got the Public with me, and shall, I trust, do very well. We are both of us, thank God, in health, and I shall, I think, make my arrangements to leave for home by the March mail."

On Monday the 27th an elaborate production was effected of the great Egyptian spectacular drama, *Azael the Prodigal*, in which Brooke as Reuben, chief of the Israelite tribe, " fulfilled," according to the *Argus*, " the conditions of such a character accurately and poetically." Efficient support was rendered by Mr. and Mrs. Heir as Azael and Jephthéle respectively. Founded on MM. Scribe and Auber's *L'Enfant Prodigue*, this piece had originally seen the light at Drury Lane on February 19, 1851, Messrs. Vandenhoff and Anderson and Miss Fanny Vining representing the above-mentioned characters in the order named.

Azael was withdrawn, after proving a somewhat qualified success, on July 6. Six nights afterwards Brooke sustained the part of Colonel Buckethorne in Boucicault's comedy, *Love in a Maze*, which aroused little or no critical attention, although a production entirely new to the Colonies. Acting continuously at the Royal until August 19, the tragedian on the 15th of the previous month appeared as the Ghost to Heir's Hamlet. giving on the 25th his first performance of Coriolanus, which proved so acceptable that the play ran eight nights. Some idea of the spell of ill-luck which had attended Brooke ever since he assumed entire control of the Theatre Royal may be formed from the following interesting letter :—

MELBOURNE, *August 26th, 1859.*

MY DEAR HEIR,

      I have up to this date lost by the Theatre Royal, since our opening of the present season, one thousand three hundred pounds, independent of my own time and services, and consider necessary to retrench in every department, in order to regain my losses. I wish you, therefore, to put your shoulder to the wheel, and see that no time shall be lost in making such alteration in the working of the Theatre as may be deemed necessary. In the first place, the carpenters must be lessened, not only in numbers but in amount of salary. In the next place, you do not require more than two male supers on the establishment, and we have ladies enough in the English engagement bound to make themselves useful. Thirdly, I think it necessary to take time by the forelock, and when a piece has a run for two or three or more nights let it not interfere with daily rehearsal, as there should be always two or three in case of any emergency. I think it absolutely indispensable to play strong dramas on both Monday and Saturday, and good Comedy in the centre of the week, and the other nights some kind of a light Comedy, backed up by broad farce. There is one thing that is a great point— that is, that the orchestra should be rung in [to] commence ten minutes before, or more, according to the length of the overture or musical selection, so that the curtain may go up precisely at the half hour; and the delay should not be more than ten minutes between the acts, except in cases of emergency. By this means the audience are not wearied, and there is a great saving in the Gas, the management of which should be well attended to by turning it off *behind* when the curtain is down, and before when it is up, and not consuming light in the back borders when not required. And now I want you to look through the present company, with the exception of Lambert and Harwood, and see who can be *dispensed* with, or who retained, upon [a slight] reduction of salaries. The stage clearers must in all cases (except modern pieces) go on as supers when required, and I expect that everybody in the Theatre as servants as well may by their services show that they have an interest in the establishment to which they belong.

      As I shall not have much time to spare, I wish you would think well over this matter and put your views regarding it on paper. There is one thing of great importance—that [is] the printing and, above all, the *posting*, which has of late been shamefully attended to. And I think the services of such a man as Mr. Younghusband no longer necessary. I would wish all bills of tradesmen and extras for the theatre should be in on Saturday for your inspection, to be paid if approved of on the Tuesday following; and by this means there can be no confusion. I would not allow one connected with the Theatre Royal to obtain anything from any tradesman without an express order from the manager, as of late things have been ordered regardless of expense. Timmins must pay 6 pounds for the privileges he has in the front of the house, or give them up. There is another thing to insist upon—fines being strictly exacted in cases of people being imperfect, sufficient time having been allowed according to length or importance of part, or any other breach of the rules and regulations of the Theatre.

I daresay there are some other things I could suggest, but cannot at present do; but shall from time to time do so by letter. But let me impress upon you—enforce economy and punctuality. Excuse the manner in which this is written. I pen it as it occurs to my mind. Think over it well, like a good fellow, weigh the importance of it, and act upon it as forcibly and nearly as you can.

> Yours, dear Heir,
>> Very truly,
>>> G. V. BROOKE.*

Hoping against hope, he strove manfully to keep the bad news from the loved ones in Ireland, and never dreamt of making his heavy losses an excuse for omitting to forward the usual handsome allowance to his mother. Looking forward with deeper and deeper longing to that "fireside muster" in the old country, and yet finding himself utterly incapable of saying good-bye to his loyal-hearted friends in the new, we find him penning a brief note, in a very shaky hand, on August 17, enclosing the customary bill of exchange and stating that he may be expected home in the *Nubia*, sailing from Melbourne on October 17 With the opening of that month, however, we find him acting again at the Royal, and seemingly entertaining no idea of an immediate return to England. On the 8th he played Rob Roy to the Bailie Nicol Jarvie of Mungall, the Scotch comedian, and for many nights afterwards was to be seen—when not interfered with by the operatic performances—in a round of his favourite characters. Beyond the production of the Rev. James White's historical play, *Feudal Times* on Wednesday the 26th (before the Governor of the Colony and a brilliant assemblage), nothing occurred at this period worthy of particular mention. Renewing his acquaintance with his old part of Walter Cochrane, as first sustained in the Manchester stock days, Brooke thrilled the vast audience by the impressiveness and power of his acting. The King of Mr. Henry Edwards and the Angus and Margaret Randolph of Mr. and Mrs. Heir were all equally admirable in

---

* Transcribed from a double sheet of commercial foolscap bearing endorsement " G. V. B. to Mr. Heir abt. Management of Theatre, 9,59," found among a mass of correspondence kindly furnished by Mrs. Heatly, the tragedian's sister. Unmistakably holographic, the document evidently forms the rough draft of the letter ultimately forwarded.

their way and contributed materially to the success of the performance.

We have now arrived at the period when an event took place in Melbourne having important bearing on the brief span of existence remaining to our hero. This was the Australian *début* at the Princess's Theatre, Spring Gardens, on Monday, October 31, of Miss Avonia Jones as Medea. Born at Richmond, Virginia, on July 12, 1839,* this promising young actress was the daughter of George Jones, the American tragedian, who, after having tasted the sweets of success at the Bowery Theatre New York, during the 'thirties, elected to figure in his later days as the eccentric Count Johannes, and in that odd capacity was amusingly caricatured by Sothern in *The Crushed Tragedian.* Possessing much force of character, Jones, on a certain anniversary of Shakespeare's birthday, is reputed to have delivered a remarkable oration at Stratford - on - Avon, and to this circumstance his daughter is said to have owed her melodious baptismal name. His wife, Mrs. Melinda Jones, who accompanied Avonia, as we shall see, on her travels, had also enjoyed great popularity on the stage in her time.

With the termination of his sojourn at the Royal, Brooke, according to a paragraph in the *Melbourne Leader,* appears to have journeyed to Bendigo to give there (on Monday, November 7) "his farewell performance before his departure for England." On the 19th following, Avonia Jones concluded her engagement at the Princess's Theatre with performances of Medea and Katharine; the latter to the Petruchio of Mr. Henry Edwards. On December 6 a complimentary benefit was tendered to Brooke at the Theatre Royal on the occasion of his resigning the reins of management into the hands of Harry Edwards and George Fawcett [Rowe]. *The Serious Family* was in the bill, Captain Murphy Maguire having his usual

* As her natal year has sometimes been given as 1836, it may be as well to point out that the actress, in a speech on her benefit night (November 19), gave the exact date as here recorded, mentioning as her authority the baptismal entry in the registers of Trinity Church, Richmond, Va.

representative. Deposing the popular comedian Harry Jackson,[*] who, after the secession of Avonia Jones, had been starring at the Spring Street house, Brooke entered upon a twelve nights' engagement at the Princess's Theatre on the 26th, and, efficiently supported by Miss Herbert, appeared in a round of well-worn characters. An old Colonial, at present residing in Newcastle-upon-Tyne, recalls to mind a fearfully hot night during this engagement when *Macbeth* was in the bill, and the pit so full that someone called out, "Rush the boxes, boys," and saw his suggestion at once put into practice. The incursion appears to have been easy of accomplishment, as by standing on the back bench the pittite could vault over into the boxes without any trouble. Much confusion ensued, bringing the play to a temporary standstill; but in a free-and-easy community such episodes were of too frequent occurrence to create any save the most transient excitement.

By way of illustrating that fine trait of large-heartedness which made Brooke so popular among his fellow-actors, Mr. W. G. Carey, a well known Australian tragedian, has put on record a slight personal experience, which evidently belongs to this period. Only a boy at the time, and the veriest tyro at that, he was cast as Lennox to the Macbeth of Brooke; and his juxtaposition with the star intensified the nervousness already evoked by an impression of the relative importance of the character. Actors can appreciate the difficulties presented by that particularly cranky speech commencing "The night has been unruly." In a condition of "funk" bordering on collapse, the novice essayed to speak his lines, with the great actor standing majestically by his side—proceeded gingerly as far as "dire combustion," and there stuck, thinking it was "dire combustion" indeed. At once a gentle whisper reached him from Macbeth, "Don't be afraid, my boy; it's all right. Go on! 'And confused events'—" Taking the word, the heart-touching kindness of Brooke dispelled his nervousness, and

* Identified in later days as a prominent member of the Drury Lane company, under the Harris *regime*.

enabled him to finish his part without a tremor. With the conclusion of the act, he lost no time in thanking the tragedian, indulging in a gush of warm but respectful gratitude, such as only a novice could feel and give expression to. " You were nervous, my boy," replied Brooke, making light of the service rendered ; " never mind that. Take this as consolation. I never knew an actor worth his salt who ever entirely conquered the feeling."

Shortly after the conclusion of Brooke's engagement at the Princess's, he reappeared there for one night only (on January 14, 1860) as Iago, to the Othello and Desdemona of Mr. and Mrs. Clarence Holt, and then proceeded on a barn-storming expedition in the country. Ominous paragraphs now began to crop up in the papers, showing only too plainly that the distress of mind occasioned by repeated misfortune had driven him back on his old habits of dissipation. Says the *Melbourne Leader* of February 4 :—" Mr G. V. Brooke has been getting into disgrace again in the country. *The Mount Alexander Mail* says neither public nor managers will much longer tolerate his eccentricities." Single performances followed at Lamplough and Beechworth ; and on the 25th *The Leader* had another paragraph setting forth that "Mr. G. V. Brooke has now disappointed the Chiltern people, who expected to have had him on the boards of their theatre on Monday. Mr. Brooke seems to be very unfortunate in regard to his provincial engagements." But the annoyance experienced by country playgoers through the vagaries of the star were as nothing to the discomforts undergone by the little band of players who accompanied him on his travels through the minor towns of Victoria. Mr. W. G. Carey relates that when Lambert, Mr. and Mrs. Younge, Avonia Jones, the tragedian, and himself arrived at a place called Tarrangower in the old days, they discovered that, in all likelihood, they should have to dispense with the services of the orchestra. Certainly there was a pianoforte — but who was to play it ? Then someone found out that the village blacksmith was the proud possessor of a violin, but lacked the

necessary skill to make it "discourse most eloquent music."
This extorted the confession from Avonia Jones that she
could play the piano a little, and, at all events, could "vamp"
satisfactorily, if someone could only be procured to play the
fiddle. Not to be behindhand, young Carey volunteered to rub
"the hair of the horse over the bowels of the cat," and the
pair constituted themselves the orchestra. The play was *The
Lady of Lyons*, with Avonia Jones as Pauline, and the tyro as
Gaspar. Having to go on the stage with the opening of the
first scene, the actress enveloped herself in a cloak before taking
her seat at the piano. But Carey had plenty of time to change,
and so appeared in *propriâ personâ* with the local Vulcan's fiddle
under his arm. "They were not musically fastidious," writes
our informant, "or I think that, besides playing the audience in,
we should have played them out again. Without bothering
about the overture to *Zampa*, or any trifles of that sort, we
gave them selections from popular airs between the acts, until we
came to the fourth, when a difficulty presented itself. Pauline
could not be expected to usurp the prerogative of Sir Boyle
Roche's bird, and be on the stage and at the piano at the same
time. But as no properly-constituted Claude Melnotte would
think of attempting to pile on the agony without the soul-
stirring strains of the Marseillaise, the predicament was an
awkward one." There was nothing for it but that Carey and
the fiddle should represent the entire orchestra behind the scenes,
and play the air as best he could. There were other ludicrous
incidents, arising for the most part out of the diminutive size
of the stage, which would have ruffled the equanimity of
most "eminent" tragedians. But no one in the company enjoyed
the humour of the whole affair better than poor Brooke, who
used to relate with great unction how his cocked hat and
feathers bade fair to effect a serious disarrangement of the sky-
borders when the battle-scarred Claude strode forth on the
boards.

Reappearing at the Theatre Royal, Melbourne, on April 9,
for the Easter holidays, Brooke played Biron in the first

colonial production of *Love's Labour Lost*, giving a personation
which, according to *The Argus*, "had fine touches in it here
and there — in the occasional gusts of humour and in the
soliloquy on Love, for instance; but he was evidently struggling
with many difficulties." Although the *ensemble* was bad—the
Costard of Harry Jackson being as pronounced in its merits as
the Armado of George Fawcett was defective—the comedy held
its place in the bills until the 14th. Followed by representations of trite pieces, *Love's Labour Lost* was revived for
one night on the 20th; and on the 24th Brooke appeared for
the first time in his powerful impersonation of Louis XI. in
Boucicault's well-known drama. In the course of an enthusiastic
notice of the production *The Argus* says:—" The portrait of the
subtle tyrant of Plessis, the master of Triston L'Hermite
and Oliver le Daim, whose character is so well known to
every reader of *Quentin Durward*, is literally drawn to the
life by Mr. Brooke, who by this impersonation has given
to the public a dramatic creation which will rank with
his Sir Giles Over-reach, his Richelieu, or even with his
Othello. Every lover of high dramatic art, everyone who lays
claim to taste or judgment in such matters, will accord deserved
praise to the artist who alone in these Colonies, and possibly on
the European stage, could produce so masterly a picture. From
first to last the living (and yet dying) Louis is before the eyes
of the audience. The make-up is perfection, and the face of
the artist wears that grim and fearful expression—a mixture of
terror, suffering, and cruelty—which, we may imagine, belonged
to the real monarch. At the end of the third act Mr. Brooke
was loudly called for and vociferously applauded." It is
interesting to note that Harry Edwards, who was the Nemours
of the production, retained vivid recollections of the tragedian's
impressiveness in this trying character up to the period of his
recent death in America. Other parts were efficiently sustained
by Harwood, Harry Jackson, Julia Matthews, and Mrs. Charles
Poole. In a word, the piece proved an unqualified success, and,
with the exception of a benefit night, held its place in the bills

until May 8. If not "the most magnificent creation ever represented" (to quote from the Melbourne advertisements), Brooke's Louis XI. was certainly the most finished of his latter-day personations; and it affords matter for regret that he was seldom, if ever, seen in the character after his departure from the Colonies.

Succeeding John Drew, the American comedian, who had been starring at the Royal in the interim, Brooke re-opened there on June 5, in his grim exposition of the idiosyncrasies of the old French monarch: and on the 9th played Iago, "for that night only," to the Othello of Clarence Holt.

A couple of days afterwards he received a copy of the following lines from an anonymous admirer:—

ON SEEING MR. G. V. BROOKE AS IAGO.

WHEN the great Poet-king the world looked through,
To find the fathom of the brain;—to guage
The inmost depths of mind in youth or age,
Ripe manhood or fair woman,—he ne'er knew,
Nor e'en could dream of a perception true,
True as his own, of the deep craft of man
Shewn in Iago! could his spirit scan
This after-time of energy and thought
'Twould light on *Brooke*, as one his truth had caught.

The subtle tempting, the observant look,
The plausible hypocrisy, the pride
Of jealous temper, the delusive guide
To wrong and cruelty, all found in Brooke
A real image. Iago never shook
From his fell purpose; never did let fall
One word of pity, but contempt for all
The means of his revenge; nor Brooke did he
Let fall one atom of consistency.

Occasionally during the season the theatre advertisements would blossom forth with "Positively Mr. Brooke's last appearance," but playgoers, so far from being "frighted with false fire," had grown quite accustomed to these mendacious declarations, and viewed them with an apathy born of bitter experience. On Saturday, June 16, *The Slave* was revived and performed, with Brooke as Gambia, until the 21st, when he appeared for the first time as Sir Bernard Harleigh in

Palgrave Simpson's drama, *Dreams of Delusion*, the occasion
being Harry Edwards' benefit. Speaking of the extraordinary
hit made by our hero in his new character, the *Argus* says:—
" The *rôle* is, in brief, that of a talented and excellent man,
who, married to a wife his junior, but in every way worthy of
him, is a prey to a baseless jealousy, of cause for which he
believes he has such clear proof that he attacks and, as he
imagines, murders the man who has wronged him. His
subsequent life is a remorse so keen that it ultimately disorders
his fine intellect, and he falls into the sad calamity of imagining
that his wife herself is mad. From this mania he is rescued
by the skill of a physician and restored to happiness. The man
whom he believes he has murdered, of course, lives, and a
powerful dramatic situation is secured by the recognition of the
two. It would be difficult to speak too highly of Mr. Brooke's
delineation of character. The make-up, the by-play, the whole
action are startlingly accurate, and more than once last night a
thrill of suppressed emotion passed through the house, so
terrible, so lifelike was it. Repeated rounds of applause testified
the appreciation of the audience. The piece is in one act only,
and it is probable that everyone in Melbourne who can will see
it, so that no more need be said." It enjoyed no sort of run,
however, and was only repeated once or twice during the season.
Next evening Brooke played Sir Lucius to the Bob Acres of
John Drew (who was about to depart from the Colonies), and
appeared for some little time subsequently in a pleasing variety
of his old characters. On Monday, August 6—last night but
four of the season—a decided novelty was afforded in the first
production in Australia of *The Comedy of Errors*, powerfully cast,
with Brooke and Harry Edwards as the two Antipholi, and
Sefton and Harry Jackson as the Dromios. In the course
of a long and very appreciative notice of the play the *Argus*
says:—" Mr. Brooke was throughout 'i' the vein'—gentle,
proud, loving, and honourable, as Antipholus of Syracuse
should be. His finished acting would have at once decided
the success of the evening, even if other elements had been

wanting." Cheers greeted the announcement by Mr. Edwards
at the close of the performance that the piece would be
repeated on the three remaining nights of the season.

After Brooke and the principal members of his company
had paid an enjoyable visit to Adelaide, they returned to
Melbourne and reopened the Theatre Royal on Thursday,
October 11, taking up the interrupted run of *The Comedy of
Errors*, which was received with all the old marks of approval
by a large and brilliant assembly. "It speaks volumes for our
colonial stage," remarked *The Argus* two days after, "that this
comedy should have been placed upon the boards so effectively.
Had the piece demanded any very high flight we could not
have looked for an Antipholus of Ephesus from Mr. Edwards,
at all like his brother of Syracuse by Mr. Brooke. The
brothers are like enough for all the purposes of the play.
Much the same remark applies to their body servants; Mr.
H. Jackson's Dromio of Syracuse being certainly superior to
Mr. Wright's Ephesian Dromio." The Luciana of the production
was Miss Dolores Drummond, who only a short time previously
had made her first appearance on the stage under Brooke's
management. "He was very kind and good to me," this
lady writes to us, "giving me much valuable instruction and
advice. I played during his last season, which was unfortunately
a loss to him, and have still in my possession an I.O.U. for a
few pounds salary owing to me, signed with his name. He
was a generous man and a kind friend." With the temporary
shelving of Shakespeare's comedy towards the middle of the
following week, Brooke appeared as Iago to the Moor of
Mr. McKean Buchanan, the American tragedian, who had
just landed with the intention of paralysing the Colonies.
Unfortunately the critics, after lavishing all their praise on the
old and tried favourite, proceeded to rail at the newcomer "in
good round set terms," among which the epithet "ranter" took a
painfully conspicuous position. Relations between the rival
tragedians at once became strained, with the result that on the
last two nights of the week Buchanan remained in undisputed

possession of the theatre, giving two very feeble exhibitions as Virginius and Macbeth. The whole affair had its deplorable aspects, although few who saw this mouthing actor in England will be disposed to deny that judgment was passed otherwise than on the merits.

On Monday, October 22, a new play, called *The Master Passion*, was produced, and, although fairly constructed, proved so tedious that only the sound work of its exponents saved it from immediate and utter failure. According to *The Leader*, "Mr. Brooke's Orseolo was excellent throughout, and eminently so in the last scene, in which the struggle between love and hate was forcibly portrayed. The actor not merely saved but made the play. With an ordinary artist the piece must have been damned." Mrs. C. Poole, who shared the honours of an enthusiastic recall with the tragedian, played splendidly as Morosina; and the performance was otherwise noteworthy as marking the first appearance in Melbourne of Miss Rosa Dunn, who gave a chaste and very pleasing interpretation of Camilla. Exactly a fortnight afterwards, *The Comedy of Errors* was again presented at the Royal, Brooke and Harry Edwards reversing their old parts by way of giving a fillip to the attractions of the play. This was followed on Saturday, November 10, by *Measure for Measure*, which was placed on the stage with every attention to detail. Voted a failure at the outset, owing to the weakness of the acting and the unredeemed gloominess of the theme, the tragedy was nevertheless retained in the bills throughout the following week with the vain hope of recouping expenses. While the critics had nothing but praise for Avonia Jones's Isabella—at all points an exceedingly powerful performance—they came down with a heavy hand on the invertebrate Angelo of Harry Edwards and the over-charged Lucio of George Fawcett. These gentlemen had, however, the consolation of being condemned in very good company. *The Leader*, after asserting that no one save Avonia Jones rose above mediocrity, while many fell considerably below it, adds, "Even Mr. Brooke, as the Duke, seemed to perform his part in a mechanical manner; and what applause he did receive was more out of respect than elicited by admiration." As a matter of fact, things were all at sixes and sevens in the theatre, and the public were soon to learn, in the most explicit manner, of the distress under which the management laboured. On Thursday, December 20, Brooke took a benefit to a crowded house, appearing, in conjunction with Coppin and Avonia Jones, in *The Honeymoon* and *The Serious Family.* After the *beneficiaire* had acknowledged a recall at the close of the performance, his quondam partner went on, and in the course of a long speech said :—" I sincerely regret that the pleasure I feel at this moment is so much counter-balanced by the distressing position of affairs under which I assume the reigns of management. When I brought Mr. Brooke out to this colony, I made a voluntary promise that I would not separate from him until he had obtained an independence. I kept my word, and last year he selected this theatre as his share of our joint property. In taking the management, he predicted many difficulties, but you will recollect that, from the spot on which I am now standing, he expressed his determination to promote the interests of the legitimate drama. I am sure everyone will acknowledge that he has carried out his promises to the fullest extent ; and there are very few persons but will regret the disastrous losses that have fallen upon himself. At that time I offered Mr. Brooke £2,000, clear of all liabilities, which were then about £8,000. How do I find him now ? Through deceit and misrepresentation, if not by something worse, he is deprived of his property for a sum of money so ridiculously below the real value that even a usurer ought to blush to look upon it. I find his plate, the presentations you so liberally made, and a portion of his wardrobe, pawned at a usurious rate of interest, which, having neglected to be paid, the things were consequently forfeited. In addition to which he is £4,000 in debt, making, in all, a loss of £32,000 since last year, besides all his earnings by engagements in Adelaide, Ballarat, and other places. How this has been accomplished remains to be explained. There are many persons who will no doubt say, ' what have we to do with this?

He should look after his own business better.' " The speaker
then went on to say that, at his old ally's earnest request,
he purposed assuming control of the theatre for six months,
and in conclusion expressed his satisfaction at the opening of a
new gasworks in the city, for the reason that " before the
house opened the collector of the Melbourne Gas Company
called here, and though this establishment has paid thousands
of pounds to that company, they threatened to cut off the gas
unless a sum of £15, the balance of the account, was paid."
The brutal frankness of Coppin, in holding a brief for his
brother, occasioned considerable excitement in the metropolis,
and evoked a wordy warfare in the papers, all " sound and
fury, signifying nothing.'

Taking advantage of a season of Pantomime which followed,
Brooke entered upon a short starring tour of the provincial
towns of Victoria, and reappeared at the Melbourne Theatre
Royal on February 8, 1861, before a crowded and enthusiastic
audience. The play was *Rob Roy*, in which the tragedian in the
name-part had the attractive support of Sir William and Lady Don
(then fulfilling a prosperous starring engagement in Melbourne)
as Bailie Nicol Jarvie and Diana Vernon. On Friday, March 15,
a complimentary benefit was tendered to Mr. J. Hall Wilton, on
which occasion Brooke, assisted by the principal actors in the
metropolis, appeared on behalf of his old agent in *The Serious
Family* and *Dreams of Delusion*. The *Argus* records that he
was received with prolonged cheering on first coming on
in the latter piece, in which his acting was, "as on a previous
occasion adverted to in these columns, distinguished for
extraordinary merit." Equally enthusiastic was the reception
accorded him on St. Patrick's Night, when he played Rory
O'More, " in honour to his patron saint," as the advertisement
has it, to the inexpressible delight of a large audience. On the
23rd following came the last performance and complimentary
benefit of Lady Don, when Brooke played Sir Lucius O'Trigger
to the Acres of Coppin and the Sir Anthony Absolute of the
veteran actor, Mr. H. Wallack, who then appeared for the first

time before a Colonial audience.   Recalled at the finish in
conjunction with our hero, Coppin indulged in a short speech,
in which he said that the engagement of the Dons had proved
the most lucrative of any under his management, excepting that
of his friend and ally, the lessee of the theatre.

Subsequently the Lyster Opera Company held possession of
the Royal until deposed, on Monday, April 22, by Brooke, who
then began a series of farewell performances, assisted by his former
colleagues, Mr. R. Younge and Mr. and Mrs. Heir.   Playing with all
his old power as Sir Giles Over-reach on the opening night, he met
with a very flattering reception, and was recalled after the second
and fourth acts, and again at the conclusion of the performance.
During the remainder of the week he appeared in well-worn
Shakespearian characters to gradually dwindling houses, but
experienced a renewal of his whilom popularity with the revival
of *Louis XI.*, "his greatest impersonation," on Monday and
Tuesday, April 29 and 30.   On Wednesday the performance,
according to the advertisements, was "under the patronage of
THE TRADESMEN, who are desirous of conveying to Mr. G.
V. Brooke their deep sympathy with his embarrassments and
appreciation of the honourable means in which he has overcome
his difficulties."   After appearing in *His Last Legs*, Brooke on this
occasion made a manly, straightforward speech, which was received
throughout with much applause.   "Ladies and gentlemen," he
said, "I attach a peculiar value to this compliment, not merely
because it is spontaneous, but because it emanates from those of
whose good opinion I have reason to be proud.   My commercial
as well as my professional character has received your approbation,
and I have to be proud of the result.   It is not my intention,
on the present occasion, to enter into a narrative of my career
in this colony.   Suffice it to say that, in the course of six
years, I have shared in its prosperity and in its adversity.   If
I have had to succumb to the latter, you will bear me
witness that I have never sought to evade the consequences
of my disasters.   I have striven to retrieve them, and, with
God's help, I have little fear of my success.   You have

generously seconded my efforts. You have imposed no hard terms, and exacted no rigorous conditions. You have met me in a frank and trusting spirit; and I hope to live to prove that whatever reputation I have made as an actor shall not be sullied by my conduct as a man. The conduct of an establishment of this magnitude, employing so many persons and entailing so heavy an outlay week by week, is necessarily attended with some risk. The receipts are diminished when the times are depressed, and, under the most prosperous condition of affairs, a theatre can only be successfully conducted by the exercise of consummate tact and the utmost vigilance. I have lost a fortune in it, but I trust that I have preserved my self-respect and my good name. I am strengthened in this belief by the assemblage which I now see before me, and although I have been so often on my 'Last Legs' there are numbers here who have volunteered to assist in setting me up again. Ladies and gentlemen, I thank you all most sincerely for this gratifying compliment, and wish you all a very good night.''

On Friday, May 3, when the performance was under the patronage of the Governor and Lady Barkly, Brooke played Othello and Terence O'Grady in *The Irish Post.* The theatre advertisement in *The Argus* of Saturday, after announcing *Richard III.* for that evening, presents the following item by way of demonstrating the utter genuineness of these farewell performances:—

PASSAGE RECEIPT.

Received from Mr. G. V. Brooke the sum of £60 sterling in full payment of his passage in the *Suffolk*, Captain J. B. Martin, hence to London, to sail 25th May.

W. P. WHITE & Co.

Placed side by side with Mr. Coleman's astonishing statement that Brooke, when he left, ''slunk aboard at dead of night like a thief and lay hidden behind the smoke-stack of the *London** till she quitted the harbour,'' this advertisement makes very interesting reading.

---

* Not launched until three years later.

The tragedian had now procrastinated to such an extent that the wits of the city began to liken him to Prior's thief, who, when on his way to Tyburn,

> "Adjusted his halter, and traversed the cart,
> Full often took leave, yet was loth to depart."

Precisely at this period the *Melbourne Punch* came out with a capital cartoon of Brooke and Coppin, accompanied by an imaginary conversation so scathing, and yet so real, that it fully merits reproduction here: -

"Scene—The Manager's Parlour.   Present—The Manager and the Great Tragedian.

"Manager: I say, Gus, don't you think it's time I had a benefit?

"Tragedian (gruffly): A what?

"Manager: A benefit, Gus.

"Tragedian: Well, I think you have a benefit every night. I do all the work, and you walk in and swallow up two-thirds of the profits.

"Manager (sleekly): But a complimentary benefit, you know—a nice little dodge to fill the house and put money in both our pockets.

"Tragedian: I tell you what it is, George, the public are beginning to tire of your dodges. You have advertised my farewell performances so often, that now I am really going, nobody believes it. I am only sorry that my easy disposition ever induced me to be influenced by your persuasive eloquence.

"Manager: It's the last time. It is really. I won't ask you any more. In fact, ever since I called Kyte a usurer he has resolved never to let me have the Theatre Royal again, and has let people know all he did for me at the time the Olympic was in progress. So the Royal and I must become strangers to each other for the time to come.

"Tragedian: Serve you right. Why didn't you keep a civil tongue in your head?

"Manager: And where were the rounds of applause to come from? But let us get back to the benefit.

"Tragedian: Ah! I don't think that cock will fight. Everybody is sneering at the passage tickets which you have put into circulation. The fact is, George, you are falling behind the age. The Melbourne public of 1861 are not a bit like the Melbourne public of three or four years back, and you don't seem to see the change. The dodges which were remunerative then won't pay now, and you oughtn't to ask me to mix myself in them. My position as an actor places me above them, and I despise them.

"Manager: Come, come! Don't be huffy. Don't turn round upon an old friend and a warm admirer in that way. Only this once, Gus, and I will never ask you again.

"Tragedian: But what do you want me to do? I'm willing to oblige you within reason; but——

"Manager: 'But me, no buts.' Look here! I have just sketched out the rough draft of two letters: one is from you to me, and the other is my reply.

"Tragedian (laughing): Well, upon my soul, George, you are the coolest hand at humbugging the public I ever came across. However, proceed.

"Manager reads:—

[FROM MR. G. V. BROOKE.]

THEATRE ROYAL, MELBOURNE,
6th May, 1861.

MY DEAR COPPIN,

Previous to the termination of my 'farewell performances' I am desirous of thanking you publicly for the interest you have taken in my welfare, and the satisfactory change you have lately made in my treasury. The most substantial recognition I can offer under the circumstances is to place the Theatre Royal and my services at your disposal upon any night convenient to yourself, believing that the 'public' will endorse my application of your managerial capacity.

Yours very truly,

GUSTAVUS V. BROOKE.

"Tragedian: That's coming it rather strong; isn't it, George?

"Manager: The British public like it strong and hot, and sweet, like a spinster's toddy.

"Tragedian: But what's your reply?

"Manager reads:—

THEATRE ROYAL, *7th May, 1861.*

MY DEAR BROOKE,

It's gratifying that a combination of fortunate circumstances will enable me to bring your lease of the Theatre Royal to a beneficial close. The treasury, however, is indebted to the attractions of Sir William and Lady Don, your own great genius and talent, and the appreciation of the public — not, as you kindly attribute, to my management. I will avail myself of your liberal offer, on Friday next, and trust you will allow me the pleasure of reciprocating next week upon the occasion of your farewell night.

Truly yours,

GEORGE COPPIN.

"Tragedian: They won't believe you wrote that.

"Manager: Why not?

"Tragedian: On account of its modesty. 'Not, as you kindly attribute, to my management,' is not at all like you, George. You are not the sort of man to hide your light under a bushel; you know you are not.

"Manager: Perhaps not; but a little modesty now and then goes a long way in our profession.

"Tragedian: 'Our profession!' I'm not a member of Parliament, thank Heaven!

"Manager: I meant the theatrical profession.

"Tragedian: To which you solemnly and faithfully bade farewell, eh?

"Manager: Tut, tut. The public have forgotten all about that. They are fond of humbug, and I can supply them with any quantity.

"Tragedian: Faith, and you may say that.

"Manager: Well, Gus, just put your name to this letter and I will get it into the posters to-morrow morning.

"Tragedian: I do not like the office, but, sith, I am entered in the cause so far, pricked to it by foolish honesty and love, I will go on. (Signs the paper.)

"Manager: That's settled. And now I'll take it to the printers. (Exit)."

During the week commencing Monday, May 6, Brooke appeared as Richelieu (under the patronage of the Mayor and Corporation); as Reuben in *Azael* (twice consecutively); as Othello (under the patronage of the local cricketers); and as Harry Dornton in *The Road to Ruin*, for the benefit of Henry Wallack. Coppin made his appeal on Monday the 13th, and appeared as Jacques and Sleek to Brooke's Duke Aranza and Captain Murphy Maguire. Constituting themselves a Mutual Admiration Society for the nonce, both indulged in sentimental speeches, burning incense at the altar of their old friendships. After referring to the reforms effected on the Australian stage by the tragedian during his six years' sojourn, Coppin suggested that "in recognition of his claims upon their appreciation of his genius and talent," they should present him with a testimonial consisting of an address on sheepskin. How this was acted upon we shall see shortly.

Among other characters represented by Brooke during the week were Fabian and Louis Dei Franchi, Sir Bernard Harleigh, Antipholus of Syracuse (in which the *Argus* says he was imperfect), and Master Walter. The last-mentioned impersonation was given on the 17th for the benefit of R. Younge, the stage manager, on which occasion Avonia Jones played Julia, and met with a very flattering reception. On the Monday and Tuesday following, Brooke appeared in *Coriolanus* and *The Lady of Lyons*, and on Wednesday the 22nd took his benefit in *The Irish Ambassador* and *The Irish Attorney*, when, in accordance with the advertisement, he delivered his "farewell address as an Irish Comedian." It ran thus:—"Ladies and Gentlemen—My countrymen are celebrated for getting into difficulties; in fact, I may say an Irishman is never so happy as when he is in trouble, and, upon my conscience, I am no exception to the general rule; for I was never in a greater state of botheration than at this moment, and I never felt so happy in all my life. The secret of my botheration is this—what am I to say to thank you all, and how am I to tell you all the delight I feel in seeing so many cheerful faces before me, and all the sorrow I feel in bidding you farewell? My countrymen will remember for what Irishman can ever forget — the mingled sunshine and showers of the heaven which bends over the beautiful Erin; and, as her skies are, so are the hearts and countenances of her people now bright with the sunshine of joy, and now dark with the rain-clouds of sorrow. My emotions on this occasion are of that mixed character, and I beg you to believe that, if my words are few, it is because my heart is full, and while I feel deeply and truly grateful, and really happy at this kindly leave-taking on your part, I also feel a pang of earnest sorrow at parting from so old, warm and true friends as those to whom I now, for the last time, in an Irish character, say farewell." On the following evening Brooke made his last appearance as an actor on Australian boards, in the character of Virginius, when the pathetic nature of the performance was considerably intensified by the regrets of the audience in having to part with their old favourite. After he had delivered another elegantly impressive adieu, and had been called and recalled until it seemed as if many of the spectators, in their affectionate enthusiasm, would have leaped on the stage and embraced him, a crumb of consolation was afforded by Coppin's announcement that, owing to a postponement in the sailing of the *Suffolk*, the tragedian would appear again on those boards, in his private capacity, at the amateur performance to be given in his honour on Saturday the 25th. Consequently, on that night *The Poor Gentlemen* and *The Spitalfields Weaver* were played by a number of local amateurs, enjoying the patronage of Major-General the Hon. T. S. Pratt, C.B., Commander of the Forces, and most of the Government Officials in Melbourne. Between the pieces Mr. James Smith delivered an address, written by Mr. Charles Bright, and emblazoned on vellum, which, together with a cheque for some £110, representing the surplus proceeds of the evening's performance, was presented to the tragedian, who made suitable and feeling response. On the following Monday a complimentary farewell benefit was tendered to Avonia Jones, who had made arrangements to visit London in company with

Brooke, in order to have the benefit of his experience in effecting her *début* there. After the performance of *As You Like It*, in which the lady star played Rosalind to Mr. Hoskin's Jacques, Brooke, assisted by Richard Younge, read a portion of the third act of Othello.

In accordance with the request of a number of the "unco guid," who were desirous of hearing him, while at the same time possessing conscientious scruples against entering a play-house, Brooke made his last public appearance in Melbourne on Tuesday, May 28, in the Exhibition Hall, the entertainment consisting entirely of dramatic readings. To mark the occasion the proceeds were devoted to the erection of a cottage in connection with the Australasian Dramatic College, which had been initiated a few months previously by the Hon. George Coppin, M.L.C.—as the tragedian's quondam partner was now entitled to style himself. Assisted intermittently, where the selection required it, by Mr. and Mrs. Heir and his old friend Mr. James Smith, Brooke gave the Dagger Scene from Macbeth, Hotspur's description of the Fop, The Seven Ages, The Night before the Battle (*Henry IV.*), besides selections from *King John*, *Richelieu*, and *Love's Sacrifice*, and two Irish readings, "The Fox of Ballybotherem" and "Paddy the Piper." Holding the attention of his audience throughout, the tragedian played upon their feelings with the same certainty that the well-accomplished musician plays upon his instrument, now commanding a painful and death-like silence, and now provoking incessant peals of laughter by the spontaneous humour of his Hibernian selections. Although the entertainment lasted upwards of three hours, there were few present who did not feel regret when it drew to a close. Two days afterwards Brooke, accompanied by Henry Wallack and Avonia Jones, sailed for Liverpool, not after all, it would appear, in the *Suwalk*, but in *The Great Britain*.

Departing, after six years of earnest unremitting labour, poorer in many ways than he had landed—wifeless, and £1,500 in debt to boot—Brooke said good-bye to the Colonies without rancour in his heart against any man. Indulging in but little self-reproach, he only retained a certain numb consciousness that the princely fortune he had gained by close attention to his professional duties had been frittered away through the blundering inefficiency of too well-trusted satellites. It had been, on the whole, the happiest period of his life; it was certainly the most important in point of histrionic influence and artistic results. Not so much a portion of his career as a career in itself, the few years passed by Brooke in Australia must be viewed now as a thing sacred and apart. That he looked upon it in some such light himself there can be little reason for doubting. We know, at any rate, that in after days of degradation and abasement, he never strove to trade upon his colonial reputation, and seldom cared to remind himself of those happier times by reappearing in such characters as had been associated in a high and peculiar degree with his Melbourne and Sydney triumphs. Returning to England a broken man, he fell back at once without a struggle into the old grooves, and with the calmness of despair took up the tangled skein of life as he had left it in 1856. Hence few of his admirers at home ever gained any save the most superficial knowledge of the extreme height to which his artistic powers had attained.

"Beaten but not disgraced," must be the verdict of those who examine Brooke's record in the Colonies dispassionately. Esteemed by all with whom he came in contact socially from the hour of his landing, he grew, as a natural consequence, to respect himself, and, up to the time when a recurrence of old misfortunes brought back all the old deplorable habits, had led a placid and comparatively uneventful life. Under the ripening influence of this salutary metamorphosis, his histrionic powers mellowed and expanded; and with the chastening of his physical exuberance came a relative increase in the subtlety and finish of his acting. Arriving with a working repertory of some forty characters, he had by dint of diligent study and forethought almost doubled the number before the period of his departure.

Of the thirty-three new personations, at least thirteen were Shakespearian, and, in directing his attention to these, the tragedian had been mainly instrumental in the production for the first time in the Colonies of a third of the Master's works. Synchronising with the more pretentious labours of Charles Kean and Samuel Phelps in the English metropolis, Brooke's managerial work in the Victorian capital, considering his restrictions and environment, was not a whit less important. Mounted as they were, without any pedantic straining after scrupulous exactitude, and yet with a care and completeness unprecedented in that quarter of the globe, these Shakespearian productions at the Melbourne Theatre Royal had an abiding influence upon the whole future tone of the Australasian drama.

Acting in a country practically devoid of histrionic tradition, Brooke became a law unto himself, and was thus emboldened to give a loose rein to those versatile instincts which, in accordance with the conventional limitations of the established tragedian, had been previously held in with a firm hand. Happily in doing this he found himself drifting before the tide of public inclination; and with the success that crowned his efforts he soon acquired two distinct histrionic identities. First and foremost, there was Brooke the tragedian—the cosmopolitan Brooke, who reached the zenith of his powers as Cardinal Wolsey and Louis XI. In sharp contrast came Brooke the gentlemanly Irish comedian—Brooke of the brogue, whose reputation in the Colonies was such as a Power or a Hudson might have envied. During his sojourn there no fewer than thirteen Hibernian characters were, from time to time, satisfactorily sustained, nine of which had been newly added to his repertory to cope with the demand for his frequent appearance in light assumptions of the kind.

Painfully conscious that Brooke had played havoc with his hopes and fortunes in the endeavour to foster a taste for the classic drama in their midst, the playgoers of Melbourne viewed his departure with unfeigned regret, and deplored his absence with constancy. Remaining the god of their idolatry as year after year rolled by, they yearned to bestow upon him fitting reward for his labours, and repeatedly sent liberal offers to induce him to return. But it was not to be. The Man was lost to them for ever. But his memory remained green, and when, in the fullness of time, tragedians of the stamp of Charles Kean, Creswick, and Barry Sullivan essayed to win the suffrages of the Colonies, it was by his standards and his traditions that they found themselves rated.

CHAPTER XI.

1861—1863.

DURING Brooke's prolonged absence in Australia a good many changes had taken place at home in affairs dramatic. When he returned it was to find theatricals at a low ebb in England, with the stage out of favour in society, and little recognised by the higher literature. Like all the other arts, the drama in the 'sixties was in an essentially transitory state, having now begun to feel the re-actionary influence of the pre-Raphaelite movement. Charles Kean's series of sumptuous archæological revivals at the Princess's Theatre had effectually stamped out the traditions of the old two-boards-and-a-passion school to which our hero certainly belonged. Even Phelps, at Sadler's Wells, deemed it advisable to float down gently with the tide, rather than oppose the rude buffet of the waves. Romantic drama was fast merging into the sensational, and high-flown comedy was about to give way to the refined mawkishness of the tea-cup and saucer school. Moreover, Fechter had dawned upon the theatrical horizon, and the growing attention to realism and minuteness of detail caused the play-going public to seek in acting for subtlety rather than breadth. Happily, with the decline of Brooke's exuberant vigour had come a corresponding improvement in the intellectual phases of his acting. This, allied with his undying popularity, contrived to render him tolerable. But it was impossible for a tragedian whose every fibre was permeated with the traditions of the old declamatory school to adopt himself satisfactorily to the doctrines of the reigning cultus; and Brooke's deplorable habits, gripping him the tighter with each succeeding misfortune, soon rendered all striving towards that end fruitless.

On his return from the Colonies our hero indulged himself with a much-needed rest among his relatives in Ireland, and at once made overtures to Mr. E. T. Smith for his re-appearance at Drury Lane. That he did not effect his purpose without considerable difficulty the following letter evidences: —

INKERMAN COTTAGE,
BRAY,
Co. WICKLOW,
October 3rd, '61.

MY DEAR SMITH,

I wish to meet you in as liberal a spirit as I possibly can, but when you talk of your being a loser by *my* proposed arrangement, you really can have no idea of my *expenses*. And unless there is a *chance* for me to make something, *I* shall be a much greater loser than *you* can possibly be.

Say we put the working expenses of Drury Lane Theatre (including the salary of myself, Miss Jones, and Younge) at Seventy pounds per night — that more than covers all the expenses named by you, with the *exception of rent*. I contend, however, that if a proprietor puts himself and theatre against the earnings of an acknowledged star, he only puts himself on a *fair business equality* with the said star. You must know yourself that there are items in your estimate of expenses that can be cut down considerably. Gas, for instance, 12,000 per night (fudge!). There are also salaries that may be essential to *you*, but will not assist my business much.

I do not want to commence my theatrical career in this country with a disagreement, and am therefore willing to concede as much as possible; but *I want no mutual friends in business matters*. I have commenced to transact my own, without intervention, and have not for some years given anyone authority to make any engagement for me without my counter signature.

If you have not faith enough in the engagement to divide with me, after *liberal* working expense, *why urge it?* If it will not pay *you*, it cannot me; and I therefore think you will meet all difficulties by returning me the memoranda I wrote to you for acceptance, sharing after Seventy pounds (£70) per night, instead of Sixty (£60), but with no other alteration.

I am, my dear Smith,

Yours very sincerely,
GUSTAVUS V. BROOKE.

Four days after writing this letter, Brooke made his reappearance on British boards, for the first time since his return, at the Theatre Royal, Dublin, playing Othello to the Desdemona of Miss Sarah Thorne. His three weeks' sojourn there proved sufficiently prosperous to put him in good heart; and he expressed great delight at the reception accorded him on his benefit night, an overflowing house having assembled to see his impersonation of Sir Bernard Harleigh in *Dreams of Delusion*.

Considering the tenour of Brooke's letter to E. T. Smith, it is not surprising to find that the company engaged in support of the tragedian, when he made his reappearance at Drury Lane on Monday, October 28, was wretched in the extreme. *The Times*, however, of the following day opined that " The acclamations with which he was received, and the applause bestowed on lines uttered with more than usual emphasis, showed that an Othello of the old school can still command a body of admirers. Mr. Brooke's style of acting, and the use he makes of a naturally sonorous voice, are so familiar to all but very young playgoers that a minute analysis of his interpretation would be somewhat superfluous. He returns home in very good case; he makes his points not only with great force, but with much deliberation, and is altogether the reversal of a non-traditional Othello. Moreover, he has a commanding figure, is earnest even to solemnity, and is, in a word, just the sort of ' noble Moor' that many people have been taught to regard as the *beau-ideal*. Without being condemned to feel their old notions violently uprooted or to bury prejudices in unwelcome oblivion, the London public may see the Tragedy move along in its old track, wishing at the same time that there was a little more liveliness in the Cassio and a little more astuteness in the Iago. But there are in Mr. Brooke the elements of a permanent popularity, and he is pretty certain of a class of admirers willing to overlook minor considerations."

Electing to stand or fall on her own merits, Avonia Jones made her first appearance in England at the same theatre, on

Tuesday, November 5, in an adaptation of the *Medea* of M. Ernest Legouvé. Unhappily, the youthful actress had been grounded in a school of tragedy fast growing obsolete, and her ponderously heavy style (which earned for her in the provinces the ungracious sobriquet of Avonia *Groans*) did not conduce to any very great popularity. Much bepuffed in advance, her *début* failed to attract more than passing attention, and was at once rated a success of esteem. "To those," says *The Times*, "who recollect the imposing figure of Mad. Ristori as she made her entrance from the rocks at the back of the stage, the slight and by no means commanding figure of Miss Avonia Jones forebodes somewhat a feeble delineation of the Colchian heroine, and though it may even be perceived that her voice is both musical and flexible and her movements generally easy and natural, the spectator is led to expect that while the pathetic side of Medea's character will be delicately portrayed, the passions of hate and revenge will not receive adequate expression. This opinion she dissipates as soon as opportunity presents itself, and in the famous 'leopard speech,' as well as in other passages, where Medea's natural savagery is brought forward, she shows an intensity and abandonment to passion which compensates in a great measure for a deficiency in physical strength. We may add that her points are made without close preparation, and that her attempts to produce those statuesque effects, which seem to be instinctively sought by all artists who represent antique personages, never betray her into a stiff, uneasy mode of gesticulation."

Continuing to appear for some little time afterwards as Othello and Medea, on alternate nights, Brooke and Avonia Jones performed together for the first time at this theatre, on Tuesday the 19th, in *Love's Sacrifice*, which held its place in the bills during the remainder of the week. A few more representations of *Medea* followed: and with the conclusion of the engagement on the last day of the month the doors of old Drury had closed for ever on Gustavus Brooke.

Some criterion of the ill-success of this metropolitan venture may be gleaned from the disastrous consequences which ensued. Not only did the tragedian find himself involved in serious pecuniary embarrassments, from which he never got thoroughly clear, but on returning to the provinces he discovered that in most places the bad news (magnified and distorted) had preceded him to unlucky purpose. Brighton, however, at the outset, proved an honourable exception to the general rule. Indeed so well attended was the theatre during his engagement there of the first week in December that the receipts averaged something like £118 nightly. Mr. Charles Coghlan was, at that time, a member of the local stock company, and among other parts played Cassio to the star's Othello. After a visit to York, Brooke, Avonia Jones, and the inevitable Younge opened at Belfast on Tuesday, December 24, in *A New Way to Pay Old Debts*, to £12 8s. 0d.! Engaged on half receipts and thirty pounds per week, the trio, notwithstanding Brooke's reputation in the capital of Ulster and the novelty of the tragedienne's first appearance, only received £44 16s. 9d. for the first four nights' performances. On the Monday following, when *Othello* was in the bill, and considerable numbers had assembled round the theatre awaiting the opening of the doors, quite a stir was created by the appearance of several men carrying poles on which were conspicuous placards bearing the undernoted announcement :—

THEATRE ROYAL.

NOTICE TO THE PUBLIC.

In consequence of a Breach of Engagement on the part of the Manager, Mr. G. V. Brooke, Miss Avonia Jones and Mr. R. Younge will not perform this evening, Monday, December 30th.

Soon the walls of the theatre were placarded with a counter-statement, and the doors remaining closed the crowd gradually dispersed. All the sympathies of the public appeared to be with Brooke, although no one exactly knew what had occasioned the rupture. Next morning the tragedian published an apology in the papers, and without deigning to vouchsafe any explanation, spoke ominously of an impending lawsuit.

Much speculation still being rife, however, in the public mind concerning the origin of the quarrel, he deemed it advisable to enlighten his friends in the following letter, which appeared in the *News-Letter* of January 2, 1862:—

MR. BROOKE'S ENGAGEMENT IN BELFAST.

To the Editor of the Belfast News-Letter.

SIR,

Feeling it due to the public that some explanation should be given to account for the abrupt and unexpected termination of the engagement I entered into with Mr. Scott in conjunction with Miss Avonia Jones and Mr. R. Younge, I now beg leave to present a brief statement of facts.

During my London engagement in November I entered into an arrangement with Mr. Scott to perform for eleven nights, commencing December 23rd instant. According to the usual custom I enclosed him the plays for performance on the first two nights, and they were duly announced. While fulfilling an engagement at York I ascertained that the funeral of the much-lamented Prince Consort was to take place on Monday the 23rd—the day on which my engagement with Mr. Scott was to commence. I immediately wrote to him stating that, under the circumstances, I concluded the theatre would not be open on that evening. Mr. Scott, however, replied informing me that he positively intended to open the theatre, and that I should be prepared to fulfil my engagement.

Consequently I arrived in Belfast on the morning of the 22nd, and immediately directed Mr. Lyon (my agent) and Mr. R. Younge (my stage manager) to obtain an interview with Mr. Scott and make known to him my feelings as to the gross impropriety of the course he appeared determined to pursue. He, however, would not yield to my feelings or opinion on the subject. Thereupon, I placed myself in communication with the Mayor (Sir Edward Coey), who, on the case being stated to him, entirely concurred with me, and the result was that Mr. Scott yielded, and no performance took place.

This was my first unpleasantness with Mr. Scott.

I continued to perform my engagement up to Saturday evening last, when my agent on calling on Mr. Scott for the fulfilment of his pecuniary obligations, he, to my great surprise, refused any settlement, but referred me to his solicitor.

I have some confidence that the plain statement of facts will justify me before the *public*; that the public will consider me fully justified in insisting upon the just and equitable adherence to the engagement I entered into at Mr. Scott's solicitation. I have thus 'a round unvarnished tale delivered.' The facts I pledge myself to. I have omitted many unpleasant details which I would be sorry unnecessarily to obtrude on public notice, and remain,

Yours respectfully,

G. V. BROOKE.

December 30, 1861.

Complying with a numerously-signed requisition from his old admirers, the tragedian, in conjunction with Avonia Jones and Mr. Younge, gave a series of readings from Shakespeare, in the Music Hall, on Monday, Wednesday, and Friday, the 13th, 15th, and 17th of January. Selections from *Othello*, *Measure for Measure*, *Julius Cæsar*, and other plays were given, Brooke on all three occasions prefacing the entertainment by the delivery of a spirited oration on the genius of the Immortal Bard. Inclement weather and the rival attractions of Barry Sullivan (who had just entered upon an engagement at the theatre) had to be contended with; but notwithstanding these drawbacks, the Music Hall was inconveniently crowded on the first reading, by an enthusiastic assembly. In a few parting words at the close of the second entertainment, Brooke announced that, in accordance with his usual practice during his visits to Belfast, of contributing something to local charities, the receipts on Friday evening would be handed over without deduction to the General Hospital. But as the attendance on that occasion was small, the cause could have benefited but slightly by his generosity.

To add to his misfortunes, the tragedian's health had been far from good since his return from the Colonies. Writing to his old friend Morris, of Ayr, from " 107 West Regent Street, Glasgow," on February 26, we find him saying—

" I need hardly express the gratification I felt on receipt of your kind note, and must apologise for not having acknowledged it sooner. But I am sorry to say that for the past month I have been suffering more or less from rheumatism—I suppose occasioned from my long sojourn in a warm climate—and I don't care how soon I may get accustomed to the fogs and bleak climate of Britain. Strange to say, I had nothing to complain of with regard to my native air, so I suppose there must be a charm in it."

Heartily welcomed by the *Herald* on making his appearance at Greenock in the following week, he was flatteringly told that time had by no means impaired his fine histrionic powers. According to the *Advertiser*, the effect of Avonia Jones's Medea

" upon the audience was intense, and the gifted actress was called before the curtain at the close of each act and received with loud, long-continued, and merited plaudits. We have never witnessed a more complete triumph."

On the termination of his Glasgow engagement, Brooke had paid a brief visit to his old and tried friend at Ayr, and on March 9, writes to him as follows from 9 Laird Street, Greenock :—

MY DEAR MR. MORRIS,

Many thanks for the umbrella. We arrived here about five o'clock and had a good house on Monday. It has done nothing else but snow or rain, and I have not been out of the house except at night when I was obliged to go to the theatre. I have been labouring under (I won't say cold) *chill* all the week ; the back part of the theatre has been cold enough, and the front part colder than I anticipated. The latter, I suppose, is attributable to the general cry, "Times are bad."

My poor unfortunate finger has been very bad. The frost got into it, and there was quite a large hole in the joint. It is, however, much better now, but like all sore places always in the way. The sun is shining to-day for the first time since we have been here, and we are going to take a walk somewhere. We shall leave to-morrow at 7·15 for Dundee, where I shall remain till Saturday morning. My arrangements are now made up till 24th of May, and thus they run :— Dundee; on the 17th, Edinburgh for twelve nights ; on the 31st, Hull for six nights ; 7th April, Newcastle upon-Tyne for twelve nights ; Easter week I shall rest ; 28th, Sheffield for twelve nights ; Monday, 12th May, Birmingham for twelve nights, ending 24th. I shall write occasionally and frequently send you papers.

With many thanks for the interest you have taken in my early career—Believe me, my dear Mr. Morris,

Yours most sincerely,
G. V. BROOKE.

The last house we have had has been £36 14s. 0d. *Oh !*

Too ill and too much out of sorts to call upon his old schoolfellow, Dr. Fox, whom he had discovered to be in practice in Greenock, he wrote him a pleasant if nervously-penned note, expressing " how happy I should have been to have had an opportunity of renewing the acquaintance of so old an associate, and trust that I may have that pleasure before I leave again for Australia, which I think will be about November."

So little of this weakness, however, did he betray on the stage that the local press continued to speak in high terms of

his acting, and in dealing with the performance of *King John*
(in which the tragedian appeared in the name-part to the
Constance of Avonia Jones), remarked that "nothing like the last
scene, in point of dramatic effect, has ever been seen at our
theatre." But alas for the probity of the critical craft! No
sooner had Brooke and his companions departed than the
Greenock Herald, as if wearied in exhausting its vocabulary of
enthusiasm, burst forth with a tirade upon the last performance,
in which the tragedian's Macbeth was compared unfavourably
with Tom Powrie's conception, and Avonia Jones (only a day or
two previously Mrs. Siddons and Helen Faucit rolled into one)
rated on a level with Miss Marriott.

Matters failed to improve with the passage of time. A
storm cloud that had lowered over poor Brooke's head ever
since his Drury Lane engagement, burst with extreme virulence
while he was at Sheffield early in May; and from that period
he never recovered his former gaiety and confidence. Under
heavy pecuniary obligations to E. T. Smith, which he had
striven vainly to meet, he at length received a telegram from
that gentleman stating that a satisfactory remittance to cover
some bills must be made by return, or "fatal results" would
ensue. Seale, Smith's solicitor, had also written a peremptory
note demanding immediate payment of debt interest and his bill
of costs, failing which, execution would be issued without farther
notice.

Alarmed at these threats, we find Brooke, on May 5,
communicating with Mr. James Morris to explain that he is
sending his secretary to give full particulars of the predicament, hoping his old friend will come to the rescue, and thus
prevent him becoming a temporary inmate of York Castle.
"Mr. Lyon," he adds, "has the proper bill to give you in
return, and if you could make it for six months it would suit
me better, as on the 2nd of June Miss Jones' engagement with
me will cease, and I shall then be untrammelled and alone."
Four days afterwards, Brooke's secretary had returned from
Scotland with Morris's two drafts for £25 each, and these were

at once sent on to London. "I am sorry to say," writes Brooke from Sheffield, in acknowledging this further act of kindness—"I am sorry to say that in consequence of my very heavy expenses, from which I shall be in a few weeks released, my tour has hitherto not proved as profitable as I had anticipated; but I trust I shall be enabled to make such an arrangement for the liquidation of the bills that may come easy to me."

Although all went well up to the conclusion of the first week of Brooke's Birmingham engagement, Messrs. Smith and Scale in the meantime had not considered the £50 remitted a sufficient "stave off." At least £36 of that sum had been ingeniously swallowed up in costs, leaving the tragedian still indebted to the tune of £79. Notwithstanding that he had intimated his intention of clearing this off in satisfactory weekly instalments, he was arrested at their suit, without further warning, on Monday, May 19, and at once hurried off to Warwick Gaol. Interrupted in the heat of a prosperous engagement, his name was immediately withdrawn from the bills without comment, and the residue completed by Avonia Jones and Mr. Younge as best they could.

Pausing here a little, it is noteworthy that among the members of the Birmingham stock company at this period was no less a personage than Mr. Bancroft, who supported Brooke during the previous week, and on the night he came of age played Allworth to the tragedian's Sir Giles. A most favourable impression was left on the mind of the young actor; so much so indeed, that when in recent years he came to treat of his early experiences in the "Bancroft Memoirs," he found occasion to speak of Brooke's acting as "of the highest kind and quite remarkable."

If Smith's vindictive action defeated its own object, he had at least the poor satisfaction of knowing that his victim—the man who had assisted in the establishment of his fortunes at Drury Lane—suffered keenly during his incarceration. Writing to Morris from "1st Class Debtors' Ward, Warwick Gaol." on

May 22, Brooke speaks in unmeasured terms of his persecutor's conduct, and, continuing, says :—

> I was to have played at Newcastle-under-Lyme for nine nights, commencing on Monday, and have now resolved to clear off liability by not being harassed. To-morrow I intend to declare myself a bankrupt and shall file my petition. I have had a most weary and annoying life lately, and I now make another appeal to send me £12 to assist me in doing what I have told you. It will relieve me from an anxious life of downright misery ; and address, "Care of Miss Avonia Jones, 103 Islington, Birmingham." I am sure you will pardon this request. I would not call on you if I could avoid it, and you are the only friend I have got that would put themselves out of the way to aid me.
>
> Believe me, dear Mr. Morris,
>
> Your very sincere and much obliged friend,
>
> GUSTAVUS V. BROOKE.

To this pathetic appeal Morris generously responded by sending a bank-bill for £20, which well-nigh miscarried, owing to his forgetfulness of Brooke's instructions. Misdirected, the letter, along with several others addressed to the insolvent actor, was stopped at the Post Office and placed in the hands of the Official Assignee. To this dignitary the sender at once made formal application, and was just in time to prevent the money finding its way into the pockets of the creditors.

Meanwhile, Avonia Jones, like a true woman, had done her best to alleviate the distress of her future husband. To one or two of his most intimate friends in Belfast and elsewhere she wrote at length, explaining his plight in terms which did equal credit to her head and heart, and showed how much she reverenced the man to whom she had given her young affections. Nor was this all. In the face of impoverished resources and an uncertain future, and despite the existence of a formidable retinue of idle and needy relatives, her one thought at this juncture was how to recompense the man who had clogged himself in endeavouring to establish her reputation. Money she had none. Brooke was already largely her debtor for salary due. But she had still some valuable jewels at her command ; and these she willingly rendered up to Mr. W. J. Reeves, a

Birmingham solicitor, as security for the costs in filing the necessary petition. Thanks to this magnanimous action, Brooke was enabled to appear before Mr. Commissioner Sanders, of the Birmingham Bankruptcy Court, on the 28th, and two days afterwards obtained his release. He then repaired to Newcastle-under-Lyme, where, from the Borough Arms Hotel, on June 1, we find him writing to Morris as follows:—

"I have suffered a good deal of wrong and annoyance lately, and when I found myself arrested for a small sum, and thus prevented from exercising my professional avocation, I thought it best to take steps to enable me to do so without the constant anxiety and fear of interruption. I therefore filed my petition, and on Wednesday obtained my discharge. The amount of my liabilities, Australian and English, comes to two thousand two hundred and sixty-seven pounds (£2,267). My first hearing is fixed for the 16th of June, and I hope after this to get on swimmingly; for it was utterly impossible for me to do anything with that great incubus hanging over me. I really cannot express the deep feeling of gratitude I feel to you for the interest you have taken in my welfare, and the very tangible proofs of kindness you have shown me."

To Brooke's credit let it be said that on the two occasions on which he became insolvent his intention was merely to free himself temporarily from the distracting persistency of duns, and not to evade payment of his debts. Previously, after returning from America with replenished pockets, he had discharged all his obligations in full; and had dame Fortune only placed it in his power, a like course would have been pursued in the latter instance. Lax and unbusinesslike as he may have been in many respects, his code of honour in regard to money matters was certainly strict and undeviating. Lending or borrowing with equal facility, he much oftener paid than received. To this integrity (part and parcel of his personal nobleness) he owed the confidence placed in him by men like James Morris, who, despite his manifold weaknesses and misfortunes, stood resolutely by him to the last.

Come we now to a lengthened engagement of note at the Theatre Royal, Manchester—one of the few oases in a desert of unappreciated strolling. Supported by an excellent stock company, comprising, amongst others, Henry Irving, Clifford Cooper, F. Everill, G. F. Sinclair, and Mrs. Bickerstaff, Avonia Jones opened there, alone, on Saturday, June 7, in *Medea*, the play retaining its place in the bills throughout the whole of the following week. Considering that seven years had elapsed since Brooke's last engagement in Manchester, it it is not surprising that a large and excited audience was attracted to the theatre, on Monday the 16th, by the announcement that the old favourite would reappear on that occasion for Avonia Jones's benefit. Having repaired, however, to Birmingham on the same day, in connection with the first hearing of his petition in bankruptcy, Brooke was detained there longer than he anticipated, and failed to arrive at the theatre for some considerable time after the advertised hour of commencing. Chafing under the delay the audience at length grew so demonstrative that Mr. Irving found it necessary to appear before the curtain and, in general terms, explain the situation. "Last evening," says the *Manchester Guardian*, "the performance at the Theatre Royal was for the benefit of Miss Avonia Jones, a lady who in the classical character of Medea has, in the course of a week, won a high place in the estimation of a Manchester audience; and when we say that to the lady's own unquestionable merits were added those of a first-class tragedian, in the person of Mr. G. V. Brooke, and that *Macbeth* was the piece chosen, sufficient has been said to indicate that an entertainment of no ordinary attraction was offered. The result was, as it deserved to be, a crowded house and a brilliant success. The reception accorded to Mr. Brooke was one of which he might well be proud. The house re-echoed with applause as he made his appearance on the stage, and throughout the whole of the tragedy the enthusiasm of the audience was sustained." Among those who assisted in the rendering of Locke's music on that occasion was our friend Mr. Dinsmore, who had seen Brooke and Helen Faucit at the old Queen's in the same play some sixteen years previously. In awarding the palm to the later impersonation, this ardent Brookite remarks that the tragedian's acting on the opening night seemingly exercised an equal charm on those behind the footlights as well as those in front. Especially does he remember that the bright particular Banquo of the occasion (who was himself subsequently to become one of the Macbeths of the century) made the most of every opportunity afforded to watch the star from a snug position in the wings.

Unhappily with Brooke's return from the genial atmosphere of the Colonies his voice had begun to show spasmodic signs of its old weakness. The story goes that on one occasion during this engagement, when Fechter journeyed from London to see the tragedian's King John, his voice was so husky as to render his elocutionary efforts well nigh unintelligible. Nothing, however, could damp the ardour of his Manchester admirers, who continued to fill the theatre nightly until July 19, and bestowed liberal applause on the stars for their presentation of a round of standard characters. Always in the van where charity was concerned, Brooke gave a performance before leaving, on behalf of the Distressed Operatives, at which upwards of £110 were realised.

Meanwhile, on the first of the month, he had written to Morris in the following strain :—" I am happy to say that things are beginning to wear a very fair aspect. I went up for my first hearing on the 16th of last month, and passed without any opposition. I have to go to Birmingham again on the 16th of this month, and have every reason to believe I shall then get my discharge. My engagement here has turned out more successfully than I had anticipated, and is consequently extended another fortnight—that is, I shall remain here until the 21st, save that I shall have to visit Birmingham and return the same evening. I shall commence at Liverpool on Monday the 28th, and have not as yet made any arrangements after, but have any quantity of engagements offered. I hope very soon to see things on the ' square,' and everyone satisfied."

Recognising that the attractions of her name were not of much additional value to the tragedian, and feeling it incumbent upon her to earn more money for the support of her mother and other relatives, Avonia Jones now elected to go her way unaided. Making her reappearance in London, in August, as Medea, at the Adelphi, she performed there intermittently until the middle of 1863, playing among other characters of importance Adrienne Lecouvreur, Aurora Floyd, and Janet Pride.

With somewhat brighter prospects looming on the horizon, Brooke had now abandoned the idea of an early return to the Colonies. Writing from " 11 Upper Newington, Mount Pleasant, Liverpool," on September 20, he says to Morris:—" Yours of the 29th ultimo has been following me about everywhere; and my peregrinations have been numerous lately. You will be pleased to hear that I got out of my difficulties with flying colours, and, despite of opposition, was highly complimented by the judge previous to my leaving the court. I can assure you that I feel myself now quite a different man; bought experience they say, is a good thing; and I am sure it will prove so in my case. For the future I feel now, comparatively speaking, free and untrammelled. I am gadding about from town to town—a week here and a fortnight there—paying off my law expenses and getting my wardrobe together, and shall commence business in *downright real earnest* on the 18th of October for a month, when I go to London, and calculate, from the terms I get, that I shall be enabled to realise between £450 and £500."

After several unimportant provincial engagements, Brooke emerged once more from semi-obscurity at the City of London Theatre, opening a protracted campaign on Monday, October 20, with a performance of Sir Giles Over-reach. A great variety of parts followed. On November 21 he played Brutus to the Cassius of Ryder and the Mark Antony of J. F. Young. In another letter to Morris, written from " 21 Bridge Road " on the previous 16th, we find him stating:—" I am happy to say that

I now begin to feel the benefit of having got rid of the tremendous incubus that I think it would have taken me a considerable portion of my life to have shaken off by paying sixty shillings in the pound. Matters look brighter now, and I look forward with some degree of pleasure to my future career. Excuse this short epistle, and rest assured that I will transmit as much as I can from time to time. Miss Jones (whose success in London, as Miami in *The Green Bushes*, has been very great) joins with me in kindest wishes to all at home."

On Monday, December 8, a novelty was afforded City of London playgoers by the production of the First Part of *Henry IV.*, in which Brooke appeared as Hotspur to Young's Prince Henry and Ryder's Falstaff. A fortnight afterwards the engagement was brought to a satisfactory close with a performance of *William Tell*. Although there were nights on which the tragedian had imbibed not wisely but too well, a wide toleration was shown to his weaknesses, and nothing of moment occurred throughout to mar the success of the campaign.

But, ah, the bitterness of these declining years! Misfortunes now crowded so thickly upon him that, with Macbeth, he might well have said, " The cry is still ' they come.' " On the verge of a great sorrow we find him writing to his friend, Mr. J. K. Jackson, the Coroner of Belfast, conveying the intimation that he was just concluding " a successful engagement in the Oriental district of the great metropolis." " I am sorry to say," he continues, " that my dear old mother has been dangerously ill for the last three or four weeks, and I have for some days past been in hourly expectation of a telegraph *(sic)* to call me to Dublin, and I am happy to say that I this morning received one to say that there was a change for the better. I shall finish here on Monday next. On Tuesday I shall play at the Theatre Royal, Liverpool, for the benefit of the ' Lancashire Relief Fund,' and shall start early on the next morning for Dublin, *via* Holyhead. I shall spend some time in Ireland, and hope to see you."

With the death of his mother, on Thursday, December 25 (four days after the above was written), departed the one great controlling influence in the tragedian's unhappy life. Recognising his loss, he sought in some measure to fill the gap by espousing Avonia Jones. The wedding took place very quietly, at St. Philip's Church, Liverpool, on February 23, 1863. Had Providence so ordained it, there can be little doubt that, in course of time, the force of character possessed by this amiable woman would have weaned him from his evil habits. But stern Necessity parted them at the height of their connubial bliss, depriving poor Brooke of his last ray of hope, and ruining the prospects of a sweet young life.

CHAPTER XII.

1863—1864.

Brooke's Decline and Fall—A Lurching, Incoherent Hamlet—In Ireland
with Mr. Bancroft—Plays Coriolanus at Dublin—The Drama in
Leamington—Avonia Jones's Eloquent Defence—Saddening Scenes
in the Provinces—A Memorable Saturday Night in Belfast and its
Sequel—How Brooke Dealt with an Extortionate Jarvey—His
Lamentable *Fiasco* at Sadler's Wells.

ALL speculation as to the future of Brooke was now at an
end. Gone were the freshness of youth, the great vigour,
and repeated misfortunes had only served to weaken a will
against which inroads had been made from an early period by
a too convivial temperament. It remains, however, sad as may
be the task, to pursue the chronicle to the end.

Accompanied by Mr. Bancroft, Mr. J. C. Cowper, and the
other members of the Dublin stock company (whose services
had been temporarily dispensed with at the Royal owing to
the advent of the Italian Opera season), Brooke paid a visit to
Cork early in the April of 1863. Appearing there during a
couple of weeks in a round of well-worn characters, his acting
evinced fitful gleams of its pristine fire; but it was with feelings
of inexpressible sadness that his old friends noticed the great
change that had come upon him.

"It was quite plain," writes Mr. J. W. Flynn, of this
engagement—"It was quite plain to everyone that Brooke was
taking more stimulants than he ought to; yet strange to say
his acting was as fine as ever (?). The people came in crowds
to see him, and though some nights it was plain to the
audience, as well as to those behind the scenes, that the actor

was under some other influence than that of dramatic
inspiration, the actor bore his part superbly, and his acting had
all the old beauty. I have told you how great he was in
Virginius. Well, the night he played it during that last
engagement he made a profound impression. In that last sad
scene, where Virginius comes upon the bronze urn containing
the ashes of his beloved daughter, Brooke's acting was
inexpressibly pathetic. As he fell forward on the urn, clasping
it to his heart with a cry of sorrow, I glanced round and saw
tears trickling down the cheeks of those around me. On the
Monday following it was *Hamlet*, and, oh! how sad a spectacle
it was! There could be no doubt Brooke was—how can I
whisper it—drunk! The fact was not to be disguised. A
feeling of sadness and gloom fell over the house—a crowded
house too—at the sight of this dismal *fiasco*, this lurching,
incoherent Hamlet. I was behind the scenes, and I knew when
Brooke was going on the stage that he had too much brandy
and that he would never pull through the play. I was sitting
in the green-room during that beautiful scene with Ophelia,
commencing 'My lord, I have remembrances of yours,' etc.
Brooke was so bad I could not bear to witness his failure.
When the scene was over the charming young actress who
played Ophelia—Miss Sarah Thorne was her name—entered the
room in a state of painful agitation. 'Isn't it too bad,
Mr. —— ?' she said, appealing to me. 'He has ruined the
scene, but I can't be angry with him, for he's the best-natured
fellow ever lived.' At that moment Brooke came into the
room, rather unsteadily, and, shaking a chiding finger at Miss
Thorne, exclaimed 'Ah, young lady, I caught you tripping
to-night; you missed your lines!' This was adding insult to
injury, after he had spoiled the scene himself by telescoping his
lines. Miss Thorne was speechless with indignation. She
looked at me and left the room in silence. 'I'm not quite all
right to-night,' Brooke said to me half-apologetically. 'I'm
not quite well, and the people in front are a bit unreasonable
sometimes.'

"In the graveyard scene poor Brooke was so palpably tipsy that there were some sounds of disapprobation from the patient audience—a hiss or some such sound. I was not looking on at the time, but I believe Brooke came forward and addressed the audience, saying, whether they blamed him or praised him, applauded or hissed, he should always respect the judgment of a Cork audience. Then the people were sorry, and sat out the rest of the play in silence. In the last scene Brooke was so unsteady that he had to be propped up at the wing to get through the fight in a sort of way. It was a sad performance, indeed, and we were not sorry the curtain fell."

Mr. Bancroft (the Horatio of the occasion) tells us that Brooke never played Hamlet again. During his stay in Cork he was very kind and hospitable to the younger members of the company, and accompanied them on several hilarious excursions to Blarney Castle and other places in the neighbourhood.

Pulling himself together, he returned to Dublin with the other actors at the close of the opera season, and began an engagement on April 27 at the old Hawkins Street Theatre, which lasted to the 16th of the following month. After playing Othello, Hotspur, and a variety of other characters, Brooke sprang a surprise on the playgoers of his native city by reviving the seldom-acted *Coriolanus* on May 16, with himself in the name-part. Rising equal to the occasion, the tragedian gave a superbly classical rendering of the haughty tribune; but, somehow, although everything was in keeping, the novelty failed to attract, and was only performed three times in all. Awaking to the merits of the production when it was too late, the playgoers of Dublin signalised their approbation of Brooke's acting as the great mob-hater, on the last night of the engagement, by calling him before the curtain at the termination of every act. Enthusiasm, indeed, ran so high on this occasion that the tragedian had to indulge his admirers with two speeches, in which he feelingly referred to his early successes there, and thanked his fellow-citizens for their ever kindly welcome. Owing to his success he returned to Dublin at the latter end of the year, "when I played with him," writes Mr. Bancroft, "as Cassio in *Othello*, Wellborn in *New Way to Pay Old Debts*, Icilius in *Virginius*, De Mauprat in *Richelieu*, and Leonardo Gonzago in *The Wife*. He was very ill during the engagement, but, as always to me, delightful and charming in his manner." Already, through the medium of the "Bancroft Memoirs," the eminent actor has told us of Brooke's great resemblance to Salvini. "His death, in *Othello*," he continues, "always seemed to me as poetic in conception as it was pathetic in execution. Acting, although not speaking, the closing words, 'Killing myself to die upon a kiss,' he staggered towards the bed, dying as he clutched the heavy curtains of it, which, giving way, fell upon his prostrate body as a kind of pall, disclosing, at the same time, the dead form of Desdemona."

Shortly after leaving his native city, we find Brooke playing two nights at the Clemens Street Theatre, Leamington, on the second of which—when Sir Giles and O'Callaghan were the attractions (?)—the receipts attained the magnificent sum of 17s. 6d.! Little wonder that the local Temple of Thespis was subsequently converted into a Chapel of Dissent! So lukewarm were the inhabitants regarding theatrical matters, that the sight of the great tragedian walking about the town in a shabby white hat and velvet jacket, prematurely gratified the little curiosity that had been aroused.

From this time onward occur significant gaps in the narrative, which tell their sad story only too plainly. Towards the end of May we find Avonia Jones writing to Morris, from London, regretting that her husband had not been able to refund the money lent to him during 1862—a state of helplessness which had given him much worry and annoyance. "Theatrical business this year," we find her saying, "has been diabolically bad, and has nearly ruined managers and actors. To pay for daily living has been the utmost the best of them could do, and *this* is why you have not received your money long ago. He is daily expecting the arrival of two gentlemen from Melbourne who have made him a very fine offer to return to Australia.

They will advance him whatever money he will require, and he will obtain sufficient to return you the seventy pounds, with his earnest thanks and gratitude to you for assisting him in his hour of need."

After Avonia Jones had fulfilled a twelve nights' engagement at the Theatre Royal, Manchester, at the beginning of June, she was joined by Brooke on the 15th, when another twelve nights ensued. Beyond the fact that Mr. Charles Calvert played Iago and Faulconbridge to Brooke's Othello and King John, there is little to chronicle in connection with this sojourn. It is worthy of note, however, that the Miss Stanhope whose name appears in the bills opposite Desdemona and other leading characters is said to have been Miss Francis Sarah (Fanny) Brooke, younger sister of the tragedian, who occasionally travelled with him about this period.

Late in July, we find Mr. and Mrs. Brooke acting at the Royal Amphitheatre, Liverpool, under Copeland. For his benefit on the 24th the tragedian played Adrastus to the Ion of his wife and the Clemanthe of Miss Fanny Addison, and appeared as Pierce O'Hara in the afterpiece of *The Irish Attorney*. Treating of the important revival of *Cymbeline* on the following night, with excellent scenery and accessories, *The Liverpool Daily Post* expresses its surprise that a play offering so many admirable opportunities for the display of sound acting was so seldom seen in the theatre. "The discussion between Posthumus and Jachimo on the constancy of Imogen, was delivered by Mr. Brooke and Mr. Cowper in a manner every way worthy of the elegance of the text, ... and in the scene in which the wager is proved to have been won, Mr. Brooke's passage, from the easy confidence of the grave but polished man of the world, to the agony of the husband bereft by a ribald's lust of his wife's purity and repute, was splendidly effective. . . . The battle scenes introduced Mr. Brooke once or twice in passages of a declamatory character in which his noble elocution was most masterfully displayed, and led up to the great conclusion—the *ensemble* scene at the end of the fifth act. Here Mr. Brooke electrified the audience by another grand display of passion, and the gradual unfolding of the *denouement* brought the play to a placid and satisfactory end. . . . . Mr. Brooke was several times recalled. He was in splendid voice, looked noble enough to be Leonatus, and acted as well as ever he did in his life. . . . . . Miss Jones, *malgré* her artificiality of voice and monotony of tone, was an excellent Imogen, and her dresses, as well as those of Mr. Brooke, were models of taste and appropriateness. We trust *Cymbeline* will be repeated and become popular; the favour in which it was last night received was an encouraging sign of reviving dramatic taste and intelligence."

"You will be sorry to hear," writes Brooke to Morris from Liverpool on the 23rd, by way of apology for not discharging his obligations—"you will be sorry to hear that business, as regards our profession, has been far from good throughout the length and breadth of our land. And in a letter of Wyndham's, the other day, he says that during the whole of his career, both as actor and manager, he never knew the Theatre to be, as it were, so completely deserted, and does not know to what particular cause he can attribute it." In conclusion, we find him saying, "I have abandoned all idea for the present of returning to Australia, and think it better to wait till Kean has finished there."

Ill-luck continued to follow him with irritating persistency. He had arranged to play a fortnight in Jersey early in August, and to repair thence to Douglas, Isle of Man, for three weeks; but the theatre in the former island was burnt down on July 31, and the other, strange to say, closed its doors a few days after. The outlook became so unpromising that poor Brooke fell into a state of collapse, and, as usual in such moods, sought oblivion in the brandy-bottle. He grew nervous and despondent, and seldom slept at nights without a lighted candle by his bedside. Worried by an expensive lawsuit, and unable to extract any definite promise from the tragedian, Mr. James Morris had in the meantime applied himself to Avonia

Jones in regard to his loan of £70—certainly too long
unrefunded. In the course of her reply, from "21 Bridge
Road, St. John's Wood," on August 9, we find the lady
saying—"Pardon my not having answered your kind letter
before, but I have been very ill, brought on by over-study and
too much hard work. I had perforce to take the two weeks
left open by the Jersey fire, as a season of rest, and hope to
start again feeling much better. I left Mr. Brooke playing in
L'pool: but I assure you it is very wearying to have to
act week after week for a mere living, sometimes not even that.
It takes all my resolution to keep my spirits up." In a second
letter from the same address, on the 19th following, she says—
"Prospects in England are very dull for the coming winter.
I would give worlds to be able to go to America. I have had
most brilliant offers, and, though a young beginner, I left a fine
reputation behind me, to which my English reputation being
now added, and no earthly opposition there, I should make a
fortune. But what is the good of wishing? I have a large
family (mother, aunt, sister, and her two children, nine and six
years of age, beside, of course, house and servants) all under
my care; and I could not get there unless I had £300; and
though I could soon pay it back with interest, despite the heavy
percentage, I could as easily fly to heaven without wings as
borrow such a sum. So I must needs submit with the best
possible grace to the anxiety of getting a mere living. Mr.
Brooke is still in L'pool, but not acting. I shall not be with
him for the next few months. I am sure he will prove to you
that all the kind things you have said of him are true."

A third letter, written six days afterwards, is replete with
interest. While showing that the tragedian was discreet enough
to hide his failings from his young wife, it effectually gives
the lie to the scandal-mongers who have hinted at estrangement.
"I received your letter to-day," she informs Mr. Morris, "and
hasten to answer it, to correct a false impression that you are
labouring under. Whoever has told you that Mr. Brooke is
dissipated, or, as you express it, indulging in 'habits too well

known,' has told you a wilful falsehood. During two years I have never known him to disappoint the public, or be in such a condition that his nearest friend might blush for him. I can see his faults quicker than anyone else, and would be the first to reprove him. You should not blame him for his non-success, theatrically, since his return to England. You should rather admire the indomitable will that has made him persevere through every difficulty, and yet to stand pre-eminent as one of the first actors of his day. You should lay the blame, where it is due, to the degraded taste for the drama that now characterises the English public. They turn aside from all that is pure, legitimate, and good, to satisfy their morbid cravings after the sensational drama. Put the ' Ghost ' that is now all the rage in London into Hamlet, and full houses will be the result. . . . . Mr. Charles Kean openly said he went to Australia because he could do nothing here, and during his farewell engagement in Liverpool he and Mrs. Kean and the party he always has travelling with him played down to £8. These are facts I know and could prove. If newspaper criticism could make a fortune I should be one of the wealthiest women in England. True, they have given me a standing as a first-class tragedienne, but that don't fill my pockets. In the same way with Mr. Brooke. He is pre-eminent in legitimate business and fully acknowledged so, but put him in a sensation drama, he would be lost. Heaven forbid I should see him so degrade himself; I prefer, far better, to see him struggle as he does now. This debt to you is a source of great anxiety to him; in fact, any debt would be, for he is an honourable man. Once before in his life he was compelled to go through the Bankruptcy Court, but on his return from America he paid every farthing that he had owed. Have you ever in all your life known a time that, work as you will, everything would go wrong with you? If you have, you can understand my meaning; if not, you may thank Heaven for saving you from an ever present, ceaseless misery. As for myself, if Mr. Brooke had a million I should go to America.

My mother is very homesick, and it is the least I can do to gratify her if I can possibly manage it. Pardon my writing thus freely, but I cannot bear that you should be under a false impression, or think ill of one who has ever looked on you as his earliest and best friend, and has taught me to do the same."

The fact that Morris's insinuation had stable basis derogates not a whit, under the circumstances, from the simple eloquence of this pathetic outburst. A couple of months or so later, the writer in *The Australian Magazine*, whose reminiscences we have already laid under contribution, chanced to visit Northampton, and, gratified by the announcement that his old stage hero was to play there three nights, repaired in due season to the dingy, tumble-down-looking place which did duty as the Theatre Royal. "The house," he says, "the dress circle excepted, was full; the pittites solid, respectable looking people, wearing, most of them, that expectant critical look which Charles Lamb regarded as the true mark of the old playgoer, but which is now as extinct as the dodo. The prompter's bell tinkles, the green curtain ascends, every eye is fixed upon the stage. Northampton is forgotten; we are in old Venice; yonder stands Brabantio's mansion; down the street in earnest discourse come Iago and Roderigo. How we listened; how we watched each movement! It was worth while to do both, for though only twenty-three years have gone since then, such actors are as extinct as such audiences. Little, indeed, did they owe to dress, still less to their scenic surroundings; but they were masters of that lost art, the colloquial rendering of blank verse—art, which not all their wealth, nor all their liberal patronage of the theatre, can secure for present day playgoers. . . . . The scene changes; we are in front of the Sagittary; Othello and Iago enter in converse. How the house roared out its welcome. There was the noble Moor; the manly form, the leonine bearing, the well-poised head, which I remembered so well. Somewhat stouter, perhaps, but in all else unchanged. So for a brief space I thought; but as the din subsided and the dialogue went on, I felt that something was wrong. On the faces near

I could see wondering bewilderment; but before I could arrive at any conclusion the brief scene ended. Next came the council chamber, with the Duke and the magnificoes; to them enter Brabantio, Othello, and their following. I could now see that the looks of bewilderment had strangely passed from the faces of the audience to those of the actors. *Vae victis!* Alas for fallen greatness, though but the mimic greatness of the stage. Every man is his own Parcae and weaves his own destiny. The simulacrum of the Othello I remembered stood before me; the informing spirit, that strange something akin to genius which aforetime glowed in the eye, thrilled in the voice, was no longer there. Ichabod! the glory had departed. Very touching, very pathetic were the reverential attempts of the actors to aid their fallen brother. All in vain. At last Iago stepped forward and made a simple, manly appeal for the fallen star; beautiful was the reticent loyalty shown by this brother of the craft. There would be a short delay to enable a substitute to dress; then the play would proceed. So the curtain fell; my last sight of the idol of my boyhood was the vision of a helpless man, head sunk upon his chest, arms hanging listless, form swaying backwards and forwards. With a big lump in my throat and deep pity in my heart I left the theatre. The real tragedy I had witnessed left me in no mood for mimic tragedy."

From every quarter came much the same tale. But while Brooke's popularity was great, and the audience generally forgiving, the iteration of such incidents did not conduce to full houses or re-engagements. "I remember going into an important theatre in the north one night," says the "Old-Fashioned Playgoer," "when G. V. Brooke was playing in *Love's Sacrifice*. Meeting the manager—one of Brooke's firmest and oldest friends—I said, 'I understand Gussy is *rather* to-night?' 'Well,' said he, 'he's *highly* mysterious'; and he was so, indeed. In the earlier scenes there was nothing very active, and he could not 'pull himself together.' All who were playing with him got their cues with perfect safety, but the public knew very little of the sense of the speeches. I have seen him play Othello in an even worse state. But Othello always kept him awake while on the stage. In the wings he would be sometimes in an absolutely somnolent condition. But at his cue he would rouse himself by an effort of will most painful to witness, the muscular development of the neck being worked in a violent manner as the head was righted and the full stature of the man attained. The struggle infused great vigour with the opening lines of the scene; but if you are told that Brooke, or any one else, 'never acted better in his life' on such occasions, don't believe it. The reaction is melancholy and usually comes before the scene is over."

Towards the end of Mr. T. C. King's starring engagement, at Belfast, Brooke appeared there for one night, on Thursday, December 24, as Othello, to his brother tragedian's Iago. Much to the disappointment of a large audience (attracted by the announcement of Brooke's last appearance "prior to his departure for Australia") the old favourite was in very bad voice, and apologised for his deficiencies in saying "Good-bye" at the conclusion. Owing, however, to his characteristic irresolution these leave-takings—here, there, and everywhere—were becoming farcical.

Returning to Belfast on Monday, January 11, 1864, he opened what was to prove an extraordinary campaign by giving an indifferent rendering of Othello. A severe cold had played havoc with his voice, and matters were not improved by his resorting to the old consoler. Acting Sir Giles, however, on the second night with much of his pristine power, he was honoured with a call at the close of the trying climax, and on appearing before the curtain apologised to the audience for first picking up the sword which had fallen near the footlights from the maniac's hand. "It is," he said, "a reminiscence of Edmund Kean. With it he played the part in the tragedy which you have just seen." Although his acting continued to present marked inequalities, nothing material happened until the following Saturday evening. *Richelieu* had been announced, and pit and gallery were crammed to repletion. A protracted delay in the

raising of the curtain caused considerable irritation at the
outset, and significantly heralded what was to follow. But,
drunk or sober, Brooke was too much the spoiled child of
Belfast playgoers to meet with anything but a favourable
reception when once the play began. As the first act proceeded,
however, it became painfully apparent that some other force
besides histrionism was lending realism to the decrepitude of
the Cardinal. Bemused with liquor, the tragedian appears to
have indulged in occasional snatches of sleep, awaking ever and
anon with a start to mumble his lines in somewhat incoherent
fashion. All went well, however, until the juncture where Julie
de Mortemar impassionately addresses her venerable protector.
Brooke had now grown completely lethargic, and not all the
efforts of the prompter could rouse him to action. Precisely at
this moment, when the calmest silence reigned all over the house,
an unlucky pittite, whose condition was equally happy with that of
the tragedian, made some *sotto voce* remark which raised a vulgar
laugh in the neighbourhood. The ears which were deaf to the
counsel of the prompter at once caught this unwelcome sound.
Rising to his feet with some difficulty, Brooke advanced indignantly
to the footlights, and said—"Ladies and gentlemen, if you wish me
to retire I shall do so. (Cries of 'No, no,' and applause.) I want
my patrons to protect me from insult." (Cries of "We will," and
"Put out the ruffian in the pit.") A scene of indescribable
disorder ensued. Notwithstanding the efforts of a couple of
policemen the offending pittite was at length forcibly ejected
into the street, and the house settled down as best it could to
enjoy (?) the remainder of the scene. During the second act the
pit and gallery appeared at loggerheads, the one hissing vigorously
while the other applauded. But the patience of both became
utterly exhausted through the long wait which followed, and
under their united protests the orchestra soon deemed it advisable
to retire with precipitation. Meantime Brooke's condition had
not improved, and when the curtain rose it was to exhibit the
Cardinal reclining helplessly in his chair oblivious of all
surroundings. Many of the audience got up to leave, while

others, more resentful and audacious, hissed. Exerting all his
energies Brooke succeeded in arousing himself, and, advancing,
said —" Ladies and gentlemen, I have been so much accustomed
to the courtesies of the Belfast public that I really cannot put
up with this." Accompanied by cries of " It is not at you they
hissed ; come back, Mr. Brooke," he then bowed and withdrew.
Amid the uproar that followed, Mr. Stinton made his appearance,
and addressing the house, said—" Ladies and gentlemen, I am
compelled to appear before you in the absence of Mr. Webb.
(Applause.) I am grieved to say that Mr. G. V. Brooke will
not again appear to-night. (Slight hisses, and cries of ' Go and
get us back our money.') Gentlemen, what can I do? We
throw ourselves on your kind indulgence." (A voice—" You'll
have it." Cheers and hisses.) During the afterpiece there were
frequent interruptions, with cries of " Bring out Brooke "; and at
length, more sorrowful than angry, the remnants of the audience
dispersed.

Brooke's appearance in Macbeth had already been announced
for the following Monday evening, but the news of this painful
exhibition occasioned the immediate return of Mr. Henry Webb,
the lessee, from Dublin, and with it a complete change of bill.
Compelled to take notice of Brooke's conduct by a withering
report in the leading local journal, this gentleman announced
that the tragedian would not be permitted to appear again under
his management until he had purged himself of his offence by
a public apology. Two days afterwards the following card was
inserted among the advertisements in the *Belfast News-Letter:*—

"MR. G. V. BROOKE considers it an imperative duty he
owes the general public (which has through life been his truest
friend) to endeavour to explain the extraordinary scene that
occurred in the Theatre Royal, Belfast, on Saturday evening,
16th inst. Severe illness and annoyance were the cause of what
took place, provoked by an open insult from some misguided
individual in the audience. Mr. Brooke is now residing on the
scene of his early triumphs, and has been constantly engaged on
his professional career without interval for fourteen years. He

feels that he requires rest, and he thinks it would be very injudicious on his part, and an insult to the public, to appear in Belfast again; but with the most heartfelt gratitude for the favours hitherto heaped on him by a Belfast public, and with the truest and warmest wishes for the prosperity of this great commercial town, and with no small amount of deep regret, he therefore announces his *Farewell*."

Nothing could have been better calculated to enlist the sympathies of the local public. Several friends who knew that poor Brooke had been nursing himself carefully ever since that dreadful night, made it their business to plead with Mr. Webb for a renewal of the engagement. At once burying the hatchet, the genial lessee and famous Dromio announced on Saturday the 23rd that Brooke had tendered his services for a free benefit to the General Hospital on the following Wednesday. Consequently, on Monday the 25th, the tragedian returned to the assault as Richelieu, acted magnificently, and was cheered to the echo by an immense audience. "For years," said *The Belfast News-Letter*, "there have been no such demonstrations of unqualified approbation as were heard last night in our ably conducted theatre, and seldom could they have been better deserved." After the General Hospital had benefited to the extent of some sixty pounds by the night set apart on its behalf, a succession of good houses followed. Appealing personally to his friends on Friday the 29th (when *The Wife* and *His Last Legs* were in the bill), Brooke, in response to a call at the close, made the following speech:—"Ladies and Gentlemen—Will you allow me to address you? I really do not know how to thank you sufficiently for the great compliment you have paid me in being present here this evening in such extraordinary numbers. (Applause.) I assure you that I appreciate your kindness in a manner that I cannot express. (Cheers, and cries of 'You deserve it all.') No one can more deeply regret than I do the circumstances which caused a disappointment during the first week of my engagement. (Cries of 'It's all right, Brooke,' 'Never mind it,' and loud cheers.) When I look back and think of the approbation and encouragement which you invariably afforded me during the early portion of my professional career, and when I now look around me and see myself surrounded by many personal friends and patrons, I have reason to believe that the good feeling, and I might almost term it friendship—(applause)—that should exist between a favourite actor and the public who patronise him, and which I congratulate myself I possess in this town, is more firmly cemented than ever. (Cheers.) There is one thing, ladies and gentlemen, that I can assure you of most sincerely, and that is, that go where I may I shall always think with feelings of intense pleasure of my career in Belfast."

Despite occasional voice failure Brooke was now in good fettle, and writes to his friend Morris from "25 Corn Market" on February 1—"You may have perceived by the papers that I have been frightening, and absolutely mesmerising, the 'good people' in the 'northern metropolis.' I have not as yet determined as to what time I shall leave for Australia, but think it will be the mail after next, 'Overland Route.'" Some idea of the respect entertained for the tragedian in Belfast, in the face of his recent escapade, may be gathered from the following incident. During his stay he had occasion one day to hire a jaunting-car for some hours, and on proceeding to settle up was surprised at the exorbitant charge made by the driver, who was well aware of the identity of his fare. After remonstrating in vain, Brooke paid the obstinate jarvey what he demanded, and at once lodged a complaint with the Police Committee of the Town Council. A careful investigation of the case followed, with the result that the brazen-faced scamp was deprived of his license for a period of three months.

After playing Coriolanus, Jaques, Hotspur, and a variety of other characters, our hero terminated an unusually long engagement at Belfast on February 13—but not before he had taken another farewell benefit, and indulged in the inevitable leave-takings. Principally supported by Miss Louise Diddear he opened a four weeks' sojourn at the Queen's Theatre, Dublin, on the following Monday, and besides repeating all his old successes, gave two performances of Cassius in *Julius Cæsar*.

Wavering in his resolution to make an immediate return to the Colonies, Brooke now determined upon once more challenging the opinion of the Metropolis. But the doors of the West-end theatres were barred firmly against him, and the best he could do was to arrange for his appearance at Sadler's Wells—an outlying theatre which had lost all repute with the departure of Phelps. Miss Marriott, who had been in occupation of the old theatre earlier in the year, opened it again under her own management on Monday, April 18, with a revival of *The Winter's Tale*. Brooke was the Leontes, and the manageress herself appeared as Hermione. On the following Saturday night the tragedian played Shylock for the benefit of the Shakespeare fund. It is noteworthy that the performance at the Winter Theatre, New York, on the same date was for the same object, the play being *Romeo and Juliet*, with Edwin Booth and Avonia Jones as the hapless lovers. Short-lived, however, was the Sadler's Wells venture, a succession of bad houses bringing the campaign to an untimely end at the beginning of May. "It was a lamentable engagement throughout," writes Miss Marriott, "for Brooke was not only out of voice, but he was not in a fit state to go on the stage any evening to do justice to himself or those about him."

CHAPTER XIII.

1864 - 1865.

WRITING to his friend, Mr. David Allen, of Belfast, from
"64 York Street, Lambeth," on September 3, we find
Brooke saying—"Sadler's Wells was a failure, so far as
concerned pecuniary arrangements, and since that I have done
nothing. Theatrical matters have been miserably dull, and I
have been dragging out lately an anxious and precarious
existence. I am resolved now to make another struggle. Will
you, like a good fellow, let me know if the theatre in Belfast
is open, or likely to be so, as I should like to go there. Your
conduct to me when leaving Belfast was kind and generous, and
I should be sorry, indeed, to forfeit your estimation. What I
can do I will do to re-establish myself in your good opinion."

Not the least mortifying of the "sad crosses" to which he
goes on to refer was the sale of all his gold and silver plate
(valued at £800), at Messrs. Christie, Manson, and Woods', on
Wednesday, June 8—an event evoking invidious comment in
the morning papers.

According to Brooke's own story, it appears that on
departing from the Colonies he was compelled to leave all his
treasured presentations as security for debt in the hands of one

of his principal creditors. Early in the year this gentleman placed all the plate under the care of a friend who was returning to England, with instructions to deliver to the owner immediately on arrival. This he had omitted to do, preferring, as he had run short of funds, to pledge the whole at a leading pawnbroker's in the Strand for £447. Not long afterwards this worthy died suddenly, and to Brooke's great astonishment he received a notification from the holders that the plate would be returned to its proper owner on payment of the loan and interest. As he was utterly unable to do this, the spontaneous tributes of three continents were knocked down to the highest bidder in the auction-room, and ultimately found their way into the melting-pot.

His promises to Mr. Allen notwithstanding, Brooke's habits showed little sign of improvement with the resumption of his professional work. Sinking lower and lower, he experienced the utmost difficulty in making engagements with any but the most inferior provincial houses. After giving two dramatic readings in Lewes and another in Eastbourne on behalf of a Roman Catholic charity, he returned to Belfast early in October, and played there successfully for three weeks. During the engagement he alternated Othello and Iago with Mr. J. F. Warden, and drew a crowded house on his benefit night to see his Sir Patrick O'Plenipo in *The Irish Ambassador.* So faithful indeed did the Belfast public remain to him that it is quite in keeping that his last appearance on the stage should be imperishably associated with the annals of North of Ireland theatricals. To this affection the *Belfast News-Letter,* in dealing with his reappearance on local boards on January 10, 1865, bears eloquent testimony, and adds—" It was particularly gratifying to find that, on the first night of his re-engagement, Mr. Brooke's mellow, manly voice betrayed none of that huskiness which indisposition and exposure to cold never fail to beget, and that its gifted owner appeared to be in the most robust health."

Dragging out a precarious existence, poor Brooke flitted here, there, and everywhere, in the endeavour to obtain engagements. Hanley, Dumfries, Whitehaven, Durham, Sunderland—all were

visited in their turn, with unsatisfactory results. Early in June
he appeared for one night as Othello, in a wooden theatre, in
Carlisle, and, although announced to perform in *The Stranger*
on the following evening, was so disgusted with his first
experience that he departed from the town at the eleventh hour,
to the intense disappointment of a crowded house. A visit to
Manchester followed; and as his name was still one to conjure
with there among a certain section of playgoers, his twelve
nights' engagement at the Queen's proved fairly successful.
Supported principally by Miss Julia Seaman and Mr. John
Pritchard, his nightly reception in the old repertory was such as
to momentarily revive his drooping health and spirits. His
confirmed admirer, Mr. Dinsmore, was behind the scenes on the
night of his last appearance in Manchester (Saturday, July 8),
and was standing very close to the tragedian when, as Macbeth,
he came off in the murder scene to receive the smeared daggers.
According to stage exigencies the time allowed the actor to
prepare himself at this juncture is necessarily brief. As chance
would have it, Brooke's dresser had left the theatre a few
minutes previously to get his evening dram, and only returned
in the niche of time. Any other "world-famous" tragedian
would have annihilated the unfortunate wight with a glance,
but Brooke merely remarked in a sorrowful undertone, "John,
why do you leave me at this critical moment? See the position
you place me in!" It is related, on somewhat doubtful
authority, that Macready, on once finding himself in a similar
predicament owing to the want of paint to smear the daggers,
incontinently dashed the dresser's head against the wall, obtaining
from his nose a sufficient gush of blood to meet all requirements.

On the same evening, according to Mr. Dinsmore, two of
the tragedian's oldest friends went behind the scenes to shake
hands and have a chat. "How are you, Gussy?" said one.
"Ah!" he replied, "bad, bad," working his fingers nervously
about his throat, and continuing in a hoarse voice —"the taste
for the legitimate drama has fallen very low in England; but I
am going to Australia, where I shall close my hands on ten

thousand pounds." He uttered the words with considerable force, accompanied by a vigorous clenching of the right hand.

Residing in the house of his old dresser, Healey, during his stay in Manchester, Brooke appeared nervous and fretful, and looked upon several petty accidents as ill-omens. The very last night he slept there he created great consternation among the inmates by shouting dreadfully in his sleep. His friends at once rushed to the bedroom, only to learn from the tragedian of a dream wherein he found himself struggling in the water, fighting for sheer life, with the danger so vivid that in his agony he screamed and awoke. This he took as a presage of coming ill, and down to the hour of his embarking for Melbourne remained apprehensive of some disaster on the voyage. Based as is the relation of this incident on evidence thoroughly sound and unimpeachable, it may be as well to point out to the incredulous that analagous cases can easily be cited. Taking only one, it will be remembered that Eliot Warburton, the novelist, gave a vivid description in "Darien," his last book, of the death of one of his leading characters on board a burning ship; precisely the fate which he himself met not long after, when upwards of a hundred souls perished in the *Amazon*.

During Brooke's engagement at the Queen's, Mr. John Coleman was acting at the Royal pending the completion of his new theatre in Leeds. Calling upon his brother actor, our hero explained that he was on the verge of appearing at the minor theatre in that town, and begged of him to give his services there on his benefit night. This proving agreeable, it was at once arranged that Othello and Iago should be the parts sustained by the two tragedians. What followed is best related in the words of Mr. Coleman. "Upon arriving in Leeds to rehearse," he says, "I saw no signs of him till the fifth act of the play, when he informed me that his wife and George Coppin would arrive in Liverpool; the one was returning from America, the other was coming from Australia for the express purpose of re-engaging Brooke and rehabilitating him in the colony.

"As usual, when left to himself, poor 'Gus' had committed numerous indiscretions. Amongst others, he had involved himself in an unfortunate connection, and was quite unmanned in contemplating the situation in which his folly had placed him.

"When I got to the theatre at an early hour that night, to my astonishment I found him (for we occupied the same room) already dressed for Iago. Except that he seemed a little more dignified than usual, there was nothing remarkable about him; it was only when we got on the stage together that I found he was *Bacchi plenus!* My impression is that, had he been acting Othello no one would have discovered his infirmity; indeed, it was impossible for him to go wrong in the Moor, but he had never mastered the words of Iago textually, and was afraid of being caught tripping with the text. The continued effort of memory muddled him, and, unfortunately, let the audience into the secret. He stuttered and stammered, and even mixed up his soliloquies in the most *mal à propos* manner. Instead of saying, at the end of the first act—

> 'I have't; it is engendered; hell and night
> Must bring this monstrous birth to the world's light!'

he substituted the conclusion of the soliloquy in the next act—

> ''Tis here, but yet confused—
> Knavery's plain face is never seen till used!'

whereupon some over-zealous Shakespearian in the pit blandly exclaimed, 'No; it is you who are confused, Mr. Brooke.' This interruption disconcerted Gustavus and put him entirely wrong. In the quarrel scene of the second act he broke down altogether. The most notable feature of his picturesque costume was a breastplate of white buckskin, elaborately prepared with pipe-clay, after the fashion in which soldiers' belts are got up. When the interruption occurred which led to the collapse, Brooke advanced amidst a tempest of yells and groans, and evidently getting a little mixed in his metaphors, and under the impression that he was acting for my benefit instead of my acting for his, exclaimed, 'You common cry of curs, whose

breath I hate, I don't care the cracking of a rotten gooseberry
for you; I am here to-night to do honour to the legitimate
drama in the person of my friend, John Coleman, and I can
lay my hand upon my heart and say——' and as he suited the
action to the word there arose a pillar of pipe-clay which filled
the stage, and evoked, I think, the loudest roar of laughter I
ever heard in a theatre.

"After this I persuaded him to drive home, under charge
of my man, while the stock leading man finished the part of
Iago; then putting on steam I rushed through the last three
acts to the best of my ability.

"I had arranged for Gustavus to be brought back just as
the curtain fell. During the interval he had tubbed and soda-
watered; and 'Richard was himself again.' He was in mourning
for the death of his mother, and was clad from head to foot in
black, black-gloved, &c. I thought I had never seen him
look so *distingué*. Placing him hastily at the proscenium wing,
on the left-hand side, I said, 'Now, Gus, will you trust yourself
entirely to me?'

"'I will do anything you wish me to do, John,' he replied.

"'Stand here then,' said I, 'listen to what I am about to
say, and, for God's sake, don't stir hand or foot till I bid you.'
Then in response to the call I went before the curtain, and
addressed the audience thus:—

"'Your voices are very eloquent on my behalf, let me
entreat you to use them a little on behalf of my friend. For
the past week I have looked forward to this night with pleasure,
but the pleasure of renewing my acquaintance with you was as
nothing compared to the honour I anticipated in acting this
part beside Gustavus Brooke, whose Othello, I considered in my
boyhood one of the greatest achievements of the English stage.
Well, to-night has been a great grief and a great disappointment
to us all; but if you knew the cause I am sure you would
condone all the shortcomings which have occurred. No one in
this building is more conscious than my poor friend that he has
failed in his duty to the poet, to you, and above all, to himself;

but you, who are indebted to him for so many pleasures of
memory, you who have so often seen him at his best and
brightest, can well afford to be generous now. He is about to
leave us for a distant country; in all human probability we
shall never see his face nor hear his voice again; he hears
every word I am saying, he is anxious to be reconciled to you;
you cannot, will not, must not part from him in anger—I ask
you, for the sake of old times, to give him one parting cheer,
one parting God-speed.'

"As I spoke the last words I stepped to the wing and led
him to the centre of the stage. Then occurred a scene which I
shall never forget so long as I live; the house rose like one
man and cheered with a mighty voice that shook the building
to its base. Men and women waved their hats and handkerchiefs,
and sobbed and cried aloud. He was himself carried away by
the general emotion; clasping my hand fervently, he made an
attempt to speak, but I plucked his arm under mine and we
retired together amidst the continued acclamations. As we
passed out of sight of the audience, he fell weeping on my
shoulder; then he gasped out 'God bless you, old fellow!'
We had five minutes' serious talk before we said good-bye, and
when we parted that night we parted for ever."

Powerless to rid himself of the limpet-like attachment of
the designing person to whom Mr. Coleman alludes, Brooke
buried himself in obscurity with the news of his wife's return
from America. She succeeded, however, in unearthing him at
Cardiff, and at once bore him away to meet George Coppin,
who was about to depart for the Colonies after fulfilling a
lengthened engagement throughout the States with Mr. and Mrs.
Charles Kean. Some months previously Brooke had entered
upon an arrangement to reappear in Melbourne under the
management of Barry Sullivan, who was then fast assuming the
position which the other had attained only to lose again.
Lacking confidence, however, he loitered, sank lower and lower,
and it was only with difficulty that Coppin, on their coming
together at Leicester, could induce him to accept an engagement

s

of two years in the Colonies. Yielding to the earnest solicitations of his wife (who found herself unable to accompany him owing to a hard and fast arrangement which her agent had concluded for her appearance at the Surrey Theatre), Brooke at length agreed to follow Coppin to Melbourne in the *London*. And the fact that she herself had chosen the vessel, was among the saddening things that afterwards weighed so disastrously upon poor Avonia Jones's mind.

Completing the circle of his professional career well-nigh where he had begun it, Brooke made his last appearances on the stage in the land of his birth. During his penultimate engagement at the Queen's Theatre, Dublin (November 20— December 2) he had for leading support another star in the person of Miss Pauncefort. Treating of his opening performance as Sir Giles Over-reach, *Saunders's News-Letter*, in the course of a laudatory notice presenting a curious contrast to most of the early Dublin criticisms, says—"The genius of this great actor eminently fits him for the part, and he has made it one of his most important characters. Mr. Brooke portrayed the ambitious, unscrupulous, passionate knight last evening in a manner that elicited the warmest marks of approval from all parts of the house. His first appearance was the signal for a loud and enthusiastic welcome, and, as the plot of the piece developed, and each incident called forth his powers, he was rewarded with the warmest marks of approval by the auditory. The upper part of the house was crammed to excess, and the pit was fairly filled, but the boxes, owing probably to the inclemency of the weather, were but sparsely attended."

Notwithstanding Brooke's solemn promise to Coleman on leaving Leeds, that he would turn over a new leaf, we find him imbibing pretty freely during his last sojourn in Dublin. Under these circumstances it was natural that a modicum of the eleven or twelve characters represented there should have but inadequate interpretation. With the tragedian at his worst on December 1, when *Othello* was in the bill, Mr. J. F. Warden, who came specially from Belfast to play Iago, found himself in the novel and extremely trying position of having to play two characters at once. The situation can best be explained in the following manner :—

Iago—" For Michael Cassio, I dare be sworn, I think that he is honest." (Pauses and looks at Othello, who is trying to steady himself. Then, after the Moor has made a vain attempt to raise his sunken head)—" *You would say*, ' I think so, too.' "

And so it continued to the end. With poor Iago thus visited for his sins it is little wonder that Mr. Warden still retains the keenest recollection of the exhaustion following upon his labours. Early in the afternoon an incident had occurred, admirably typical of Brooke's unbounded good fellowship and camaraderie, particulars of which were first given to the world by Mr. John Coleman, on the authority of Mr. T. C. King, in a sympathetic contribution to the *Shakespearian Show Book*. Owing to the fact that one or two serious errors of detail crept into the original narrative, we deem it expedient to relate the story from our own standpoint.

During Brooke's sojourn in Dublin he was grieved to find his old comrade-at-arms, T. C. King, lying there seriously ill and with but slender chances of recovery. No matter how tiring the rehearsal or seductive the pleasures of the moment, Gus, never allowed a day to escape without putting in an appearance at the bedside of the sick man. Flowers, fruits, wine—the best that money could purchase—were all in their turn lavished upon the invalid. Accompanied to King's apartments on the last Friday of his stay by Harry Webb, the actor manager, and Tom Powrie, the Scotch tragedian, Brooke, as usual, turned the talk into a cheery channel, and after a few minutes' desultory conversation, abruptly addressed his companions in mock-authoritative fashion with " Now then, boys, clear out ; I want to speak with Tom."

When the two were left alone, Gus, leaned affectionately over the bed, and in a subdued voice said, ' Look here, old man a fellow can't be on his back so many weeks without getting under the weather." Then quietly thrusting a bundle of Irish pound-notes into King's hand, he continued, "Take these as a parting gift. I wish they were a hundred times as much." But the seemingly moribund one, knowing full well that Brooke could ill spare the money, and that he had no personal reason for anxiety, as his children were earning good salaries, gratefully but firmly refused the present. Too much vexed at the rebuff to expostulate, Brooke placed his arms round King's neck and said, "Kiss, old fellow. Good-bye, God bless you." This spontaneous action at once reminded the invalid of "Kiss me, Hardy," and ill-attuned to bear strong emotion with composure, tears streamed liberally down his face.

Tired of waiting outside, Macbeth and Dromio now returned to the sick room. Resuming a feeble attempt at mirth-making, Powrie struck an attitude and said, "When shall we three meet again?" to which Webb responded with "There are four of us, you old duffer." Then all three bade King a cheery good-bye, and subduing their laughter, filed quietly out into the passage. Through the door, left slightly ajar, the sick man heard poor Brooke's voice for the last time, and woful was the message. "Poor Tom," were his words, "I fear he's booked for kingdom come. We shall never see him again." *

Lying between life and death for several weeks after Brooke's departure, King eventually experienced a turn for the better. Meanwhile his resources had become exhausted, and in view of the importunities of dunning tradesmen, he recalled with regret his impulsive refusal of Gus's proffered gift. Idling at home, unable to take an engagement, he saw in the papers dread accounts of the loss of the *London*, and for many days participated, with hosts of others, in the

---

* At this juncture in the original narrative Mr. Coleman has clearly over-reached himself. He represents King as saying, "and they never saw me again, for in less than twelve months these three men, full of health and strength and vigorous life, had met the great mystery face to face," etc. A reference to any of the old *Era Almanacks* would have shown that Webb died on January 15, 1867, and Powrie in the August of the succeeding year. Indeed, the sketch is chronologically inaccurate throughout, and "weeks" may be substituted for "months" wherever the latter crops up.

anxiety to learn whether his old playmate had shared the
fate of the engulphed passengers. About the time that all
doubts were set at rest by public confirmation of the sad
rumour, Mrs. King, after the manner of industrious house-
wives, was one day bustling about dusting the room, and on
turning her attention to an old fashioned tea-caddy standing
laden with dust on the bookshelf, startled her husband by
exclaiming, "This is just like you, Tom. Always telling me
you haven't got a shilling left, and here, like a magpie, you have
been stuffing this dirty old tea-caddy full of bank notes."
Taking the notes nervously from his wife's hands, King, to his
great amazement, saw "Gustavus Vaughan Brooke" written on
the back. "Gus's Legacy" Mr. Coleman has aptly styled this
trouvaille, in seeking a title for his sketch; it was certainly all
he left to any person in the world.

On repairing to Belfast to fulfil what was fated to prove his
last engagement, Brooke was accompanied by his wife and
younger sister, the latter of whom had determined upon voyaging
to the Colonies for her health's sake. Opening at the old Theatre
Royal on Monday, December 4, as Othello, the ardency of his
acting was marred somewhat by the ravages of recent intemperance
which had played havoc with his sonorous voice, rendering it at
times harsh and monotonous. Furthermore, his memory was
occasionally at fault. Mr. Edward Terry—then stock low comedian
at Belfast and the bright particular Roderigo of the evening—
relates that in the third scene of the third act he mixed up
part of Iago's speech in the opening scene of the first act with
Othello's lines, in the following odd fashion :—

> "I'd whistle her off, and let her down the wind
> For daws to peck at."

To his credit be it said, however, Brooke was completely
abstemious during his final performances in Belfast, and from
first to last let nothing in the way of liquor cross his lips,
save and except an occasional glass of claret. In this he was
largely influenced by the soothing presence of his wife, who,

although not required in Belfast in her professional capacity, was sufficiently sensible of her error in hearkening more to the claims of her mother than of her husband, not to leave him again until he had finally boarded the *London*.

Appearing successively as Matthew Elmore, Virginius, Richelieu, Master Walter, and Macbeth, Brooke played to uniformly good houses, and was efficiently supported by the local stock company, which, besides Mr. Terry, then numbered among its principal members Messrs. J. F. Warden and W. E. Mills, the lessees of the theatre; Mr. F. Young, Mr. J. G. Swanton, Mrs. Mills, Miss Jenny Bellair, Miss Julia Leicester, and the sisters Polly and Maggie Findland. On Tuesday, December 12, when the performance was under the patronage of the Marquis and Marchioness of Downshire, the star displayed his comedy powers by giving impersonations of Sir Lucius O'Trigger in *The Rivals*, and O'Callaghan in *His Last Legs*, to an overflowing house. His acting on that occasion was distinguished by great care and painstaking, even in minor detail; but most of his old admirers had their pleasure lessened by a distressing sense of the efforts put forth to overcome the feebleness and inflexibility of his voice. In face of these drawbacks, however, Brooke evinced a keen appreciation of the humours of Sheridan's maiden comedy, and was tickled to such an extent by the ludicrous figure cut by Edward Terry as Bob Acres in the duel scene, that he turned his back on the audience, and literally shook with suppressed laughter.

On the 15th *The Rivals* was repeated, with *Catherine and Petruchio* as afterpiece; and on the following night Brooke appeared in *The Wife* and *His Last Legs*. *A New Way to Pay Old Debts* was in the bill on Monday the 18th; and on Tuesday the star played Shylock and Sir Patrick O'Plenipo in *The Irish Ambassador*. The two-act comedy was repeated as afterpiece to *The Stranger* on Wednesday; and on Thursday *Othello* was performed, with Brooke as Iago, and J. F. Warden in the name-part. For his farewell benefit on Friday (when he received half the receipts, taking only a third on other nights) our hero elected to appear as Edgar, in J. W. Calcraft's drama, *The Bride of Lammermoor*, and as Captain Murphy Maguire in *The Serious Family*. It was certainly a strange coincidence that on this, the penultimate night of his appearance on the stage, Brooke should have fastened on a play written by the manager under whose kindly auspices he had first blossomed forth in Dublin. But a stranger thing was to follow. In one of the intervals during the performance the tragedian, on sauntering up to the prompt corner, was startled to find hanging there a copy of the bill announcing his final appearance, and headed in bold letters—

L A S T   N I G H T

OF MR. G. V.

B R O O K E .

"Last night," he said, in a saddened undertone, half to himself and half to the little group of actors standing about, "it seems like sounding a fellow's death-knell."

Little did he reck that in the course of a few short weeks the same mournful bill, reduced in photographic fac-simile, would be treasured by his old friends as a fitting memorial of his greatness.

Saturday, December 23, 1865, marks Brooke's final appearance on the stage. Responding to an enthusiastic recall after a vigorous performance of Richard III., the tragedian took his leave in a few spontaneous words entirely characteristic of the man. "Ladies and gentlemen," he said, "with this night finishes my professional career in Belfast, for a long, very long time to come. I fervently trust by the favour of the One Providence that I may at some distant time be enabled to return to a town where I may professionally or unprofessionally mingle with my friends in Belfast again. I now take an affectionate farewell of you all, wishing from my heart continued prosperity to this magnificent city."

Dingy and tumbledown as was the scene from which G. V. Brooke made his last exit, the time-honoured boards of the barn-like edifice in Arthur Square were not without classic associations. Kemble, Siddons, Cooke, and Kean had all fretted and strutted their hour there in by-gone days. And it was not a little singular that the quondam "Hibernian Roscius" should have ended his picturesque career within the walls which had encompassed the marvellous Betty boy's first audience. Fully a score of years have elapsed since the historic old theatre was razed to the ground, and during that period two more commodious structures have successively occupied its site. Gone too, for the most part, is the Old Guard of playgoers, with their cherished memories and fine enthusiasm for the legitimate. Another generation has sprung up, knowing little and caring less for the traditions of the playhouse. Still the respect entertained for the memory of Brooke has descended reverently from father to son, and amid the clangour of commerce and strife of contending opinion sheds a hallowed radiance over the theatrical precincts of this puritanical city.

CHAPTER XIV.

1866 – 1867.

The S.S. *London*: her Cargo and Defects—"Mr. and Miss Vaughan" Embark at Plymouth—Unhappy Results of Brooke's *Incognito*—The Legend of the Baffled Sheriffs' Officers—Detailed Account of the Voyage—Death of Miss Brooke from Heart Failure—Gustavus Lends a Hand at the Pumps—He Refuses to go in the Boat, and Sends his Farewell to Melbourne—Verses Commemorative of his Noble Ending—Reception of the News in England and the Colonies—The Poolbeg Memorial Lifeboat: an Ephemeral Memento—Avonia Jones Heartbroken—Appears at the Surrey in *East Lynne*—Returns to America and Dies there—Her Father and Mother Reconciled over her Deathbed.

THE *London*, in which Brooke had quietly arranged to voyage to the Antipodes, was an iron screw ship of some 1,429 tons register. Built at Blackwall, Middlesex, in the summer of 1864 for Messrs. Money, Wigram, & Sons, she was classed Aa1 at Lloyd's, and in the opinion of Lloyd's surveyor (as expressed at the Board of Trade inquiry in February, 1866), "was in all respects a good vessel." Other equally competent authorities, however, considered her too long and too deep for her beam, added to which she was practically over-masted.

On preparing for this her third voyage the *London* was laden with cargo, in the East India Docks, consisting of railway iron and casks of agricultural implements, to the value of well-nigh £125,000. Freighted with a similar quantity of iron to that borne on her second voyage (when no particular stress of weather was encountered) she carried in all 1,808 tons, or 39 tons less than on the previous occasion. These facts to the contrary notwithstanding, there can be little doubt that the dead weight on the last sad voyage was excessive. About 348 tons of railway iron were packed nearly solid in a space of fifty-six feet in length by twenty-four in breadth and five in depth. Had the vessel not been overburdened it is reasonable to infer she would have risen satisfactorily to the heavy seas encountered in the Bay of Biscay, instead of floundering in their trough. It is certainly strange that next to no one foresaw the terrible risk incurred, although the reproach which resolves itself around the oversight is softened by the circumstance that the loadline had unhappily been placed ridiculously high.

Leaving the docks in charge of a Trinity House pilot early on the morning of December 28, the *London* called at Gravesend to take in live stock and baggage, proceeding towards Plymouth on the 30th. A heavy sou'-wester, however, soon sprang up, causing her to drop anchor before nightfall at the Nore. There she remained until the grey streaks of morning arose on the New-Year's day of 1866. Shortly after resuming her course more squally and unsettled weather was experienced, culminating in a delay of several hours at the Mother Bank. Later on the strong winds from the S.S.W. were accompanied by a succession of heavy seas; but beyond lurching a little the vessel behaved admirably, arriving safely at Plymouth early on the morning of Friday, January 5. Here, by way of renewing her stock, she took in some fifty tons of coal which, after a practice then followed by Australian bound steamers, were stowed away in bags on deck, mostly around the steam chest and engine room hatch. At Plymouth, likewise, were the remainder of the passengers embarked, Brooke and his sister Fanny (registered on the first-class list as "Mr. and Miss Vaughan") among the number. This significant falsification of names, coupled with the fact that few knew of their departure, led to much unhappy conjecturing after the disaster. It was in the first place confidently asserted that the tragedian had never sailed in the ill-fated vessel; this was no sooner set at rest than up sprang an uglier rumour to the effect that he had met his end while eloping with an abandoned woman. To this calumny

the broken-hearted widow made pathetic reply,* pointing out
that she had accompanied her husband and sister-in-law on
their last sad journey to Plymouth, and, as a matter of fact,
had only put off from the *London* a few short minutes before
the lifting of the anchor. She might well have added that in
her firm resolve to follow at an early date, she had rendered up
to the tragedian the few treasures saved from the wreckage
of years, and when the news of his death arrived, had nothing
to retain in his memory save a hastily scribbled note and a
soiled collar.

As Brooke was not the man to travel *incognito* from mere
motives of delicacy, the only reason that can be assigned for the
course pursued was the natural desire to escape from the pressing
attention of his creditors. Whether this be true or not, a legend
exists to the effect that Brooke had some difficulty in getting on
board without arrest, and even then thought it advisable to lie
perdu until the anchor was lifted. The story goes that two
sheriffs' officers clambered up the vessel at the eleventh hour and
informed Captain Martin they had warrants for the arrest of the
tragedian, of whose whereabouts they were perfectly assured.
Nothing daunted by a fruitless scrutiny of the passengers' list,
these vigilant worthies demanded the commander's assistance in
the execution of their duty, and were told in reply to search the
ship from stem to stern without delay. " If you find him take
him off by all means," said the captain. " If not, take yourselves
off as speedily as possible, for there is much to do here, and we
cannot be impeded in *our* duty." Then began a vigorous search
on the part of these limbs of the law—upstairs, downstairs, and
possibly in " my lady's chamber.' But all to no purpose; the
disappointed pair had perforce to confess themselves mistaken;
and, with a poor attempt at concealing their chagrin, took their
departure. And what of Brooke during this anxious period ?
No sooner was the coast clear than he is said to have emerged
from the fo'castle disguised as a sailor, only to utter profuse

* See her letter in *The Times* of February 17, 1866, under signature
" Avonia Brooke."

expressions of gratitude, in a choked voice, to the gallant, warm-hearted commander.

What degree of truth attaches itself to this yarn will probably never be known. Colourable as it appears we cannot unreservedly accept all the details of a narrative which implies that the heroic captain figured as a quibbling accessory to an evasion of the law.

Tarrying in port, in accordance with the sailors' superstition, until a few minutes after twelve o'clock on Friday night, the *London* steamed away from Plymouth, with seven boats, 163 passengers, and a crew of 89, of whom fifteen were foreigners. Although Captain Martin was afterwards blamed (by those who did not take into consideration the great expense of delay and other contingencies) for sailing at a time when the barometrical indications were anything but favourable, the weather was fine and calm at the outset, and continued so until Saturday afternoon. when it began to blow hard. There can be little doubt, however, that a severe storm had been explicitly foreshown. We have evidence of this in the transference of several passengers at Plymouth from the *John Duthie* to the *London*, the latter being deemed the more seaworthy of the two. Both sailed much about the same time, but by a strange irony of circumstance, while the seemingly safer vessel foundered in the Bay of Biscay, the discredited one passed scathelessly through the ordeal, and, but little delayed by the stress of weather, reached Sydney in safety. Sunday came, and with it no abatement of the south-westerly winds. The seas, too, began to increase, but the *London* steadily pursued her course, steaming along at the rate of eight knots an hour. It was blowing so hard, however, by eight o'clock on Monday morning (January 8) that the captain gave orders to stop the engines, lift the screw, and extinguish the fires. The wind moderating with the approach of evening, steam was again got up, and the reefed spanker and staysails set. Brief was the respite. Before midnight the main topmast staysail had been carried away, and from that period onwards the gale raged unceasingly, increasing in velocity down to the last dread hour.

About nine o'clock on Tuesday morning the jib-boom was carried away on the starboard side, followed shortly afterwards by the foretop, top-gallant, and main-royal masts, which hung down aft from the rigging aloft. Strenuous efforts were made by the crew to cut away these swinging dangers, but owing to the heavy seas which kept sweeping over the vessel (one of which washed away the port lifeboat), it was found impossible to effect anything more material than the securing of the foretop mast. Nothing of sufficient gravity had as yet occurred, however, to cause fears to be entertained for the ship's safety. The engines continued to work well, and but little water had been shipped. In fact, no serious note of alarm was sounded until the middle of the evening, when the persistent incursions of the seas occasioned the battening down of the hatches.

At length, deeming it advisable to turn the ship round and run for Plymouth, Captain Martin gave orders at three o'clock on Wednesday morning to set the engines at full speed. It was blowing a complete gale at the time, and no sooner had the instructions been obeyed than a heavy cross sea struck the vessel, washing away the starboard lifeboat and staving in the starboard cutter. With only four boats remaining the prospect was far from reassuring.

To add to the general misfortune some of the coals which had been packed around the engine-room hatchway broke out of the bags, and in rolling and floating about soon blocked up the lee scupper-holes. This, of course, militated against the escape of deck-water; a source of danger considerably aggravated by the circumstance that the vessel was provided with no gutter way, having instead a box spirketting on the weather deck. Still sticking manfully to their task, the crew contrived shortly after noon to get in about twenty-five feet of the flying jib-boom, which they placed alongside the combings of the engine-room hatchway, firmly securing one end to a stanchion. Unlucky arrangement! All afternoon the doomed ship laboured greatly, and kept taking in green seas over the port side. With the scuppers stuffed up, the water on deck soon became deep enough to float the imperfectly secured flying jib-boom, which in beating about contrived to weaken the fastenings of the engine-room sky-light. Owing to the damage thus effected, this portion of the vessel offered little resistance to the succession of heavy seas encountered about eleven o'clock p.m. (lat. 46.8 N., long. 0·87), and on being borne away left the water free to pour down into the engine-room. Ten minutes after this appalling mishap the fires were quite extinguished and the massive machinery silenced forever.

It needs no great powers of imagination to picture the anguish and agony of suspense suffered by the passengers at this terrible juncture. Albeit the hatches had been nailed down five or six hours previously, the deck-water found its way into the state-cabins with alarming persistency, and had now accumulated to such an extent that the bedding in the lower bunks on the starboard side was being washed from the berths. Terrified by the sight, all the first-class passengers assembled in the saloon where the Rev. D. J. Draper, a Wesleyan divine, strove fervently to administer spiritual consolation to those who felt unprepared to meet their Maker. A knot of earnest women gathered around reading bibles with the children; and now and again all would unite zealously in prayer. Powerful, indeed, was the effect of the good minister's exhortations, for soon an epidemic of calm resignation cast its spells over the anxious, maintaining its sway until the last dread moment.

Although something like a score of the crew were lying below, ill or hurt (many of the foreign element skulking to their berths and refusing to work), hopes of saving the vessel had not yet been abandoned. With the putting out of the engine-room fires, Angel, the third officer, summoned most of the male passengers on deck to assist in covering the gap made by the carrying away of the sky-light. Sails were brought up and with difficulty nailed over the opening. Mattresses and other bulky objects were piled on top as additional security. But all to no purpose. Nothing could have withstood the seas which kept pouring over the vessel with alarming violence and persistency. Observing how fruitless were their efforts, many of the passengers went below and, with a determination born of despair, spent hours at a stretch in attempting to bale out the lower saloon by passing up buckets of water.

Meanwhile, God in his mercy had cut short the suspense of at least one of the passengers. Troubled with heart failure, Miss Brooke's vitality proved too weak to resist the shock. Watching over her tenderly to the last, Gustavus lost all grip of the world—all desire for self-preservation—with the closing of her eyes for ever. Giving no thought to himself, he rushed on deck to do what he could for the others. Owing to the washing out of the fires, no use could be made of the powerful engine pumps; but the ordinary deck pumps had been rigged without delay. It was a difficult and highly dangerous task to work these in the face of the violence of the elements, and volunteers were none too plentiful. Brooke, of his own free will, at once decided to lend a hand. Bareheaded and barefooted, attired only in a red Crimean shirt and trousers, with his braces fastened belt-like around him, he laboured untiringly at the pumps, and time after time revived the drooping spirits of his companions by the almost superhuman energy with which he applied himself to his task.

All through that terrible night the pumping, and baling, and bootless covering of the engine-room hatch-way went on. But, do what they would, the water continued to gain ground, and soon brought the horrible consciousness that the ship was gradually settling down. Nothing daunted, however, the captain preserved a brave face until five o'clock on the morning of Thursday, January 11, when the stern ports were driven in, and the water poured freely through the apertures into the lower saloon. Totally disabled by this crowning misadventure, the ship rolled helplessly in the trough of the sea, continually swept by the merciless waves.

It now became the captain's sad duty to inform the ladies that nothing short of a miracle could snatch them from destruction.

But religious consolation had robbed death of its terrors; and by one and all the dread message was received with surprising fortitude. A serio-comic incident, however, followed on the heels of this intimation. No sooner had the word gone forth than one of the male passengers lugged a heavy carpet-bag on deck, causing the captain's grave features to relax for a moment at the absurdity of anyone thinking of personal property at such a crisis.

When daylight came Captain Martin ordered the remaining boats to be cleared, and by nine o'clock the starboard pinnace, capable of holding fifty persons, was swung outboard. Six of the crew got in, but the boat was lowered unevenly, and a heavy sea coming to leeward filled her as she hung in the davits. Hence when released she shot her bow under the ship and sank like a stone, the occupants scrambling up again into the *London*, aided partly by the ropes hanging alongside and partly by the advent of a heavy sea. A few of the sailors then endeavoured to clear away the port iron boat, but getting little help from the others, who deemed the task hopeless, had to abandon their efforts. Finally, the port cutter was provisioned with bread, water, brandy, and champagne, and lowered without mishap a few minutes before two o'clock in the afternoon. Sixteen of the crew and three passengers eventually got in. Happily there was little disposition to overcrowd the boat, the sinking of the pinnace having acted as a wholesome corrective. Revolvers were freely displayed by many of the passengers remaining on board, most of whom declared their intention to shoot themselves rather than meet their death in the manner imminent.

Everything now being prepared in the boat, one of the sailors hailed the captain as he walked meditatively up and down the poop deck, and asked whether he intended to accompany them. "No, King, I do not," he replied; "I am going to remain on board." And then, with considerable forethought, he gave them their course "E.N.E. for Brest, 190 miles; the nearest land."

And Brooke? Just as they were pushing off, Gardiner, the assistant steward, observed him leaning with stern composure against the half-door of the companion way. There he stood calmly surveying the scene, with his chin resting on his hands as they grasped the top of the door, which swayed slowly to and fro under the pressure. "Will you come with us, Mr. Brooke?" shouted Gardiner, pity welling up in his heart for the man who had toiled so bravely. "No! no!" replied Brooke. "Good-bye. Should you survive, give my last farewell to the people of Melbourne."

By this time the water had poured through the cabin windows to such an extent that the sea was flush with the top of the poop-deck, and the bodies of drowned women and children were to be seen floating about in the vessel. On putting off, just as they had drawn their knives to hack at the hands of those who might be disposed to cling to the gunwales, the sailors were startled by the agonising shrieks of a handsome young lady, who screamed out an offer of " A thousand guineas if you'll take me in." But it was too late. Already the swirl of waters round the stern was so excessive as to betoken the near approach of the end. Millions would not have tempted the occupants of the boat to return and brave the dangers of the suckage setting in. As they rowed slowly away, many of the passengers, anxious that someone should survive to tell the tale, waved their handkerchiefs and cheered as best they could. Straining their eyes back eagerly as the distance grew greater, the men saw that the ill-fated vessel was sinking rapidly by the stern. In fact the stern rose so high out of the water three minutes after their departure that the keel was visible for a moment as far as the foremast. Then the cutter went down into the trough of the sea, and when she had climbed a hill of water, Olympus high, no trace of the *London* or of the remnants of her living freight was to be seen; nothing but an awful gulf of dark whirling water.

Next day the survivors were picked up by an Italian barque and carried to Falmouth, and not long after some of the sailors gratified public curiosity by appearing at the City of London and other theatres, where Brooke in his time had played many parts.

T

The awfulness of his fate, combined with the Spartan fortitude with which he met it, formed sufficient excuse, at the heat of the moment, for the sporadic outburst of elegiac verse in which the tragedian's death was commemorated at home and abroad. Unfortunately the picture was somewhat distorted by the glossing of the fact that cowardice was more the exception than the rule in that last dread hour when "mute horror strode the deck."

With Dr. Corry one can agree that—

> " Faults, if any, are forgotten ;
>   Virtues now alone appear ;
> As choice gems in darkest setting
>   Shine more lustrously and clear.
> Brooke has passed away for ever !
>   But our lips shall name with pride
> One who, in that hour of danger,
>   Feared not death, but nobly died."

But one could have wished that a little of this poetic fervour had been bestowed upon the memory of Captain Martin, who, with reputation at stake, continued to preserve a brave face, and throughout all those days of maddening suspense bore himself with conspicuous nobleness and self-abnegation.

It were idle to attempt to divine, as some have done, the innermost thoughts of the hapless tragedian in that last sad hour. For some years previously he had uncomplainingly fought an uphill fight against Fate; and under the blow dealt at him through his much-loved sister he resigned himself to the inevitable. *Felix in opportunitate mortis*, might we not well say? He had lived the best of his life, and, no matter how bright the future outlook, nothing but shallows and miseries could have been his portion. Far better than to lag superfluous on the stage was it to die thus nobly, with his memory embalmed in our minds, as

> Victor from vanquished issues at the last,
> And overthrower from being overthrown.

When the news reached England and the Colonies, sorrow for the fate of poor Brooke seems for a time to have dwarfed the magnitude of the disaster. In Australia, where he had always been looked upon as the Father of the Drama (his failings only rendering him more popular with the excitable inhabitants), the sad intelligence threw an unexampled gloom over the entire country. Printed in large letters within a deep mourning border, his last words were to be seen in a conspicuous position in every shop window.

While Brooke's old Melbourne friends were busily engaged in getting up a memorial fund, those at home had set well on foot a similar movement. Acting upon the suggestion of the Cardiff correspondent of the *Era*, who, in a letter to that journal under date January 24, 1866, pointed out that a lifeboat would form an appropriate memento of the actor's ending, a committee was formed to carry the proposal into execution. This consisted of Messrs. Benjamin Webster, Joseph Jefferson, J. W. Anson, Paul Bedford, John Billington, J. L. Toole, Clarence Holt, and Lieut. Gilbert, R.N. Subscriptions soon began to pour in all over the country (Belfast alone contributing some £90), and the money thus derived was satisfactorily supplemented by numerous memorial performances at Dublin, Manchester, and elsewhere. A noteworthy tribute was the publication of a lyrical ballad, entitled "The Wreck of the London," by Mr. John A. Herand, the well-known dramatist and critic, the entire proceeds from the sale of which went to swell the memorial fund.

Shortly after being launched with due honours at Dublin, on September 20, the *G. V. Brooke* was presented by the Committee to the National Lifeboat Institution, whose controlling members very appropriately placed it for service at Poolbeg.

Fitting, indeed, was the attempt to write the actor's epitaph "in water." Taken figuratively by those who saw in the noble new lifeboat—

> "No selfish monument of useless stone,
> But one which in all honest hearts will ever live."

the words must now be read with saddening literalness. Opposite the hundreds of pounds so freely and generously subscribed, nothing material remains to perpetuate the memory of Brooke. After about fourteen years' service, the memorial lifeboat was replaced by another, of which it could *not* be said that

> . . . "Many a rescued one through it had heard Brooke's name,
> And lived with grateful heart to speak his fame."

Detractors of the tragedian must stand abashed when confronted with the result of his sad taking-off upon poor Avonia Jones. The shock at once threw a settled melancholy over her spirits, from which she never recovered. Sleep forsook her. For weeks after the loss of the *London*, although continuing to fulfil her arduous professional duties, she never went to bed, but sat up night after night with wearied eyelids, attended only by a single friend.

When the blow fell it found her actively preparing for her appearance at the new Surrey Theatre in a dramatisation of *East Lynne*, specially written for the occasion by Mr. John Oxenford. Struggling to keep faith with the public, she attended long and trying rehearsals at a time when she had scarcely broken her fast for days, refusing to hearken to those who judiciously advised postponement. It is not to be wondered at, therefore, that her acting on the opening night was nerveless and dispirited, or that throughout the engagement (decidedly successful notwithstanding) she showed little of the sonority and force so characteristic of her style in earlier days.

The legend still flourishing vigorously in America to the effect that Brooke's last words were, "My dear Avonia," probably had its origin in the circumstance that Mr. C. A. Elliot, of Trinity College, Cambridge, in strolling along the beach at Brighton on Thursday, March 15, 1866, picked up a wine bottle containing the following message written in pencil on a torn

---

'It appears that the entire moneys accruing to the Brooke Fund from subscriptions, performances, etc., were £292 16s. 0d., and that the residue of the sum necessary for the purchasing of a lifeboat was furnished out of the funds of the Lifeboat Institution. During her brief career the *G. V. Brooke* was instrumental in saving the lives of some thirteen people.

envelope:—"11th January, on board the *London*. We are just going down. No chance of safety. Please give this to Avonia Jones, Surrey Theatre.—Gustavus Vaughan Brooke." Sufficient testimony of the genuineness of the note was given by the shock experienced by the disconsolate widow on recognising the well-known handwriting.

As if to make assurance doubly sure, Brooke had addressed a second note to "Warden, Belfast Theatre," similar in drift to the other, but containing the pathetic postscript:—"Do what you can for poor Avonia." This too was washed ashore on the South-east coast of England and transmitted to Mr. Warden, who gave the bottle and its contents a place of honour in the box-office of his theatre until the building was unfortunately destroyed by fire.

Concerning Avonia Jones, little remains to be said. The end quickly came. On leaving London, she fulfilled a series of engagements in the provinces and then returned to America. Fearing the worst, her medical advisers at once ordered her to Cuba; but while preparing to depart, rapid consumption got in its work unerringly and carried her off at the early age of twenty-eight. She died at her father's residence, No. 2 Bond Street, New York, on Friday, October 4, 1867, and was buried in Mont Auburn Cemetery, Boston.

Poor Avonia! One possessing such a generous, earnest, and withal affectionate disposition, was deserving of a better fate. Yet happy and peaceful was her ending; for over her deathbed she had the satisfaction of seeing her long-estranged parents join hands and become sincerely reconciled.

INDEX.

ERRATA.

Page 14, line 4—For "Pizzaro" read "Pizarro."
Page 42, line 9 from bottom—For "Whiteadder" read "Whitadder."
Page 133, in headline—For "Calaynos" read "The Betrothal."
Page 213, line 7 from bottom—For "hy" read "by."

Printed by W. & G. Baird, Royal Avenue, Belfast.

www.ingramcontent.com/pod-product-compliance
Lightning Source LLC
Chambersburg PA
CBHW020851020726
47497CB00005B/1348